The fie...
which you...
phy." This...
ful laser be...
so tiny tha...
photograph... ...match the vibrant colors and radiant
glow of a hologram.

So look for the Zebra Hologram Heart whenever you
buy a historical romance. It is a shimmering reflection of
our guarantee that you'll find consistent quality between
the covers!

LOVE'S SWEET INNOCENCE

"Tanya," Ashe murmured in a painful whisper,
but when she looked up she was met with a sardonic
smile. The taunted mask was wiped from his face by a
muttered curse as Ashe lowered his mouth to capture
hers. He moved with exquisite slowness at first; then
all his restrained power broke loose and his mouth
grazed hungrily over her lips, her throat. A flooding
excitement Tanya had never experienced washed
through her.

"Ashe, please, help me lie down. . . . I—I'm so
shaky . . . I don't think I can. . . ."

He scooped her up in his arms, hugging her
fiercely against his chest while burying his face in her
flowing tresses. All barriers had been swept away like
scattered leaves by a tumultous wind. He lowered his
lips to hers and kissed her more urgently than before.

"Ashe, my sweet darling, Ashe, love me, oh love
me," she begged.

"As God's my witness, Tanya, I love you," he
whispered against her gently rounded breast.

Then he could think of nothing else as Tanya's
silken body writhed and bucked in sweet ecstasy
beneath his. He knew that this night—their wedding
night—would be one they would never forget. . . .

THE BEST IN HISTORICAL ROMANCE
by Sylvie F. Sommerfield

BETRAY NOT MY PASSION (1466, $3.95)

The handsome sea captain's hands felt like fire against the raven-haired Elana's flesh. Before giving her heart she wanted his pledge of everlasting love. But as the prisoner of his fierce desire she only prayed . . . BETRAY NOT MY PASSION.

TAME MY WILD HEART (1351, $3.95)

Fires of love surged through Clay's blood the moment his blue eyes locked with the violet of Sabrina's. He held her bound against him with iron-hard arms, claiming her honeysweet mouth with his own. He had bought her, he would use her, but he'd never love her until she whispered . . . TAME MY WILD HEART!

CHERISH ME, EMBRACE ME (1711, $3.95)

Lovely, raven-haired Abby vowed she'd never let a Yankee run her plantation or her life. But once she felt the exquisite ecstasy of Alexander's demanding lips, she desired only him!

TAMARA'S ECSTASY (1708, $3.95)

Tamara knew it was foolish to give her heart to a sailor. But she was a victim of her own desire. Lost in a sea of passion, she ached for his magic touch — and would do anything for it!

DEANNA'S DESIRE (1707, $3.95)

Amidst the storm of the American Revolution, Matt and Deanna meet — and fall in love. And bound by passion, they risk everything to keep that love alive!

Available wherever paperbacks are sold, or order direct from the Publisher. Send cover price plus 50¢ per copy for mailing and handling to Zebra Books, Dept. 1714, 475 Park Avenue South, New York, N.Y. 10016. DO NOT SEND CASH.

TEXAS TIGRESS

SONYA T. PELTON

ZEBRA BOOKS
KENSINGTON PUBLISHING CORP.

ZEBRA BOOKS

are published by

Kensington Publishing Corp.
475 Park Avenue South
New York, NY 10016

Copyright © 1985 by Sonya T. Pelton

All rights reserved. No part of this book may be reproduced
in any form or by any means without the prior written
consent of the Publisher, excepting brief quotes used in
reviews.

First printing: December 1985

Printed in the United States of America

This is for I. R. "Nig" Hoskins, Sheriff of Bastrop County, the oldest known working sheriff in Texas, three times elected to office. He is still going strong. And, as always, for John, one of Nig's Deputies.

È il Sol dell'anima,
la vita e'amore. . . .
Love is the sun by
which passion is kindled.

Part One

Came the Spring with all its splendor,
All its birds and all its blossoms,
All its flowers, and leaves, and grasses.
—Longfellow, "Hiawatha"

Chapter 1

The gentle sun was only five minutes above the horizon when the occupants of the little house began to stir. Tanya Hayes bustled in the kitchen corner, dipping her large wooden spoon into the barrel of flour. She was making sourdough biscuits to go along with a breakfast of salt pork and eggs.

Tanya kept right on mixing the dough while she half-listened to her younger sister and brother argue over who was going to wash up first. Tanya, an early riser, had washed herself while it was still dark outside.

Wiping her slim fingers on her old, bleached apron to free them of flour dust, Tanya paused, this time to gaze out the window. The bluebonnets were just making that God-given metamorphosis from bud to bloom and the trees were decked in a hundred different shades of bright and soft green. Nature's paintbrush had splashed whites, yellows, and reds over the budding March landscape, wiping away winter's dull browns and grays, while purple windflowers, snowy pink blooms of the lantana with their yellow eyes, mountain laurel and magnolia, peach, and plum blossoms added their own magnificent color to the onset of nature's rebirth.

"Willow Margaret, you just about done in there?" Tanya called, reluctant to turn from gazing out the window. "I sure would appreciate some help in here."

"Yes, ma'am," came the soft reply from the other room beyond the curtain.

Again Tanya caught herself staring out the window. In her mind's eye she could see the well worn path that wound from the creek to Sundance. Out front, where the long drive extended to the road, it would be lined with dogwoods that bloomed in white profusion. Each spring she had wandered along the path, halting to feel the delicious rays of warm sun bathe her face when she broke from the woods and beheld the house she had always loved. Tanya had loved it ever since she had first seen it as a child.

She had not gone to the big house in a long time now. She had buried her father two weeks ago and had sat on a stool by the window in the little house, mourning, alone, while her sister and brother went out, to do the chores, or Sammy to play and Willow to walk. She had laid her tired head on her arm, mourning her father's passing.

No, she wouldn't cry, not now, not ever. She would find a way to get along somehow.

It was time, Tanya decided pushing her stool away from the window, time that she left the house and got some fresh air. Besides, it was spring.

The Texas sun was higher and it had grown considerably warmer. Everything was hushed and dewy and apple blossom fresh. Tanya took her time, picking her way along the creek and then gingerly crossing the slippery stepping stones to the other side. As she climbed the short incline memories came to her, along with a young man's voice:

"I'll come back, missy, when you're all grown up"—he'd laughed in that easy way of his—"and you better be waiting."

Tanya had waited. Five years, and still Ashe Brandon had not appeared. Or was it more like six years gone, she wondered.

The sun accented the faint glistening ripples in the water, and it touched her cheeks as she walked. Tanya's eyes traveled along the creek where the moss was already forming and she smiled, tossing her long, dark red hair.

What would Ashe Brandon think of her now if he came upon her here? She had been a willowy fifteen-year-old, with freckles, long unruly braids; and she had looked shyly downward and shuffled her scarred brown shoes in the earth when he'd spoken to her.

Remembering, Tanya smiled. She had been unable to look directly into Ashe's eyes, but she could remember them—hooded, hazel-green eyes, sometimes changing to stormy gray without a moment's warning. He had been her very life and breath.

Tanya now came to stand beneath a spindrift of

shade, where the newborn buds of a purple-flowering tree shielded the path from the golden sunlight of day.

Before her stood the Brandon house, the white throne of the Sundance property, its flower beds, ornamentally arranged in different shapes and sizes, sadly neglected as were the grounds about the blazing white structure. The house was badly in need of a coat of paint, for patches of gray showed through here and there when one stepped up for a closer look.

Tanya's dark-lashed eyes moved forlornly over the house and grounds. An ache of acute loneliness settled in her, and she hugged herself as if she were suddenly coming down with a chill.

Oh, Ashe, why have you stayed away so long? she asked the wind that whipped about, seeming to imprison her legs and the hem of her skirt, pulling, beckoning her forward as if it, too, was lonely.

Ashe Brandon's handsome face was growing dim. Six years ago she had her first dream of Ashe, a dream that had shaken her thin frame awake to an awareness of his masculine scent, his aura, his almost tangible manliness.

Her fresh teen years had been filled with thoughts of him, her life an entrancing miracle when he was around. But she was twenty now and her life was wasting away.

Just last night she had dreamed of Ashe Brandon, but she hadn't recognized him. He had changed so much. The dream had frightened her, for he had been different. His hardened face had looked as if it had never known a smile. Waking up, she had felt as though a sharp blade had cut her deep.

12

He hates me, she had thought in her dream. She had reached out to touch and caress his face, to search out the sharp planes and deep hollows, but he had dissolved like a melting wraith and Tanya had brought her tear-stained cheek back down to the pillow.

Now she broke from the shade, and when her eyes had adjusted to the glare, she drank in the sight of the two-story, plantation-style house, its large timber pillars, axe-hewn, and the galleries that ran its whole length. Inside, she knew the hearths and mantels were of marble, and the floors were luxuriously carpeted with only a foot of gleaming wood at the borders. Dainty walnut pieces mingled with the heavier, more masculine mahogany, and Pete Brandon's antiques graced every room. Proudly he had shown her one piece, when he had still been alive, a cabinet on a stand with Oriental pictures painted in gold over the lacquered black background. She had loved it, as she loved every bright and shadowed corner, every whitewashed wall and bit of oak flooring at Sundance.

Tanya wished she could go inside and clean the house. Only Clem, one of the few remaining ranch hands, went inside to check the house now and then, to make sure no wandering vagrants camped within, he'd told her.

Clem would allow no one else inside, and Tanya respected his wishes and did not question him, believing this to be a dying request of Pete Brandon's.

There was a mystery here, but Tanya had never expressed her wonder to Clem. The old man had been indulgent of her pressing need for food and had

13

offered her the use of his milch cow. Besides he had buried her father. He owned a shovel. Tanya did not.

Tanya's gaze roamed the sweep of sadly neglected land. She remembered other days, pastures full of cows and fine horses, and gardens stretching as far as the eye could see. Her heart turned over once again.

Pete Brandon was gone. Her father, Rob, who'd been the foreman was gone too. All the ranch hands but Clem were gone. The house needed care, willing men, a woman's gentle touch, and love. The grounds had once been carefully landscaped, but now weeds grew everywhere tangling the once lovely flower-beds.

Damn you, Ashe Brandon, Tanya cursed his memory. No, she thought, not his memory, but the uncaring man he had become. Her heart wrenched painfully against her ribs as she wondered if she would ever set eyes on Ashe again.

She inhaled deeply. Spring brought the traveling scents of apple and locust blossoms, and with them more memories. She could almost hate Ashe Brandon. *Almost*. But as a little girl, she had adored him, had fallen in love with him when she had just turned fifteen.

Tossing her gleaming mane of dark red hair, Tanya thought: What is wrong with Ashe . . . and what has become of his younger brother—she could not recall his name, something to do with a bird, almost an Indian sounding name.

All of a sudden, after all these years, Tanya did not love Ashe Brandon any longer. His handsome, boyishly rugged face was growing dimmer and dimmer. Maybe it was better this way. . . .

With her father gone and her funds nearly depleted, Tanya wondered where she would go? What about Willow and Sammy? She should have married one of the neighbor boys, she guessed. They had certainly pursued her when she was invited to attend a dance or a barbecue, but she had always pictured Ashe Brandon walking straight up to her, coming to the rescue, and gallantly taking her hand for a dance. His hand was dry, not clammy and moist like the paws of the overstuffed lads who vied to dance with her.

Willow, younger than Tanya by two years, felt the same way about the neighbor boys. Why weren't there any halfway decent-looking young men in the county?

"What are we going to do now, Sis?" Willow had asked her just the other day. "How are we going to stay alive?"

Samson, the youngest, had joined in. "Yeah, Tanya, are we goin' to starve to death now Pa's gone?" The brown eyes of the lad, which matched his freckles, had stared up at Tanya.

"No, Sammy, we are not going to starve. I'll"—she almost gulped—"*we'll* make out, stay alive—somehow."

"Are you goin' into town like you said to borrow from Granger's store, on credit or somethin' like that?" He had tugged on her slim hand, "Are you, Sis?"

"Yes, Sammy. Mr. Granger will give us credit." For a moment Tanya was silent, and then she added, "Clem is helping us out too, don't forget. And I'll get a job in town, if I have to. . . ."

15

Tanya had averted her face as she'd bitten down on her lower lip. She was scared. She wondered what sort of job would pay well enough to keep the three of them clothed and fed, and under a roof. She was greatly saddened that neither Willow nor Samson would be able to go back East to school as she had, but she had gone when Rob Hayes was still alive.

As the sun became warm, deliciously so, on the back of her neck, Tanya brought her wanderings back to reality and the sight before her. The house she had always loved. . . . Again she was poignantly reminded of Ashe. He was part of all this, the essence that would breathe renewed life into the soul of the house and the land, Brandon land.

Oh, Tanya thought, if Ashe would do that he would also bring Tanya Hayes back to life.

Tanya swept her long hair onto the top of her head, digging into her deep pockets for pins to keep it there. Still, she felt moisture at the nape of her neck. The loose strands coiled around her flushed cheeks, made her magnolia white skin come alive and they contrasted vividly with her sapphire blue eyes. Later, when she returned to the house, she would make a long braid of her hair; it was cooler that way.

As she walked about the yard, Tanya was unaware that someone was watching her from the cover of the side of the house, a young man who thought a fiery-haired vixen in dyed blue calico had appeared on the greensward.

"Damn if she ain't a sight." Talon Clay Brandon sighed to himself. Carefully he kept himself hidden where she couldn't see him.

Even though Talon Clay did not especially care for

16

redheads—he'd had his share of them—Tanya Hayes got prettier each time he caught sight of her . . . spied on her. He had caught a glimpse of a golden-haired girl chasing a red-haired lad and pulling him away from the house by tugging on his ear. She had been smaller, like a tiny porcelain figurine, less endowed with curves, and Talon did not realize the blonde was kin to Tanya. Later, Talon promised himself, he would ask Clem to fill him in.

Talon Clay stood in troubled silence. He was supposed to meet Carl Tucker here, so they could take the loot back to Clem's bunkhouse to stash it. The young outlaw shifted his low-slung holster, tugged his hat lower to shadow his face, and waited for Tanya Hayes to end her morning stroll and go back home. He stayed in the shadows of the big house, concealed by the vine-covered trellis on the lower gallery.

Glancing around from under her lashes, Willow held her breath as a tiny butterfly lit on her shoulder and then took flight as she exhaled. Its powdery yellow wings fluttered as it made its carefree way toward another human.

The butterfly skimmed Talon Clay's wide shoulders, leaving some yellow dust there, and then rose gaily to the roof of the house. With his eyes, Talon followed it, then, slowly, he looked back across the greensward.

As the fragile girl came into full view, he held his breath. The radiance of her angelic smile was just fading, her small oval face becoming serious. He could hear her voice ring out, clear as a bell on Sunday morning.

"Sammy is in trouble again," she told Tanya. "He's got a thistle in his foot . . . again . . . running barefoot. You told him not to, Sis."

Talon nodded, softly muttering, "Be Jaysus!" The little blonde had said "Sis." Now he had his answer; he wouldn't have to ask Clem—at least not about that. But there were some other questions that needed answers. Talon looked up to the sky; it was bright blue.

"Are you coming?" Tanya called back, hurrying to the edge of the woods. She paused there, watching Willow bend to pick a wildflower and hold it up to her pert nose. It was pretty, a cluster of tiny purple bells with yellow stamens.

"I'm going to walk a bit, Sis," Willow said, thinking what an absolutely glorious day it was. She called over her shoulder, "Do you mind?"

A worried look crossed Tanya's face momentarily, then vanished. "Just don't stay too long. You promised to peel those potatoes for me." She tossed one more searching look about the grounds before stepping onto the path.

"I promise," Willow replied, mesmerized by something straight ahead in her line of vision.

She is too wonderful to be real, Talon thought warmly. He broke from cover and walked toward the dainty blonde as soon as Tanya Hayes left the clearing. "Howdy," he said. His deep drawl was sensual and he kept his eyes trained on the girl who had frozen into a slim statue as soon as she'd caught sight of him.

Finally willing herself to move, Willow shaded her nut-brown eyes from the sun. "Do I know you?" Her

18

eyelids blinked for the first time since she'd sighted this young man. "Am I *supposed* to?"

Talon smiled, a friendly disarming smile, as he stood before this enchanting slip of a girl. He took in her tiny, golden-haired beauty, and he was so bold as to note her small breasts and to wonder about her age. When she cocked her perfectly shaped head, his heart did somersaults in his chest.

"Your hair is long like mine." Willow, in her trusting way reached out to finger a strand that lay over his shoulder. Her eyes slipped to his bronzed throat; then she jerked back as if he had been holding a red-hot branding iron out to her. "Why?" she asked him.

"Why?" Talon stepped closer to breathe in her special perfume, delicate and feminine like the sweet voluptuous signals she was sending him. His hair, not quite as long as hers, swung forward to brush his shoulders. "Why do I wear my hair so long, or why is it so close to your own color?"

Talon shook his head as if he couldn't believe all this loveliness was standing before him in the flesh, flesh he didn't dare touch. "Hello?" He waved a hand in front of her staring eyes. "Is anybody in there?"

"My name is Willow," she offered pertly, "and your hair is whiter than mine."

"Howdy, Willow," Talon said, masculine depth in his voice. The world seemed to have stopped spinning, yet he couldn't seem to see past the curtain of Willow's golden tresses. "You're right there, Miss Willow. You got gold dust in your hair, and I ain't."

"You *have not*."

"I stand corrected," he said in an easy drawl. "I

19

have not got gold dust in my hair.'' He showed her a white grin in a sun-browned face.

Willow's curiosity was aroused, for more reasons than one. "What are you doing here on Sundance property?" she asked, taking in his dusty, travel-stained clothes.

"Uh"—he glanced around, his green eyes lazy and hooded—"just passing through, you might say. What're you doing here, Willow?"

"I live here." She tossed her flushed cheek above her shoulder. "Back there, but it's still on Sundance property. You here to see Clem?" she asked, her eyes trained on his unusual, almost ivory-colored hair. When he turned a certain way, she noted a pinkish tint among the heavy strands.

"Yeah," he said quickly. "Yeah, that's right." He began to step away from her, his movements pantherlike and smooth. "I'll have to be going now, Miss Willow."

"I—I still don't know your name."

He shook his head, tossing his long hair back over his shoulder. "Best you don't," he said, thinking of the butterfly that seemed to have been born from the silky envelope of her hair. It had come to him bringing a part of Miss Willow with it. "So long. . . . *Damn!*" he swore as he spotted his partner in crime riding across the greensward toward them.

Willow's mouth dropped, and as she stepped back out of harm's way, a strong arm was wrapped about her waist. "You'd better go now, Miss Willow," the young stranger said into her ear, his breath warm against her flustered cheek.

God you're lovely, Talon thought. She was so close

20

he could kiss her if he chose and be away before she thought twice about it.

Suddenly Talon leaped onto the huge lathered mount that had pounded over to them, barely missing Willow before she'd been pulled out of the way. As the man who was wearing a red kerchief sped away, Talon called back, "Go away, Willow. Don't tell . . ."

Trying to catch her breath—it had become little gasps when the young stranger had touched her—Willow stood, spellbound and bewildered as the mounted pair sped away.

Gone, she thought, gone like mist from a lovely golden dream, her handsome rugged stranger. He had said, "Don't tell," but what exactly had he meant by that warning? she wondered. Her heart began to beat faster, stronger.

Willow stepped back until her skirts brushed the lower branches of the pecan tree, the newly formed buds shading her somewhat. Her brown eyes grew larger, and her skin prickled, not from the keen pressure of the branch she had wedged herself under, but because of the sight before her.

Two more horses galloped into the yard, the mounted men carrying a small chest between them. Willow wondered briefly why they hadn't dropped it somewhere.

Peeking from her sun-dappled hiding place, Willow watched the scene unfold, the quiet yard of Sundance quiet no longer.

Horses went to and fro, Willow's head doing the same. She rubbed her eyes hard and wondered if she were only seeing things, like in a fast-moving dream or a nightmare. . . .

She sought her young man and found him, the yellow-haired one who was urging the others toward the line of bunkhouses behind the house. He was different—angry, domineering, dangerous. Willow was afraid of him, and of what he was doing.

From the sun-dappled edge of the woods, the blond cowboy—Willow hated to think he might be an outlaw—the almost pretty half-man, half-boy, led a horse from concealment and, in one fluidly skillful act of motion, hopped aboard the buckskin's back.

The men raced for the line of bunkhouses, Clem's in particular, Willow thought as she remembered what the blond stranger had told her. Had he actually told her, or had she by some magical method read his mind? she asked herself. What he had been thinking had seemed to flow from his brain to Willow's, and she blushed now in remembrance of the warmth that had passed between them.

Alone now, Willow stepped from her cover and, shading her eyes, gazed in the direction of the woods that concealed the bunkhouses from view. Like puffs of dangerous smoke, the men had vanished into the dark camouflage of the trees.

Willow's heart caught. Was Clem afraid of these strange men? What were those four men hiding in that chest? She shivered to think just what it could be.

At Clem's bunkhouse, Talon was chewing on his lower lip as the old ranch hand showed them where to hide the loot—beneath the false floor. "Brance used to hide his belongings here," Clem said, lifting the dusty piece of carpet that resembled petrified wood. He looked up as Tucker and the others lowered the heavy chest. "What you smilin' fer, pretty boy?" he said to Talon.

Talon, relieved of his tension, laughed low. "Did Brance ever have the notion to hide a pretty girl down there?" His green eyes coruscated like emeralds under the sun. "After sundown, I mean."

"You feeling like a horny toad over some new gal, Clay?" Clem called the young man by his middle name instead of his first on special occasions.

Frank popped back inside the door. "Rangers are comin', I told you, Clay, and you jest keep jawin', first with that gal and now with old Clem here."

"Texas Rangers?" Clem's eyes grew large.

Talon laughed. "There ain't no other kind, Clem." He shook his head, his ivory blond hair spilling against his taut cheeks. There *is not* no other kind," he laughingly corrected himself. "Hey, did that little, yellow-haired gal back there go to school back East or somethin'?"

"Yeah . . . or somethin'." Clem eyed the young man with one narrowed red-veined, blue orb. "You met little Willow, did you? Thought so. Her sister Tanya did teach Willow. Tanya's the oldest of them. She went back East to school, not for very long though, cuz her old man, her pa, he come down with some sickness of the belly."

"Sorry I can't chew the fat some more, Clem, but we gotta be running." Talon saw Frank and Butch waiting for him at the door, but he couldn't resist one more question, "How old is Miss Willow?"

Clem scratched through the few gray hairs left on

23

his head; then his eyes bulged. "Hey, you ain't been messin' with her, have you, Tal?" He looked around as if he expected a Ranger to leap from a dark corner. "No? That's good, 'cause she's a downright sweet gal and never did mess around with no boy afore, I know that for sure. She's near eighteen years," he finally disclosed.

"They must be the Hayes children." Talon shook his head and then stared down at the floor as if he had all the time in the world to chat. "She's sure a little slip for near eighteen year."

"Makes your heart giddyup, eh?" Clem looked around again and sidled closer to the young man to whisper, "You're a wanted man, boy, so don't you be messin' round that pretty gal. 'Sides, you could never give her nothin', unless . . ."

Clem, with a wistful eye, looked out the window toward the greensward of the big house. Talon followed Clem's line of vision and his heart wrenched beneath his leather vest and shirt.

"Yeah, know what you mean," Talon said. "If only Ashe would come back to Sundance. . . . He's the one with the legacy." He stared down at the hand clamped over his mouth, sealing off any further disclosure.

"Yore pa didn't leave you out, Tal." Clem's lips moved closer to the lad's ear. "There's a safe hidden in the house somewheres, in a room no one ever saw. Yore pa hid it damn good. Told no one, he did. He jest told me he had it hid there, that's all. You find that safe afore your brother and it's yours, boy."

"No," Talon said hotly, stepping violently from the older man's side. "I might be an outlaw and rob

24

folks, but not my own flesh and blood, Clem. I love my brother, though we ain't been very close over the years. I don't even know if I remember what Ashe looks like; he has one of those changin' faces, you know?"

"I knowed you wouldn't rob your brother, Talon Clay, even though the devil kept tellin' me you would've." He shook his head. "I don't know where your brother's hid himself all these years. Last I heard he was fightin' in the bloody Mexican War. Can't understand it. Ashe never lacked horse sense afore, leastways until that woman come along."

Like an angry cat, Talon's lips split in a snarl. "Don't ever be mentioning Garnet Haywood again, hear? Good." He stuck his head out the door, calling softly to Carl, "Seen any rangers coming yet?" Then he laughed.

"Nope." Carl Tucker sounded bored. Actually he was waving the others away so he could eavesdrop on Talon's conversation with Clem. The others had frowned suspiciously, but they hadn't questioned Carl's odd behavior. As a result, Carl had picked up a few pieces of information.

Clem moved to the door. "At least you come back to say a few words over your father's freshly dug grave. Dadblasted Ashe never showed his handsome face for over five years now." Clem hung his grizzled head. "That big brother of yours must have got himself killed, I know it for sure."

"No!" Talon bunched his slim, squared fingers into a tight fist. "No, Ashe's not dead. He's out there kicking butt right now. He's too damn rough and tough to get himself killed. Maybe he found himself a

25

gal somewhere and got hitched up with her or"—
Talon looked aside—"or something."

"Naw. You was always the one for the gals, you li'l
booger," Clem gave a hearty chuckle. "Saloon gals.
You still got a hankerin' for tainted stuff, Tal?"

Through the greasy window, Talon could hazily
make out the magical place near the big house where
he had stood not ten minutes ago with the cameolike
girl who'd made his outlaw heart race. The redhead,
Willow's sister, she was damn beautiful—serious,
earthy—but Willow, with her eyes brown as pussy-
willows, staring up at him so wide-eyed and
innocent, intelligent too, that tiny girl had made
holes in his heart. They would never mend either, not
until Miss Willow touched him with those lily-white
hands—touched his chest, not with anything desir-
ing in mind, just touched his heart there. Much more
than that could never come to pass.

"That's all I'm good for, Clem, tainted stuff.
Wouldn't know what to do with a delicate little angel
like Willow Hayes."

"Damn, Talon Clay, the rangers are hot on our
tails!" Butch called from the wooden porch outside.

Chapter 2

Willow stared at the dusty track leading toward the bunkhouses, her head swimming from all the activity she had just witnessed. She could still feel the fiery heat at her waist where the young stranger had left the imprint of his strong embrace. The musky smell of him still clung to her clothes. The soft valley separating her small breasts tingled. Her heart thudded hard.

Eventually she felt her feet begin to move onto the path and out of the bright sunlight. Willow wanted desperately to see the blond stranger again. She compared his touch with that of other young men and the others came up short. She had been kissed lightly before, at barn dances, at barbecues, and on the Fourth of July; and she had wondered why those kisses had left her feeling cold and empty. Now she knew the reason. It was not so with this young man with the dusty clothes and low-slung hat. He hadn't even kissed her, hadn't touched her intimately, yet Willow had felt all warm and excited just looking at him. Funny little darts had shot through her chest and down her arms.

How could I be in love, just like that? Willow asked herself.

She was just heading down the incline when the thunder of horses' hoofs reached her ears again. Willow spun about and ran to the tree she had hidden under before, disbelief written on her face as three more mounted men rode past her. "Lordy be," she exclaimed softly, "what is Sundance coming to?" She watched the men dismount, two of them, while one went on ahead. Then it hit her: These three are looking for the others . . . no wonder the blond stranger had begged her to be silent.

Hunkering down, her curiosity keeping her there, Willow stared as one man walked boldly in the back door and then came out several minutes later. He was looking the place over while his gloved fingers caressed the prettiest pistols Willow had ever seen. She noted his snug khaki trousers, his leather boots with scuffed toes, then his large felt hat.

Willow frowned, silently asking herself, "Now where have I come across their kind before? If they are searching for the others . . . No. She shook her head. They just couldn't be rangers. She hadn't seen any around in a long . . . Of course! When pa was alive they had taken a trip down to San Antonio. There had been a chicken fight, Mexican style. She shuddered just to think of it. The Texas Rangers were there, for San Antonio always needed some sort of military force. It had to be guarded constantly and other rangers often went into San Antonio to rest their horses and enjoy a little amusement. She had even seen one strolling in the part of town that was inhabited almost wholly by Mexicans, and a pretty *señorita* clung to his arm.

"Tanya," Willow said aloud, suddenly thinking of her sister and how she disliked Texas Rangers.

Keeping low, Willow scurried to the path and down the hill, gingerly stepping across the creek on large slippery stones, then running up another hill toward the little house. She burst in the door.

"Tanya!" She stopped short.

"Ouch!" Samson hollered. He was perched on the table while Tanya, resting one knee on the puncheon bench drawn up before the boy, was just straightening with the tiny blade of a splinter pinched between her fingernails. "Does it still hurt?" Tanya asked her brother, watching him rub it gingerly between two fingers.

"Naw," he said bravely, hopping off the table, "not anymore. I'm goin' back outside to play." He started off toward the door but was pulled back by a swift tug on his ear.

"No you don't," Tanya said.

Now Samson was rubbing his ear. "Why?" he said. He watched her expression for a moment and then giggled. "I kin go outside, but I have to go get some milk from Clem?"

"*No!*"

Both Samson and Tanya turned to look at their sister, staring at her as if she had appeared at the precise moment she had spoken. Samson cocked his head, wondering at his sister's strange mood. But Tanya, older and wiser by several years, read something into Willow's oddly flushed cheeks and

29

the wild look in her usually calm brown eyes. Tanya broke the silence at last.

"Sammy, take the pail to the garden and fetch me those potatoes." She looked at her sister again, saying, "Willow promised to peel them."

"Yes'm!" Samson said, going out the door lickety-split. "Should I wash 'em outside too?" he called from the other side of the door.

"Yes," Tanya said, "please."

"Yes'm!" Samson hopped from the porch.

Having contained her curiosity for a time, Tanya now turned to her sister and was about to hear Willow out when Samson appeared at the open door again, asking, "How many potatoes?"

"Six," Tanya said at once, watching as Willow's mouth snapped shut in exasperation. She kept her eyes on Willow as she heard the lad counting on his fingers as he hopped off the porch once again.

"There's rangers up at the big house," Willow gave vent finally to her excitement.

Unblinking, Tanya stared at her sister for a moment before she casually went over to the fireplace. The crane squeaked noisily when she swung the heavy kettle off the fire. As if she hadn't heard her sister, Tanya poured the steaming water into a large metal basin, added the juice of barks and berries, then dropped in a few items of clothing and began to stir the mixture with a large stick. As she gazed fixedly at the faded clothes already taking on color, Willow came to stand beside her.

"I said there's rangers—"

Tanya broke in softly, "I heard what you said." She halted her stirring to look up at Willow. "What

30

do you want me to do about it? Go up there and invite them down here for supper?"

Holding her chin high, Willow turned away. "You could; then we could see what they're up to. If you did, maybe they would stop snooping around."

Tanya stabbed her stick into the clothes, lifting a dress to check its color. "I don't care what they are up to," she said tersely, "and I don't care if they starve to death." She transferred the dress into a bucket of cold water at her feet. "If they are rangers, as you seem to believe, then they are welcome to snoop around Sundance. I don't own it."

Willow spread her finely boned fingers. "What if"—she paused to take a deep breath—"what if they are looking for bandits?"

Tanya laughed shortly. "On Sundance property? Hardly," she said. Suddenly she studied her sister closely. "There is something else, Willow. What is it? Did you see someone else besides these wicked rangers?"

"Wicked!" Willow laughed. "They keep the law and order and peace. Pa said they fight the Indians and the Mexican bandits to keep us folks from getting hurt. Pa said they are gentle men, men who can ride straight up to death and look it in the eye."

"They have a reputation as troublemakers," Tanya repeated what she had overheard while in San Antonio. "General Taylor has said they are a lawless set. They participate in the fiestas and fandangos at Mexican homes, and are usually uninvited! And"—she looked down into the basin—"and they are sexually unrestrained."

"Sex," Willow said thoughtfully. "I know what

31

that means. But what does the other word mean?"

Tanya took a deep breath before saying, "You'll know if you ever meet that kind of man." Her eyes lit up with blue fire then. "They are trespassing!"

"Sis, don't you think they're looking for something? Ain't it crossed your mind?" Willow said, forgetting all the proper grammar her sister had taught her.

"The only thing they are looking for is something to eat if they, as you say, are chasing bandits this far from San Antonio." She thought for a moment, then, wrinkling her brow into a frown, said, "Or some fun." She took her pa's rifle down from its rack. "They are not going to find it here."

A confounded look crossed Willow's pert little face as she followed Tanya. "If you go up to the big house and show your face, maybe you are going to run into some trouble."

Tanya whirled on her.

"Well"—Willow shrugged sheepishly—"if you think they are so . . . uh . . . unrestrained"—she said the word slowly, as if she were afraid of it—"then aren't you kinda walking into a fire that's already lit?"

Wielding the rifle that was hers now, Tanya snapped, "I'll light a fire all right, right under their lecherous hides!"

"Confound it!" Willow breathed to herself. She puckered her soft pink mouth. Lecherous must surely have something in common with the word "unrestrained" if she knew her sister Tanya. And she did. . . .

Tanya had not had an easy life here at Sundance

property, having to be mother to her and Samson. Because Tanya was the eldest, she'd taken on her shoulders the responsibility of raising them, mostly Samson, and that could be a chore. Samson was a handful at times!

Tanya had a quick temper, but like foxfire it came and went. Mostly she was gentle and kindhearted, besides being the prettiest woman in those parts, and Tanya loved babies—animal or human.

Now Willow tagged along while Tanya scrambled down the hill, took the creek bed like a deer, and climbed the hill on the other side. Tanya's red hair matched the fury building inside her, the long fat braid of it hanging down to her softly curved hip. Willow halted right beside Tanya when she paused to look around, and she could feel her older sister's heat.

"I should've kept my big mouth shut," Willow ruminated aloud before she ducked beneath a branch. Tanya had set off again. Maybe, just maybe, time would be on her young man's side and he would escape the rangers, she thought. She should reveal which way he went but she couldn't bring herself to turn him in.

Willow blushed. Already she was thinking of the outlaw—she was almost certain he was that— thinking of him as her young man. It'd be a dream come true if she ever spoke to him again, alone as they had been for a few, wonder-filled minutes.

"Sis," Willow said, grinning to herself, "if you're in such an all-fired hurry to bushwhack them Rangers and run them off, then why're you shivering? Afraid to face the lecherous devils, huh?"

"I'll take that, ma'am."

"*Oh!*" Willow and Tanya gasped simultaneously, as the rifle was snatched from Tanya's unsuspecting fingers.

Ashe Brandon, closely watching the young woman, reached for her wrist and pulled her gently from beneath the spreading arms of the oak. Willow followed her sister, her eyes never leaving the big man who had to be a Texas Ranger. Willow was certain of it. She could spot their authoritative manner a mile away.

A playful spring breeze whipped at the wheat-blond hair that hung beneath the man's felt hat, and Tanya stared, transfixed in time.

He glanced at his fellow ranger and then back to her. "McNeil," he said over his shoulder, "see what you can find out at the bunkhouses."

"You know where they are?" McNeil asked, wondering how.

"Sure do. I sent Farley back there. I'll take care of this matter here." His cat-hazel eyes swept from the rifle in his hand to the young woman's face. "Follow the beaten track to where the row of flowers ends."

"You mean the weed-eaten flowers," McNeil said, catching the narrowing of his fellow ranger's eyes and his stern profile. McNeil had seen Ashe laugh, but he didn't look too happy at the moment. Lightly he said, "Sure you'll take care of this matter here?" He swept the young ladies one last admiring glance. "Sure will," McNeil added.

The ranger was staring right into Tanya's mist-blue eyes. "You weren't planning on using this on us?" When she didn't answer, he slid his eyes to the smaller, light-haired woman.

With the tip of a forefinger between her lips and her tawny eyebrows lifted gently, Willow jumped when the ranger shifted his attention to her suddenly.

"Was she?" he asked.

"Was she what?"

Puzzled, Ashe Brandon stared at the two young women. He had ridden with Captain John Hays and had faced Comanche braves, he'd dodged Indian arrows efficiently, faced Mexican spears, been tried and tested. Yet he was totally at a loss as to what to say or do with these two kitten-eyed females staring him down. "Was she going to bushwhack us?" he asked Willow, thinking she would be the one to speak up first.

Spun back into time, Tanya could only stare at Ashe Brandon, thinking, *He doesn't remember me.* She was sorely disappointed. Tanya blinked out of her daze. How could she have run Ashe Brandon off his own land? She said the first thing that came to her mind.

"Are you hungry?"

With a deep chuckle, Ashe lowered his head; then, with the bore of the rifle, he poked his hat up so that a strip of lighter skin showed on his forehead. As quickly as his smile had appeared, it was gone, and his eyes narrowed in suspicion. As he looked them over, trying to discern their sincerity, Tanya took the time to look him over. Carefully, she searched his sunbrowned face, then regarded his wide, relaxed shoulders, his buckskin covered chest, snug khaki trousers, and the long-boned fingers lightly rubbing the butt of the rifle he held close to his thigh.

Yes. As her dream had cautioned her, Ashe Brandon had changed. She sensed that he was totally indifferent to his past and to anything that had to do with his past.

This is where you belong, Ashe Brandon, here, here at Sundance, not off killing wild Indians or Mexicans or bandits—or chasing women, she wanted to scream at him.

Instead Tanya stiffened as his eyes raked her face. His gaze didn't linger on the rest of her. He quickly lowered his dark lashes and that was it. She felt a flash of hot embarrassment go through her as she realized he had been talking to Willow, asking her questions, while she, Tanya, stood in a half-daze looking him over as if considering how he felt toward her.

"Haven't seen anything suspicious, Mr. Ranger," Willow was saying. She swayed then and he reached out his free hand to steady her. "Oh, I feel faint. . . ."

The other men arrived just in time to see their fellow ranger scoop the dainty blonde into his arms. He handed his rifle to one of them, asked the redhead a question, and then set off down the hill. The rangers shrugged and then followed him.

Tanya lingered a moment longer at the wooded crest. Just that morning, she had wondered what the next day would bring. That next day had not even come, but more had happened than she could handle.

Chapter 3

Willow peered from one half-closed eye, then promptly closed it. Poignantly, Tanya watched Ashe Brandon gently lay her sister down in the bedroom. Points of sunlight broke through the window slot, dappling the toes of his scarred boots with tiny diamonds of light.

A thrill shot through her when she looked up.

Ashe's eyes shifted over to the red-haired woman. He bit back the compliment that struggled to escape from his lips at the taunting reminder of that flashing red hair. Instead, he said, "I asked you before: Does she usually faint like this when she's excited?"

"She's not excited," Tanya said, unconcerned over what was merely another of Willow's sly little games. But she couldn't figure out the reason for this duplicity.

Ashe Brandon glanced to the girl and back to Tanya. "She's not in the family way then?" he said brusquely.

"She's certainly not."

With those curt few words, Tanya returned to the main room, leaving the curtain to slap Ashe Brandon's sun-browned face. But he caught the curtain in the nick of time, just as he was stepping out, and he missed the impish grin of the girl on the bed.

Now the young outlaw would go his way, free, Willow thought happily.

"Yes, ma'am!" Rand McNeil was answering Tanya as Ashe entered the room. "After a steady diet of jerked beef, that sounds mighty good, ma'am!"

Tanya could feel Ashe Brandon's eyes following her every move, and she wasn't so ignorant of man-woman relationships that she didn't know he was admiring her. She tingled all over as she asked him, "Would you like some pone? I can warm it up, and there's fresh vegetables and—"

"We won't be staying." Ashe moved closer to the table and Tanya. "We got work to do," he added, hearing his fellow rangers groan. "Gonzales. McNeil," he said, and waited for them to file out the door to fetch the horses.

Tanya's taut stretched nerves vibrated when she was left standing alone with Ashe Brandon. Their eyes met, and held. Tanya shivered as Ashe Brandon's hazel eyes grew bolder, but he was studying her as if he still did not recognize her as someone from his past—not fully, at least. Finally, Tanya thought she could detect a slow flicker of recognition. It was fleeting, however.

"We'll have to be going now, Miss . . ." He paused. "It is Miss?"

Tanya fought back the tears threatening to mist her eyes. She stiffened and nodded for she was at a loss for words, even one solitary word.

Slowly Ashe pulled his head back, indicating the girl hidden behind the bedroom curtain. "Don't you think you ought to look in on her, make sure she's all right?" he asked, a mysterious green light moving in his flecked hazel eyes. "She's been awful quiet in there."

"Willow," Tanya emphasized the name, watching for another flicker of recognition, "she's okay. She's just—"

The rickety screen door slammed. "Jumpin' Josie, Texas Rangers!" Samson exclaimed, burtsting into the room, his face smudged, his hands dirty, his eyes growing wider by the second at the sight of a third ranger. Samson caught the man looking guilty as he dragged those green-gold eyes from Tanya to him, and the boy, in his innocence, read something else into the look. "You are a ranger, ain't you?"

Then Samson stared at the .34-caliber Colt neatly tucked into the man's belt. It was called the "Texas." Samson knew that because his father had told him about firearms, especially the six-shot .34-caliber pistol which only rangers carried. Yep, Samson had this man pegged for sure.

Ashe Brandon smiled. "I am," he confirmed, "but let's keep that a secret."

"Samson," the boy filled in proudly, "just like Samson in the Bible, yessir!" He stared at the ranger then, as if waiting for the man to tell him something.

"Go right back outside and wash your hands, young man, before you come in this house again,"

Tanya ordered crisply, her eyes an angry blue.

"Awww," Samson groaned, but he obeyed, grinning over his shoulder at the handsome ranger as he left.

"You didn't tell him your name," Tanya said, whirling on the man after Samson had gone out. "Don't you even remember that? I thought rangers were supposed to be polite and all that." The words tumbled unheeded from her lips and she stepped back, touching the table with the backs of her shaking legs. "Don't you remember promises you make either? How about the girl you promised to return to, after she was all grown up?"

Ashe's eyes roved boldly over her, telling her she was just that, all grown up.

Tanya moved to the other side of the table. "Why did you have to stay away so long, Ashe Brandon?"

He stared at her. He hadn't thought too much about the Hayes girls. They'd been cute as bedbugs, freckled, and one in particular had always tagged along wherever he went. Her hair had been a brilliant splash of red, always worn in the tight braids that her pa Rob had made her do up every day. Ashe remembered that. He hadn't seen all that much of the younger one, but she'd had lighter hair, like his and his younger brother's. Willow, that was her name, the little girl with the Scandinavian looks. The baby—the boy, Samson—he recalled seeing only on one occasion.

"Tanya," Ashe said gently now. "I'm real sorry I don't recall those words, much less promising I would come back for you." He reached out to lift her thick braid, carefully feeling the silken texture of it

40

and wondering how her hair would look unbound and flowing free about her shoulders. Then he allowed the hank to slide from his fingers and return to her waist. He stared into her misted eyes. "I never look too deeply into myself, Red, and never try to remember the past. There's no place or time in my life for romance, Tanya Hayes."

"So, you remember my name at least," she said, her voice well controlled. "But I suppose it's necessary to know everyone from here to Austin and back on down to San Antonio in your line of work. Right, Mr. Ranger?" She stared down at the table, away from the unfeeling eyes. "No time for romance? That's not what I've heard, Ranger, not with all the tall tales about your kind burnin' all the proper ladies' ears." She gave him a haughty Eastern look. "Infamous tales," she added.

"Miss Hayes"—Ashe Brandon stressed her name— "I'll set you straight on a few things before our relationship goes any further and we become more than passing strangers, because that's what we are, Lady, nothing but. You and I knew each other briefly a long time ago." He shrugged languidly.

"A long time ago!" Her heart was mending fast and her anger rising. "You call six years a long time ago? Oh, long enough for you to forget everything, even a girl's broken heart, I see."

"For my 'kind,' it is." He smiled politely. "The time element, I meant, not the other. You know," he went on, "you're mighty pretty when you're angry, Tanya Hayes. Might be someday we can get to know each other better."

He cordially tipped his hat and, without further

41

ado, stepped outdoors. Tanya's feet took her to the door, where she looked out to see Ashe Brandon hunkered down beside Samson. He was telling Sammy something in private, Tanya could tell. Samson smiled and gave a whoop at what the ranger had told him.

"My name's Ashe," the man told the boy; then he nodded to Gonzales who had led his horse over.

Worshipfully Samson watched the man named Ashe. A fellow ranger, a Mexican, had brought the buckskin gelding to the tall man. Ashe seemed to be in charge. He tipped his hat to Tanya who was watching from the porch; then he shoved a booted foot into a stirrup, pulled himself into the saddle, nodded to the boy, and rode away with McNeil and Gonzales following.

Tanya watched until she could see them no longer and then she turned to go inside. Samson followed close on her heels.

"Ashe's goin' to be comin' back this way," he said, studying the lustrous braid hanging down Tanya's back. "Reckon he'll be mighty hungry by then, huh, Sis?"

"He said that?" Tanya faced Samson now. "Sammy, you said he's coming back. What about the others? Is Ashe Brandon coming back alone?"

Samson giggled at all the questions being fired at him by his older sister who was usually so reserved.

"Oh, he ain't comin' back right away, Sis. Said it'll be a week or two. Him and the others are busy chasin' bandits. He thinks they might've holed up around here somewheres. This is not his usual job, y'know. He's mostly an Indian fighter or an agent. S'pect he

42

rides with Captain John Hays."

"Hays?" Tanya said.

"I guess so. Pa said it was spelt almost the same way as our name."

Samson tagged after his big sister as she began preparations for their meal. "You think Ashe will really come back? You think he was tellin' no lie?"

Tanya paused for a split second in her labors. "It will suit me just fine, Sammy, if Ashe Brandon never comes back."

Tanya went to the fireplace at one end of the main room, saying over her shoulder, "I don't put any trust in Rangers, and neither should you."

The outer door slammed, telling Tanya that Samson hadn't heard the last of her sentence, but Willow had taken in every word from where she stood in the curtained doorway. Hiding her worry, Willow bolted across the room and ran to fetch the potatoes for their supper.

Tanya turned just in time to see her sister going out. Her shoulders sagged in a weary fashion, then she straightened and went back to her work, recalling only that Ashe Brandon had forgotten to "set her straight on a few things." After all the foolish things she had angrily blurted out, she doubted she would ever see Ashe again. At least, he would not come by especially to see her.

Five minutes after he had left the Hayes place, Ashe Brandon sat his horse and stared wistfully at the sadly neglected house and grounds of Sundance. He remembered when it had been a self-supporting

43

ranch. It still could be, he thought. Sundance could be brought back to life. Sundance was his . . . and Talon Clay's . . . wherever his brother was.

Gonzales rode up just then. "Rand is combing the area back of the bunkhouses. We have not seen any sign of the *bandidos*. You want to keep looking, or shall we go back to the ranger post? I think that Captain John will be waiting for us."

Keeping his eyes on the big house, Brandon said, "You've questioned the old man, Clem?"

"He knows nothing. I think he was very nervous." Gonzales shrugged. "Maybe he does know something, maybe not. Maybe he is frightened, that is all. Why do you not talk to him yourself, Ashe? He knows the Hayes women."

An emotion coiled within Ashe Brandon's chest, one he had never known in all his years of ranging, something he had left behind long ago when his mother had still been alive. Inwardly he recognized it, but he attributed the sensation to poignant memories aroused by being on the Sundance property . . . Brandon property. He thought of Garnet Haywood who had forced him and his brother from the house when she'd married Pete Brandon. Half-buried memories, painful . . .

"What is it?" Gonzales asked.

"You and McNeil go back to the ranger post," Ashe said, still staring at the house but having no desire to go inside. "Get word out that the outlaws might be heading north."

"North? How do you know that?"

"They won't be heading back in the direction of the robbery, not toward the southbound Stage."

Gonzales rubbed his jaw thoughtfully. "What are you going to do?"

"Stay holed up here for a while," Ashe said, thinking of Tanya Hayes. "They might just come back this way."

When McNeil rode up on his bay, Ashe Brandon told his fellow ranger of his plan; then he watched the two rangers head south before he rode over to the long-unused stable and put his horse up for the night. Having settled his mount, he made his way toward Clem's bunkhouse, never glancing back at the big lonesome house or the path that led to Tanya Hayes.

Willow ran up the hill fast as her slim legs could carry her. With supper over and her chores completed, she had stolen from the yard while Tanya was in the back room resting with a book and Samson was playing in their bedroom with the toy wooden soldiers Clem had carved for the boy.

As the big house came into view, Willow glanced over one shoulder and then the other before she started to cross the yard. But she had gone no more than two steps when she caught sight of the tall, blond ranger stepping from the stable, his powerful and attractive body cast in bronze by the slanting sun rays.

"Damn," Willow swore softly and ducked under the spreading arms of what was becoming her favorite tree. Certainly it had been her usual haunt on this day. As she watched the ranger's long, easy strides carry him in the direction of the bunkhouses,

Willow almost giggled out loud. Poor Clem. He had had his full share of strange visitors this day!

"Oh, no." Willow sobered. She had prayed fervently that her handsome blond stranger was far away by now. Though she had to admit curiosity had tugged her back to this spot . . . and something much much more. She had wanted to play a favorite childhood game—make-believe. If she never laid eyes on the young man again, never felt his presence touch her heart and soul as it had this day, she could always make-believe.

Sometimes, Pa used to tell Willow, if you squeeze your eyes shut tight and wish for something real hard, when you opened your eyes your wish just might come true.

Willow tried wishing. But when she reopened her eyes all she saw was the ranger's tall, buckskin-clad frame, disappearing into the trees.

Willow stepped back onto the path leading home, her delicate features saddened. She pushed back threads of fine, spun-gold hair from her face with the back of her hand so they wouldn't stick to the tears on her cheeks. The path before her swam. Through the green- and gold-laced mist, the beautifully rugged face of her handsome stranger smiled at her.

Wishes do come true, Pa, she thought. But why, oh why, she wondered sadly, couldn't you touch them.

Chapter 4

By late afternoon the undulations of the hill country and the guardian pines to the east took on brown creases and green wrinkles that were exquisitely highlighted by the low-angled sun.

A spur of hill extended down from where Willow sat Clem's horse, a strange and shivery sensation holding her motionless. Since she had met the blond stranger, since he had first stared at her with those bold green eyes, Willow had thought of nothing else.

Now here she was, dressed in masculine clothes—dusty old shirt and trousers and hat—all of them borrowed. She didn't know who they belonged to, but they had hung on a peg in the saddle and harness room at Sundance.

Now she was seeking her blond young man, to tell him of the ranger back at Sundance. Or was she only kidding herself? She wanted to warn him, true, but she also wanted to see him again, to feel the shivery wonder of those green eyes flame-licking her face and body.

Spurring the old gray mare on, Willow rode up and down the rugged hill country, knowing that soon she would have to turn back, for the spring grass and wildflowers were turning a vivid crimson in the setting sun. It wouldn't be long before darkness set in, making the low, jutting rocks and prickly cactuses dangerous obstacles in the horse's path.

But the air smelled of dewy earth and sweet grasses, and not a breath of wind stirred her hair. The moon's color would soon be like that of the yolk of an egg, a vibrant contast to the starry, blue black Texas sky. This would be a night for lovers.

Up ahead, under a field of cottonwood, Willow saw them. They were resting their mounts, wary and watchful. There were three of them. The fourth man was absent, which led Willow to believe that the blond was vigilantly scouring the area. Dismounted, the gray mare tucked behind her, Willow crept up behind the thick bole of a tree, and waited.

Willow hadn't decided what she would do when she met the young man face to face once again. Perhaps she just wanted to watch him from afar. She told herself this was why she had dressed in the masculine clothing, so he would not recognize her. It did not occur to her at the time that it would be dangerous to dress as she had.

Pungent smells of damp earth, pastureland, ponds, and woodbine reached her, wafting on the night air. She was too intent on watching the area around the men to sense a presence right behind her and stealthily creeping up.

With Willow unprepared, the attack came hard. Her horse's alarmed cry came too late. Willow would have screamed, but her face was covered by an iron-muscled hand.

Clutched from behind, her arms pinned flat against her waist, she could feel a hard chest curving into her back. A whimper of pain escaped her. She felt that her back would be crushed by the viselike hold. Afraid of that, Willow began to fight the man holding her, or maybe it was a bear. She had heard of bears, but she'd never seen one. The hold slackened just a bit, but the voice in her ears was frightening.

"Damn you, boy, I'm gonna teach you a lesson for spying on us!"

He pushed Willow to the grassy earth and stilled her helplessly frantic struggles with his body. Newly familiar sensations exploded in her when his hand pressed against her rib cage, his angry, gruff voice saying, "You carryin' a weapon, boy?" The rough hand came to a complete halt on the pointed rise of Willow's chest. Then it went over to examine the other breast. He stopped again. "Be Jaysus!" He rolled off the dainty frame he'd thought was a lad and jerked the trembling body to its feet.

Off balance, Willow could only half-crouch while the dusty hat was swept from her head and her crowning glory tumbled forth in a spill of splendid moon gold. "What did you expect?" Willow snapped. She snatched the hat from his nerveless fingers and dusted the thing off on her bagged-out trousers.

"Not this," Talon Clay mumbled. Yanking down the mask that had concealed the lower half of his face, he stared at the golden ghost she made from the waist up. Next he said dumbly, *"You."*

"Yes, me," Willow said, more gently this time. "I came to warn you not to return to Sundance. There's a ranger just awaitin' to bushwhack you and your friends."

Now Talon chuckled. The soft sound reached her ears like silken thunder, reverberating through her very nerve ends.

"One ranger?" Talon snorted. "Shoot, that's a laugh, Miss Pussywillow." His partners were coming up to see what all the scuffling and grunting had been about, but Talon Clay waved them off and they left with grinning faces. Carl Tucker's eyes narrowed, and then he, too, made his way back to the concealment of the cottonwoods.

"Mighty obliged to you, miss," Talon said, "but what you wearing those duds for?" He watched her shrug prettily and thought she was the most charming sight he'd ever come across or tangled with. "You afraid you might be recognized coming to warn me, huh?" He reached out and ran a finger over her softly rounded chin. "Cat got your tongue, Pussywillow?"

"Tell me your name?"

He heard her soft, pleading tone, and it wrenched his outlaw's heart. "Clay," he said, "that's my middle name."

"What is the first?" Her hair swung out and she swayed toward him.

Talon stepped back just a little, having no desire to touch her again. "Can't tell you that now, little one."

"Clay," she murmured, leaving out I love you. But she did, Willow knew this with all her heart. There would never be anyone else for her, ever.

50

He stood before her, a still portrait of rugged maleness, a dangerous young man, a man who walked with a swagger that a lady of the evening would call a sensual rolling of the hips.

"You tiny slip of woman," Talon said, "I don't want to be hurting you."

"Clay, Clay," Willow said with a whimper in her voice. "Why won't you kiss me, hold me, Clay? Please touch me. I'll die if you don't!"

"No you won't." He moved an inch closer. "I won't let you, sweet, sweet thing."

Her pussywillow-brown eyes begged, and Talon tipped his hat back from the line of sweat that had moistened his brow.

"Lord, you don't know what you're askin'. I'm bad, honey, real bad, and I've been with all kinds of women."

Willow did not even flinch at that.

"And," he went on, trying to frighten her, "I've done everything there is to do with them. A man couldn't get lower than I've been, darlin'."

He reached out to run a coarse, tanned finger along her fine chin. "You're so damn perfect, like a tiny doll carved outa porcelain."

"Clay . . ." Willow tilted her head to press her cheek against the roughened back of his fingers. "You feel so good, Clay. You make me all shivery inside."

Talon Clay squinted as if peering into a hot ball of noon sun. "Oh Lord, honey, don't say those things. You make me want to do bad things, wrong things to you. You're too good for the likes of me. I'm cut out and fashioned all wrong for you, Willow. We . . . we just wouldn't fit together right."

With the sun cutting a red-gold swath across her forehead, Willow rose to the balls of her feet and pressed her petal-like lips gently to Talon's cheek. The outlaw's hands hovered above her shoulders as if her heart held him at gunpoint, his dark calloused fingers itching insanely to grip her, to cup her sweetness.

"Honey, oh sweet Pussywillow, if I touch you," his voice shook badly, "if I kiss you, that won't be the end of it. I'll have to taste you all the way. If not today, then another time. That's the way I am." He looked down into her vulnerable face, saying, "Then there's the fear."

He kept on looking into her moist brown eyes with a seriousness new to his personality, his expression growing very grave.

"You don't have to be afraid I'll break, Clay. I'm very strong."

Willow dared to brush her soft lips against Talon Clay's and at the exact moment he felt her moist velvet flesh, his hands crashed down upon her shoulders. But they didn't stay there. His silky blond hair swung forward under his hat as he leaned over her, gripped her small cheeks in back, and brought her lips fully against his. All along his tall, lean frame he shivered. He sucked the sweet nectar from Willow until she was so weak that her knees began to quiver and then collapse. Then he pulled her up hard against himself, feeling her woman's depression meet his hardness.

Talon sucked in his breath. What it must feel like to be a finger of rock under the relentless high noon,

Talon Clay suddenly knew. He knew, for sure. He smiled happily against her lips, thinking Willow must share his discovery too.

"Let me down, Clay." Willow pulled her lips away and squirmed.

Talon's smile was lopsided. He continued, however, to hold her a little longer, and his voice was husky and quavery deep when he finally spoke, looking her hard in the eyes.

"I told you. I warned you, Pussywillow, that I would frighten you. I've never known the ways of a vir—"

"Clay." She cut him off. "Put me down." She pointed. "Over there."

He peered along her steady finger. "What?" He stared, stunned, over to the bright bedding of long-fallen leaves, some stained a bright red, some brassy yellow. His knowing eyes came back to hers. "Willow, sweet darlin', you don't know what you're asking for." He shook all over, hot perspiration appearing above his lips.

"Yes," she said firmly. "Yes I do."

He looked over his shoulder, making out three figures dimly through the cottonwoods. "They're waitin'."

"They'll wait."

Willow took his hand, guiding it to cup her through the baggy trousers. Then she tossed her head back and pressed down the back of his hand. He made an animal sound in his throat. It welled up, screaming for release, when she innocently, shyly said, "I've got honey for you, Clay. Please make love to me and make the hurt go away."

He set Willow down so hard that she thought her teeth would shatter. "What do you know about making love?" He glared. "Tell me!"

Talon Clay's fingers burned and ached where he had touched her. He shook her. Tears glistened in her eyes, the last splash of light melding them into golden sundrops. Terribly ashamed, Willow hung her head and the sunny tears rolled off her chin.

"Nothing," she muttered.

Then she whirled and ran, sped headlong, her heavy tears blinding her, so ashamed that she could never face the man—the total stranger—who had become her undying love in one day. One miserable day!

Talon stared after her, but he didn't move from the spot. He was frozen. His sensuous fire had turned to stone-cold apathy in a few seconds.

"Damn it Willow," he said, wiping still-hot perspiration from his upper lip and forehead. He whistled for his horse, and at once the honey buckskin came. He did not cast a glance in Willow's direction as she rode off, but mounted and wheeled the horse, executing the turn so sharply his boot dragged in the grassy earth. He hailed his partners and proceeded to head in the direction of the closest town—a town where he would find a saloon.

The way was dark save for a splattering of moonlight here and there, and Willow's flesh-pink mouth was drawn down, sullen. Shadows reached out from the trees, shadows that the climbing egg-yolk moon created, shadows that frightened the young woman out of her wits and almost from out of her saddle.

"The man in the moon must be having a good laugh, huh, Pa?" Willow said aloud, patting the gray mare to reassure herself that she had company. "You always said he has a good chuckle on spooky nights like this one when he comes out to play games on folks." She glanced up briefly, then back down to the rocky rolling terrain. "Yep, he's sure grinnin' from ear to ear tonight, Pa." She gulped when a hoof clacked loudly over a stone. "Easy there, girl, easy now, watch your step. Shoot," she aped Clay, "there really ain't nothin' to be afeared of." She shivered. "Nothing. *Oh!*"

A section of a tree bole detached itself and came floating toward her—or so frightened Willow thought. At that moment a calm, easy voice reached her like a soothing balm. But the voice spoke Spanish.

"Miedoso?" He asked her if she was afraid.

"Sí!" Willow exclaimed. *"Quién es?"* "Who is it?" she asked as the shadowy figure approached. The horse, a buckskin, was darker in color than Clay's, yet the horse seemed familiar to her.

"Ashe Brandon. Remember?"

"Of course," she said, watching him fall in beside her. "Why did you speak Spanish? Are you keeping a low . . . a low profile or something like that?"

"You said it right, Miss Willow." His eyes rolled downward, across her face, then back to the path before them. "Watch out for that cactus on your side." He waited until she had reined in a bit. "I didn't know who you were until you spoke. You

55

looked just like a little brown Mexican in that getup, your hair tucked up inside, the hat shading your little face. I thought I might have to bring a runaway back home instead of escort you to your place. So tell me, Miss Willow, why are you dressed like this? And how do you know Spanish?''

Feeling secure now, Willow laughed. "The first question is none of your business, Mr. Ranger, and the second is easy."

When she chose not to explain, Ashe said, "How are you at brewing coffee?''

"Wouldn't know. Tanya always makes the coffee and tea. Besides," she said, looking downward, "we don't have any coffee."

"I see." He paused thoughtfully. "Are you going to answer my question or do I remain forever in suspense?''

"Spanish is a second language to most folks in Texas."

"True," he said. "A few basic Spanish phrases. But you, Miss Willow, have stayed around here most your life. Why, I don't believe you've ever been out of Sweetwater Springs or Bastrop County for that matter."

"I've lived in Sweetwater Springs all my life, mister, at Sundance. I love it and I never want to leave." She sighed wistfully. "I just bet you can't guess how I learned some Spanish, can you?''

Ashe Brandon peered at her through the darkness, then back at the moonlit trail ahead. "Your sister," he said softly, "Tanya."

"Nope!"

He wanted to talk about Tanya, but to do so would

make Willow curious, then nosey, and then gossipy. All women were the same, he had discovered.

"Where do you think?" she asked, too quickly.

"Aha, so it wasn't a person." He laughed softly. "It was a 'where.' I know, it must be San Antonio."

"You guessed it, Ranger. Everyone there speaks Spanish, and if you don't, you're in a heap of trouble."

Ashe smiled. How true, he was thinking. He remembered a night in a San Antonio hotel and a pretty *señorita*. If he hadn't known Spanish, fluently, he would have had a hard time explaining to an enraged husband that his wife had deceived this ranger into believing she was "to be had at any price." The man had been a hulking bear of a Mexican and the woman . . . well, she hadn't been worth losing his life over. No woman was worth that, he thought. Besides, the whole affair had left him with a sour taste regarding easy women. Always they had to be unmarried—and not liars. But that had been before, before he had returned to Sundance. Now, all of a sudden, he was beginning to like the feel of it here, now that Garnet Haywood Brandon was gone.

"Here we are," Ashe said, reining up his horse forty feet from the little house. He smiled to himself, waiting.

"Oh no," Willow said. "Not here. You see Sis don't know that I . . . uh . . . that I went on this little ride."

Ashe Brandon frowned. "You afraid of your big sister?"

"No, it's not that." Willow looked toward the little

57

house. "She won't talk to me if she's put out over something I've done. She just ignores me, if you know what I mean."

"I do." Ashe set his horse into motion once again.

"Hold on there!" snapped an angry voice from the shadows. The voice became a woman who stepped onto the path, a woman whose lovely face was set in a scornful mold. "Willow, I heard your voice, you aren't fooling anyone."

"Miss Hayes, I can explain—" Ashe began, but he was cut off by a catlike hiss.

"So, it's Ranger Brandon," Tanya ground out, sweeping her rifle up to her shoulder and leveling the ancient weapon expertly. "I'll kill you right here for dallying with my sister, you lecherous bas—" She stopped abruptly, having no desire to swear even now. "Come down from that horse, Ranger, easy, and don't make any sudden moves." She jerked the long-barreled hunting rifle higher.

"Tanya," Willow cried, afraid for Ashe Brandon now. "You don't understand, Sis."

"Oh, I'm sure I do. It's you who is too innocent to understand what's going on here." Tanya, emotionally overwrought, poked her rifle in the air carelessly. "Where did you get those clothes, Willow? Did he find them for you? I suppose he found a nice nest to tuck you into for a few hours while he dallied with you?" The harsh question was hissed through gritted teeth. "Willow Margaret, you'd better not lie. Are you still unsoiled, or not?"

Willow was shaken by her sister's inference that she had had sex with a man. Her face reddening, she recalled how deliciously close she had come to doing

58

just that with Clay. Her blond young man was a fire in her blood. She loved him. Oh God, how she loved Clay!

Unconscious tears came to Willow's eyes at the thought that she might never see Clay again, never have him touch her, never be loved by him. She groaned, not knowing she did so aloud. How was she ever going to be able to face Clay again if he came back to make good his threat, that he wouldn't be able to stop once he had kissed her lips!

Mesmerized, Tanya stared hotly at the tears coursing down her sister's cheeks, stared through her own scalding tears, unable to see clearly through the swimming mist. Too late, Tanya realized her mistake.

"I'll take that, Miss Hayes," Ashe Brandon said.

"Not again!" she shouted, reaching out viciously only to come up hard against the barrel of the rifle now turned sidewise to her. She kicked at his shins. "Damn you, Ashe Brandon! She kicked again, making contact this time, hard. He flinched.

"Take your sister," he began, "your *unsoiled* sister, home, and learn what you can from her. I'm not guilty of touching a hair on her head, Tanya, but I"—he shook the gun—"I want some answers myself."

She pressed her lips together in a taut line. "Like what?"

"Like just what she was doing out there in that getup. She sure wasn't playing soldier boy or hunting for jack rabbits, not by the look on her face when you mentioned dallying in the hay."

Willow stepped forward now, her little face

pinched. "Just what do you think I was doing, Mr. Ranger?" she asked, this time acting a bit too big for her britches.

"I *know* what you were doing, Miss Willow—or what you came close to doing." He started to walk away, leading both horses. As they both stared after him, Ashe Brandon tossed back, "Just *who* you were *almost* doing it with is what I aim to find out. Good night, ladies."

Chapter 5

The soft thrumming of rain on the low roof of the little house was constant. Smoke billowed from the chimney like a giant ghostly hand, its fingers twisting, entwining; and the redolent smell of pine and smoke mingled with that of the wet earth.

Tanya stood at the window, the orange glow of the fireplace behind her filtering through the thin cotton of her flimsy nightgown. She tossed her head in a savage, angry gesture, and her eyes were deep sapphire jewels staring out into the early morning gloom.

Ashe Brandon had vexed her so that sleep had eluded her all night long. She couldn't believe that she, Tanya Hayes, had once been in love with the man, this imperious ranger who provoked her to no end. Twice now, he had snatched her Pa's rifle from her, and he'd treated her with no more respect than he would show to a common criminal. There would not be a third time, she promised herself.

Tanya turned back to the room and went to pour

herself a mug of the cider she'd been warming in an earthenware jug on the hearthstones. Cupping her hands about the mug, she took a seat and, leaning her elbows on the table, stared into the golden flames licking the new log she had placed there earlier.

Since Willow and Samson were still asleep, Tanya was using this time to think matters over. There seemed no help for her dilemma. If she had the money to do so, she would take her brother and sister and depart from Sundance as soon as possible. She had nothing, however: no horse of her own, no carriage or wagonbed. All of her earthly possessions rested in this little house to which she had come as a young girl.

Tanya heaved a sigh. She could barely remember the small town in California where she'd lived as a girl, their poor pa looking after them after their mother had up and left them.

Taking a sip of the cider, Tanya lowered the mug to the table and gripped it tight. Her mother's face had grown dim through the years and she didn't even recall her name, only Pa's tears and the fact that he'd never mentioned her mother's name since the dark day she had gone away. He had called her Ma, and his children had known her only as that.

"Sis, I'm hungry."

Samson padded into the room and climbed onto the bench beside his big sister. She offered him a good-morning smile while she ruffled the tufts of red hair sticking up from his mussed head.

"What were you thinkin' about, Tanya?"

"Just things, sweetheart."

He screwed up a corner of his mouth. "What

kinda things?"

"Oh," she said thoughtfully, "how much I love you."

He scooted closer and laid his rumpled head against her breast. "I love you too, Sis." He took her hand in his and toyed with her long, tapered fingers. "Do you still love Willow too? I know you were mad at her last night 'cause you didn't talk to her when she came back with you. Why was she wearing those clothes?" He wrinkled his freckled nose in a boyish grimace.

"You know what?" She lifted his head, cupping his cheeks on either side. When he shook his head, she said, "You ask too many questions, young man."

Samson hopped off the bench, took a cup from the shelf, and poured himself a generous portion of apple cider. He turned, smiling at his sister as he warmed his backside at the stone hearth. His eyes strayed from her to Willow who now stood in the bedroom doorway, yawning and stretching wide, her yellow cornsilk hair flowing from her white throat to her pointed breasts and on down to her waist.

Samson gawked at Willow; then he blurted out, "You look just terrible, Sis! Are you sick or somethin'?"

"Samson!" Tanya rose from the table, brusquely swiping up her mug. "Go to your room immediately and get yourself dressed." She addressed Willow next. "Willow, take your things and come to my room and dress. We'll have that talk now."

"I wanted to wash up," Willow said, as if she wished to delay an ordeal.

"Wash up in my room." Tanya walked over to the

hearth, put her mug upon a shelf, and swung the crane supporting the heavy pot off the fire. "I've heated water."

"It's boiling!" Willow squeaked, after snatching her clothes from her chest. "I'll scald myself!"

"Ha-ha!" Samson stuck out his tongue and flicked the curtain shut in Willow's face.

"Samson, behave," Tanya called through the curtain, "or I'll take the switch to your hide."

The freckle-faced lad poked his head around the curtain. "You never done that afore, Sis." His reddish-brown eyes had grown wide at the mere thought of physical punishment.

Tanya carried the huge black kettle to her room and emptied some water into the blue-flecked metal washbowl. "There's always a first time for everything," she called through the wall, eying Willow as she said the words.

Plopping herself on the feather mattress, Willow said, "You wash up first, Tanya, you're the eldest."

Tanya nodded and, free from embarassment, began to strip. They were used to washing and dressing together, ever since Willow had become a woman and needed to do so away from Samson. At times, though, Willow and Samson argued over who was going to use the first water heated up in the morning since there was only one huge kettle between them.

"I'll go heat up some more water, Sis," Willow said, beginning to rise from the bed on which she was reclining.

"Never mind. There'll be enough. It's cold in here and I'll be done soon." Tanya ran the small sliver of precious soap over the cloth and proceeded to wash herself quickly all over. When she was done, she rubbed her body briskly with a rough linen rag and then reached for her slip and blue cotton dress. "Willow," she began while she dressed, "who did you meet last evening when you went for a ride on Clem's mare?"

Willow rolled from her back onto her stomach and picked at the patchwork quilt with suddenly nervous fingers. "No one you would know, Sis. Just a drifter who was passing through Sundance property the other day." Her soft brown eyes took on a dreamy look then, their expression changing quickly from worry to ecstasy.

"You are," Tanya paused, searching for the right words, "you are still untouched, I pray?"

Willow stared at Tanya's lovely breasts and thighs clad only in a chemise and a long petticoat, not really seeing her sister at all.

"I am, Sis, honest to God." Willow sighed dreamily. "He's the most beautiful young feller I've ever laid eyes on. His hair is the color of mine, worn long, and he wears the tightest pants I've ever seen."

"Willow!" Tanya said, scandalized that her little sister should speak in such an open fashion about a man. Adjusting the bodice of her dress over her full, soft breasts, she asked, "Where did you meet him?"

"First time?"

Tanya paused at the last two buttons, her hand falling to rest on her hip. "How many times have you met this young man then?"

"Two times." Willow's eyes rolled heavenward.

"You should not be alone with a total stranger. It's

not proper, Willow Hayes. Things—things can happen, even in a short time, you know."

Willow laughed softly. "Not when he won't even touch me, they doesn't."

"Don't."

"Don't, then." Willow puckered her pink lips and bounded from the bed to begin undressing. "Tanya," she began boldly, "don't you ever want a man to touch you? Not any man?"

A crimson blush spread from Tanya's white throat to her cheeks, making her appear even more lovely than she already was. "Perhaps," Tanya said, turning to the curtain, her eyes wistfully sad. "When the right man comes along, that is." She bent to scoop up the clothes that needed laundering, paused, and then placed the dirty clothes in the corner atop her wooden chest. "This will have to wait till a sunny day. It's too chilly and damp outside to be washing clothes even on the porch."

Just then the sun peeped through, making Tanya's words sound foolish, but the steady drip-drip of raindrops on the roof announced that it would be high noon before she could do the laundry. The clothes would take too long to dry if she hung them out before the sun had burned away the moisture from the air.

"Tanya, Sis!" Samson called from the main room. "Ashe Brandon's here to see ya," he said. He continued cheerfully, "he brung some coffee from his saddlebags, and cornmeal from Clem!"

A bright red color, this time a heated flush, spread over Tanya's suddenly alert countenance, and her hands fluttered about her hair like nervous little birds trying to bring some semblance of order to their nest. But actually her hands were working busily, flying through her long red hair and braiding the heavy hank which she finally tied at the end with a strip of material.

"Hmmm," Willow hummed, stepping into her yellow calico after having dried herself off. "Does this ranger happen to be the same Brandon whose pa owned Sundance? He don't—he doesn't—look familiar to me." Willow paused to tap her chin. "But then I would've been too little to remember Ashe Brandon, though you might remember him 'cause it seems to me this here ranger's the same feller you used to tag after." She smiled mischievously. "Why are you blushing so, Sis?" She giggled beneath her hand. "Are you pining for that tall, handsome ranger, Ashe Brandon?"

"What?"

Tanya spun to face Willow. Their faces were level as Tanya leaned forward to peer into her sister's laughing brown eyes. "What would you know about that? And just exactly what, Willow Hayes, do you mean?"

"Oh . . ." Willow buttoned up her bodice, working slowly with the tiny buttons there. "It's when you care a lot for someone and he makes you feel warm and shivery all over just lookin' at him. Your stomach tickles, way down, and your chest get hot and hard. Then it begins to hurt if he doesn't touch you, Sis."

Heat burned Tanya's cheeks and she had a hard

time swallowing. She placed her hands on Willow's shoulders. "Has your young man touched you intimately? Has he, Willow?"

Willow stared into her sister's blue eyes, studying them thoroughly. "Yes." She peered down at the floor, then up again. "But I drove him to do it, Sis. I couldn't help it. I swear nothin' more than that happened. He was mad at me, madder than a wet hen." She hung her head dejectedly. "He treated me like a loose woman, Sis."

"Can you tell me his name?" Tanya asked, beginning to feel a headache coming on.

"Clay." Willow turned toward the bed, ashamed of her actions the day before. "That's all."

"We'll talk later."

With that, Tanya left Willow alone to her thoughts and went to greet Ashe Brandon, steeling herself for the questioning she knew was to come.

"Mornin'," Ashe said when Tanya entered the room, his eyes scouring her from head to foot, slowly, maddeningly. He took in her freshly scrubbed appearance, his attention resting on the faint bluish tinge beneath her eyes. It attested to the fact that she'd slept little the night before. He'd had a time of it finding sleep himself.

"Good morning," Tanya said, primly and properly. She went directly to the small table beside the hearth and from the shelf above it took down the ingredients she needed to prepare soda and buttermilk biscuits. Her nose twitched curiously in response to the delicious odor wafting from the hearth. "Coffee? You made coffee?" She turned to

Ashe Brandon.

"In my job one learns to prepare food and drink quickly while on the trail." He smiled down at Samson, ruffling the lad's hair, and Samson smiled back happily as he munched on the beef jerky Ashe had given him. "It should be done by now," Ashe said, indicating the pot.

Half-conscious of her motions, Tanya took down two mugs and poured coffee for Ashe and herself. She placed hers on the small table beside her fixings, then brought Ashe's steaming mug to where he sat lazily watching her every movement. Samson grinned with boyish happiness, but he watched the odd behavior of Ashe and his sister, wondering why they were looking each other over so. Samson took a bite of the jerky, chewing hard and swallowing before he blurted, "I saw Tucker's cats matin' just last week. You should have just seen that old tomcat—"

"Samson!" Tanya whirled, her cheeks afire, her doughy spoon threatening the lad.

"It's only nature, Tanya," Ashe Brandon drawled; then to change the subject he said, "I brought your rifle back." She looked over her shoulder to where it hung on the two pegs. "Don't think you could have hit the broad side of a barn with it, though, dirty as it was inside. Cleaned it up for you"—there was a smile in his voice—"just in case some lecherous stranger gets too close."

"What's lechrous mean, Ashe? I never heard that word afore." Samson looked curiously at the smiling ranger.

"It means a dirty old man with only one thing on

his mind," he told the lad, lifting one corner of his crisp mouth in a lopsided grin.

The lad's red eyebrows rose knowingly. "You mean like old Clem? Is he lechrous?"

Ashe Brandon laughed aloud, showing a row of even, white teeth that contrasted with the bold tan of his ruggedly lean face. He looked over to where Tanya was washing her spoon off in a small pan because she had dropped the utensil on the floor only a moment before.

"Clem's not a stranger," Tanya said, avoiding Ashe's eyes. Furiously she began mixing the batter, the motion twitching her hips and drawing her guest's hazel eyes as the sensuous movement increased. Ashe shifted on the bench, his body a plenitude of warmth.

"Holy Cow!" Samson exclaimed. "What's happenin'?"

Seeing where the lad's eyes had lowered to and rested, Ashe grinned at him in a most pleading manner, and, thinking quickly, said, "Samson saw a buck and a doe out the window just now, didn't you, Sammy?" The warning glint in his eyes dared the lad to say otherwise.

"Well,"—Tanya shrugged—"what's so unusual about that?" She put the biscuits into the oven, secured the door, and turned to face them again.

This time Samson was leaning on the table, cupping his chin, and staring up at Ashe Brandon in a most unusual way. Ashe looked very sheepish, almost embarrassed, and Tanya wondered briefly if the two were sharing some secret.

"What sort of mischief is this?" she asked, but silence greeted her. "I must have flour on my face or in my hair." She walked over to the mirror which hung crookedly on the wall. Straightening the thong that fastened it to a nail, Tanya peered at her reflection but found nothing amiss. However, she was most surprised at the delicate flush that stained her cheeks and the half-wild look in her eyes.

"It's what the creatures were doing that caused Samson to shout," Ashe said, squinting a warning eye at the lad while Tanya's back was to them.

"Yeah," Samson said, suddenly catching on and believing this to be a man's game that had nothing to do with women whatsoever.

Oh, Samson, Ashe thought upon seeing that the lad considered this was a game. Oh, lad, in a few years you are going to remember this conversation and laugh. Ashe's eyes wandered back to Tanya, taking visual pleasure in the curve of her back and the slim fingers that fussed with her hair. Feeling his gaze like the touch of flesh-and-blood hands, Tanya whirled to face Ashe Brandon.

"I see," she said, grateful that Ashe was taking the lad in hand, believing that he had restrained Samson from blurting out a crude remark as he had earlier. "Thank you." She couldn't bring herself to say Ashe.

Willow entered the room by the time the biscuits were ready, and she helped her sister by bringing out the butter—which Tanya had made, thanks to Clem's cow—warmed over fried apples from the day before, and coffee. The delicious coffee made it a real

71

feast for one and all. Even Samson had half a cup of the steaming black brew.

The younger woman kept her eyes averted from Ashe Brandon's measuring glances. They swept over her far too often for comfort. She knew the interrogation could not be avoided, and it made her uneasy to think that she was going to be forced to lie for Clay's sake. She kept glancing at her sister, praying that Tanya would not reveal her young man's name. Tanya caught on and nodded when Ashe's head bent to listen to something Samson was saying for his ears only.

When Tanya rose to clear the table after the meal was finished, she bumped into Willow who had jumped to her feet at Tanya's movement. Placing a hand on either side of Willow's shoulders, Tanya gently pushed her back down onto the puncheon bench. Resigned to her fate, Willow sat demurely, folding her suddenly clammy hands on her lap.

"Samson," Tanya said, taking his empty plate. "Go outside now, please, and ready the tubs for the wash. You know where the dirty clothes are kept."

"Awww, do I have to?" Samson said, but he was already climbing back over the bench. He knew, by the determined look in her eyes and the set of her shoulders, that his big sister would brook no argument. "You know what, Sis," he blurted out, stalling, "you forgot to say the graces."

"So I did," Tanya said. She stopped halfway across the room, her hands full of dirty plates.

"Can we say them now?" Samson wondered if this was the proper thing to do. His sister nodded and

Samson climbed back onto his seat. "Can I say them?"

Tanya's face split into a charming smile. "Go ahead."

"I have to hear this!" Willow said, already bowing her head.

Ashe cleared his throat, but he bowed his head just the same, grinning as his eyes met the one eye with which the lad was peering up at him. Then Samson closed both eyes and Ashe followed suit.

"Dear Lord," Samson began, "thank you for the blessin' of this food, and the nourishment to our bodies, and thank you"—he faltered before going on—"for the food what we already ate! Amen!"

One and all smiled as Samson hurried out the door, slamming it shut in his haste to be away before the red blush reached his ears. And suddenly, while Tanya's back was turned, Ashe Brandon leaned forward to stare into Willow's eyes.

The force of this ranger's character hit her between the eyes. The gentle lines of Ashe Brandon's face had vanished, and the charity he had shown her the night before was gone too. She no longer felt safe and secure with Ashe Brandon about. She felt that he was going to eat her whole, chew her up and then spit her out like so much Willow fluff.

"Willow," he began, gently enough, "all I want is for you to answer me one question."

He smiled and Willow felt like a turkey at a Thanksgiving shoot.

"Shoot," she blurted, then she changed her mind quickly. "Just one question, and that's all?"

Ashe didn't stand on ceremony, but whipped out the question. "Who were you with last night?"

"Tanya. Samson."

"Before that, Willow. You know what I mean." He spread a lean hand on the table, adding, "Late afternoon, if you prefer then."

"You."

His fist crashed down. "You know exactly what I mean. I want you to stop playing cat-and-mouse games with me." His hand came up and she flinched, but he merely rubbed his chin impatiently. "Young lady, this is serious business we're talking about here. Three men, maybe four, robbed a stage three days ago. And do you know what else? Can you guess?"

Willow shook her head, her eyes wide and fearful. "No," she softly said.

"A man was killed." Ashe's eyes became hard, the lines about his mouth brittle. "An innocent man, Willow, one with a wife and children. He had a newborn baby waiting for him back home."

Willow gasped and Tanya rushed over, her eyes gone wide, every nerve quivering in her body. "Baby," was all Tanya could mutter. She pictured a tiny boy or girl in this harsh country without a father's sustaining strength to lean on. She knew all too well what it was to be without a mother, but she couldn't have managed without her pa. It struck her how very helpless they would become when their clothes were full of patches, their feet bare, when they had only food from the garden, no supplies from town when the few dollars she had set aside ran out. I'll have to get a job somehow, Tanya thought.

Then she chided herself. Here she was worrying

74

about how they were going to go without when a baby had just lost its father!

When Tanya looked down at her sister's golden head, she saw an amazing sight.

Ashe Brandon had come around to their side of the table, and cradled in his arms was Willow. She had fainted, and this time it was genuine.

Chapter 6

Willow finally came to, blinking, hearing Tanya speak her name over and over. Sun was streaming through her little window, the big cottonwood outside creating swimming patterns across her bed. Rolling her head, Willow stared first at her sister and then at the ranger hovering behind Tanya. Ashe Brandon looked anything but sorry that she had fainted dead away!

Then the reality of what Ashe Brandon had revealed to her swept all else from Willow's brain and she was left with a sinking feeling. Clay, a murderer!

"It's not true," Willow murmured, snatching the wet cloth that had been draped over her forehead up in her shaking hand.

"I'm afraid it is, Willow," Ashe Brandon said softly. "Now, can I have that name?"

Willow was feeling miserable, for she suddenly realized she would never see Clay again. It was her own fault for falling in love with a man she already knew was an outlaw. Now he would be locked up or, worse, hung for murder.

Adamant, Willow said, "He didn't do it, I just know he couldn't have murdered a man in cold blood, much less two men." She looked up into the impatient cat-hazel eyes. "His name is Clay, and that's all he would tell me. Honest to God."

"Clay?" Ashe muttered, gone stone cold. "What does this Clay look like?"

"He has hair like yours and mine—blond— and—"

Trembling excitement washed over Ashe. "Has he green eyes, very green?"

Lifting herself from her reclining position, Willow sat with her legs tucked beneath her. "Yes! Green as new summer grass. You know him?"

"Clay . . ." Tanya said, almost to herself. Then louder, "Talon Clay." She looked at Ashe. "Could he be? . . ."

All the tension seemed to leave Ashe then, and the taut lines in his face relaxed into a tender expression. His impatience was gone. "Talon Clay Brandon," he said. Then, "My brother."

But Willow, unlike Ashe, had become even more confused and frightened. Her chest was now so tight that she felt she was being smothered. She waited, knowing what the next question was going to be.

"Willow," Ashe said, smiling now, "was Talon, I mean Clay, was he alone?"

He and the others had been running from this man, this ranger who stood before her now, Ashe Brandon, Clay's very own flesh and blood. Oh Lord, what now? Willow trembled all over inside.

"We were alone," she said, knowing this was not a lie. They had been alone, those two times, and Ashe Brandon had not asked what she had seen.

"Did you see anyone else?"

Oh, no, Willow groaned inwardly. Here comes the lie, just one teeny one. She meant to find Talon Clay and ask him for the truth. He would tell it, she knew. He was not a bad man. He might rob, but he wasn't a killer at heart.

"No."

"Thank you, Willow." Ashe Brandon turned brusquely to leave the curtained room. "You don't know how much this means to me," he said, pausing before dropping the curtain. "I haven't seen Talon Clay for nigh onto six years now."

Willow affected a cheery smile. "He must have come home looking for you, right?"

"I aim to find out." He tipped his hat as he put it on. "Ladies."

When they were alone, Tanya said to her sister, "Well, I'm sure glad that's over with. Willow? What's wrong? You aren't looking too happy about the matter. Ashe Brandon is here looking for outlaws and Talon Clay certainly couldn't be one of them. Could he, Willow?"

"Of course not," Willow said, then to brush over the lie, she blurted, "I sure hope he's not." Not the murderer, at least, she told herself silently.

"I'm going to get busy, see what I can rustle up for dinner. You tidy up in here and then go see if Clem has gotten those eggs from Rankin's. He promised us some the other day."

"Eggs," Willow murmured, but she brightened when she thought of going to see Clem. The old man just might have some sorely needed answers for her— If he would talk. Willow had a sneaking suspicion that old Clem was in cahoots with the outlaws.

After Willow had completed her chores, she took her shawl down from the peg and left the little house. She tossed her golden hair back and turned to run across the yard and down the hill to the creek. Tanya watched her go, wondering at the girl's moodiness.

Tanya washed clothes that afternoon, Samson helping with the emptying of the large tubs; and when the wash was done and hanging on the line, Samson went wearily to the room he shared with Willow. Tanya decided she would have to do something about that, for it was time Willow had her own room. The main room was large enough to provide an area for Willow. A curtain strung across the width of the room would give her privacy.

Since Samson was studying Tanya's arithmetic book and doing his figuring on an old slate, Tanya decided to slip away to the creek and bathe in the cool, clear water. She reflected that it was fortunate she had been able to teach her little brother how to read, write, add, and subtract. The school was too far away for him to attend.

The afternoon had warmed considerably by the time Tanya set out from the house, soap and a cloth in hand. When she'd last checked on Samson he had been asleep, his strong, boyish hand resting on the arithmetic book, his ciphering printed out in a neat, clear hand across the old slate.

The woodsy world was alive with birdsong, the soft melody of the creek, and the sunshine filtering down through the gently swaying branches. Tanya reached her private spot and shed her clothes. Hanging them over a low branch, she smiled at a little brown bird that cocked his head, watching her. She walked slowly into the cool water, fresh from the spring rain, and shivered. Goose bumps broke out on her flesh and Tanya was almost tempted to get back into her clothes, run back to the house, and renew the fire. But this was her own special place. Here she could be alone and renew her thoughts. She wanted to relish the time, however short.

Clad only in the chemise that reached down to her thighs, Tanya quickly headed toward the spot where the sun warmed the water. Dipping her cloth in the water, she wrung it out and began to wipe her skin free of the sweat that had accumulated while she did the wash.

A splash across the creek reached Tanya's ears and she looked up. Before her stood Ashe Brandon, his chest bare, naked as the day he was born and just as surprised as she was.

"Well, well." He chuckled. "Fancy meeting you here."

While she gasped and tried to cover herself by splaying one hand at her chest, the other at the top of her thighs, Ashe Brandon just stood there, a grin splitting his handsome face from ear to ear. Unable to move or mutter one word, Tanya found herself staring at this fine specimen of manhood, her eyes dropping from the flare of his wide shoulders down to his tapered waist, then to the Vee of dark blond hairs leading to the imposingly bold evidence of his masculinity. His pants were of a light material raggedly cut off at the knees and she blushed at seeing so much manly leg. She dragged her gaze back up and found no help there either, for his hair, bright as a sun-kissed field of wheat, swung forward as he moved. She thought he looked like a Greek god come back to life, walking, walking ever slowly toward her. . . .

At first, Ashe Brandon had not been able to credit what he was seeing. Then she had moved from beneath the shade of an overhanging branch and into the yellow splash of sunlight, alive, not the dream of a man who had abstained from lovemaking for far too long to be comfortable in this situation. There was a very pressing need arising just now. If he thought he had been aroused while looking at her standing before the mirror in the little house, he was ten times more so now. How would she react to that? Ashe decided he was not going to be the one to turn coward and run. In fact, he found himself impelled forward like a Texas vulture toward its prey.

Mesmerized, Tanya stared into gray-green irises flecked with the topaz of a richly hued gem, and she realized, with a start, that he was standing right before her.

"Tanya," he said softly, "you're beautiful."

"I—I . . ." She could only stutter. She wanted to say she thought he was beautiful too, but somehow that wouldn't sound just right, nor would it be proper.

"Tanya," he breathed her name deeply this time.

When Tanya finally spoke, her voice came out just as whispery as his. It was as if they shared a secret and spoke low, even though no one could hear but nature.

Recovering some composure, she told him, "If you touch me, I'll kick you right between the legs, Ashe Brandon."

"I'll try my best not to." Even as he said this he reached out to run a finger along the flushed slant of her cheek.

"You lied," she said, jerking back.

He stepped closer, aware that she might very well make good her threat to wound him in a place that was very vulnerable, especially at this moment. "I said I'd try"—he shrugged—"not that I wouldn't."

"Your kind always lies."

"My kind, Tanya?" His eyes burned into hers.

Tanya could feel the heat being released from the corded muscles of his long thighs. She was suddenly assailed by a nostalgic remembrance of other sunlit days of long ago. She'd encountered the same long planes of Ashe's face, the implacable features. She studied him now in fascinated admiration as she had when she was a shivery-kneed girl.

With icy politeness, he asked her again, "What kind is that?"

Not liking the sound of his voice now, she averted her flushed face, saying, "Never mind." She had already gone over this ground once with him, and she had no desire to point out again the areas in which he had aroused her distrust. It was too painful to speak of that.

"You were a starry-eyed girl back then, Tanya," he said and heaved a long, impatient sigh.

Tanya was stunned that he could have so easily read her thoughts. She lapsed into silence.

He gave a short laugh. "I assure you, Tanya, it was never my intention to hurt you. Can't you believe that?"

"No," she answered dully.

"How can I undo the damage?"

"Just go away, Ashe Brandon." She was trying to sound calm, but with him standing so near that she could feel his hot, shaky breath on her forehead it was all she could do not to fall against him and melt.

Tanya could not know how strongly Ashe's own senses were responding to her nearness, her mere presence. He saw her as a lovely girl waiting, pining for her first love, and his mouth twisted in bitter regret. She had placed an impenetrable barrier between them. He was only randy right now, he tried to convince himself. This was the only reason he was trying to get through to her and melt that icy façade.

Tanya's heart leaped when his heated regard fixed on her moist, parted lips. She didn't know when he made the movement, but she could feel the muscles of his long thighs, bunched, as he had stepped closer to her. Tanya sensed the tension in his big man's body, and a sudden desire rushed through her own body, heating every part of her. A fierce coil of flame was curling in her belly, and his lips were coming closer and closer.

Ashe could see pale lavender flecks, like stars at

night, swimming in the deep blue of Tanya's eyes. He wanted to love her, here, now, with the lubricating water swirling about them; quickly at first so as not to prolong her hurt, then slowly, over and over gently. The fiery thought reverberated through his brain.

"Now, Tanya, now," Ashe found himself muttering as his lips brushed hers.

"Tanya!" Samson called from the hill. "*Tanya!*"

In confused alarm, Tanya stepped back, her fingertips pressed to her throbbing lips. They were on fire. She stared at Ashe as a short, soft curse issued from his mobile mouth.

Whirling about to see if Samson could view them from the hill, Tanya was relieved to realize that her brother was too far away to see anything. Judging by the intensity of his tone, Samson would have to walk a ways through the thick brush and trees before he caught sight of them.

"I think you had better—" Tanya bit off her words when she turned and found that she stood alone. Then she giggled behind her hand at the sight of a flash of muscled white leg disappearing into the brush on the other side of the creek. She knew he had left the water with all due haste so as not to be caught standing there in the near buff with her.

Shivering, but not from cold, Tanya reached the clearing that led to the little house. She was surprised to see Samson standing with a tall, lanky man in dusty, travel-stained clothes. Samson waved, and the young man with him turned toward her.

"Tanya," Samson called. "Guess who's come to

visit?'' Before she could even look the man over and venture a guess, Samson said, "Carl Tucker!''

The sight that greeted Tucker's gray-blue eyes was highly pleasing, for he had remembered Tanya Hayes as a freckle-faced kid wearing unruly braids. However, Carl had never forgotten the fiery red of her hair. Now Tanya had grown into a beautiful woman, her face creamy perfection, her curves a tantalizing promise any man would long to caress. And Carl Tucker did suddenly long to do that.

"Hello, Carl," Tanya greeted the tawny-haired man who was their neighbor, Dan and Janice's son. A long time had passed since she had last seen Carl.

"Howdy, Miss Hayes." Carl smiled widely to conceal the lust he had felt heating his face and smoldering in his eyes moments before. "You're lookin' real nice, Miss Hayes, hardly the freckle-faced girl I used to play with. Remember when I used to pull your braids?" he said with a chuckle.

"I . . ." Tanya faltered, still warm and shivery from her encounter in the stream with Ashe. "Yes, I suppose I do remember that, come to think of it. Will you join us for a cup of coffee and some cornbread?"

"That's most neighborly of you, Miss Hayes."

Tanya laughed over her shoulder, leading the way to the house. "You can call me Tanya, Carl, but not 'Red' like you used to." Ashe Brandon crossed her mind. "I don't much care for the nickname anymore." Ashe had called her that on the day he returned to Sundance.

"I'll take your horse, Carl," Samson offered, taking the reins Carl handed over to him. The lad tied the bay mare before the little house. "This old hitchin' post is gettin' a lot of use nowadays. Right, Tanya?"

Tanya laughed shortly. "Right."

A quick squint wrinkled the corners of Carl's eyes momentarily before he asked, "Why's that, Sammy?"

Pausing on the porch, Tanya thought she had detected a hint of suspiciousness in Carl Tucker's tone, but she decided she had only imagined it.

"Have you been home?" Tanya quickly asked Carl before Samson could answer. "I mean," she said, catching the sudden swing of his head toward her, "I meant, you've been traveling far and wide . . . it seems." She flicked her eyes from his dusty clothes to his tired horse. There is something wrong, she told herself, but she couldn't put her finger on it.

"I've been away," Carl said. "Yeah, I guess you could say that."

Samson followed them into the house, his boyish curiosity getting the best of him. "Where've you been, Carl? I have a hankerin' to hear about adven— avent—"

"Adventures," Tanya supplied, going to the hearth to begin brewing coffee. "Don't you be rattling your tongue off, Sammy, and questioning Carl Tucker to death."

Carl ruffled the lad's red hair. "You go right ahead, Sammy. I've a hankerin' myself." His eyes swept Tanya and came back to the lad. He had more than one hankerin', Carl told himself. First things first, though, and then there would be time for Tanya.

"I can tell you're hungry, Carl," Samson said. "I

can tell by the way you're eying Tanya fixin' up some grub for us."

An imperceptible stiffening of Tanya's back escaped the notice of both lad and man. She kept right on preparing the coffee and the cornbread, whipping up the slab of butter, and taking in every word Carl Tucker spoke. He would slip up somewhere and reveal the true meaning of his visit, she just knew it. All she had to do was to wait.

Carl Tucker had a nice way about him, Tanya had to admit. He told Samson many tales—Tanya would bet most of them were untrue—and sat on the porch after they had finished their cornbread, his coffee resting on his knee. He tilted back his chair and his hat, and Tanya began to rest easy when his eyes ceased to rove over her.

"That coffee tastes like more, Tanya," Carl said, his smile pleasant.

"I'll take your cup." Tanya rose from the bench where she'd sat bathed in the glow of the sun.

"Ashe brought the coffee," Samson blurted out just as Tanya was going inside. She paused inside the door, listening to what Samson had to say next, but it was Carl who spoke.

"Ashe?" Carl drawled lazily. "Ashe who?"

"Ashe Brandon." Samson laughed. "Don't you know him?"

Carl knew him all right. "He's a Texas Ranger now, ain't he, Sammy?"

"Yep!" Then Samson began to ponder. How

much should he be telling Carl Tucker? Maybe, just maybe Ashe didn't want too much gossip going around about him. He had been secretive about certain things, even around Tanya, so Samson decided not to answer too many questions having to do with the ranger. "He was here today," Samson offered, looking aside.

"Well," Carl drawled, "I suppose there ain't nothing so suspicious about that. Ashe Brandon used to live here at Sundance, but now that his ma and pa are gone . . ."

Tanya frowned, wondering about those words. He'd made it sound as though Ashe had nothing to do with Sundance now that his parents were dead. He knows, she thought, just like everyone else around these parts, that Ashe Brandon has given up everything to do with his past. Ashe is a ranger now, and nothing else seems to matter to the man.

"I'll be back soon," Carl was saying to Samson when Tanya finally emerged from the house, steaming mug in hand. "Do you want to take your coffee with you?" Tanya asked with a friendly smile.

Carl untied his bay mare. "I want to get home before sundown." His smile was warm. "Keep it warm for me, Tanya."

Biting her lower lip in thought, Tanya watched Carl Tucker ride away. What was the man up to? she wondered, looking down at his cup. Before she went back inside, she tossed the steaming liquid over the porch railing.

*　　*　　*

Willow returned from Clem's but all she brought was eggs—no answers to ease the torment in her mind. Clem had seemed suspicious of her and of the reason she was asking him so many questions. He had said that he had seen Clay, and he'd acknowledged that his full name was Talon Clay Brandon. There was no hiding it now, the old man had thought to himself, now that Ashe Brandon was aware of his brother's "visit" just the other day. Willow and Clem shared a dangerous secret, although each was unaware of the extent of the other's knowledge.

"Here's the eggs." Willow placed the shawl holding the eggs gently on the table and plumped it up into a nest so they wouldn't roll off.

Silence greeted her.

"*Hellooo*," she called out the back window. Pulling her head back inside, she wondered whether Tanya and Sammy had taken a walk to Pa's gravesite.

Coming back into the main room, Willow pulled up short and gasped. "W-Who are you?" She gaped at the huge, lanky man filling the doorway and remembered she had left the door open wide.

"Well, well, well," Carl Tucker drawled out, expressing his surprise loud and clear. "Ain't you a pretty little thing now." He rubbed his stubbled chin. "Say, ain't you the gal that met Clay, all got up in shirt and pants? I knew you was a gal after he tangled with you and tossed you to the ground."

Angrily, Willow puffed up her shoulders, snapping, "What else did you happen to see? But first, tell me what you're doing here." Then her heart leaped in sudden joy. She stepped closer, thinking there would be no danger in doing so. "Did Clay send a message?" she asked, hope lighting up her brown eyes.

Having seen too much woman flesh when he was not able to satisfy his craving for it, Carl went crazy and grabbed Willow by the shoulders, his mouth crashing down over hers, his thick tongue pushing through her soft lips into her mouth. Then his big body leaped into action, grinding against her, unmindful in his lust-crazed brain that she whimpered and struggled, crying out as he hurt her with his huge, roving hands.

Willow finally managed to wrench her bruised lips free. "Stop it," she panted. "Leave me alone, you bastard!"

"Heh, heh." Carl chuckled. "You'd better be giving me what I'm hankerin' for, little gal, else you're never going to see Clay alive again."

She choked back a sob on the back of her hand. "Wh-what do you mean?" If only she could stall for time . . . She called his bluff. "You wouldn't kill Clay because he's your friend." Willow backed up, slowly moving toward Tanya's bedroom, and the open window there.

He laughed again. "Clay's no friend of mine, at least not now that I see what we're going to have to be fightin' each other for. He's going his way anyhow, back to San Antonio and a pretty Mex girl waitin' for him there. Says he's going to settle down, get married to Conchita." He backed her, so he thought, into the bedroom. "He'll be back here, though, to get some more of what you give to him the other night in the shadows of them cottonwoods." Carl moved his hands to begin unhitching his pants. "He told me you put up real good, free for the askin', to anyone."

"Not to the likes of you!"

Willow spun and very agilely climbed through the open window, dropping to the ground below. She pulled her skirts after her and laughed out loud, for the sheer joy of having duped the lecherous—now she knew what that meant—man. Instantly she heard a thud. He had tripped on his pants, his *whoosh* of breath announcing that he had fallen flat on his face. She could just see his bare behind, his desire utterly squelched when he'd crashed.

Willow did not wait around to witness the man's red-faced embarrassment when he emerged from the house. She went, instead, to find Samson and Tanya.

"What was Carl Tucker doing back at the house?" Tanya asked her sister, seeing Willow approach and Carl putting spurs to his horse and ducking beneath the overhanging branches of a live oak.

"Trying to rape me," Willow said nonchalantly.

Sapphire blue eyes paled considerably.

Samson asked, "What's rape?"

"Go to the house," Tanya ordered, her eyes smarting from the sudden burn in them. "Go now, Samson."

"Big words, secret talks all the time," Samson mumbled, running ahead to chase the birds pecking in the yard.

Tanya led Willow into the taller unbent grasses off to the side of the yard. Before Tanya could speak, Willow blurted:

"So that's Carl Tucker. Wonder what Janice Ranae would think of their son, the rapist. He's probably the murderer Ranger Ashe wants. I hate that bastard." She winced then touching the bruise already forming on her shoulder, "He hurt me."

Studying Willow, Tanya could see that the girl was suddenly becoming a woman, a woman with explosive wants, needs, emotions, and of course, the frustrations that accompanied them.

"What did he do to you?" Tanya wanted to know.

"He bruised me, that's about all." She grinned slowly, mischievously. "I bruised him too, right where it counts . . . and just at the time when it hurts most I'd wager!"

Tanya shook her head, almost smiling. "You kicked him!" she guessed.

"No." Willow laughed. "He fell right on his face. All tangled in his pants and"—she grinned impishly—"bare assed!"

"No," Tanya breathed.

"Yep. That's where his hind end is, if you ask me, right on his face!"

Tanya sighed. "Well, you don't look as if he harmed you."

"Oh, he did, all right."

"How?" Tanya looked concerned now.

"His words," Willow gulped. "It's what he said Talon Clay said about me. He made it sound," she began to sob, "sound like I'm no better than

93

a whore. . . ."

Her last word emerging as a long feminine wail, Willow clutched her skirts and flew toward the house, skirting Samson as he careened toward her pretending he was a horse. Willow flared up, stopped dead in her tracks, and whirled the lad about by the shoulders. She slapped him soundly across the face and Samson stared after her when she continued on her way to the house.

He was still caressing his smarting cheek when Tanya walked over to him. "What'd she do that for?" he asked his sister, looking up at her in a fashion that said he was endeavoring to be brave in this situation.

"Because," Tanya began, tossing an arm across his shoulder and walking him to the porch, "that's what love does to a woman."

Gaping, Samson looked up at his big sister. "Willow loves Carl? He's too big for our little sister."

Tanya laughed at that, but explained the truth of the matter to Samson, "Willow is in love, at least I suspect she is, with Ashe Brandon's brother, Talon Clay. I'm not certain, only time will tell."

"Oh." Samson continued for a space, then said, "You know what?"

Tanya shrugged. "I give, you tell."

"I don't ever want to love a woman."

"Why not?" Tanya stopped, looking down at the lad.

He shook his red head. "Why would I ever want to go around causin' a woman all that pain?"

"You'll understand when you're older," Tanya said, wondering why boys had to grow up into men. She supposed for the same reason girls had to grow up into women. The two went together like fire and fuses on the Fourth of July, and God must have meant human nature to be just like that. She shivered, wondering what it would be like when she and Ashe came together finally . . . for that, too, was as inevitable as the Texas sun!

Chapter 7

As the last of the night gave way to morning, Ashe Brandon packed up his gear, fastened his rations to his saddle, mounted his buckskin, and rode on through the rugged hill country. It was his second day out on the trail.

A spring breeze whipped at Ashe's wheat-blond hair, and the loose buckskin jacket he wore flapped at his sides. He had been riding for two days now and should reach the ranger post in San Antonio by nightfall if all went well and he didn't meet up with any roving Comanche bands like the *Nermernuh*, the "People". He had slept with his clothes on, ready to spring into action and fight if the situation warranted it. It was victory or death. He never asked for quarter, though he sometimes gave it—but not to the *Kwerharrehnuh*. He hated them most and struck at them for vengeance.

How long ago it all seemed now.... He could vaguely remember, when his mother had been captured by the *Kwerharrehnuh*, enslaved, tortured,

97

and returned only to die not long after. They had exchanged her to secure the release of a Comanche boy. Then Pete Brandon had remarried, almost before Martha's grave was cold. Pete had married Garnet Haywood, the woman who had come all the way from Monterey, California when she'd heard one of the biggest Texas ranchers was advertising for a cook, a "good" cook, Clem had told Ashe. And Garnet had been a good cook, but she had taken Pete away from his children when they had needed him most.

Ashe had hated her, almost as much as he hated the Indians who had taken his mother away. Now he ground his teeth together, in remembrance. While Martha was still alive, Garnet had come up to the house after she'd fed the ranch hands. Ashe had thought she was too pretty, a silly gold-haired woman with blue eyes, eyes that flirted with his father. Ashe recalled the arguments Martha and Pete used to have over Garnet, the jealousy and bitterness. Young Ashe had come to hate Garnet Haywood, but Talon Clay had been too young to notice this. There was something always strange about Garnet, Ashe reflected, like she had been hiding something, a secret. Oh yes, she had been pretty . . . and younger than Martha.

When Garnet had moved into the house as if she'd already owned it, Ashe had moved out. He'd taken his belongings to a vacant bunkhouse. Talon Clay had tagged along, but Garnet always fetched him back to the big house.

By living with the ranch hands, Ashe had come to know a thing or two about ranching, and before he left Sundance he had been working hard with them. Then, suddenly, his brother went to live with the Tuckers. Garnet had been ailing, Pete had explained. She couldn't take care of the wild boy. Ashe, she didn't have to worry about. He'd always taken care of himself, even as he did now.

Just before he had gone away, there had been some trouble between his father and the Tuckers whose land bordered the Brandon strip. The ranch hands had said there was a border war going on, and cross fencing had had to be put up so ranchers could prove their property rights.

Just yesterday Clem had told Ashe the rest of the story. Talon Clay had stayed on at the Tuckers, but Garnet had died of consumption. Pete Brandon had become a gruff man, acting older than his years, always riding the range alone. Not long after that Pete had followed Garnet to her grave.

Ashe shook his head. It seemed everyone was dying at Sundance, from one thing or another. He had guessed, even before Clem had said so, that the foreman, Rob Hayes, had passed on not too long ago. Ashe told himself that he should have expressed his condolences to Tanya Hayes, but it seemed their conversations never lasted long enough to become friendly and personal. He laughed shortly.

A thin smile pressed Ashe's lips together. Tanya . . . she wore the stars from the night skies in her eyes, and unless he was mistaken, he had a pretty good idea she wanted him. He chuckled and tried to switch to safer thoughts.

Tanya Hayes, he was thinking, don't you be trying to win my heart.

True, she had been the first thing on his mind that morning. He was even considering moving back into the big house and settling down to ranching—making Sundance the place it used to be. Even better.

He warmed as he visualized the scene of Tanya and himself standing in the creek several days ago. He'd had the desire to do more than just stare holes in her—but he hadn't the time. He had some outlaws to catch up with and a brother to find before he returned to his normal duties. He shrugged. After that? Who could tell? Maybe back to John Coffee Hays and fighting Indians and Mexicans. Maybe not. It was all up to the wind and where it took him.

Ashe rode beside a swollen creek, his eyes on the smoke-blue distance, his mind and his barely controlled desires racing on ahead to the proprietress of Gray's Boardinghouse, the delectable Larrisa Gray, one of San Antonio's most beautiful of ladies. He could hardly wait. . . .

Up the creek, not far away, a young man's face turned sharply, his powerful back straightened, and he stood erect, slowly, slowly.

"Someone's coming!" Talon Clay hissed, but his voice carried. His long blond hair swung over his shoulder in a silken slide as he turned to the men with him.

Like alarmed creatures, his three companions came to their feet, each reacting to the warning in his own way. Butch held a rifle in his arms, his young, handsome face alert; the stamp of the outlaw, however, was plain upon him. The other two men grinned, as if enjoying the threat of danger immensely, one even spitting on the ground in a swaggering manner.

Four pairs of eyes watched as the man pulled up his horse, swung a leg across the horn of the Mexican saddle, struck a match, watched it flare for a moment, and then lighted a *cigarro*. His hand was steady, but they could not see Brandon's eyes, narrowed, roving the country about him, watching, waiting, alert.

A hand touched Talon's shoulder. "What sort of ranger smokes *cigarros?* Thought they all chawed tobaccy." Butch laughed, his teeth even and wide.

"Dangerous kinds," the thin outlaw said. "He's loaded, too, packin' a six-shot Colt, a sonofabitchin' shooting machine. The rangers bought 'em all up down in Galveston."

"You don't know your down from your up," Butch said.

"Hush up!" Talon Clay ordered, swinging around his one-shot pistol; one shot was all Clay needed, for the pretty blond lad was a deadly shot. "I'll show you boys where the up is with this here if you don't shut your flappers!"

"Stuff it," Frank said to Butch. "That's Ranger Ashe, the meanest ranger."

Then Frank froze, already feeling the knife prick at his back, the blood welling from the wound in his shoulder after he and Ashe had tangled. But Frank smiled, for he had outwitted Ranger Brandon and had got away before the mounted gunman had delivered him safely to the jail door. Of course, Frank couldn't really fault the man for eying a pretty, dark-haired lady driving her wagon into San Antonio, and he just bet Ashe had followed the lady home that night . . . five years ago maybe.

"He's grown mighty big," Frank said to Butch. "He's been following Jack Hays for five years around San Antonio now, been one of a handful of the captain's men that's the heart of the force. He's Talon Clay's br—"

"Shut up!" Butch leaned over to whisper in Frank's ear. "Think Clay don't know that? Of course he don't."

Frank blinked, shook his head.

Butch went on. "Don't you know when a man wants to forget? Fool. You think Clay would stick around to be snared like a jack rabbit in a trap?"

Talon Clay stared across the creek at his brother. His brother, yes. So it *was* true he had been a Texas Ranger all this time. Talon had tried not to think this was so, but now, as he stared, every line, every feature was there, although subtly blurred by the distance that separated them.

Butch broke into Clay's thoughts. "He hunts for you."

Viciously, Talon Clay whirled on the man. "He hunts for *us!*" He laughed softly then, his anger quickly burned out.

In the last month they had made ten raids, each more successful than the last, yet Clay was depressed. Butch could sense it. Their outlaw band had been dwindling away this past week. With Carl Tucker gone into hiding, at home of all places, they were down to the present four. Butch swore under his breath. All because Carl Tucker had gone and killed a man when they held up that stage . . .

"I can feel the heat," Frank said, shuddering, even though the ranger had pressed on. He watched the man's back, ramrod straight and proud in that fine Mexican saddle.

"What does it matter?" Butch said. "Dead men can't talk."

"But we stashed the loot back at Clem's. The old man don't know Tucker done in an innocent man for what's in that chest." He looked at the ranger's slowly fading back, the buckskin's swishing tail. "This Ranger Ashe ain't no fool. He's caught up with three other outlaws, murderin' outlaws, and seen them hanged."

"What does it matter." Butch laughed. "We have been hunted before and we'll be hunted again. So?"

Talon Clay's eyes moved across the rolling hills, and he frowned against the glare of the afternoon sun, shielding his eyes with one long-boned hand, a beautiful hand for an outlaw, a woman had once told him. He came to his feet, lithe as a cat after a nap, deciding there were better things to do than lie about in the sun all day.

"It's time to move on," was all Talon Clay said, but his gaze went back in the direction thay had come, where a pair of pussywillow-brown eyes stared back at him from the rolling terrain.

Released! He was no longer a ranger. With this ringing in his ears, Ashe Brandon strode down the street to where his horse was tied at the hitching rail outside the cantina. He glanced at the swinging green doors, thinking of drowning his troubles in drink, then he remembered there was a beautiful lady waiting—Larrisa would always be waiting—at Gray's Boardinghouse.

He mounted the buckskin gelding and rode a couple of blocks north, where he dismounted again. He looked up, pausing, undecided. His imagination was playing tricks on him, creating a charming picture of a woman with fiery red hair, coral lips just waiting to be kissed, creamy skin, eyes blue as the dawn sky. But this was not Tanya Hayes.

"Ashe Brandon!"

A frown puckered the tan skin between his eyes, and they narrowed keenly on a dark-tressed woman who was tall and slim, with deep-set blue-gray eyes and sweeping arched brows.

"Larrisa."

Ashe's eyes strayed hungrily to the deep cleft Larrisa invariably exposed. Ashe wondered briefly if others found pleasure in the warmth of Larrisa's body. She always wore printed silk dresses. The one she wore today was plum colored.

"Hello Larrisa," he said, and she frowned delicately.

"You don't look all that happy to see me, Ashe."

Larrisa kept her regal stance, her dark, lustrous hair piled high atop her proudly held head. Ashe knew her hair would soon come tumbling down and he would run his fingers through it, smelling the clean fragrance of her freshly washed tresses.

Like a queen, she led the way into the house and into her parlor, but as soon as she had entered she spun about to enter Ashe's welcoming embrace. "Tell Larrisa what's wrong, big boy," she purred voluptuously.

Sweeping up a bottle of brandy and two glasses, Larrisa led Ashe to her bedroom, to her soft feather mattress. They conversed softly for a while, seated comfortably on the bed as was their custom on these visits, each sipping a glass of brandy. He told her then.

"I've been let go."

That said it all.

"Oh," she said, "not a ranger any longer?"

"That's right." He took a sip of the fiery liquid. "Men with families were retained, but"—he shrugged languidly—"I've got a pile tucked away in the San Antonio bank."

"I think the money is of little concern to you?"

"You're right." He sighed. "It's not the pay I'm worried about. Hell"—he laughed—"I'm not worried at all."

He reached for her, but Larrisa stayed his hand. "There is more. Do you want to tell Larrisa?"

"It's Texas I'm angry with, Larrisa, not Captain Hays."

"Why is that, my darling?"

"Lack of money."

"What?" Larrisa blinked black-lashed eyes. "Are you tipsy, Brandon?"

"The politicians in Austin, it's all their fault."

"Oh?" She lifted a delicately penciled eyebrow. "Why is that?"

"The company has been cut, Hay's company." He stared into the amber liquid as if hating it. "It's not Jack's fault."

"You mean John Hays? His nickname is Jack?"

"Right."

"I am sure"—Larrisa wrapped her perfumed arms around Ashe's neck, took his glass to set it aside—"very sure, darling, that you will be ranging again, very soon." She tapped his lips with a painted fingernail, pressing him back against the plump pillows then. "Who knows, you might not want to go back."

Larrisa's breasts jutted against the thin material of her plum dress, and hazel eyes gave them full attention as she stood to undress.

But Ashe did not see Larrisa as she moved toward him. Another woman took her place and he imagined a spill of magnificent red hair; long, ivory legs; slim arms. This was the way he envisioned the woman who had come, like a splendid wraith, into his life. Ashe's breath, which had come evenly, slowly, now began to speed up.

The knocking became insistent, drawing the couple on the mussed bed from their languid kiss and into awareness of the world outside the passion-drenched one they had entered not long before. Actually, Larrisa had been more transported than Ashe and she wondered at this, for her handsome lover had never been one to lag behind in their lovemaking. No. Ashe had always been more than eager to couple with her and he'd always been totally involved . . . until now. This time, however, she had been the one ravenously attacking him, her body shamefully soliciting responses while his enthusiasm was less than keen. Therefore, this interference,

106

at a time when Larrisa thought she was just gaining ground, made her resentful and annoyed. She jounced from the bed, leaving Ashe to stare after her and wonder at her unusual anger.

"Who in hell could that be!" Larrisa snapped, jerking on her watered silk wrapper. She glanced at her lover before answering the summons and was annoyed to see him staring at her as if he'd never seen her before this moment. "Well, Ashe Brandon, what are you staring at? Haven't you ever seen what a woman's like when she's been called to the door just when . . ." She faltered, flustered, unable to go on.

Ashe rose to his elbows, his face achingly handsome to Larrisa at that moment. "Just when what, Larrisa?" His voice dipped, making him sound bored. It was not really a question he asked, so there was no need to wait around for an answer. He rose from the bed, reaching for his shirt and pants.

"No, wait Ashe." Larrisa rushed to him. "I didn't mean for it to sound so, so—"

"So desperate?" He worked at the buttons on his shirt, finding himself quite calm despite his situation. "I'm sorry, Larrisa." He shrugged, causing the material of his shirt to strain across his wide shoulders. He looked at her. There was nothing else to say, nothing but that he was sorry.

"Why?" she asked, grinding her teeth beneath her rosy painted lips as a knock jarred the walls of her house. "Is the whole damn town out tonight?" She whirled to the door as if hollering at it. "Where are the boarders?"

When she came around again, Ashe was looking at her with the same strange expression she'd seen moments before. He could hardly believe that this woman was sweet, lovable, caring Larrisa. Or was he just beginning to see Larrisa as she really was, rather than as the woman from whom he'd sought release all these times—the release her voluptuous charms provided.

"I really don't think I have to explain my inadequacy to you, Larrisa." He smiled into her pained expression. "Really I don't."

"Ashe Brandon, after sharing my brandy and my bed all these years, you've got some balls telling me that!"

He pressed a finger to her rouged cheek and slid it down to her chin, dragging her face downward in the process. "That is something I never realized about you, Larrisa Gray. Just that." He dropped his finger and swung away from her to reach for his boots. He had never cared for a cussing woman, but he had not noticed this trait of Larrisa's before.

Afraid of what he was saying, Larrisa tentatively touched her face, wondering if she had suddenly begun to age all that much. No. Just yesterday she had gone to visit a friend at a ranch outside of town and had dallied with a handsome vaquero in the stable before he'd "fixed" the spoke on her sulky—a present from an enamored gentleman from New Orleans. The vaquero Miguel, had told her that she was young and beautiful. She had been grateful for such kind words, and for the way Miguel had appreciated her gratefulness. After a time, in the sweet-smelling hay, Larrisa and her new lover had desperately found each other. Now Larrisa had another thought.

"Ashe," she said, not bothering to rush to the door just yet, "it may very well be my fault today. You see, just yesterday I met this—"

Larrisa suddenly went pale as Ashe placed a finger over her lips and shook his head slowly. "No fault of yours, Larrisa." He hooked a finger in the collar of his buckskin jacket and flung it over a shoulder. "See, love, I met this girl that I used to know. . . ." His words dwindled as he strode down the length of Larrisa's hall, leaving the proprietress to wonder what he'd said at the last, if anything.

Larrisa watched Ashe Brandon go. Then, as she headed down the hall, he just nodded to her curtly, as if he had merely been a customer of hers, and then he closed the door, closed it in her face, giving her no explanation regarding the man who had been banging on her door in such a ferocious manner. She rushed to the front window, brushed the dainty lace curtain aside, and watched Ashe Brandon walk down the street with a man she knew was a fellow ranger, one who probably had come to seek Brandon's aid. She'd known they would not let him go for long; Ashe was too good for that. He had been too good for her too. She watched him leading his horse, striding with that lazy, rocking gait she had always loved— watched him walk out of her life.

Larrisa went to her cupboard, took down a fresh bottle of brandy, opened it, and picked up a glass. Then she went to her favorite chair in the parlor and proceeded to get good and drunk. "Here's to you, Ashe Brandon." She hoisted her glass in salute. "The best of the Texas Gunmen!" Larrisa grinned at the bottle she clutched by its neck, pressed it against her thigh. "May he never die!"

Warm, languid air immediately surrounded Ashe as he stepped down the stairs from the boarding-house, and he knew without a shred of doubt that he would never come this way again.

"Someone wants to see you," the lieutenant said. "Let's go for a walk, Ashe."

"Right." Ashe Brandon was all for it.

He strode alongside the officer, aware of the admiring, sidelong glances he received from sultry, dark-eyed girls. Even clad in his dusty buckskins, Ashe made a handsome sight, his heavy guns sagging at his slim waist, the clean-limbed buckskin gelding following behind him. But Ashe had lost his taste for pretty women all of a sudden, except for the one who had lodged in his heart, the one with shimmering red curls and a sweet, gentle way about her—when she wasn't all fired up over something he had done. He was determined to do something about that, and soon.

"What I need is a hot bath and a shot of good whiskey," Ashe said to McMullen.

"Tequila, you mean!" The lieutenant laughed heartily. "Ashe, Taylor's mustering several of Hay's Texas Rangers into the national service. The captain's just returning and he wants us in our respective locations to guard the frontiers." He looked over to the main square. "Here he comes now."

110

"Us?" Ashe said, his eyes following McMullen's gaze.

Just then a dark bay warhorse trotted proudly into the main square of San Antonio, and an impressive man dismounted from it in a single lithe movement, his intelligent dark eyes flashing.

The lieutenant turned to Brandon before Captain John Coffee Hays could approach, saying, "You're one of the best men Hays's got, Ashe. Why'd you walk out like that? What fired you up? Shoot, we didn't want to let *you* go."

Ashe could only shake his head at realizing how befuddled one small woman could make him. "What an ass I am." He laughed out loud. "Damn."

When Hays stuck out his hand and shook with Brandon's, Ashe's pride swelled within him. "Guess I didn't want to stick around and hear that I was being let go." He shrugged. "My six months with the ranging company were up, anyway."

Feeling Brandon's warm, steely grip, Captain Hays said, "Ashe, whatever made you think we'd let you go." His black eyes gleamed. "I've been looking for you since I was told you picked yourself up out of that chair in the station and walked out as if you hated the world—so it was said." Captain Hays smiled. "You haven't gone and fallen for some pretty *señorita*, have you now? Is that the reason for the misunderstanding?"

"Not a pretty *señorita*," Ashe said, shaking his blond head with the high felt hat atop it. "A redhead." He found himself telling Hays of his feelings before he knew what he was saying. "A beauty," he added, feeling good about the announce-

111

ment now that he thought about it.

"A redhead," Captain Hays echoed, beginning to lead the way across the main square. "Real beautiful, you say?"

"That's right, sir." Ashe grinned playfully. "And wait till I tell you her name."

Chapter 8

Rosa's Cantina was even more crowded than usual. It was nearing midnight and San Antonio had settled into its usual drinking, gambling, and wenching—in that order. The sharp scent of highly seasoned Mexican cooking mingled with the stink of sweat and strong drink, and the air was dense with smoke.

A young man, his dusty hat slouched low over his forehead, his raw-honey hair spilling across his hunched-up shoulders, sat alone at the table in one corner of the room. His stubbled face was pulled down in a sullen frown; his deep green eyes were narrowed, devoid of expression. A tall smoky bottle of tequila sat before him, half-full.

Vaqueros in high-crowned sombreros, gay-striped serapes slung across their shoulders, moved in and out of the cantina's swinging doors. Uninterested and utterly bored with his surroundings, Talon Clay watched the goings-on, ignoring the intrigued glances of passionate, dark-haired girls and the soft

Mexican endearments directed his way. All the fair-haired young *hombre* could think of was Willow Hayes. *Willow* . . . Such a little thing, Talon Clay mused. She, that lovely slip of a woman, had the power to evoke dreams in his waking hours, not to mention bittersweet torment during the restless nights when her gentle image tortured his burning brain, churning his loins. He had even forgotten all about his latest *querida*, Conchita. . . .

Suddenly Talon Clay slouched down further, the action automatically tipping his hat lower over his forehead, as he'd meant it to. Ashe Brandon, of all people. Why now?

When Ashe entered the cantina, his hawk-keen eyes were immediately drawn to the travel-stained young stranger seated by himself in one corner of the smoke-filled room. Ashe was not a man to ignore the opportunity of speaking to a stranger in town, especially if that man might come up with some sorely needed answers.

The ranger paused to light a slim brown cheroot.

Talon Clay was grateful for the dirt he had accumulated over the past several days—it hid some of the taut planes of his features—but he kept himself hidden beneath the slouching hat, giving the impression that he was dog-tired and just wanted to be left alone. He heard boots saunter up to his table . . . and he waited.

"*Amigo.*"

"Yeah," Talon drawled lazily.

Ashe's voice dipped so his words sounded more like a challenge than a question. "Mind if I join you?"

Swiftly, Talon peered up with one tired eye; then, returning to his former position, he stated, "Nope."

Drawing up a chair, Ashe Brandon sat. He gave the young stranger a thorough appraisal, but there really wasn't much he could tell about the man, except that the slashes grooving the sides of his mouth were like Talon Clay's. That was about all . . . until he made out the bright color of his hair. Even in the shadows and despite the dust, Ashe could tell it was the color of pale cornsilk. "Never seen you around before," Ashe said in a conversational tone.

"Have a drink," Talon offered, lacing his black-gloved fingers over his chest. "If you're thirsty," he added, indifference obvious in his deep voice.

The smoke from the man's cheroot drifted indolently into Talon Clay's face. He coughed—just once.

"Not thirsty." Ashe drove away the grinding urge to take this insolent-tongued youth outside and dunk him in the water trough. He'd never cared to talk to a man who hid his face behind a low-slouched hat. Usually, if that was the case, the man had something to hide. "Are you"—Ashe expressed his assumption out loud, as was his custom—"hiding something, stranger?"

"If you gotta know," Talon said lazily, opening and closing an eye, "I'm hidin' from a woman. She claims I'm going to become a *papá*, and I say she's plumb loco. Know what I mean?"

"Sure." Ashe suppressed the chuckle welling in his throat. "I know just the kind of woman you're talking about." Implacably, he went on. "Where've you been lately, *amigo?*"

115

"Up and down the Hill Country." Talon emitted a weary affected cough. "Why?" He shifted in his chair, mute testimony that he had gotten himself an aching backside from riding long distances. The absolute truth of the matter, however, was that Talon Clay never got butt-sore, not since he'd turned six years old.

"I'm looking for some men, that's all. Maybe six, maybe seven." Ashe Brandon looked the younger man over more closely, noting the dusty blond hair, the untrimmed sideburns that trailed along a lean cheek. "Maybe four."

"Why?" Talon asked. "What's your game?"

"Can't you guess?"

The muffled reply came, "I know who you are . . . *Rinche*."

Just then a shadow fell across the table. Ashe knew at once who owned the huge frame, Greasy Joe, Rosa's henpecked husband. Talon Clay chose that moment to look into Ashe's face. However, he afforded Ashe merely a glimpse of a dirty stranger. Still there was something. . . .

Talon realized the vivid color of his eyes would be a dead giveaway, but that remained a secret in the shadows, which also obscured his unshaven, dirt-streaked countenance. And what about his features? he thought. Would Ashe recognize him if he got a good look? Someone, Talon could not remember who, had told him that the Texas Ranger was a quiet type, but deliberate, a gentle sort who could gaze calmly into the deadly eye of a cold-blooded murderer, divine his thoughts, and anticipate his action. But Talon Clay was not a murderer like Carl

116

Tucker, nor could he ever become one. Someone else had said that the Ranger was a man who could ride straight up to death and court it with a devil-may-care attitude. Now, looking at Ashe, Talon could see that this was so.

At that moment, Talon experienced a swelling pride in his brother's work and in the man himself.

"Eyyy, *Rinche*," Greasy Joe said boisterously, addressing the Ranger. "I will bring you a clean glass, no?"

"No," Ashe muttered. "I'm not drinking."

Talon jerked upright, sliding his chair back as he did so. *What the hell have I got to hide? My brother won't suspect that I'm linked to the Wild Bunch.*

Ashe stiffened at the sudden unexpected movement, his long-boned hand already flinching toward his Colt.

Greasy Joe stopped in his tracks, then tried to shuffle his hamhock feet backward, out of harm's way, but the moment was too tense. Actually, no one moved. Even the smoke seemed to cease swirling in the room.

"What?" Talon said, tipping back his hat. "Not drinkin' with your own brother?"

The frozen stare on Ashe's handsome face melted like a sudden spring thaw. *Damn!* He'd thought there was something achingly familiar about this rugged young man. Relaxing his gun hand, Ashe slammed it on the table and then extended it to the gloved one across from him. Startled for a moment by the series of swift movements, Talon rose and leaned forward. Ashe did the same.

"Well, I'll be a son of a gun! It is you!" Ashe

exclaimed, a sharp nostalgic pang piercing him as he recognized that set of roguish green eyes, eyes that could belong to no one but his brother, Talon Clay. "Where the hell've you been?"

Talon laughed and returned the hearty handshake. Then, with a wide handsome grin, he peeled off his worn black gloves and clasped Ashe's hand.

Almost sheepishly, Talon answered the question, "Tryin' to stay alive like everyone else. Eatin' jerky, drinkin' black mud, sleepin' out on that hard rock mattress of Mother Nature's. What've you been up to? Say, let's sit down a spell and get reacquainted!"

Ashe chuckled, "You'd think we were distant relations."

"Yeah."

As both men realized they had stood to shake hands, they laughed aloud. Joe headed back to his bar, shaking his meaty head and sighing with relief, to fetch a glass for *Rinche* Brandon.

Ashe's nose twitched curiously. "What do you say we fetch you a hot bath at the hotel first?" He grinned. "I know just the room."

"You wouldn't happen to know Conchita," Talon said, "Would you?"

"Sure. She scrubs my back . . . and," Ashe smilingly went on, "that's *all*. She's a nice girl but a little too young for my taste buds." His eyes narrowed suspiciously. "Why?"

"Ah." Sheepishly, Talon scratched beneath his hat. "Let's get us a different room, way down the hall in the corner, what do you say?"

*   *   *

118

Greasy Joe stood in stunned silence at the vacant table until it finally registered on his dull-witted brain that his customers had taken themselves elsewhere. Straightening from his bent position over the table, he swiped up the two glasses he had sat down, and grasped the bottle's neck in a meaty grip. He returned to the bar where Rosa was cursing vituperations in rapid fire Mexican at his head and shouting for him to shake the *polvo* from his plodding feet. Joe tossed up his jiggly fat arms. *"Maldito sea!"* he said. "Never a moment's rest."

"That gang is about the worst bunch of outlaws this part of Texas has seen in a long time."

His jaw slackening, Talon Clay unconsciously nicked himself with the recently honed blade he was using to shave. He peered into the wavy cracked mirror positioned on a board over the steaming tub in which he was immersed. Then he swore under his breath.

"Like the wind you can't catch," Ashe went on, "and as free, so they think, this Wild Bunch."

Evasively, Talon said, "When will you be heading out?"

Ashe laughed. "Ready to see the last of me for another five or six years, my brother?" He ground out the cheroot he had been smoking, grimacing at the acrid taste of the thing.

"It's not that," Talon began. "I've got to meet a man in La Grange about a . . . horse." He pushed himself up straight in the huge wooden tub. *"Be Jaysus!* If I got a sliver again . . ."

Coming around to the open end of the flimsy partition, Ashe gestured toward the shaving mug and then the murky water in the tub.

"How the hell can you shave in there?" He shook his blond head and chuckled. "Didn't anyone ever teach you to shave while standing before a mirror? You come out cleaner, you know."

Talon giggled playfully and reached over the side of the tub. "See here, *Rinche*," he said, his grin wicked, his body as handsome as that of the nude cowboy in the painting that hung crookedly above Conchita's bed, "I've got some nice clean water if that's what's botherin' your proper sensibilities."

"What?" Ashe ducked, thinking he was going to get doused.

Hoisting the bucket high as he rose from the water like a lean, gleaming Greek god, Talon Clay whooped, dipped to his knees, and then tipped the water over his head to rinse his long, slippery body clean of the facial hair that had stuck to him along with the lye soap scum.

Ashe shook his head and stepped to the door, pausing to look back at his comical brother. Dripping and wonderfully naked, Talon saluted him with another clean, bright grin.

"See you back at Sundance in seven days! Maybe less."

Ashe tipped the brim of his felt hat. "Right. We got some talking to catch up on. And you had better not disappoint me, or I'll come looking for you." He stepped into the hall and heard Talon Clay call after him.

"Wild horses couldn't keep me away!"

120

Ashe was thinking the same as he shut the door on Talon's grinning face, only he was seeing a redhead. Talon, meanwhile, stepped out of the tub and yanked a bleached linen cloth from the edge of the bed. He had misty visions of a tiny, golden-haired blond, but he knew he would never be able to love her, only to look at her.

Part Two

April is the cruelest month, breeding
Lilacs out of dead land, mixing
Memory with Desire, stirring
Dull roots with spring rain.
                    —T.S. Eliot

Chapter 9

At first the humming of bees was strong; then, as the sun pulled its radiant face beneath a shrouded sky, the buzzing insects sought their hives.

It was late afternoon and the heavy blue-gray overcast had a scent that forewarned of rain. Unaware of anything but the peace of the moment, Tanya sang softly to herself as she dried her red tresses beside the creek. Through the trees, the buckskin color of a horse could be seen intermittently before a low whinny reached her ears. Ashe Brandon owns a buckskin, she thought. But she had to make sure. She reached for the long gun lying within arm's reach.

"Who's there?" Tanya called sharply.

When Ashe Brandon parted the bushes, *very carefully*, she was waiting with her rifle at the ready. "Oh," she said. "What are you doing here?" Placing the rifle beside her, Tanya busily finished braiding her hair into a long, neat hank of gleaming red.

"I like your hair much better loose." He strode into

125

full view, leading the buckskin. "Much."

"Were you watching me bathe?"

"No." He grinned, glanced at the sky. "I came too late for that, but I wish I had been here sooner." He cleared his throat. "Believe me."

Tanya could not help but smile, albeit a bit reproachfully, as she twirled her red braid into a loose bun at the back of her neck. He watched her, thinking she looked like a fetching portrait of a wood nymph, while Tanya began to lace her doeskin boots with her smooth, long-fingered hands. Her hands are beautiful, he thought, womanly, just like the rest of her.

"Do you always swim alone like this?" His voice was a lazy drawl.

"I thought I was bathing?"

"Well," he said with a loose shrug, "bathe, dip . . . whatever."

"You know I've come here almost all my life."

He hunkered down, flicking a finger to the brim of his hat and bringing more of his handsome face into view with the motion. Perceptively, he looked at the damp place where the material of her bodice stuck to her flesh. His gaze lowered a fraction, went to the right, then the left, and he said, "Do I?"

"You forget awful easy." She poked her smooth-fleshed chin into the air in a defiant gesture. "Nobody comes this way much, and if they do"—she patted the rifle—"I've got this."

Ashe's face changed then. Suddenly it seemed he wanted no part of the Sundance property, of the past he had left behind. He was lost, in limbo somewhere. He looked at her again, thinking, *She's more a part of*

Sundance than I am.

"I used to come here," he said, "if you remember."

"I suppose I do." She looked aside, feeling his eyes and the first warm raindrops tickle her skin. "I try not to, though . . . at least, not anymore."

"Why?"

Why do I try to forget you, Ashe Brandon? Tanya felt hurt move inside her as she saw his eyes swirl darkly with some emotion she could not name.

He had moved closer to her and they were now sheltered beneath the tallest trees on the bank of the creek. Ashe's nostrils flared because the rain gave the air a curious quality . . . or was there a magic current passing between him and Tanya . . . maybe it was both.

Tanya and Ashe gazed at each other, both lost in different thought images.

"It's good to look at you, Tanya. I mean . . . there's a good feeling inside me just being near you. . . ." He regretted speaking so openly immediately.

A tentative smile stretched Tanya's lips, fleetingly, then it vanished. "I used to feel the same about you, Ashe."

Ashe coughed to stifle a groan; then he extended a finger and ran it along her delicate jawbone. "You are very pretty when you smile, lady. I wish you would do it more often."

"I would"—she tossed her bright head—"if I had something to smile about."

He gazed down at her, his expression grown very serious.

"Have I hurt you, Tanya?"

"Hurt?" She turned aside, blinking hot tears back.

127

"How long did it take you to forget me? Two months? Three years? Five?"

"Never."

"Never?" Her gaze shot back to his unsmiling face. "I don't under—"

He felt the softness of her cheek as he laid a gentle hand there. "I think I've carried your memory in my heart all these years, Lady Red, and I've just lately realized it."

"I have a hard time believing that." She shook her head, breaking contact with his stroking fingers. "I'm sorry."

"I'm here now," he murmured, and her heart skipped a beat.

With that, Ashe stood and walked over to his horse, taking down the blanket roll from the buckskin, Lágrimas, who was contentedly cropping the rain-dewed grass. When he turned to face her again, he softly added, "I'm real, Tanya, no ghost."

His gentle and true statement made her feel she had spoken very rudely. He was here. *Ashe Brandon was here in the flesh*.

Still, before Ashe could spread his blanket on the ground, Tanya rose to her feet, intending to return to the little house. "I have to get back. . . ." His eyes halted her. "I . . . otherwise Willow and Samson will . . . worry."

Unceremoniously, he shed his jacket and she could not help but watch him closely, noting the play of muscle and sinew beneath the black shirt he wore. Then, ceremoniously, Ashe spread the blanket over the dewy blades of grass, in a spot well protected from the soft, perpetual rain that was falling outside the shelter of the trees. "I've been up to the house." He swung around slowly to face her. "Willow said you'd probably come to the creek for a . . . dip." Lazily, he grinned, watching her wide eyes closely. "They won't worry, not as long as they know I'm with you . . . and they do." He glanced down at the blanket and then back to her. "Would you join me for a spell?"

The falling mists refracted and multiplied the greens into a thousand different hues until it seemed as if the gray-blue sky itself took on pale tints of the soft, elusive green which tinged the heavy clouds. Tanya slowly nodded in acquiescence and sank down to sit with her legs tucked beneath her. The blanket felt warm, inviting. She studied the water below, which mirrored the lacy green of the trees and the slanting, gossamer mist of rain. Tanya sighed, attuned to the magic beauty of this bit of paradise and of the wet green earth. She was lost in the moment, not caring what tomorrow might bring. Ashe Brandon was back, beside her, and that was all that mattered for the time being.

With eyes that glittered like a tiger's, Ashe lowered first his body then his face to Tanya. "A kiss," he murmured. "Would you care to oblige me?"

"I . . . I don't know." She felt sad. Suddenly she remembered the heartbreak, the emptiness of promises made and broken.

"Sweet Tanya, let me hold you for a while," he said in a husky, mesmerizing tone. "I need you."

She tilted her head and looked up into his ruggedly lean, strong face. "I'm not a woman of easy virtue, Ashe Brandon."

He gently placed a finger on either side of her chin and gazed deeply into her eyes, running the palm of his other hand along her flat stomach. "I know," was all he said.

In a heartbeat, Tanya turned into his arms to offer him her soft, dewy lips. Masterfully, gently, Ashe Brandon reawakened the flame of young love in Tanya as he kissed her first tenderly, then, as he grew ardent, roughly, his mouth slashing across hers, quickening the pace of her heart.

Like magic, Tanya was swept up and away by the passion he ignited in her. Ashe circled the softest part of her lips, opening them up, then plunging his tongue inside. She moaned softly, pulling back a little even as she touched his tongue tentatively with her own. He broke the contact by lifting his head and looking down at her.

"Lady Red, you are disturbing me very much, you know." He smiled wistfully. "Deep inside, I'm churning like a wild horse."

The words were out and Tanya felt that moment was sensusous and unbelievably sweet. She had always known Ashe Brandon would make her feel like this, all glittering movement inside of her. Now she could feel his strong heartbeat accelerate against her breast as she clung to him, flooding excitement washing through every single fiber of her being.

"Ashe"—a little sob escaped her—"I missed you . . . you don't know how much."

He hugged her against his chest, pulling her closer until their bodies meshed. "Lord, I missed you too, Red." He leaned back on an elbow to look at her closely. "What's wrong? You don't like me calling you Red?"

"It's just that . . . well, that day you last called me Red"—she paused—"I was very angry with you. I hated that name!" Her voice cracked on a wretchedly embarrassing sob.

"Easy, girl." Ashe stroked the back of her neck, laying the flat of his large hand over the braided bun of her shining hair. "You had every right to be, I guess." He watched as she closed her eyes, her lips parting naturally, softly, invitingly. He began to sensuously massage the nape of her neck, his long fingers relaxing the cords that led to the gentle slope of her shoulders. "Does that feel good?"

"Hmm, yes." Tanya opened her luminous eyes to see that a tawny drift of hair had fallen over his forehead. "Make me feel good, Ashe. Please make the hurt go away."

His gaze swiveled to the hand pressed beneath her heart, its fingers moving as if she would lift the pumping organ from her chest and offer it to him. As his lusty physical urges grew apace, Ashe debated with himself as to how much Tanya Hayes was willing to offer him. Had she ever known a man physically? He thought not.

Having come to a decision, Ashe leaned over and began to nuzzle the softest part of Tanya's throat. "Oh, lady," he whispered deeply, a groan starting in his throat, "I'll do more than that." Groaning steadily now, a low soothing sound, he opened her mouth with his devouring kiss, his tongue stroking the inside erotically. "Help me, Tanya. Help me make you feel good. Show me, love"—his lips moved to her ear—"show me."

Stretched out upon the blanket, gazing up into his glittering eyes, Tanya was torn between sweet desire and fear. "I don't know what to do." She watched his gaze play lightly over her lips, her throat. "I'm afraid I have never, never—"

"Been intimate . . . with a man."

"Yes." She looked aside and then her eyes flew back to his. "I mean . . . no, I have never—"

He pressed a long finger against her lips, stilling their nervous motion. "I'll make love to you, Tanya"—he slowed down, then cleared his throat softly—"but you, will have to tell me when to stop." His eyes seemed to be telling Tanya that he wouldn't want to when that time came.

"Don't you know when . . . when to stop?" she asked shyly.

His tanned finger ran from her softly parted lips down to her chest and stopped there. "I know when, love, the only question is how. Already I can tell I've never desired a woman this badly before." He laughed softly. "It's overwhelming, Tanya."

"I know how difficult it can be to struggle against one's feelings, to . . ."

"I know that you know that."

"You wouldn't take me by force?" As she asked this, little shivers of bewildering excitement ran through her. "Would you?"

He laid his head back and chuckled. Then he gazed at her once again. "It sounds like you're asking me to do this terrible thing to you."

"No!" she cried out, then she added more gently, "Heavens no." Her cheeks flushed and her eyes fixed on a pearl button on his black shirt; and it was then

that Tanya realized Ashe had worn his best outfit to come and see her. This made her very happy and even more excited.

When her eyes finally lifted, Ashe smiled a secret smile. Then his eyes shifted, grew serious. The gray in them lightened, the green and gold glittered like shards of crushed gemstones.

"I couldn't promise you I would not, because you're different, lady. I've never wanted a woman so badly that I had to force her. But with you"—he shook his head, shifting his blond hair—"I'm not going to promise you anything—not that I'll stop, not even that I'll go on for that matter." He shivered in his manly heat. "I can make you feel good, Tanya, that's a promise."

Suddenly apprehensive, Tanya turned onto her stomach so she would not be forced to meet the piercing gaze that seemed to enter her body and make it tingle. Her head was spinning. Ashe was not thinking of her head, however, nor was he looking at it. His desirous eyes were focused on the gentle swell of her buttocks. It was all he could do not to reach out and fondle her firm globular contours.

"What are you doing?" Tanya asked abruptly, not turning about to see for herself.

Ashe moved then, to rest his long body on one side, his elbow crooked, his face close to hers. Smiling, he reached out to trace the outline of her ear, his fingertips playing with the sensitive lobe. His eyelids slowly closed as he leaned over to kiss the sensitive spot beside his fingertip; then he took the quivering earlobe between his lips. Rolling the nub against his moist flesh, Ashe breathed into her ear, hotly, causing Tanya to suck in her breath at the new sensations building in the lowest region of her pelvis. He was creating havoc with her senses, stimulating the flow of her blood; and her heart pumped against her breastbone, vibrating almost tunefully.

Just when Tanya thought she was going to swoon from the pleasure Ashe was giving her, he lowered his lips to kiss the corner of her mouth, but it was his hand, now below her waist, that was making her heart go wild, her galloping pulse race. The hand had slipped down to cover her hipbone and gently pressed her lower torso to the blanketed earth. "Ashe? . . ." Tanya began.

"Tanya . . . hush," he said, and she gasped as erotic sensations overwhelmed her. Now the merest brush of his hand made her feel like screaming because of the almost painful ecstasy he evoked in her. Tingling currents of desire washed through her while Ashe kissed her, cupping her buttock more intimately than before.

"Ashe." She came up for air, panting. "What are you doing to me, Ashe?"

"Nothing much, yet, lady . . ."

"I think we should stop now . . ." Her tiny, involuntary whimper surprised her and she shut her eyes against the pulsating hazel gaze boring voluptuously into them. "Before it's too late . . . Ashe."

"Tanya, darling, I can't." His arms closed about her and hugged her tight, and his fingers fanned out across her back to pull her, shivering, against the hardness of his body. "I'm already inside out, love." He rolled her to him then, to shape her softness more intimately to the contours of his manhood.

With the hardened reality of his desire so close, Tanya began to tremble and a multitude of frightening apprehensions entered her mind. She wanted him, but not like this, not without the blessing of God. Only in marriage would she give herself to a man. Not to any man . . . only Ashe.

Fervently aroused as he was, Ashe struggled for control of his lust, but the sweet taste and smell of Tanya was driving him mad. She was like a luscious ripe peach he would love to devour whole. Still, he held himself in check, only because he deeply respected her wishes and would not dishonor her by forcing himself upon her. But Tanya, now being rolled over onto her back by the firm pressure of his hands, thought she was certainly in for a ravishing, especially when she saw the ardent look in his gaze.

"No, Ashe . . ." Tanya murmured, weak as a newborn kitten from all his burning kisses and caresses.

"Lady Red . . ."—Ashe's voice was tender as he lowered his lips and then pressed them softly onto her dainty chin. "I won't hurt you, ever again." He moved up to nuzzle the corner of her lips. "Never . . ."

Beneath her fingertips, she felt the muscles of his chest taut and hard. "But . . . you said you could not promise that you'd be able to stop."

Ashe splayed a warm hand over her middle. "I can make the hurt go away," he said, moving his hand a little lower, "if you let me." He waited for her almost imperceptible nod. "Trust me?"

Again she nodded. Then she rolled her head on the blanket as Ashe moved his hand slowly upward to cup the underside of a breast already swollen beneath the bodice of her dress. Tanya's intake of breath was a sharp hiss. She gazed into his eyes trustingly as two fingers scorchingly rested on the budding tip of her breast and began to apply a firm pressure, back and forth. Tanya found herself instinctively arching her back and was not shocked by her own immediate response. She was discovering a new realm of experience as her untried sensuousness came into play, and the look of savage hunger on Ashe's face made her realize what it was to fully arouse a man's desires.

As for Ashe, he stared at Tanya like a starved man, his desire for her overpowering.

Tanya cried out, from surprise, wonder, fear, and hot pleasure, as Ashe came boldly against her and she felt the hardening pressure of his manhood. He kissed her with more force than before, cupping her buttocks in large hands that trembled a little, sucking her lips and tongue, thrusting and wresting his own in and out of her moist mouth, while his hips moved rhythmically.

"*Ashe*," Tanya whimpered when his hot, wet tongue circled her ear and then thrust itself inside. "Ashe . . . please."

He knew what she wanted.

Ashe lifted his head to look down at her and Tanya hazily saw that the rain dew had stolen into their haven and honeycombed his wheaten hair, but the moisture dotting his forehead and upper lip was his own.

"I know how to bring you to ease, love," Ashe said gently, "but you have to trust me, Tanya. You have to . . . relax."

She blinked worriedly up at him. "Will it help you too, Ashe? I mean . . . oh, I don't know what I really mean." She rolled her head aside to hide her embarrassed face.

Ashe smiled to himself, but he said to her, "No, it won't help me much. In fact, I'm afraid it will only cause me more . . . pain. Tanya, don't be concerned for me. I know you don't understand what I'm talking about but you will some day, love, you will, and by that time I think—at least, I *hope*—you will have become mine." Ashe halted there, wondering just what it would take to make Tanya completely his, to hold, and to love. Well, he would not think on that now.

"Tanya! *Tannnyaa!*"

"Oh!" With a guilty start, Tanya came to her elbows and busily tugged at her skirt which had been hiked up high on her legs. She looked reproachfully at Ashe, but following his innocent laconic shrug, she could do nothing but smile at the irony of the moment.

"Willow is calling," Ashe whispered, heaving a disappointed sigh.

"I know." When Tanya attempted to rise from the blanket, she found that her limbs were a bit wobbly. Ashe's hand shot out and helped her to complete the movement; then she was standing with him beside her. It had stopped raining and the air was fresh, full of wonderful earthy smells.

"You'll have to go." He watched her closely, his lips wreathed in a tender smile.

"I will." She picked up her things and started up

137

the hill. She was suddenly very embarrassed over what she had almost let him do. Whatever it was, Tanya realized that it would have been very intimate, involving a part of her most secret self. "Good-bye, Ashe." Sadly, she wondered when she would see him again.

"See you in the morning, Lady Red," he called after her.

"Really?" She paused on the hill, a happy smile appearing on her flushed face.

"I'll be here."

"You will," she said, feeling almost silly.

"For sure."

Chapter 10

Tanya stood alone on the low-browed hill, her intense jewel-bright eyes staring into the growing pink and gold in the west, watching the land emerge from the dew-kissed shadows of the night.

Night mists had gathered in the low spots and now they hugged the massive tree trunks. The creek slowly became visible, wandering in a blurred, unbroken line of pinkened silver through the green and carmine-brown hills. Far in the distance the black pyramids of great pine forests became distinct as the warming Texas sun at Tanya's back rose higher and lavished its earth-glorifying rays far and wide.

Still Tanya had not moved.

Then, like a beauteous icon come to life, Tanya broke her silent vigil, the pungent aroma of the stable galvanizing and guiding her slim, dark figure through the empurpled shadows of the lower reaches which the sun had not yet touched.

Clem was leading the gray mare out to the corral

just as Tanya emerged from beneath the spreading pecan tree. The mahogany red of her hair caught the old man's eyes first and he thought to himself how fast the years had flown while this lovely girl had grown to womanhood. He had to shake his grizzled head to clear it, because for just a fleeting moment he was sorely reminded of another. He thought seriously of this. Little Willow Hayes had provoked an even stronger memory when he'd studied her face and dainty movements the day before. Now Clem blinked and the distasteful vision of Garnet Haywood fled; in its place stood Tanya Hayes.

"Up bright 'n early, ain't you?" Clem said, watching Tanya walk over to pet the gray mare and stroke its charcoal mane. She murmured the horse's name: "Dove."

Tanya pertly jerked her head up. "Yes. Have you seen Ashe Brandon this morning? I was meaning to ask him to come along with me for a ride." She laughed then. "I mean, if you don't mind my borrowing Dove. I . . ."

Just then, before Tanya could finish her request, the back door of the sun-bathed house swung open and out walked Ashe. How handsome he is in the early morn, she thought. His hair was softly tousled, his muscle-rippled chest bare and glistening as if he'd just washed up. His hazel eyes found her and narrowed lazily, sensually, as he warmly recalled the violently sweet kisses they had shared the day before and the pleasure he had wrapped her in. There had been only one thing missing: complete fulfillment.

As if in a trance, Tanya watched Ashe Brandon push his sinewy arms into the shirt he had been carrying moments before. "Good morning," she called cheerily to him, flushing softly at the remembrance of the wonderful hour she had spent with him in the spot she had recently given a name: Raintree. A shelter from the rain. Her—now *their*—special place.

"So, that's where you went off to last night," Clem said to Ashe. "The big house. And here all the while I thought you went galavantin' off, ridin' into the sunset again."

Ashe walked over, his long strides eating the distance like nobody's business. As he approached, Tanya felt the warmth of his ardent gaze rove her womanly form and she was happy she had washed her best green calico frock and had donned it early this morning. She knew she looked pretty, for the mirror had told her so. *Lord*, she thought, *I must look absolutely beautiful in his presence!*

"Tanya." His lazy-lidded eyes made love to her as he meant them to. "You're up—"

"Bright and early," Tanya finished for him. She laughed charmingly, and Clem joined in.

The old man bent and slapped a dusty thigh. A tawny brow lifted. "You two got a secret that's being kept from me?"

"It's just that it is such a beautiful day already, one should be up bright and early." She faltered, then went on briskly. "And I thought you might like to join me in a ride, Ashe." She looked to Clem for help. "That is, if Clem wouldn't mind my borrowing the gray mare?"

"'Course not!" Clem took his cue and began to amble over to the garden. "Dove needs her exercise anyhow. I gotta do some work in the garden, so don't worry none about me." He waved over his shoulder. "You young'uns have yerselves a good time."

After Clem had disappeared into the garden on the other side of the trees, Ashe spread his fingers over Tanya's back and pulled her into his embrace. "I missed you, Lady Red. Lord, one night of tossing and turning, and I couldn't wait to see you again." He looked into eyes that shimmered brightly like morning dew. "And here you are, sweet witch, right in my back yard waiting for me," he chuckled, "bright and early."

Tanya spread her slim hand over his chest, gazing up at him with obvious yearning. "Ashe? Are you here to stay?" Hope drifted in her bright blue eyes and her thoughts were like sunshine and shadow.

Ashe lowered his face and planted a soft kiss on her forehead, causing shivers of pleasure to spread along Tanya's spine. "I won't always be here, Tanya, but I'll sure try my damnedest to come home as often as possible . . . and I sure as hell want you waiting here for me."

"Ashe!" Tanya pushed herself to arm's length. "Are you telling me you're going to move into the house and start ranching again?"

"That's right." He smiled into her happy eyes. "I don't know if I'll be ranching right away." He stroked his chin thoughtfully. "That takes time, a precious commodity I'm short of . . . and there's the subject of funds. Clem told me Pete hid a safe in the house, full of notes from the sale of cattle and the drive money. Before he told me, I checked my father's bank account in Galveston, but there was nothing there. Last night I tried to discover the 'secret room'

142

Clem is talking about, but I'll be damned if I can find it. As for right now, in a few days I'll have to be meeting with my captain. There've been Indian raids along the Brazos." He sighed like a man with pressing matters on his mind. "In addition to the ranging duties I'll have to be attending to, I'll have to be going to Mexico City with John Hays soon."

"*Los Diablos Tejanos*," Tanya said, smiling up at him playfully.

"How did you know?"

"How do I know the Mexicans call rangers 'The Texas Devils'?" She tossed her head and looked him square in the eye. "I've been to San Antonio, you know. Do you love a fandango? Yes? I've heard this also, that your Captain Hays himself can often be seen whirling around with some fair *señorita*."

Warmly Ashe appraised her from head to foot. "Will you attend a fandango with me? Good. The Rankins are going to be having one in two weeks. His son, Almanzo, is getting married." Seeing a tender look come into Tanya's eyes at the mention of marriage, Ashe smiled and lowered his head.

When Ashe's head tilted, Tanya knew what he intended. Her face changed color and her pulse accelerated as their flesh made contact in a soul-stirring kiss, Ashe devouring, she offering. The two mingled and became one, each starved for the other.

His tongue caressed the velvet folds of her lips, urging Tanya to open them, and when she did, he plunged inside. Tanya felt her knees go weak. She leaned into him, feeling the strength of his heartbeat which, if she stopped to think about it, his heart was pounding as furiously as her own. His hands came up to cup her chin on either side, his palms resting on the thumping curve of her throat.

"I've got a hankering for your sweetmeat, Lady Red."

"Ashe . . ." Tanya protested feebly when one of his hands slid downward, the fingers pressing the underside of a breast. "We can't. Clem might see. . . ."

A spurt of raw hunger flamed through her chest as his lips nuzzled the ivory column of her throat, then pulled away. "You're right," he said in a strained tone. "If we don't stop now, I'm going to take you into the house and stretch you out on a bed upstairs." He murmured this against her lips, groaning deeply then and telling her of his intense need of her. "Would you like that?"

Her head, flung back a moment ago as he kissed her throat and fondled her aching breast, now came forward to rest on his chest. "Yes, Ashe," she said, softly and breathily, "someday."

His forehead furrowed as he studied her.

"Someday hell!"

"Ashe! What are you doing!"

He had scooped her up, whirling her about in a flurry of green calico, and was now making his way toward the back door which was invitingly open. Her hands were twined about his neck, her arms resting on his chest and feeling the powerful muscles there. His manliness acted like a narcotic on her untried body. But where was he taking her? she wondered frantically.

He stopped in the doorway, and Tanya experienced some uneasiness as his passion-drugged eyes bored into her very soul.

"Are you serious?" she asked.

"Very."

"Ashe!" Tanya squealed. "Put me down!"

"Not on your life, Lady Red," he replied in a terrifyingly pleasant tone.

"Ashe Brandon . . . you can't do this!" When she began to push and shove at his chest, she felt the muscles beneath her fingertips become taut and hard. "You're going too far!"

He chuckled. "There's no such place."

Hardly believing Ashe was doing this, actually carrying her off to a bedroom to do only God knows what to her, Tanya began to struggle, writhing and scissoring her legs in the air while thrusting herself against his unyielding chest.

Ashe groaned when Tanya's soft breasts surged and rubbed erotically against him and his already sorely strained restraint broke in two. He was searing with heat! Sweat dotted his upper lip. He did a strange thing then. Setting her down in the middle of the hall, he began to trudge back in the direction they had come.

"Where are you going?" Tanya stood in trembling puzzlement, watching his retreating form, noting that he walked with some difficulty.

"For a ride!"

"I thought we were going together!" She paused, perplexed. "Well?"

Ashe returned, looking boyishly handsome and sheepish. "My horse has a sore leg."

"Well . . . how can you go for a ride then?" She was even more puzzled.

He seemed to be pondering this for a moment. "I'm taking the wagon into Bastrop Springs."

"Oh." She stared around, at the inside walls which were plastered white. They looked creamy and cool. "I don't understand you, Ashe." She looked away at once when his frowning gaze contacted hers. "I really don't," she said again, more softly.

"I *am* serious, Tanya." He turned away, began striding the length of the hall. Then he returned, to stare down into her bewildered blue eyes. "You're very lovely, Tanya Hayes. Too lovely." He gave a cursory shrug. "Will you clean my house while I'm gone?" he asked her.

Still confused, Tanya nodded.

She was a woman in love and she would do anything Ashe asked her to do . . . anything at all.

Chapter 11

The morning flew by. After tidying up the sitting room, Tanya sat and rested for a spell, wondering what to do next. She felt a sense of pride as she looked around and saw what she had accomplished with just a flimsy old broom and some oily dust cloths she had discovered in the corner of a cluttered closet. Of course, she hadn't dusted the furniture yet, for she wanted to get Ashe's permission to touch those prized pieces that had been in the Brandon family for hundreds of years. She could tell they were antiques.

Seated on a large, sheet-draped chair, Tanya leaned back and found herself staring up at the ceiling. Its border was painted with a design of climbing yellow roses and green vines that trailed slightly onto the upper wall. She could not remember ever having been in this room, for Pete Brandon had seen his guests, out on the gallery where the passageway running along the exterior wall made a shady retreat from the hot summer sun. There trumpet creeper with its spectacular orange and scarlet flowers clung to the trellises, and other climbing, flowered vines abounded.

Somewhat weary from her labors and from rising well before dawn, Tanya closed her eyes and drifted into delicious slumber. Her mind began to wander . . . back in time. . . .

A lovely golden-haired woman with flirting blue eyes, eyes that were not flirting at the moment, but scowling and scolding, stepped into Tanya's misted vision. She was ordering the red-haired girl in braids to stay in the house with her little sister and her baby brother. By doing so, however, the woman only whetted the girl's curiosity, and when she went into the back yard of the clapboard house, the nine-year-old could not restrain herself. Leaving her sleeping sister and brother in the bedroom, she violated her mother's—yes, her mother's—command and went to peer out the window. Tanya's bewildered eyes scoured the yard, and there, in the overgrown garden, she found the golden-haired woman. Her mother was not angry now. The girl's breathing quickened as she took in the couple partially obscured by the shadows of the tallest bushes. The woman—she was standing on tiptoe—writhed scandalously against the stranger . . . a man who was *not* Tanya's father, but another, just another man she had never seen before. . . .

"Mmmm . . . Oh!" Tanya's eyes flew open and quickly skimmed the lovely young face bent over her.

The face in the dream . . . almost identical to this one hovering before her . . .

"What are you doing here, Sis? You left the back door open. I thought you might be in here because I couldn't find you anywhere else."

The visions evoked by the disturbing dream waned, but Tanya's heart still throbbed against her breastbone. She repressed a frown and smiled sleepily into Willow's startled face. "What are you doing here?" Tanya murmured.

"I just asked you the same question."

"So you did." Tanya smoothed her wrinkled skirts as she stood and stretched languorously. "How long have you been standing there?"

"Not long." Willow glanced back over her shoulder, then grinned sheepishly. "I followed the footprints in the layers of dust in the hall. Whose prints are the big ones?" Willow asked, sucking one side of her rosy cheek inward.

"What?" Tanya's face suddenly assumed a velvet pink hue and all she could do was stammer. "W-Wait a minute, if . . . if you think . . . Willow, there is no one else in here with me."

A masculine chuckle sounded from behind the sisters. "But there *was*." The voice was deep and rich and full of feeling.

"*Aha!*" Willow exclaimed, turning about as a tall rugged form became visible in the dimness of the hallway. Now it was Willow's turn to do the questioning. "So, Ashe Brandon, *Rinche* Brandon, how long have you been lurking about? Catch any *bandidos* or Comanche warriors while you were away?"

Ashe smiled as he came into the room. He halted, towering over the petite blonde. "In fact," he said smoothly, tweaking her pert nose, "I just now returned from town. If you must know, there was a message to send and some supplies that needed picking up. I did both errands in record time." He shook his head slowly, then said in a conversational tone, "Poor Dove, she just isn't what she used to be. She's plumb tuckered out."

"You nasty man," Willow said with a charming laugh. "Don't tell me you drove that poor horse to death. What's wrong with your buckskin?"

"I . . ." Ashe grinned sheepishly. "Guess you could say I was in an all-fired hurry to get back to Sundance. Lágrimas has a sore leg, but he'll recover in no time. He's never let me down yet when I needed to be moving on. He's one hell of a horse."

"What's Lágrimas mean?" Willow said the Spanish word perfectly, her eyes shifty brown and sly. She waited.

One of Ashe's tawny brows lifted in mock curiosity. He had a very good idea what she was up to. "Tears," he said, eying the little woman closely. She had known *rinche* meant Ranger. . . .

"Ha!" Willow snorted in an unladylike fashion. "No wonder!" she hooted. "One hell of a horse. *Poor horse.* I betcha named him that because he cries every time you mount him." Ashe scowled playfully and began to back Willow toward the hall. "You'll have to be giving Dove a new name," she declared.

"And what would that be?" Ashe stood before Willow, his hands cocked at his lean hips. "Well?"

"Deforme!" Willow called back, running down

150

the hall and out the back door. "Because that's what Dove is now that *Rinche* Brandon rode her into the ground!" she shouted back, all breathless giggles.

"She's paying me back." Ashe stared down the hall with laughing eyes. "I just know it."

Tanya came up to stand beside him, a curious smile on her soft lips. Ashe looked down at her, already forgetting the playful moments with Willow. A vein throbbed at his temple, his cheeks grew taut, and his eyes full of sport before, were now passionate.

Tanya was still smiling softly, however. "Ashe, what does *deforme* mean?" She was beginning to feel breathless because he was staring with such deep intensity into her eyes. "I know," she guessed, for it was so simple. "Deformed!" She laughed. "Oh, poor Dove . . ."

Now Ashe was coming for her, snarling low, "Not you too . . ."

"No, that's not how—" He caught her then and Tanya cared no more for words, only for Ashe's kiss which plummeted her into a breathless, giddy world where only the two of them existed.

After a bit of romantic dalliance with Ashe, Tanya cleaned and cooked while Ashe hovered in the background doing his own chores. His warm gaze returned to her often, and she caught him smiling hungrily when she looked up from some task. At times he walked over to plant a lingering kiss on the nape of her neck, surprising her and causing tingles to race up and down her spine. Then leaving her in a quiver, he would saunter away, and she would

151

struggle to compose her emotions after the pleasurable agitation he had created.

Tanya prepared a meal for all of them, Clem included, cooking in a huge fireplace equipped with iron pots and pans. The plaster on the interior walls of the adobe kitchen had been applied in the traditional Mexican manner. It was composed of a special white clay that had been ground on a *metate* stone, moistened to the consistency of thick paste, and then applied with a wad of sheep's wool. It was a joy to prepare a meal in the adobe kitchen because it stayed much cooler than the corner she cooked in at the little house. But she hadn't minded the heat, not as long as there was enough food on the table when she'd finished preparing the meal.

Tanya remembered times when they had had little more than cornbread, molasses, and milk from Clem's cow. Now, today, Ashe had brought back a veritable spread for the long puncheon table that sat outdoors beneath the huge oaks and cottonwoods. Tanya had prepared it, with Willow's help, while Clem, Ashe, and Samson had waited beneath the spreading branches for the food to be brought out.

"We're havin' us a real feed, whoopee!" Samson hollered when the ladyfolk finally stepped outside carrying trays laden with steaming foodstuffs. "Where'd you get all these provisions, Ashe?" He eyed the big man at the table, his expression almost worshipful. "Are you rich or somethin?"

"Hardly!" Ashe laughed; then he looked up to see Clem returning with a dusty jug. "Home-brew?"

"Yep. This here's real booze, young fella."

Grinning handsomely from ear to ear while he

pretended to hold an aching head between his hands, Ashe said, "Do I remember that stuff!"

"Want a snort?" Clem hoisted the bottle high in the air.

Ashe raised a splayed hand. "Later," he said, but doubtfully. "After there's some food in my belly. That hooch is firewater!"

"Hah! It'll curdle milk into buttermilk all right!" Clem hooted, then poured himself a healthy tot while Tanya walked over to his side of the table and snatched up the firewater. She set it at the far end of the table. "Not another swallow until you eat. I don't want you soused before you enjoy the meal."

Ashe smiled at her wisdom and Samson giggled behind his hand.

"Bet you never knowed how I can hold my liquor, girl." Clem chortled with glee. Watching her eye him sidewise, he touched his nose gingerly. "I didn't earn this grog blossom from swilling milk and honey!"

"Aww, Clem," Samson drawled. "You're funny when you've had one noggin!"

"The milk is in the crock," Tanya told Willow. "In the kitchen. Would you get it please?"

"Should I bring the cornbread now?" Willow called over her shoulder as she set out for the adobe kitchen. "If you would," Tanya answered.

Gay streams of laughter reached Willow when she paused, at the other side of the house where the kitchen was located. With her arm wrapped around the slim post of a sapling, she listened, feeling melancholy all of a sudden. A bird sang. The plaintive sound pierced her very soul while tears misted her eyes. He should be here . . . *Talon Clay*

153

belongs here. An ache started in the region of her breast, a restless, incessant longing.

Somewhere, close by, a mockingbird sang a sweet, soulful melody.

"My *love,*" Willow breathed, warm tears wetting her flushed cheeks. She listened then, growing inexplicably excited as the seconds passed.

The songbird repeated each phrase of a complex plaintive air several times before taking up another. Willow sighed, drying her tear-salted cheeks. The beautiful song, full of sweet trills, fluted notes, and liquid phrases was rich and melodious. It filled Willow's young heart with a nostalgically wistful yearning.

As if on cue, against a backdrop of scintillatingly resplendent descending sun a rider could be seen traversing the long, curving drive out front, while the last notes of the mockingbird trilled away.

"Is it? . . ." Willow's heart skipped a beat. "It must be . . ."

He was dusty and travel stained, but he let out a lusty whoop and a holler when he saw the gathering rise from the long table and begin to wave him in. A party—he chuckled—just in time . . .

"Talon Clay?" was all Tanya said, looking from the grinning rider back to Ashe Brandon. He nodded yes, never taking his eyes off the brother who steadily approached.

A flash of bright pink calico showed around the big house, and cornbread and biscuits plopped onto the thick grass. Willow's hands were clamped over her mouth in unbounded joy. Very shaky but happy beyond describing, she recovered and bent to place the still-clean breadstuffs on the platter. She began to walk toward the table, her knees quivering like a jelly, her eyes lowered on the biscuits and cornbread.

Talon Clay saw her and his heart stood still.

"Willow, you forgot to bring the milk," Tanya said, laying out the boiled beef and Irish potatoes, the latter from her kitchen garden.

Unconsciously Ashe took the huge bowl of green beans and onions, his eyes never leaving his brother's flushed face. Then he noticed Willow who stood dumbstruck at the end of the table.

"Willow?"

"Oh, I'll go fetch it right away, Tanya." She tried not to gaze into the eyes of the beardless young man standing at the far end of the table, as if he didn't want to get too close to her. "I'll fetch the buttermilk too."

Talon had fixed his gaze on Willow at once, as soon as she'd come around the corner of the house, feasting his eyes on her like a starved man. He could not pretend that he was unaffected by her presence, no. He was rather shaken by the sight of Willow, for he had kept her in mind ever since the first moment he had beheld her dainty form. He could look at her; that was all. And she knew what he was, Talon was pretty sure of that . . . if nothing else.

"I'll go with you," Talon Clay found himself saying, and all eyes swung to him.

"What?" Ashe said, but no one heard him. Then he remembered that Willow had met his brother before, right here at Sundance, but he did not let Talon Clay know the extent of his knowledge. Something held him back, but he did not acknowledge it for what it was yet. He was just happy to see his brother, alive and well. "Ah . . ." Ashe waved his hand in a nonchalant air. "Go ahead, what's keeping you? Willow just might be needing help with the heavy crock."

Already walking on ahead, Willow felt Talon Clay's presence beside her when he caught up. She stared straight ahead, shyly avoiding looking at him. Not yet, she didn't want to gaze into those eyes just yet. Anyway, she was supposed to be feeling angry over what he'd bragged about to Clem Tucker. Of course, he might not have said those awful things about her, but he might have been acting big around his sidekicks. What she didn't realize at that time, was that Talon Clay had never bragged about his conquests, yet everyone had found out sooner or later that he was a ruthless and indifferent lover.

In the distance, wildflowers grew in abundance along a split-rail fence silhouetted against a blaze of orange sky. In the sunset, shades of evening were taking hold, fuschia and heliotrope streaking the sky in bold sweeps of breathless color accented by blue and lavender. While the backdrop, the verdant earth, was deepening into a heavy layer of deep purple and charcoal gray.

"We'll have to bring some lanterns back with us," Talon broke the silence.

Keeping her petulant chin in the air, Willow said, "It won't be dark for some time yet." Nonetheless, her eyes glanced at the darkening woods. "How've you been, Talon Clay?"

"Oh, just fine." He smiled at her profile. "How about you?"

156

"Okay."

"You're looking real good, Willow." He slanted his eyes downward, recalling the silent communication that had passed between them when he'd ridden up and heard the mockingbird's song. "I've been thinking about you."

"You have?" Her heart sped up; then her spirits sank at his next words.

"Yeah, a little."

"Here," Willow said shortly, stepping into the humid warmth of the kitchen. "You take the crock and I'll get the freshly churned buttermilk." She lifted a small crock, one that Clem had brought by earlier.

Without taking his eyes from her, Talon lifted the big crock by the thick ears on either side. Being so near the man of her dreams and having him stare at her so, Willow thought she would faint. Blood rushed to tint her cheeks a breathless petal pink, and the lock of gleaming hair that fell across one cheek looked like a skein of yellow silk on cherry velvet. Shifting the crock into one arm, Talon Clay lifted a hand to brush the wayward strand back, tucking it behind her ear. Willow prayed she would not swoon there in front of him, but his hand went back to the crock and she breathed more easily.

"You," Talon Clay said, "are like no other woman I've ever met, Pussywillow. I wish . . ." He lowered his bright-colored head to one side. Then he shrugged, at a loss for words for the first time before a woman. There was something so pure and golden about Willow that he often wondered if she was just putting on airs, like a lot of women did. Not long afterward, they changed, after they'd got a man where they wanted him. Talon had seen some of his friends reduced to poor excuses of manhood when they'd thought love had come calling, and he'd learned to read most women like a book.

His gaze lowered. Willow . . . he could not judge rightly. He only knew that she was different from the others he had known. A stab of pain and loss wrenched him as Talon Clay knew without a flicker of doubt that there would never be a future for him and Willow. He was quiet now, but there had been times when he'd been hard and ruthless, robbing folk while they eyed him with suspicion and dread. He had been with too many free-swinging, careless women who had known him for the outlaw he was. He had been born with an evil nature, and he didn't want to stain this lovely slip of a girl whose heart showed in her eyes.

"Talon Clay?" Willow broke the silence. "You said you wish? . . ."

She looked up at him with soft brown eyes, not knowing how very lovely and vulnerably innocent she appeared at that moment.

I love the shine in your hair when it catches the light. Talon wanted to tell her this and so much more, but he held himself back.

"I wish we had met sooner. Now"—his voice was oddly strained—"now, darlin', it's too late for us."

With those words piercing her heart, Willow watched Talon walk out the door, taking a part of herself with him. She shivered, but not from cold.

Slowly, each step harder to take than the one before, Willow followed Talon to the long table. She

158

was beginning to understand why he'd said it was too late for them. He'd missed her a little, true, like one misses a friend, a new one at that, but the truth of the matter was that she could never hope to compete with the older, more sophisticated women he had mentioned, had warned her about. Oh yes, he *had* warned her not to become involved with him. She was a fool! His heart was promised to no one in particular, but his body? . . . Talon Clay was a young man who took his physical pleasures where he could, and she had the terrifying feeling that he usually sought out an older woman, one who would not cause him terrible embarrassment by her ignorance of lovemaking—a woman who would not be awestruck by his own proficiency.

Besides, she thought, angry tears threatening, he probably is a murderer and if he is anything like Carl Tucker I want nothing to do with him!

Hanging her head lower, Willow realized the cold, hard truth: She could never win Talon Clay's heart. She was just not woman enough for the likes of him. She was nothing but a child in his eyes.

Chapter 12

Lanterns had already been lighted about the perimeters of the table by the time Willow and Talon Clay came back with the milk. They sat down to join the others in the meal that was just beginning, the blessing being said by Tanya.

She spoke softly but loudly enough so that all around the table could hear, and when she arrived at the part where she said, ". . . and thank you, Lord, for all the dear company gathered here . . . ," Ashe Brandon found her hand beneath the table and gave it a tenderly warm squeeze. "Amen," she concluded.

"Amen!" Clem and Samson exclaimed collectively, both reaching for the bounty spread on the table while they spoke. "Eat up, boy!" Clem said, reaching for a chunk of bread and cheese. "There's hasty pudding afterward." He directed a wink at Ashe and Tanya.

"Hasty pudding!"

"There is," Tanya began, a suspenseful twinkle in her eye, "also something Ashe brought back. It's made from oats, raisins, brown sugar, and honey." She smiled at her little brother then. "And something called chocolate!"

Samson almost swooned. "Chocolate! *Yum!*" He rolled his eyes, staging a swoon backward over the bench. Clem caught him just in time. "I ain't had no chocolate in a coon's age!" Samson straightened, his large brown eyes already roving in search of the mentioned sweet.

"You *haven't* had," Tanya corrected.

"I have not had," Samson said with a sniff, instantly adopting the air of a lad who was heir to an English dukedom.

"Very good," Tanya said, laughing along with Ashe who was chuckling over the boy's antics. "You should be in the theater, Samson. Don't you think so?" she asked Ashe, but he was quiet now. She looked into his eyes while Clem and Samson kept up a string of lively, inane chatter.

"Yes," Ashe said hollowly. "He should."

But Tanya had caught Ashe studying Talon and Willow, the one seated beside him, the other across from him. Tanya could not see Talon Clay unless she leaned forward or back, but she knew he was seated beside Ashe. As for Willow, Tanya knew something was troubling her.

All life seemed drained from Willow. She was listless, disinterested in the delicious fare spread on the table and in all that was going on around her. There was no trace of a smile on her face in response to Samson's antics, nor did she laugh when Clem related a funny story.

Clem glanced about the table, leaned forward, and

took in Willow's dejected expression. She looked like an angel whose wings had been suddenly clipped. Clem shifted his eyes to Talon Clay. The young man, in no mood for gaiety, sat woodenly, staring at Willow's bent head, looking as if he would like to pounce on her and tear her apart. Clem sat back and cleared his throat.

"Make a clean plate, Sammy." Clem nudged the boy in the ribs. "Hah! Ashe's a hearty eater. Just lookit him, how big and tall he's growed. Talon Clay's a big 'un too, just like you're goin' to be, if . . . *Say*, you ain't dreamin' about that there chocolate are you?"

"Awww, Clem," Samson drawled, "how'd you know?" He bent his red-haired head then and attacked the last potato with mock relish, already eying the hasty pudding beside his dish so he could eat it up real quick and get some of Ashe's chocolate.

As soon as Tanya ate the last bite on her plate, Ashe leaned closer and laid an arm across her shoulders. Questioning blue eyes lifted to meet hazel ones.

"What do you say we go for our walk now?" Ashe squeezed Tanya's upper arm to emphasize the real meaning of his words. He lazily dragged her eyes with his; then he grinned across at Willow—she was looking straight ahead at nothing in particular. He grinned, too, at his brother, who was lounging back on the bench, staring up at the sky, again at nothing in particular. Ashe had been struck by an idea, the most pleasant one that had ever popped into his head. He realized he was being a bit hasty but he proceeded.

"Well," Ashe said loudly, slapping Talon on the

163

flank, "how about you younguns cleaning up this mess. Seeing as you two haven't offered anything to this celebration but—"

"*Celebration*!" all but Talon and Willow exclaimed in surprise. "What celebration?" Tanya asked Ashe, her eyes beginning to mist over due to the premonition she was having. When he did not answer at first, she said, "Ashe?"

"Well," Ashe drawled, almost shyly. "First I guess I've got to ask you if . . ." He bent over to whisper in her ear. "Tanya, being near you, I"—he rushed on then—"I think we're going to have to do something about this. . . ."

Her misted eyes swung around to question him, mutely saying, *What, Ashe? What?* Ashe cleared his throat and tried again, this time a stronger conviction in his voice.

"I know what I feel," he said, very low in her ear, his eyes watching Samson lean closer until the boy was almost in his pudding. "What I feel for you is more"—he slid the chocolate confection that he had dug from his pocket across the table—"is more than, ah, lecherous, and I . . . I've always *adored* you, Tanya Hayes. Will you marry me?"

Samson, chocolate wreathing his mouth, jumped up and down on the bench, shouting, "I heard what Ashe Brandon said . . . *Ashe loves Tanya, Ashe loves Tanya,*" he said in a singsong voice, licking his lips and grinning impishly.

"W-wait a minute," Tanya stammered. "Did you say 'marry'?" When he nodded once, firmly, Tanya choked on a happy sob. "Ashe Brandon, you want to *marry me?*"

"Sure do, Lady Red."

If Ashe Brandon had shot her between her bare toes with his Colt pistol, Tanya would not have been more surprised than she was at this moment. She wanted to pinch herself to find out if she was awake, but she needn't have, for Ashe placed a hand on her back, and drew her close to his side. He was warm and alive, and she was not asleep!

Ashe lowered his head, whispering, "Lord woman, if we don't get hitched up pretty soon, I am going to behave in a most ungentlemanly manner and take you into the woods—the darkest, deepest part—and no one will see hide nor hair of us for two years." He chuckled lustily. "We'll be living in sin."

"*Two* years!"

The others looked on, more curious than ever— even Willow and Talon had perked to attention— while Ashe shushed Tanya with a wildly wonderful kiss that shook her to the very core. Then Ashe cupped her happily flushed cheek in his large hand, gazing at her with a sweetly voracious hunger in his gray-green eyes. "Tanya Hayes"—this time he spoke loudly enough for everyone to bear witness, "will you marry me?"

"Yes!" Tanya fell against his chest. She sighed, hugging him tight, never wanting to let go for fear he would vanish. She pressed her smiling lips into his tanned throat, whispering fiercely, *"Yes, oh yes."*

Part Three

If love were what the rose is,
And I were like the leaf,
Our lives would grow together
In sad or singing weather.
—Swinburne

Chapter 13

Tanya's wildest fantasies had burst into flight! Her heart was soaring higher and higher. Ashe had asked her to become his bride and she could not yet believe the thrilling words that sweetly reverberated in her mind like wild, wonderful bells. Ashe loves me . . . *loves me*.

Of course, he had not actually said that he loved her, but Tanya knew that loving and adoring were much the same. So why should she worry over such a petty thing? Ashe wanted her for his wife and that was all that really mattered. He would tell her he loved her soon, she was sure of it.

After clearing up the table, Clem and Talon Clay each took a lantern to walk Willow and Samson back to the little house. Ashe and Tanya were still strolling hand in hand beneath the silvery moonlight. The ephemeral clouds scudded by the smiling face of the moon, and night breezes wafted about Tanya's skirt, stirring the hem.

"Listen," Tanya said. The mockingbird was

169

singing again, its trill coming from the low hollows in the hills. "It's so beautiful."

"Just like you," Ashe said deeply, *"mi amor."*

"Oh, Ashe," she murmured against his buckskin-clad chest. He had just called her 'my love.' "You have made me the happiest woman in the world!"

"And you've made me the happiest man"—a lazy smile curved his lips—"by accepting. Do you know what a great feat you've accomplished?"

"No." She smiled, shaking her head. "What?"

"Texas Rangers don't ask women to marry—"

She spun around to face him, cutting off his sentence, "Oh, the woman does the asking. That's how it works with arrogant gunmen?"

"—at least," he went on as if she hadn't said a word, "not those I know. Well," he conceded, "maybe a *few* have a family."

"Ashe, are you serious?"

"I am, Tanya. And it'll be a while before we can actually hold the wedding. I want a nice one, for you, Lady Red. Now we can begin to make plans." He led her to the front of the house, onto the colonnaded porch. Looking up at the fan-shaped transom, Tanya felt a thrill much like that a bride would experience crossing the threshold. "Let's go inside and start there." He grinned down at her, his teeth flashing whitely in the lantern's glow.

The flash of pleasure, Tanya knew, came from the tone of Ashe's voice and from what his words seemed to imply. She was correct, for no sooner had they stepped inside, bumping into a sheet-draped table in the foyer, than Ashe quickly set the lantern down and turned to pull her into his arms.

A bewildering combination of excitement and alarm washed through her, yet then Tanya could not help but surrender to the overpowering tug of desire Ashe's kiss brought to life. The silvery moonlight stole in through the transom window, illuminating their faces, and Tanya opened her eyes slowly when the kiss ended abruptly. Her eyes flew wide then, her breath snatched away by the blatant expression of passionate hunger on Ashe's manly features.

"I want you," Ashe said, his voice oddly strained.

Afraid of the bold, virile stranger Ashe had become, Tanya began to inch away from his chest, stepping to the left.

"No," he rasped. "Stay."

She halted, looking up at him. Pierced by the fierce sting of desire, Tanya swayed to the side and he caught her, holding her tighter and clamping her to his chest while his free hand roamed up and down her back, cupping her buttocks and pulling her up against his rigid thighs. "You want me too, Tanya, I can tell."

"Yes, I want you," Tanya told him breathlessly. "But I also want to wait, Ashe . . . do you know what I'm saying?" She toyed with the buttonhole of his leather vest. "I guess you could say I'm old-fashioned, but it means so much to me." She heard him sigh. "Ashe?"

His arms loosened their fierce hold. "I know, Tanya. I guess that's one of the things I like about you. You're good—pure—and you're special, the kind of virtuous lady a man wants when he marries. But Lord," he said with a half-snarl, "it's going to put some strain on this body to be around you and not be able to make love to you"—he smiled—"all the way."

Gaily Tanya escaped the circle of his arms, whirling and calling over her shoulder: "Do you want to join me . . . upstairs?" A dazed look crossed his face and she laughed provocatively. "Well?" she said, sliding her hand up the oak balustrade.

Swiping the lantern from the shelf, Ashe playfully snapped, "Do you want to find out what it's like *not* to be old-fashioned?" He followed her up the stairs, eying the swirling patterns the wheeling lantern light created on her swaying skirts. "Damn." Ashe gulped down the knot in his throat.

"Did you say something?" She sauntered along the hall, her old-fashioned sway catching Ashe's eye once again after he regained his footing at the top of the stairs. Shyly, Tanya asked him, "Is there a nursery up here?"

Holding the lantern high, Ashe made out the bright flush staining her delicate cheekbones a cherry color. "A nursery? Aren't you getting ahead of our plans just a little?" He placed the lantern on a sheet-draped table nearby, again reaching out to draw her into his arms. "First things first, Lady Red."

His arms in midair, holding nothing but the light breeze Tanya had created, Ashe watched her dance away. A slow, disbelieving smile broke out on his handsome face and he chuckled softly to himself. So, she wants to play games. . . . He followed the evasive figure down the hall and to the right when she turned down a shorter hall.

"There's no nursery here," Tanya called in a singsong voice. She paused in one of the doorways then, motioning for Ashe to come over with the lantern. "Oh, Ashe," she breathed, quickly going over to kneel beside a baby-blue crib. Pink and white flowers and young animals were painted cheerfully on its curved ends. The cradle was held solidly in position between two tall stanchions that formed a bridge underneath, the bed rocking gently when it was set into motion. "It's lovely," Tanya said, a gentle wistfulness in her low voice.

Tight-lipped and staring into the shadowed corners of the room, Ashe did not lower his gaze after the first glimpse of the cradle. He remained motionless. Finally twisting about to look up at him, Tanya stared, shocked by the cold, emotionless mask that greeted her.

"Ashe . . ." She came at once to her feet, growing apprehensive. "What's wrong?"

"This was *her* room," he ground out, his nostrils flaring, his brow lowered angrily. He gazed around, snarling, "I should have come in here sooner . . . and gotten rid of all her things. I forgot to lock it up."

"The room, you mean?"

"Yes," he mocked her sweetness, *"the room."*

"Ashe, I don't understand any of this. Lock it?"

"Yes, damn it, can't you hear?"

She stiffened, glaring right back at him. "But why? Whose room was this?"

"Jezebel's, that's who." He leaned down toward Tanya and glowered into her shocked face, as if she were the very one whose memory he so despised. "My dear mother died, right here in this house, because of that teasing tramp who sashayed about here. She always had it in her evil mind that she was going to take over Sundance, as mistress, once she got rid of Martha."

"Who"—Tanya paused, almost afraid to go on—"who was Martha?"

"My *mother*."

"Oh." Tanya's eyes grew wide with wonderment. "Who was the other woman?" Again she was almost afraid to ask.

"Garnet Haywood."

"Garnet," Tanya echoed hollowly, staring back into the past. For some odd reason the name struck a familiar chord, yet she could not remember where she had heard it before. But upon hearing the name Martha, she wondered why Ashe's father had never mentioned his deceased wife . . . or the other woman. She had never heard that he had married twice.

"Tanya." Ashe reached out to pull her into the circle of his arms. "Forget it. I . . . it was something haunting me from the past. She has nothing to do with us now. We'll make this house a happy one again, you and I."

"But the ghosts of the past still haunt you and hurt you," she declared.

"Not for much longer." He kissed her, murmuring against her lips. "You'll make me forget . . . I just know it."

They kissed and caressed for several minutes in the hush of the big silent house, while outside the crickets made romantic night music to serenade them. The lantern's yellow light flickered and danced on the wall, making Tanya's hair glow like a brighter, willful flame. If the flame inside her were only let out, Tanya knew it would set the whole

174

house on fire.

"Uhmm, Lady Red." Ashe nuzzled his face against her forehead. "We'd better quit this foolishness now." He moved back from her, dropping his hand from her waist and rubbing it up and down his tight buff breeches. His thighs ached as he touched them and he suddenly knew that he had never hankered for a woman this badly.

Grinning handsomely, Ashe said, "I'll take you home now." He lifted her arm carefully, as if she were made of china, adding, "I'd *better* take you home now."

"It's such a beautiful night," Tanya sighed, walking in the overgrown yard beside Ashe. They were taking the long way to the little house, as they occasionally had in years past, when the branches of the Yagua had been swollen after a floodlike deluge. For the last several years the creek had not been all that high, so Tanya wondered now why Ashe was taking the long way. "We could have gone the shorter route," she told him, her hand through the crook of his arm as she studied his virile profile.

"We could have." He looked down at her with a grin. "But it's longer this way and like you said, it's a beautiful night. Besides, now you won't get your skirts wet when we cross Emerald creek."

Tanya's laugh tinkled in the warm night. "How *gallant* of you, sir. Will you spread your coat—in this case your shirt—and allow me to walk across on it so the hem of my skirt will not be dampened?"

Ashe squeezed her hand. "Do you know what I think?" He watched her shake her head. "You were out East too long and got your pretty head full of all

175

kinds of fancy notions about gallantry and such." He walked along with her, his scarred boots and her high-laced shoes stirring the moonlit mists at their feet. He stopped and, with one hand whirled her to face him, pulling her torso against his chest. "I'd spread just about anything at your feet"—his mouth was close to her lips which opened and closed in a breathless stir—"even my heart, for you, Lady Red. Lord"—he kissed her lingeringly—"but you're in my blood!"

Tanya squealed then, for Ashe had scooped her up into his arms while still clutching the lantern. Gallantly, he carried her across the narrow neck of the creek, but he made no move to put her down when they reached the other side. Tanya began to squirm out of his grasp, looking up at him a bit reproachfully.

"I remember what happened the last time you carried me like this." She stopped her struggles. They were useless anyway, for he just held her all the tighter. "I thought . . ."

Ashe's gaze roamed her lovely face, narrowed on her halting lips. "What did you think? That I was going to take you into my house and have my way with you?" His smile faded at her stunned look. "Did you?"

"Yes," she admitted, turning her face aside.

"You're right, you know." Her face whirled back to him. Ashe laughed, a low sound in his throat. "At least, ma'am, that's what I wanted to do more than anything else in the world."

Tanya felt her feet touch the ground, *almost* touch the ground, that is, for she felt that she was floating on air because of his nearness, the slight touch of his big, warm hand. Everything about Ashe Brandon made her feel, and sometimes act, like a giddy schoolgirl with her first crush. She knew that soon he would be moving on, but she hadn't realized how soon until he spoke when they stopped beneath the spreading branches of the cottonwood that grew beside the little house. No lights shone and all was quiet within, telling them that Willow and Samson were already asleep.

"One more kiss," he said, setting the lantern down and reaching for her as she willingly entered his embrace. Following a long, lazy kiss that created wave after wave of pleasurable sensation as his lazy hands traced the curves of her body, Ashe lifted his lips and gazed down into her face for what seemed a small eternity. "Did you like that?" he asked, still palming a raised nipple through her bodice. "There'll be more to come," he told her, "but we'll be in a predicament if we don't stop now, Lady." He was silent for a moment; then he said, "I won't be here when you wake in the morning. I'm heading out"—he chuckled low—*"bright and early."*

"When will you return?" she asked a little sadly, feeling lonely already.

"Hopefully in about two weeks. Can you wait for me that long?"

"Yes, I think I can manage that." She fought to keep her voice from cracking.

"Don't look so forlorn, sweet," he said, tracing a long finger over her delicate jawline. "I'll be back. And you keep taking care of the house while I'm gone." He leaned forward after backing away a step, to kiss her softly, once more. "It's going to be your house too, one day. You'll be mistress of Sundance."

Mistress of Sundance. Sitting Indian fashion in the middle of her bed, Tanya unpinned her long hair and brushed it until it snapped and crackled in the glow of the single lamp. The wonderful events of the afternoon spun through her mind, stimulating her senses and recalling the glorious moments when Ashe had sat beside her, the suffusion of colors as the evening sky changed from dusty pink and dark lavender to deep gray and nugget gold, the tingles of delight he had sent up and down her spine. Ashe's face had been boyishly handsome yet virile when he had accidentally brushed her bosom in reaching across the table. "Excuse my elbow, ma'am," he had said.

It struck her then that a wedding date had not been set. Tanya panicked for a moment; then she smiled, knowing there was really not anything to worry about.

Chapter 14

The sun rose beyond the massive cottonwood, setting its wide-spreading branches ablaze. Within several moments, there was no looking at the tree; it was a molten ball of coruscating fire. Yet the sun rose higher, higher still, to bathe the landscape in breath-taking pinks and golds.

Flailing one arm across her face, Tanya awoke to the soft glow that filtered through her little window like bits of powdered gold dust. Suddenly she was sitting up in bed, feeling strangely guilty for not having awakened sooner.

She rose swiftly, eager to be about on this fine day. Preparing for her morning ablutions, she heated water and then shed her cotton nightgown and lathered herself with the bayberry-scented soap she had made last autumn.

The day was going to be warm and sultry, for the new leaves on the trees surrounding the big planta-tion house were already drooping by the time Tanya reached it. She had prepared breakfast, eaten with

Willow and Samson, and then had set out to cross the creek and climb the hill.

She dusted the halls and cleared the upstairs storage room, to allow better access to that area. Now she was ready for a break. Wiping an arm across her brow, she perched on a trunk beside a pile of old newspapers she had placed there in want of a better place to put them. The newspaper on top caught her eye and she spread out the *Texas State Gazette*, dated 1849, to read what the editor had written:

No bride ever joined her fate to that of her lover with a less selfish zeal than that which Texas has joined herself to the United States. Yet no lover has ever treated his bride with more cruelty and coldheartedness than the United States has treated Texas. Want of protection, scorn, *and efforts to rob her of her dowry*—all mark the faithlessness and deception of her lover.

Tanya continued to scan the paper. The complaint was that the United States was not protecting the frontier, not sending enough soldiers to Texas, and yet not permitting the Texans to protect themselves by deploying the rangers.

There were constant pleas for mounted men and endless complaints about the use of infantry, which was as out of place in Texas, another writer declared, as 'a sawmill on the ocean.' Because the government would not place the rangers in the field, the officials in Washington were charged with being indifferent to the Indian atrocities. The reporters obviously felt that the life of a Texan was held in no more regard at Washington than a bit of codfish.

George Wilkins Kendall wrote:

I see that the Comanches are still continuing their forays upon the Texas borders, murdering and carrying off defenseless frontier settlers who had been granted protection . . . the Comanches must be pursued, hunted, run down, and killed—killed until they find we are in earnest. . . . If Harney can have his way, I cannot but believe he will call in Hays, McCulloch, and all the frontier men to pursue the Comanches to the heads of the Brazos, the Colorado, and even up under the spurs of the Rocky Mountains. Harney can take the dragoons with him, but for the light work he must have Texas Rangers. Without them, even he can effect but little.

Tanya looked away from the paper, at nothing in particular. Ashe must have been with John Coffee Hays at that time. It was painful to wonder whether Ashe had been one of the rangers appointed as executioners. Or had he been employed as one of the federal Indian agents—those who had to gain the friendship and hold the confidence of the Indians? Because they did this, they often incurred the ill will of the whites. Making a treaty with a tribe, or several tribes, is a task that tries the patience of the agents,

Tanya thought, but getting either the whites or the Indians to observe the treaty is even more difficult. She decided that Ashe must have been an agent, for he had a special way with words and he had told her at the table that he knew the languages of several Indian tribes.

Later, while Tanya was seated on the porch swing that Clem had repaired just the day before, Samson regaled her with a tale. The lad had become quite knowledgeable on the subject of Texas Rangers and Indians in the short time Ashe Brandon had visited with him.

"He fought with Hays in the summer of '54 in a battle with Indians," Samson was saying. "There was a ranger force of only sixteen men and they come upon sixty or seventy warriors near the Llano River! The rangers, Ashe Brandon along with them, closed in with these new revolvers and killed twenty-two Indians. They lost only one man!"

Samson waited eagerly for her question.

"How many rangers were wounded?" she asked with a slow smile.

"Only four of 'em!"

"Not bad." Tanya nodded.

"Ashe Brandon was a scout and a guerrilla fighter too. He taught me how to spell guerrilla, which is different from g-o-r-i-l-l-a."

"Was Ashe wounded?"

"Nope. Not never."

"Not ever," she corrected.

"Not even once," Samson giggled and rose from the wicker chair. "I'm going to go see if Clem needs any help in the stable. He said maybe I could ride

Dove in the corral today."

"Be careful," Tanya called after him. She was glad that Samson possessed an inquiring mind, and she knew that Ashe would be good for the lad. Samson needed someone to tame the wildness in him, and Ashe Brandon was just the man for the job, though Tanya hoped Ashe would not use too heavy a hand when it came to discipline.

Humid warmth was descending on the land like a heavy gloved hand so Tanya decided to rest right where she was for several hours before returning to the little house and preparing the evening meal. She knew that Willow was straightening up and making up a corner for herself in the main room of the little house.

Tanya let her eyes scan the length of the soaring colonnades and drift to the decorative wrought-iron grillwork, then she closed them. She sighed. She had always loved this place, it was like home to her, so peaceful, like a piece of Heaven itself. The smell of purple wisteria came to her on a sultry stirring of air. Soon, she knew, the wisteria would become huge masses of flowers cascading to the ground at the far end of the porch where the green, louvered shutters shut out direct sunlight from the sitting room. The shutters were adjustable and admitted light and ventilation. She could just imagine a husband beside her in that room, a babe in her lap. She knew now she would always be waiting here for Ashe to come home. He would be away for long periods of time, even when he quit the rangers and began ranching again, but this did not matter as long as she could be with him, even for a short time, and have his masculine vitality beside her like a nourishing aura. Just thinking about him caused a flush to sweep up her long, willowy legs. It kept rising, over her slim curves and right up to her cheeks and ears. She felt hot all over.

Tanya was aware of nothing but her vision of Ashe's countenance, the remembered power of his arms about her, his warm lips descending; so engrossed in her daydreams was she that when the wagon approached the house she remained in a dream state, her eyes closed to the world.

A burst of feminine laughter broke into the ardent wanderings of Tanya's mind. It came from down the lane. She opened her eyes, aware that a wagon steadily approached. Who could this be? she wondered. A hand flew in frantic haste to her hair, tucking back the unruly, recalcitrant strands that had escaped her long braid while her other hand busily tried to ease the wrinkles from her skirt. Clearing her throat and breathing deeply to clear the flush from her body, she rose to greet these unexpected visitors.

A woman with short, frizzy blond hair stood in the wagon. She handed the reins to the man beside her as soon as the wheels had ceased to roll. "Tanya Hayes, Lordy, is that you?" Janice Ranae Tucker called out as her feet touched the ground before the colonnaded porch. "I do believe it is." She came to stand before a much-surprised young woman, her pale blue eyes searching the disheveled countenance of her neighbor. "I thought you and your family lived in the little house." She looked around, surveying the now-tended grounds. "Don't tell me that you've gone and become the mistress of Sundance?"

"Well, I—" Tanya stopped abruptly, her cheeks flushed. "Not yet, Mrs. Tucker."

"I'm sure glad not yet, because we sure would be put out if we weren't invited to your wedding." Reaching behind her, she pulled a giggling girl out into the open. "Tanya Hayes, you remember Hester, don't you? I know it's been a long time since we last visited. Lordy, nearly three years. Hester, where are your manners? Can't you say hello to Tanya Hayes?"

"Well, Mama"—Hester impudently tossed her tawny-maned head—"you do chatter so that there's hardly an opening for me to greet our neighbor." She looked at Tanya now, her eyes giving the slightly older woman a bold once-over. She decided that Tanya Hayes resembled those pretty, French chambermaids in her cousin's house in New Orleans. "How lovely it is to see you again, Miss Hayes," Hester chattered on, "although it *has* been a long time, like Mama says. I must be the same age as your sister Willow." She gave the area surrounding the house and the balcony above a quick scan. "Where is she? And, *oh*, I hear that Talon Clay is here too. I haven't seen him in over six months now, and I'm certain Talon Clay will just jump with joy when he knows I've come visiting. Do you have any refreshments?"

"Hester Louise Tucker!"

"I'm sorry, Mama, I forgot my manners. But I'm just so thirsty!" She flounced her lilac skirts around her white-stockinged legs like an impudent child.

"You should remember your manners, Hester Louise. I didn't send you to New Orleans for nothing, you know." Janice Ranae patted the curls fried to a crisp by her daughter's new curling iron, one of the many gifts her cousin in New Orleans had lavished upon Hester at her departure. "Hester's refreshed my memory on a few of the finer points of the social graces, you know. It's so easy to forget when one moves to a rugged country such as Texas, don't you think, Tanya Hayes?"

Tanya finally found the time to blink. She gazed from mother to daughter, wondering which one was the more flighty. But she, too, must not forget her manners, she reminded herself. "I really don't remember too much about the town we left behind in California," Tanya said slowly, trying to think of what refreshments to offer her neighbors. "When we first arrived in Texas, we settled in the Piney Woods. That was before we heard of the rancher who was looking for a drover. My father was a drover before he became foreman of Sundance. Well," Tanya said with a breathy laugh, "let's go inside, and I'll see what I can come up with in the way of refreshments. I left a pitcher of lemonade in the hall." She whirled around to face the Tucker women, smiling a little from embarrassment at what she was about to say. "I don't really think it proper of me to invite you into the house. You see, I am not Ashe Brandon's wife yet and he most likely would not appreciate my inviting neighbors into the house . . . just yet."

"Fine," Janice Ranae said, not trying to hide the haughty tone creeping into her voice. "We, Hester and I, will just sit out here on the porch while you bring the refreshments out. Hester"—she addressed her daughter, who was looking away from Tanya— "go out and tell the drovers to rest the horses in the stable, out of the heat."

"There—" Tanya bit the angry words off, saying instead: "Go right ahead and make yourself at home in the shade." She stressed "at home," but she was certain they had missed the issue entirely or had ignored her. She had been about to mention that there was plenty of shade at the side of the house beneath the cottonwood, but she shivered to think of the sight that would greet Ashe if he happened to arrive home unexpectedly . . . like today. Would he think she was taking too much upon herself by moving into the mistress of Sundance position as soon as he rode out? How embarrassing it would be to have those hazel eyes sweep the visitors and then come to rest on her accusingly. Accusing her of what? she asked herself. Wasn't she as good as Ashe's wife already? No . . . not yet.

Telling herself that Ashe would find it delightful to find his lady seated on the porch sipping lemonade with their neighbors, long unseen neighbors at that, Tanya smoothed her hair, pinched her cheeks, which had grown somewhat pale in the past several minutes, and served her guests the lukewarm lemonade. How fortunate that she had seen fit to make a huge pitcher of lemonade before leaving the little house, although it was far from being spring cooled now. If only she could excuse herself to go ask Willow to bring up a platter of cornbread and dewberry jam . . . As it was, Tanya discovered that this would not be necessary.

"No thank you, Miss Hayes," Hester said in her sugary voice, "we've already eaten. But perhaps later? . . ."

The lemonade having been drunk down to the very last drop in the pitcher, the three women sat beneath the shade of the cottonwood, the dappled sunlight turning strands of Tanya's hair the color of liquid fire.

Janice Ranae's pale eyes narrowed as she fanned herself with a wide-brimmed straw hat, and she said bluntly, "Tanya dear, a man with a family cannot spend his time riding the wild frontier."

"I have heard that rangers do not marry," Hester put in. She really was not all that interested in the conversation; she just wanted to see Talon Clay. She remembered his passionate kisses, sometimes bruising, on her body; her senses stirred and her blood began to race in her veins. Never had she felt such desire as she had with Talon Clay; even the drovers, Jake and Frank, could not make her feel such a fierce urgency.

Tanya forced herself to shrug lightly and smile at Janice Ranae's cool remark. "Ashe won't always be a ranger," she said, unaware that the older woman saw the happiness that radiated softly from her lovely face when she spoke of Ashe Brandon.

Hester's eyes widened as she regarded the slender, dainty form just emerging from the trees and walking up the gentle slope. As the petite blonde neared them, Hester noted that the soft pink of her frock suited her honey-pale hair and fawn-colored eyes, but in Hester's firm opinion, it was not appropriate for the early-summer day. The sleeves were much too long, the bodice overly modest, and the hem, *mon dieu*, the girl could trip over it if she held herself less erect than she was doing.

"This must be little Willow Hayes," Janice Ranae gushed as the young woman came to stand before them, her gentle eyes full of curiosity.

"Hello," Willow said, her eyes sliding over to the girl who appeared to be the same age as herself.

For one timeless moment their eyes met, Willow hoping that the two of them could become friends, Hester seeing only a rival for Talon Clay's attentions. Although the two had known each other for a long time, living so close, Hester decided, looking at the innocent face before her, that Willow had not been broken in yet, and she intended to make dead sure Talon Clay was not Willow's first lover.

In a chilly voice, Hester said, "You must be awfully warm in that frock, Mademoiselle Hayes." Tossing her tawny head, she postured before Willow in her best Southern belle pose.

Mademoiselle? After finally getting an eyeful of the lovely dress the other girl was wearing, and of her shiny, curled hair, Willow asked abruptly, "Are you French? I've heard that word *mademoiselle* before." She looked toward her sister before going on, missing Hester's momentary gape at hearing her perfectly accented French. "It means miss, doesn't it?" Willow said carefully, using her best English and being careful not to sound too untaught.

Smiling her haughtiest and not happy at all that the other had bested her French accent, Hester pulled herself up so she could look down upon the slightly shorter Willow. "*Oui*," she said, sniffing through her turned-up nose.

Janice Ranae stepped closer, leaving Tanya on the porch alone. "We are your neighbors. Of course, you

189

wouldn't remember. You were too young last time we visited, or"—she thought a moment—"maybe you were out playing in the woods. Yes, that's what you were doing, and we heard your big sister scolding you just as we were leaving."

Forgetting her genteel manners, Willow blurted out, *"Tuckers . . .* you're the Tuckers." Her voice lowered and she blushed profusely. Then she remembered Carl, his bruising paws mauling her, and her friendliness drained from her face, leaving her countenance nearly as haughty as that of the other young woman. She began at once to notice flaws in the personalities of their two guests. Besides, she had a strong feeling they were after something, maybe even *some one,* and her suspicions proved true when next Hester spoke.

"Where's Talon Clay? He only stopped home once in the last six months, and I so do wish to see him. Do you know where he is?"

Now Willow realized she had a terrible enemy, by recognizing the covetous look in Hester's green-gray eyes. And she knew this would be so for some time to come. There was going to be a battle. One woman would come out the winner . . . and, of course, there had to be a loser. Then Willow brightened: Talon Clay wanted no woman. She smiled inwardly. At least he didn't think so . . . Not yet.

"Talon Clay will be along soon." Tanya softly interrupted their exchange, stepping forward to join the other women. "Willow, I hope you have started some dinner? Talon and Clem must be near famished after mending fences."

Walking a few steps from the house and turning

away, Willow smiled. Over her shoulder, she said, "Why don't you all come down to the *little house* for something to eat. There's plenty to go around . . . if you all like leftovers from the night before." That should make the haughty pair blanch—leftovers.

"Have the drovers bring the wagon around, missy." Janice Ranae went on as if the mention of leftovers didn't bother her at all. She proceeded to give her daughter a little shove when the girl had not moved. "Go on, tell them and we'll meet you down at the . . . little house."

"I don't remember where the little house— Oh, if it isn't Talon Clay!" Hester whirled in a flurry of fine muslin and cambric, her curls and breasts bouncing. "Go ahead, Mama, I'll have Talon Clay walk me to the Hayes' place!" She raised her skirt on either side as if she were a sprinter leaping into the midst of a minuet already in progress, the invisible couples swirling about on spring-green grass.

Willow trudged down the hill and splashed through the creek, carelessly getting the hem of her skirts wet, not even bothering to use the new stepping-stone bridge that Clem and Talon had erected two days before. She mocked the air around her:

"*Oh*, if it isn't Talon Clay. Go ahead, Mama."

Controlling her surly temper by a single thread, Willow entered the house and began to slam things about, pots and pans. Eying one big pan in particular, she envisioned the haughty head she'd like to clobber; then, as the hot waves blasted her from the open oven, she took a deep breath to steel herself for the hours to come.

It was cooler out on the porch, and so dinner was served there. With Talon's help, the long puncheon bench had been brought out, and this was where all were seated when Clem finally broke away from whatever he'd been doing in the bunkhouse and came down to join them. As soon as Willow sighted the old man coming up the slope, she rose from her end of the bench where she'd sat, her dish on her knees, surreptitiously eying the two at the other end. She called a greeting to Clem.

"Hurry up, Clem, if you want to get some of what's left"—she eyed the young woman with the voracious appetite—"before it's all ett up."

"Oh," Hester piped up, "Willow says the most quaint things, doesn't she?" She fluttered her lashes at Talon Clay who seemed to be eating up every morsel of feminine affection she flirtatiously tossed his way.

"Look at this!" Janice Ranae almost yelled at Talon's head. "Both my boys come back. How about that!" She slapped the blond boy's knee, never mentioning the whereabouts of her other "boy" Carl, nor would she on this visit. Carl had been in an ugly mood ever since he'd arrived home after his long absence from Saw Grass, their lovely ranch, despite the house's faded exterior and the progressively crumbling state of the outbuildings.

Shaking her head where no one could see her, Willow entered the main room and went over to the kitchen area to fix Clem a plate of her special beans with beef. The spicy odors of garlic, chiles, and tomatoes were deliciously released when she lifted the lid from the huge black kettle. Before turning

192

about to go back outside, Willow felt a presence close behind her. Knowing who was there stirred her senses and weakened her leg muscles. She turned then, to encounter passionate eyes, very dark, very green, outlined by thick, spiky lashes.

"Those are the most delicious beans I've ever eaten, Miss Willow," Talon Clay said, humorously surprised to see her eyes become like thunderheads pierced by lightning.

She puffed up her shoulders, and spoke in a painful constricted whisper. "I'm not *Miss* Willow, Talon Clay Brandon. I am Willow, just Willow."

With a muttered curse, he brought his hand up to tilt her face. He was about to say something and then thought better of it. He knew it would do no good to ask what bothered her. She had not spoken two words to him since he had walked out of the adobe kitchen the day of his homecoming. "Can't we be friends, Pussywillow?" he said, for want of something else to say. Besides, he did want to be a friend to her—if he could be nothing more.

"Don't call me that either." She turned back to her pot, then questioned him coldly over her shoulder. "Do you want some more beans, or not?"

"I've had enough."

With a toss of her head, Willow seemed to shake off the biting words. She picked up Clem's plate and abruptly turned toward the door. But she halted before going one step, for there stood Hester, and across from her, Talon Clay leaning a shoulder negligently against the door jamb.

She would go through them if she had to plow her way. With my chin up too, Willow thought determinedly. Not even excusing herself for barging through, Willow did just that, but she was very sorry for her hasty action. For when she came through, Hester chose that very moment to step forward and block Willow from going to the left. Willow had to turn right quickly or else knock Hester down—not a bad idea, she had thought—but she twisted about and came up hard against Talon Clay.

With their bodies pressed so close, even for a few seconds, Talon's face contorted with pain and Willow's vision blurred. The two were painfully aware of each other. In silent communication, they stared. Then Talon Clay's mouth curved into a sad half-smile, but the rest of his face was rigid. A shiver shook Willow to her very toes; then, just as quickly as it had come over her, the spurt of desire vanished.

"Willow," Talon broke the spellbinding silence. "You can bring the plate down now."

Hester, a hand pressed daintily over her mouth, began to giggle. But it was a nervous laugh, for Hester had caught the highly emotional moments, had felt the tension between the two. It was a live thing. If she didn't work fast Talon Clay would soon have Willow Hayes in his arms—very soon.

An embarrassed pink climbed from Willow's throat to her cheeks as Talon brought the hand holding the plate down. Cradling the plate gently, he whispered, "I don't like having that hanging over my head, Willow."

Willow snatched the hand holding the plate from his. "I don't suppose you much like having anything hanging over your head." She stared back into suddenly threatening eyes. "Do you?" she dared.

Willow's breast ached for her heart thumped a painful tune as she whirled from the door, coolly allowing her eyes to flick over Hester and letting her know exactly what she thought of a woman who flaunted herself around a man, making sly little movements meant to arouse and excite until a man could take no more.

A small frown played between Tanya's brows as she watched Willow come onto the porch and try her hardest to smile while she handed Clem his almost overturned dinner. She sighed and gave Janice Ranae her undivided attention once again, but she was growing weary of the chatter of cattle, of the newest meat on the market, of the drive to Galveston, and so on.

Willow's gaze was painfully riveted on long, tan fingers winding about shapely white ones. Talon Clay sat very still, perusing Willow while she watched him unthinkingly stroke the palm of Hester's hand.

With a lump growing in her throat, Willow thought bitterly, here it comes. She could not hear what Hester and Talon Clay were saying for a strange buzzing was occurring in her head. Was she going to faint—die?—because of what was going to take place? Willow turned her face downward to stare vacantly at her tin plate.

Excusing themselves for a walk in the woods, Talon set out with Hester, but when they entered the trees that promptly swallowed them from view, Hester turned at once to come into his arms. Talon gazed down into the woman's hollow eyes. Just as he was closing his own, Hester's lips pressed urgently

195

against his, and he envisioned a pair of lovely, haunting pussywillow eyes.

He tore his mouth from hers, snarling, "Let's get out of here!"

Hester's hot, bruised lips quivered passionately as she breathed, "Talon Clay, whatever do you mean? I thought you wanted to—"

"I do! But not here," he said, roughly pulling Hester after him as he pressed deeper into the woods, then dropping her hand briskly as if she were diseased. "Take your clothes off," he ordered in a dead-cold tone, starting to shuck his shirt.

She planted her hands on her hips. "Wait a minute, Talon Clay. I'm not some painted whore whose legs you can climb between any time you want to. I want to be wooed and courted, like I was in New Orleans, before I—"

"Before you what?"

As Talon Clay waited for her answer, he recalled the way Willow had kissed him and pressed herself cautiously, innocently against him, and his loins tightened now as they had then. She had wanted him, and he had sent her away. He clenched his jaw, looking right through the "easy" woman before him and envisioning the one he wanted more than anything he'd ever wanted in his life. He wanted to fill Willow with pleasure, until she screamed out her love for him.

"Love?" Talon caught himself, unaware he was speaking out loud.

"Love?" Hester said, giggling and tossing her tawny curls about her passion-flushed cheeks. "Yes, Talon Clay, yes. But first I want you to 'make love' to

196

me. You know, touch me, kiss me— *Talon Clay!* Just where the hell are you going?"

With her mouth gaping, Hester watched the tall, lean form go back the way they had come, and within moments he was swallowed by the juxtaposition of the full leafing trees.

Hester buttoned up her bodice, wondering if she would ever understand men and their crazy, shifting moods. Talon Clay! Sometimes she thought that handsome lad played harder to get than a woman!

Chapter 15

Gray dawn found Ranger Brandon many miles closer to his destination, but it seemed he had been riding south forever.

To his left, on the eastern horizon, a roseate hue appeared. It was reflected from the treetops, and its glow crept ever so slowly down the dark boles of the oaks and cottonwoods and tall evergreens, spreading its ethereal paleness of color across the land until Ashe felt the radiant morning beams touch his whisker-bristled face.

Like a kiss, Ashe thought.

He murmured, "That sure feels good, Lady Sun." He chuckled at the whimsy of his pun. "Lady Sun . . . Lady Red." Red was the hue of his lady's hair, the lady with the crystal-blue eyes. Oh, Lord, he could make up a song to sing to her.

He reflected back to the unforgettable day when they had first kissed, remembering how they had tarried, the beautiful sounds of falling rain, and the verdant earth, so sweet-smelling because Tanya

Hayes had been there to lend more sweetness to the air. Something triumphant had rung in her laughter. Her charm had grown *on him*.

A strong, almost violent power had taken hold of his heart that day, and he had felt it in his blood. She was like a wind of flame. When he had embraced her it was more than a hot lashing of greenhorn passion that flushed his face and suffused his body. It was an inexpressible hunger—a yielding to something much deeper and more far-reaching than he had ever known with any other woman. No woman had ever done to him what Tanya Hayes did. He felt like a savage when he kissed her!

Passions which have been dreamed and relived during an entire day's ride are powerful ones, and that night, with his fingers linked behind his head, Ashe stared at the ceiling of stars and moon above his head, pleasurably envisioning his wedding night— his and Tanya's.

Ashe Brandon's blood stirred hotly as his mind drifted to that night in the near future. He imagined his fingers freeing that beautiful hank of shimmering red hair, bringing her face close to his. In dreaming sensuality, he saw her silken, long-limbed body writhe to absorb the muscles of his own form, the hardness of his thighs; saw her hips rising to meet his thrusts and take him into her melting warmth. He would be gentle, careful to arouse her until she was panting for him to take her. Tanya Hayes was a virgin and this pleased him greatly for he knew how

200

to be a tender lover. His long-boned fingers rubbed his Colt methodically as he smiled and thought. At first I will be gentle; then, when she becomes a woman in the sense of lovemaking, I will show her the ways of fiery, passionate love.

With these glorious visions dancing in his head, Ashe rolled over onto his side, rolling with his blanket around him and trying to get as much sleep as he could. But that blessed relief was not to come for yet another hour.

When the sun rose again, Ashe was already on the trail. The mist clouds rolled over from the woods to be stirred into ghostly shreds by Lágrimas' hooves. Soon the sun would burn away the mist and gleam golden against the blue sky. Ashe feasted his eyes upon the wildness and beauty of the Texas landscape, the glorious shades of green, even in the cruel thorny plant of the cactus. He was now in the southwestern corner of the Great Eastern Woodland, on the Louisiana side. Ashe had been to Mississippi, Georgia, and other Southern states, and he had found that they did not differ from East Texas in climate, general appearance, or in vegetation.

Soon he would reach the level prairie region where trees were scanty and there was tall grass. From the forests to the plains, and back again to the forests of long leaf, short leaf, and loblolly pine. His mind drifted back and reflected on the time when he was a boy growing into a man.

Ashe Brandon now realized that his long hours of toil at Sundance had molded his spirit, in some immeasurable way suiting him for the dangerous, hard-riding life of a Texas Ranger before he had set out to become one. So, in those first days out, he made friends, a wealth of them, mostly men—hard men and great men who had changed the color and direction of his life. He thought back on his first days as an Indian agent.

The Indian agents had exercised what influence they could over the native and resident Indians through councils and treaties, but Ashe Brandon's patience had been strained sorely during those years. The intrigue, the hypocrisy, the concealment of the real purposes of his fellow agents, the lying and the cheating, and the importance of saving face were the same in the forests of Texas as they were at Portsmouth or Paris or London. Some bands, usually of Comanches, would not come to these meetings at all, having no confidence in white men or in their own ability to outspeak them in council.

As a Texas Indian agent, he had pursued the ungrateful task of dealing with primitive people, had worked for months to bring the Indians into a council, only to have all his efforts thwarted by some wild rumor set adrift by an unscrupulous trader.

When the Lipans came into council they would report that the Comanches were hostile and making ready for war. The agents realized that the Lipans feared and hated the Comanches, that they wanted to join the Texans in making war on them, partly to take revenge on their enemies, and partly to have the opportunity of visiting San Antonio and other towns.

At that time Ashe was in one of the three

companies of rangers who had established headquarters at Corpus Christi while ranging the country from Goliad to the Rio Grande for six months at a time. These companies had been called in because of Indian depredations. In the Nueces and San Patricio counties, people had been captured, wounded, and killed; and over a thousand head of fine horses had been stolen in that same area.

The ranger tradition prevailed: Each ranger had to furnish his own horse, saddle, bridle, halter, and lariat; while the government supplied each man with a percussion rifle, a pistol, and ammunition. By 1850, there were five companies with seventy-nine rangers in each.

From then on, the border was fairly quiet for three years, partly because the United States was undertaking to establish the Indians on reservations in Texas. However, during the last year of Governor Pease's administration there was considerable activity.

That activity was part of what Ashe Brandon was now involved in. He had been appointed one of Callahan's Rangers, ordered to range in Medina and Bexar counties. He'd taken the field with the understanding that this time they would be furnished with arms, horses, and ammunition, but since the state treasury was empty, provision of these necessities depended on the act of a future legislature, as did his pay. Ashe smirked at that thought, knowing the dangers that lurked ahead when Texas Rangers were sent into the field with no provision for their maintenance and without assurance of payments for their services.

And how right he was, for the evil consequences of such a system were not far off.

Before Callahan's Rangers reached Eagle Pass, in pursuit of a party of Lipans, they fell in with a band of men led by an adventurer who called himself W. R. Henry. Ashe rode beside him now, his head cocked to one side, listening.

Henry grinned widely as his gaze returned to the unbeaten path. "I made camp on the Leona in July," he was telling Ashe. "I issued a call for volunteers to aid me in overthrowing the Mexican government."

Took a load on yourself, Ashe thought, but he only nodded when Henry looked over to see if he was being attentive. Henry went on.

"I used to be a Texas Ranger. I was engaged by the government during an Apache campaign. Yeah," he said with a vigorous nod, "that's for sure true."

"I believe you," Ashe said.

"Before leaving the federal service, I wrote to the governor of Chihuahua. I asked for a job fighting Indians in Mexico."

"You wanted to fight Indians?" Ashe said, making it sound more like a statement than a question.

"Hell"—Henry wiped his face with the dirty sleeve of his jacket—"I was willing to fight on either side of the Rio Grande." His laugh was a loud snort. "Besides that, I'd fight for any damn country that needed my services."

Ashe said nothing in response. He knew where W. R. Henry's loyalties lay.

Naturally, when Callahan's Rangers had come riding through on the trail of Indians, it had seemed only natural that Henry and his men should join in the chase. As Ranger Brandon looked from Callahan to W. R. Henry, something convulsed his gut. He wouldn't know until much later what this strange, foreboding feeling had meant.

The combined force, numbering one hundred twelve men counting Ashe (though he would rather not be counted among Henry's crowd), crossed the Rio Grande at Eagle Pass; it was nightfall. On the following day they rode toward San Fernando where the Indians were encamped.

Ranger Brandon chewed off bits of jerky, in turn relaxing and steeling his body for battle, knowing it would not be long in coming.

They met, in battle, a large body of Mexicans and Indians, losing four of their own and suffering seven wounded. The sunset that night was blood-hued as the Mexicans retired wearily toward San Fernando. The Texans headed for Piedras Negras which, after another grueling day, they captured.

"Callahan told the Mex officer that he was going to hold the town until the Indians are delivered"— Henry spat out a dark brown stream of tobacco juice—"or defeated." His grin was ugly.

Brandon recalled the officer, a rotund runt of a man with a swarthy complexion but strong as a bull. "Has he appealed to the Texans to come to his aid?" Ashe asked the man.

"Yep. He mentioned the Seminoles and Mescaleros. They're a thousand strong under Wild Cat and other leaders."

"I wonder what it would be like to climb as high as I can see," Ashe muttered to himself as he lounged back against a scrubby gnarled tree.

"What?"

"Nothing."

Another day dawned, and despite his bold talk, Callahan found it impossible to hold Piedras Negras in the face of the growing Mexican forces. Retreating to Texas would be dangerous for the Rio Grande had risen and had cut them off.

"What are you going to do now?" Henry asked Callahan, who had been plundering the Mexican town. "And where's Ashe Brandon? Did he desert?"

Callahan shrugged. "Must have." He hunkered down with a tin cup in hand. "I'll tell you what I'm going to do. . . ."

Ashe Brandon sat his horse atop a small barren knoll on the other side of the swollen river. He wore a wide sombrero, and a dull-colored serape was thrown casually about his wide shoulders. His legs were wet and damn cold, his borrowed boots sodden. His saddlebags bulged with his regular attire.

He watched the flames lick at the town of Piedras Negras for a time; then he nudged his horse away from the miserable scene. He realized that Callahan had been urged on by a desire for plunder, but he had also been drawn on by the adventurer W. R. Henry, Ashe decided.

He sucked at his lower lip. He should have had his wound tended to instead of letting it go this long. He looked down at the throbbing teeth marks in his hand. Just before he had thrust his knife into the Comanches's stomach, the warrior had attacked his other hand, sinking his teeth into the flesh like a feral animal. Then the brave's half-naked body, the blade sunk hilt-deep into it, had jerked, stiffened, and crumpled to the earth to lie still.

Returning to the ranger station a week later, Ashe Brandon had received medical attention to further the healing process he had begun with herbs for which he'd traded some coffee to an old Indian woman he'd met along the way. She had recognized the bite of Nermernuh. He had laughed when the toothless crone had grinned, thinking she might have been jesting with him, for who could tell a Nermernuh bite from a Pehnahterkuh.

Ranger Brandon had caught up with the story that had preceded him. He'd told the man in the station how much he knew, and together they had pieced the whole story together: in order to cover their plundering of the Mexican town, Callahan and Henry had set fire to Piedras Negras and had crossed the river under the protection of the flames.

After a week or so, the whole incident had come to a head. The burning of Piedras Negras was wholly unwarranted, and it resulted in the dismissal of Callahan from the Texas Rangers. Ashe had stayed on, knowing he was correct in his assumption that it was dangerous to send Texas Rangers into the field without providing for their maintenance and survival. Besides, without the assurance of payment for services rendered, who could really blame J. H.

Callahan. Nonetheless, there was little doubt in Ashe's mind that W. R. Henry had been the instigator of the unfortunate situation.

The sunny weather had broken, settling into a drizzle that made Ashe wish he had brought another jacket along besides the unlined buckskin. Now it would have to do.

He was downstream of Plum Creek with only the pleasant smell of wood smoke in the air and his horse for company. All the slopes were enshrouded in a gray blanket, and while he sat beneath a canopy of trees and watched, they grew darker and colder. His beans, cooking in a pot hanging over the fire, were almost ready. Meanwhile, he chewed on a strip of dried meat, his last.

His fire was making a lot of smoke, so he doused it with dirt and ate his beans. A hard chunk of bread and black coffee completed his meal, the bread had been given to him by a pretty Mexican girl in Piedras Negras. He hoped she and her parents had escaped before the blaze fired their little two-room house.

The meat had been stringy, but he was used to a steady diet of jerked beef and venison. He sipped his cruel black coffee, staring, watching the rain quit and the moon peek through wispy shreds of clouds. Lágrimas snorted and whinnied.

Ashe jerked his head, blinked, and rubbed his eyes. "What the? . . ." He stood to his feet and bumped his head on a low-hanging branch. Then he sat back down, telling himself he must have been seeing things. He had to have been! A white Arabian stallion just did not appear out of nowhere!

As the moon made another appearance, Ashe saw

it again, on a hill above where he had camped, a magnificent white stallion. Again Lágrimas snorted and whinnied to the other horse, the white stallion sending a defiant whinny back. This was no dream, and he was not under the influence of the Texas moon. The stallion was real but as elusive and untouchable as the moonbeams he stood under.

Chapter 16

The true meaning of Carl Tucker's last visit was finally, revoltingly, made clear to Tanya. Now she, too, knew the most graphic sense of the word "lecherous."

Furiously Tanya mixed the batter for biscuits, imagining Carl Tucker swam inside her bowl. She would add Janice Ranae and her daughter too, especially after their last visit. *Visit*. For more than a week now, that word had been overused at Sundance. "Look who's coming for a visit again!" said Samson. "Oh Lord, not again!" Willow replied. "Well, if this don't beat all crow, the Tuckers are back!" Clem had snorted just yesterday. You'd think they had moved right next door. And Talon Clay, he walked about silent as a cat.

Carl Tucker had come along this last time, and he'd had the nerve to ask her to Rankin's fandango, after he had practically ravished her sister, and while he was raping her with his roving eyes. The man was a lunatic. He should not be allowed to run loose!

"Have you already promised to go to the fandango with someone?" Janice Ranae had asked Tanya as she'd sipped her coffee, her fourth cup.

"Of course! I am being taken there—all of us are"— Tanya had laughed—"by Ashe Brandon. Clem says Talon Clay is buying a brand new wagon from Joel, the carpenter in Bastrop Springs. Oh, I can hardly wait to go, I'm so excited." She'd turned to her sister, who'd been fiddling with a wood carving of a stallion Clem had fashioned for her. "Willow, won't it be just too wonderful?"

At her last words, Carl Tucker had risen and stormed from the yard, beating his horse's flanks all the way to the main road. Blessedly, Janice Ranae and chatterbox Hester had taken their leave not long after that, not too soon for those who resided at Sundance.

On the way back to Saw Grass, five miles from Sundance as the crow flies, much longer by the road, Janice Ranae had sat glumly, snapping at her fidgeting daughter and at the drovers for talking too loudly or laughing too much. She wanted to think matters over more clearly. Her plans were going awry.

Janice Ranae had hoped and prayed that Ashe Brandon, being in the dangerous line of work that he was, would somehow be killed; then Sundance would go to Talon Clay. That lad might be their son, considering the way Pete Brandon and his fancy second wife had cast the boy aside. Such a shame that had been. She had known by the look on the ten-year-old's face that something very strange, and damaging, had gone on in that house. Talon Clay had climbed into a shell every time Garnet's name was mentioned. Above all, Talon had been sensitive to everything that went on around him. His first steps into manhood had been painful, and then, almost overnight, she had noticed the change in him, had recognized that rugged contours had taken over his formerly boyish, almost pretty, face. Only when he was around horses had the boy seemed reasonably happy.

Janice Ranae knew that Carl and Talon Clay would be friends again, even though they had had their differences lately. Hadn't they gone off together to seek adventure? But now her prodigal son had returned, and she knew her godson—she thought of Talon as her godson—would come back to the nest when he and Carl settled their argument. Then, when they got Ashe Brandon out of the picture, everything would be theirs. The Sundance property would be joined with the Tucker's, and they would own the biggest spread around—one of them anyway. There were several large ranches.

The woman's knuckles whitened as she clutched the reins tighter. Now there was a new problem: Tanya Hayes. And it seemed as though Ashe Brandon just might return to stay. If there was a wedding in the making, then all would be lost. Somehow, with the help of Carl and Hester, they would tear those two lovers apart and make damned sure a wedding would not take place.

With a nasty, cunning smile, Janice Ranae turned her thoughts to the upcoming fandango. She was going to have to take Hester and Carl into her confidence, and they were going to have to work fast!

Up ahead, Carl Tucker was just wheeling his horse into the long drive that led to the rundown stable at Saw Grass. Reining up before the red, double doors, Carl remained mounted and reached for the tobacco in his shirt pocket. He looked around at the shabby grounds, faint distaste visible on his rather crude face. He wanted better. *Hell*, he deserved better. And I'm going to get it, he thought, picturing the Sundance property in his mind. When the lands were joined . . .

Imagining Tanya Hayes seated beside him in the big house at Sundance, Carl felt his belly harden and the muscles in his chest grow taut with unsatisfied lust. He passed his hand over his beard-stubbed face, making a rasping sound, and then another sound intruded. Wheels were bumping over the rutted road leading to the entrance to Saw Grass.

Goose flesh prickled Carl's skin as he watched the wagon approach. The gleam in his mother's eyes reminded him of what a good shot he was. As the wagon rolled to a stop, mother's eyes meeting son's, their devious minds met too. They knew what had to be done. First, a bit of snooping over at Sundance . . . inside the house. This was where he felt that some damaging secret, one having to do with Garnet Haywood, Garnet Haywood Brandon, would be discovered, and he was just the one to make the discovery. If that failed . . . He caressed his gun.

Much later that evening, Carl Tucker returned, very excited, to his mother's side. It had been a moonless night and so his dirty work had gone undetected.

"Ma, I got the letters—*Garnet's* letters!"

With her threadbare housecoat wrapped around her, Janice Ranae entered the kitchen, padding ungracefully in her sleepy gait. "Good," she said, pulling up a chair and plopping into it. "Now we'll have to think of a tall story to go along with them." She chuckled. "It'll have to be a good one." She pulled her chair closer to her son's, saying, "Let's see what you've got."

Chapter 17

The moving light of dawn brightened the earth a section at a time, first touching the highest hills with orange while the misted green forest waited beneath a sea of blue half-light. The first bird songs were being warbled; the skylark soared, singing in flight, until it was a mere speck alternately fluttering and sailing in the gilding sky, still pouring out its joyful and melodious song.

Tanya stepped outside the door to the little house, tossing her slim arms wide to the new day and embracing the lovely morning. While she had been abed, she had longed for coolness, because her dreams of Ashe had created a fever in her blood. Now she found herself shivering in her thin nightgown and wishing she had some of that heat back. Dreams of Ashe certainly warmed her, but it was her bed and a different kind of warmth she longed for now. Nonetheless, she must dress and see to the day's business.

Although Tanya was famished after the long

night's fast, she was too excited to eat. Rankin's fandango was only a few days away, and Ashe had promised to return before then. Suddenly, her heart fell dejectedly. *What will I wear to the fandango?* She had no dress. Willow had her dress ready, the one she'd been stitching on for a week now, a lovely pink and white frock. Tanya wondered where Willow had acquired the lovely eyelet lace that adorned the neckline and the sleeves. She would have to ask her about that—later. There was just too much to think about and do for the time being.

"Wait a minute . . ." Tanya said aloud. *Why not?*

"Willow." Giving the girl's shoulder a shake, Tanya waited for her tawny silk lashes to lift. They did, but only a crack. "Willow, where did you get the lace for your pink dress? I haven't much time. Willow?"

"Hmmm? . . ."

"Willow—the lace. I need some of it." She rolled over the slim white shoulder, and was mildly disturbed to note that her sister was naked. "Willow, are you sleeping in the buff? Completely?"

"Yep," Willow answered groggily. A slim arm snaked outward and raked through the long tangled mass of golden hair. Her brown eyes finally opened, her lips lifting at the corners in a lazy grin. "What's wrong with that, Sis? Ain't you ever slept in the raw?"

Tanya finally came out of her daze. It was as if she had just seen Willow grow from a girl to a woman. "But in the buff?" she said aloud. "Aren't you a little chilly?"

Under the patchwork quilt, Willow rolled onto

her back, her mischievous brown eyes smiling into her sister's mildly shocked ones. "It feels good," she said, snaking under the covers and chuckling like a deep-voiced lad.

Her hands on her hips, Tanya tossed back her head and laughed, laughed until her sides ached. "In the buff," she said, going to the curtain and shaking her head. Thoughtfully she nibbled her lower lip before she asked, "Willow, do you have any more of that lace?"

"Lace?" Willow rubbed her eyes and acted as though she was not awake enough to comprehend the question. She had never thought that question would be put to her, and now that it was, what was she going to say? Could she tell Tanya that she had stolen it from the secret room she had discovered in the big house? Along with the ribbons, laces, and lovely gowns she had found, there were other things—letters, documents of some sort, and other papers.

Willow had to think fast, but what was she going to say? She would have to lie, tell another white lie, like the one she had told Ashe Brandon. Come to think of it, this lie was going to have to be a whopper.

"I've got more," Willow said excitedly, dragging the quilt with her as she sat on her haunches in the middle of bed. "I, uh, I got it—lots of it—from an Indian. . . ." Now what? Willow wondered. What Indian would travel around trading such fancy items? Usually they kept such things for themselves, for their women. "Uh . . ." She faltered; then her big brown eyes lit up and she blurted out the story she had just dreamed up . . . part of it anyway. Neither young woman noticed Samson enter the main room.

While Willow told her concocted story, Tanya shook her head and nodded, but her mouth fell into an astonished gape many times during the telling. She wondered if Willow had started to sleep in the buff after she had met her new Indian friend. Horrors! "Willow, what has—What did you say his name was?" Tanya had already forgotten in her frantic worry.

"Nightwalker." The very moment Willow said the name, she felt a thrill of premonition course along her spine. Then she laughed at herself. Surely, there could be no such Indian . . . *of course not!* Even if there was, she would never meet up with him.

Tanya took to the tall tale like bees to a succulent bud. She knew a little about the tribes, however, so she asked Willow which tribe he belonged to.

Willow, already straightening her curtained corner of the main room, slowly said, *"Kwerharrehnuh."*

The most arrogant and fierce tribe—Comanches. Tanya had heard that some Comanches practiced a form of ritual cannibalism—a grisly, ceremonial remnant of a harsh past. She told her sister this, and Willow, knowing more about Indians from her long talks with Clem, set Tanya right.

"All Texas tribes," Willow said, "except that one. They may torture whites savagely, but I never heard of one eating folk, and not their own kind in a ritual. And they always respect the one who is brave— Indian or white."

To keep her sister satisfied, so she would not become unduly worried, Willow set out to stretch the falsehood, that she had met the Nightwalker, never fully realizing how deeply enmeshed she was becoming in something that would someday be not far from the actual truth of the matter. At the time she could not comprehend just what the fabrication would set into motion because she had no idea how closely entwined her story was with another's.

Willow began: "Nightwalker's parents had come out of the mountains of Montana to roam the Black Hills of South Dakota. They were Kiowas and very warlike. Before Nightwalker was born, of course, his father met a beautiful girl, daughter to one of the most fierce Dakotas, or Sioux. After Nightwalker was born, his people, his father's people were harassed by the Sioux, and they threatened to kill Nightwalker, who was a baby then. The chief's daughter was put to death, but the baby was spared." Seeing that Tanya was thoroughly entranced by her story, Willow went on, also enjoying herself immensely.

"Where did they go then?" Tanya wanted to know, but Willow was already speaking by the time her sister's mouth closed. "Nightwalker's father took the babe with them, though his wife was very jealous, and had children of her own to think about." Staring but not seeing, unable to understand the compelling wave that was carrying her story on, Willow faltered and then continued. "They were harassed by the Cheyennes on the west, and so the Kiowas began to move south. They began to live in the way of the Comanches, hunting bison on the Plains. With them were the Kiowa Apaches. Nightwalker's parents then moved into Comanche country. It was here that his adoptive mother tried to do away with Nightwalker, taking him into the High Plains hunting grounds.

221

But a Comanche war band was moving through and the chief of that tribe saw her. Pole Cat slew the woman and took the Kiowa Sioux as one of his own, to take the place of a son he had lost."

Willow bit her bottom lip in thoughtful reflection, feeling strangely melancholy. At first she had been afraid of the tumultuous power of the tale she had been telling, believing it to be of her own fabrication, but now she realized she had been retelling the story that Clem had told her. What had started out as a fairy tale was now the truth about a young man's history, and the one part that was a white lie, a teeny one, was the fact that she had never really met this Nightwalker. There were some other things that Clem had not related to her that she had put into the story, and she tried to tell herself that she had only made them up. Why then did she have this strange, unaccountable feeling that this was truly the way it had been for young Nightwalker?

Tanya sat forward, unaware that she was sitting on the edge of the bed with her arm wrapped about Samson's shoulders. The boy's eyes were large and he kept repeating the words *"Holy cow,"* in a breathless voice. "What happened then? Tell us, Willow, hurry, I want to know!" he urged.

Willow shrugged. "That's about it . . . but for one thing."

"Yes?" Tanya was just as curious as her little brother.

"Nightwalker was the first of many that followed." She went to her knees then and began dragging a box out from under her bed. Holding up her treasure, she lifted the slatted lid and out poured ribbons and French laces fit for the likes of a duchess.

Samson wrinkled his nose at all the fancy stuff. He wanted to hear more about the one called Nightwalker. "How many is he?"

"How many?" Willow said, not looking up at Samson who lay on his stomach on her bed, his chin propped in his freckled hand. "Oh, he is the fourth one, I guess. Yep, here it is!"

With her mouth gaping, Tanya lifted the gorgeous length of lace from Willow's hand and imagined it dressing up the bodice and sleeves of her best summer frock, a blue gown, one of the few dresses she had bought when she'd visited the Boston shops.

Just then the sound of boots scraped across the porch and stopped right outside the door that Samson had already opened to let one of Tucker's cats inside. Speaking of the cats, Tanya had a pretty good idea that one of the Tuckers was dropping the poor, mistreated creatures off on the road near Sundance.

Peeking outside the curtain, Tanya felt her insides churn into mush, her knees go weak, and her heart begin to beat a crazy tattoo. *"Oh, Lord . . ."* she breathed.

"Lady Red, with the blue, blue eyes," the voice, achingly familiar, husked across to her, "come here."

The party was on its way to Rankin's fandango. Tanya's frock had been completed in time, and Talon Clay's new wagon had come in. So, right now, they were all seated in it, singing songs. Dove's ears twitched to the tunes as the big buckskin swished his tail to shoo away the flies. Once in a while Lágrimas would nicker an answer when Dove let out a snort at the sight of other humans in wagons, and before long there were some wagons in front of them and several strung out behind, all headed toward Rankin's fandango.

They had left the San Antonio Road, the road that had once been known as El Camino Real when the area had been claimed by Spain and Mexico. It had had its first beginnings as an old Indian trail, and now, as yesterday, the road served Indians, gold seekers, priests, merchants, slave traders, outlaws, armies, settlers, and murderers. In 1828, James Goacher had gotten a commission from Stephen A. Austin to blaze a trail through this area, and by 1832 there were over three hundred families settled along the San Antonio Road, most of them near Brown's Mill. When Texas had won her independence from Mexico in 1836, land grants were effected for those who had fought for the Republic and this led to a rapid increase of settlers in this land of rolling hills, farms and ranches, post oak woods.

Knowing this area had belonged to Mexico, Tanya asked Ashe, "When did this land first become a part of the United States?"

Ashe smiled, stretching out his long legs in the bed of the wagon, his arm slung about Tanya's shoulders. "In 1803," he began. "It was considered to be a part of the Louisiana Purchase from France. But Spain also claimed all of the Texas coastline as far north as the Sabine River."

"How was the argument settled?"

"It was not settled, and when Mexico won her own

independence from Spain in 1822, Mexico just took over the Spanish claim.''

"When did the settlers come in then?'' she asked. ''And how?''

"The first legal settlers in this area resulted from the grant Stephen Austin obtained from the Mexican Governor Trespalacios in 1820. Then a man come along by the name of Shaw. He had been given a section of land in Austin's Colony as a reward for service with Sam Houston. He met a friendly group of Tonkawa camped in what's now called Burleson County, and settled there as a surveyor.'' Ashe grinned boyishly. "Any more, Lady Red?'' She snuggled next to him. "That's sufficient for now, Ranger Brandon.''

Seeing the festivities were in full swing, the party from Sundance realized they were a little late. But wagons and buggys were still arriving, so they were not the only tardy ones. In fact, people would be coming and going all that day and night, Ashe informed his companions.

As Tanya watched, she saw that this was so. Like magic, the conveyances streamed in, usually two-wheeled carts piled high with gifts and food, and drawn by oxen. Brightly dressed men and women, both sexes riding astride, arrived on horseback, laughing in gay abandonment. Music flowed out to greet them, the musicians romantically thrumming and throbbing out wild, tempestuous notes.

With a roguish grin, Ashe slipped his arm about Tanya's waist to pull her even closer to his side. "Happy?'' he asked, smiling down into her glowing sapphire eyes.

"Yes," she softly told him. "I remember the last party I attended, when Pa was alive." Her eyes misted in poignant remembrance of times past. "The young people, both Anglos and Latins, danced the Virginia reel and waltzed from three in the afternoon until dawn. There was a wagonload of roasting corn, and loads of other vegetables and watermelons, and cantaloupes."

"You like fruit?" He kissed the column of her neck, his eyes dipping to her scooped bodice, thinking of the "fruit" he would love to sample. She nodded. "I'll bring you all the fruit you want," he said. "Just tell me when. I know just the man I can get cantaloupes from. Say, we can grow our own. What do you say to that, Lady Red?"

She giggled softly. "I've tried. And the largest watermelon I've ever gotten from my garden was the size of a broom ball."

Ashe picked up her hand, looking deeply into her eyes as he kissed her palm. "I know how to grow them big." His eyes dipped to her muslin-draped stomach.

"Ashe!" Tanya laughed. "You've got your mind back in the house at Sundance—in the nursery."

To that he said nothing, only settled back, his arm slung about her shoulder and riding there gently as the wagon bumped along to Rancho de Rosa. Tanya was disappointed by his reaction, for she wondered why Ashe still avoided the subject of their wedding date. He had been the one to bring up sex and babies this time, so she couldn't understand why he hadn't gone on to discuss their wedding. She felt a little dejected and her spirits lowered a bit, but at least, he had asked her to become his wife. When would he mention love? Should she take the initiative herself? As of yet it was a hard decision to make. Maybe she would know later, before the evening ended.

The spicy odor of chiles, garlic, and tomatoes, assailed their senses, but Clem was the first to mention Mexican food. "Cain't wait to sink my teeth into some fire-hot frijoles and tortillas! OOoee!"

"Awww, Clem, you'll dunk your head in the first water trough you come to after you've had only one chile!" Samson hooted and hollered, attracting the attention of a few very young *señoritas*. These pretty dark-eyed girls who were about Samson's age were already gauging who would be the first to teach him the fandango. Samson blushed nicely and raised his hat.

As the party alighted, Talon Clay finally took a good look at Willow, and what he saw caused his jaded heart to turn over. Her hair, like fine gold dust, was swept back, just like her older sister's, and her pretty pink dress, the one he had seen her wearing before, was now adorned with lovely eyelet lace. He could take Willow, any time, whenever he wanted to. Poor willow-eyed creature, she was his for the taking; it was in her eyes. She would never tell him no if he had it in mind to make love to her—and he did think about it all the time. Who would stop him if he led her to the stable and took her in a dark corner there?

Respect for Willow Hayes won out, however, and Talon Clay looked aside. As she went around the front of the wagon, he tried to tell himself that the part of him that desired her was the part that also didn't want to seduce her. Somehow, seeing her as

227

she was today, so vulnerable and innocent, he decided that the time wasn't right . . . and maybe it never would be for them.

"See you later, Talon Clay," Willow shot back to him. Then she purposefully lifted her chin and let her eyes wander over the handsome Latin men already eying the blond beauty, dark lights sparkling in their eyes.

"Damn." Talon clenched his teeth. He looked back to be sure the wagon was empty before he brought it around and headed in the direction of the stables. God only knew what kind of wreck he'd make of her life if he let his hot-blooded passions get hold of him. He could take her, in a snap, and forget her the very next day. She would be willing, for he knew Willow wanted him something fierce. He wasn't mistaken about that. But, hell, he didn't want to hurt her, not Willow. However, he could tell that she needed some watching tonight. Otherwise, some other dude might get the same ideas he had and lead her off to some dark corner.

Tanya and Ashe walked into the courtyard, their party following close behind, except for Talon who would be joining them in a short time.

"Holy Cow, this is better than a hoedown or a barbecue!" Samson exclaimed, his eyes shifting back and forth as he realized he was being trailed by the pretty little *señoritas*. One flashed into the corner of his vision and he caught her standing impudently near, her black eyes saucily flippant, but when he grinned brightly over to her, she giggled and ran back to her friends.

"Where is your friend, Guy Rankin?" Tanya asked

Ashe. She was a little nervous about meeting Ashe's friend for the first time, but she realized this was unnecessary as soon as Guy came over. His manner was pleasant, his face amiable and ruggedly handsome.

"Good to see you again, Ashe," Guy said, pumping his hand. "And who is your lovely companion?" Dark blue eyes sparkled in a deeply tanned face. "I've never met this one before," he jested, winking at Tanya.

"This is Tanya Hayes." As Ashe introduced her, he pulled her forward. "She lives with her sister and brother at Sundance, in the little house. They've been there close to ten years now, I'd guess."

Though Tanya smiled and shook hands with Guy Rankin, the numbness of shock held her in its cruel grip. Ashe had not introduced her as his future bride! Oh God, she felt sick. This could not be happening to her, not now. After waiting so long for his love, she could not bear to have it dangled before her, clutch it for a moment, and then have it cruelly wrenched away again.

Tanya did not even hear Ashe making the other introductions, for she was in a state of acute misery. Indeed, she felt that life would soon end for her. Willow's soft voice was a buzz in her ears, as was Samson's, and Clem's, and there was another she could not recognize. It was Talon Clay's, and he was watching Tanya and wondering what had caused her dazed look. Frowning, Talon Clay moved closer to Ashe. He was about to ask what was wrong with Tanya, but just then, the betrothed couple came over to be introduced to the newcomers to their party.

"How-de-do!" Clem said to the handsome couple, his robust greeting finally bringing Tanya's eyes up from the cold ground on which they had been fixed.

Tanya's eyes rose from polished black boots, to black skin-tight trousers and a flaming red sash tied about a slim waist. Then her dull stare dropped again. The young man, no doubt the groom, was the tallest, lithest, specimen of manhood she had ever looked upon. On his boots, he sported silver spurs. Now he was saying something to her, and she looked at him, blinking, then finally found her voice. Ashe was taking all this in, with a frown.

"I'm sorry, I didn't catch your name." Tanya felt like a fool. Glancing over to Ashe, she straightened her spine; then she looked right back into the blackest eyes ever. She regretted having done so at once.

"Almanzo Rankin," he said, dropping her hand after brushing a soft kiss across her palm.

A brisk, playful wind set the gaily colored lanterns strung about to swinging. Tanya experienced a sensation of danger at being this near Almanzo Rankin. When he had looked at her, ever so briefly, yet admiringly, she had found herself staring into reflective black eyes that seemed to read her mind. A flicker of gentle understanding had crossed his taut-boned features, making her wonder if he had read the misery in her heart. He was as handsome as Ashe, but the difference in their coloring—Almanzo's coppery, Ashe's tan though fair—gave each a different cast.

After being introduced to Almanzo's bride-to-be, Tanya found herself relaxing somewhat when Ashe handed her a glass of *naranjada*. She was not imbibing tonight, she rarely did. Feeling even better when Ashe moved to her side and possessively hugged her waist, she shoved her fears aside and endeavored to enjoy herself.

"She's beautiful," Tanya breathed, unconsciously drawing Ashe's attention to the bride-to-be. To keep herself from sounding too eager to become a bride herself she said, "I forgot her name already. It's so unusual."

"Ellita Tomás." He plucked another strong drink from the tray being proffered to the guests, and quaffed it as if it were merely cool beer. He had things on his mind all right, but he was in no mood to destroy Tanya's fun just because he was worried about their future together. He had already asked her to become his wife, and fool that he was, he had not even found his inheritance yet. It was hidden in the house somewhere, so Clem had told him, but where, *where?*

Tanya gazed dreamily at Ellita Tomás. The bride-to-be wore a lace-trimmed white satin gown with enormous puffed sleeves, and a four-layered organdy canezou billowed above her waist. Her high mantilla decorated with tiny-faceted, glittering diamonds made the picture complete. Tanya thought Ellita looked like a Spanish *princesa*. But for some odd reason the girl looked sad. Or is it fear just beginning to surface in that lovely face, Tanya wondered, or am I only imagining it?

"He is the adopted son of Guy Rankin and his wife, Rosa," Ashe was saying. He looked at Tanya strangely before he realized she had been carried away by the lovely picture Ellita Tomás made.

"Who is? . . . Oh, you mean Almanzo." Tanya caught sight of Willow then, staring in rapt fascination at Almanzo. The girl couldn't seem to keep her eyes off him. Across from Willow, Talon Clay stood, looking uncomfortable in the white shirt Clem had starched for him, his ivory-blond hair Indian long. He typified the godlike beauty of perfect manhood, yet he watched little Willow as if he feared she would vanish into thin air.

"What happened to his parents?" Tanya asked.

"One of them was Kiowa Sioux, his father I think, for the name was Nightwalker . . . yes, that was it." Ashe went on to say that Almanzo was next in line to inherit the name, should he choose to live like an Indian. "Tanya? What's wrong? You look a little pale all of a sudden. Do you want something to eat?"

"How did Nightwalker—I mean Almanzo—come to live here on Rancho de Rosa?" She was feeling a little dizzy and wanted to sit down.

Mesmerized and shaking, Willow stared at her "make-believe" Indian. He was not only real, but frighteningly so to this girl who had thought he was but a figment of her imagination. His eyes and hair were the same color—black. Black as a moonless night. He was slim hipped and wide shouldered, and his movements were pantherlike, soft and sure footed. When he shook hands, his movements were lightning quick. He gave an order in Spanish just then, and Willow felt faint. As she collapsed, two vaqueros rushed forward to catch her. Her eyes had wavered to the left just before she'd passed out, and she'd seen two bright green eyes staring at her. In her swirling brain, the vision began. A pure white

232

Arabian emerged, blowing and stamping, from a misted wood, but Nightwalker was not astride it. No. This was a blond Indian, his long flowing hair melding with the white horse. Around his ivory-tressed head he wore a black headband. His chest was naked, but he wore fringed buckskins and mocassins. She knew him, for his eyes were as green as the most verdant landscape.

Chapter 18

Food was piled in high heaps on the straining tables that stood to one side of the clearing. In addition to salads, vegetables, breads, and fruits, several tables were devoted to whole spit-roasted cattle, deer, and pigs. Sweating men were now hoisting yet another brown, crackling pig into place. As knives bit deeply into the tender, succulent meat, fatty juices oozed through the wooden planks to the ground.

That was the first sight Willow beheld when she finally roused and opened her eyes—that and the fire-illumined face of Talon Clay who was bending over her. Holding a jug of water, he tipped it to wet the rag he'd been using to wipe her face, his green ice-sharded eyes were assessing her in a cold way that seemed to hold no concern. To Willow's hazy way of thinking, he seemed disgusted with her swoon.

"How could I help it!" she snapped at him.

His expressionless assessment continued to rake her as his voice roughened perceptibly. "You're as skinny as a newborn fawn. Don't you ever eat?" He glanced over to the table that groaned beneath its burden of foodstuffs. "I'll get you a plate, *Miss Willow*, and then—"

"And then . . ." She began to finish the sentence for him, but then she saw Tanya's concerned eyes on her so she bent forward to whisper the rest. "And then, you get your skinny rear away from me, you hear?"

He straightened, tossed the rag at her, and began to walk away, saying over his shoulder, "As long as you're feelin' so spunky, get it yourself—*Miss Pussywillow.*"

"*I will.*" When she looked up to see Ashe and Tanya hovering around her along with some other guests, all of them looking like concerned vultures, she treated the group to a taste of her volatile temper. "What are you all *gawking at?*" She tossed her head like a snarling tiger cub, loosening long strands of hair that fell, like yellow sun rays, around her face, and her brown eyes smoldered.

Tanya sat down beside Willow while Ashe motioned to her that he was heading for the table where the liquor was being served. He smiled at her winningly and blew a kiss over his shoulder as he walked away. Suddenly Tanya was feeling much better; she could even smile cheerfully now. She turned to Willow, who was ignoring everything, and everyone, but before she spoke to Tanya she noticed the string of handsome caballeros vying for Willow's attention. It wasn't long before Tanya was being asked to dance herself, and she thought, why not? Ashe seemed to be enjoying himself, chatting with the trio of pretty, laughing, *señoritas* who had joined the group of men he'd been talking with.

"Willow," Tanya called over her shoulder as she was being led into the clearing, "you be sure to get yourself something to eat. Promise?" She felt herself being tugged along and she laughed because she felt young and gay.

On the fringe of the crowd, Ashe was not entirely thrilled by Tanya's sudden gaiety. What was she trying to prove? he asked himself as he accepted another drink from the server at the table. As he stood there and watched, nodding curtly to those he'd already met, Tanya danced one dance after another—and he drank one drink after another. When he could see her no longer, the crowd about the dancing couples having grown, he strode in the direction of the clearing.

In the ensuing minutes, after he'd found a break in the laughing and cheering crowd, all of Ashe's attention was centered on the scene before him. His facial muscles grew taut as he watched a handsome young *hidalgo*—that one fresh from Spain—teach Tanya, his lady, his betrothed, the fandango. Indeed, urged on by clapping hands and the passionate strumming of guitars she was doing very well—so well, in fact, that the *hidalgo* spun her about and changed the step. Tanya followed gracefully, looking like a gypsy as her red hair began to fall about her flushed cheeks. Ashe had never seen her like this. As the music grew even wilder, *olés* were being tossed at her, cheering her on, and when Tanya began to snap her fingers high above her head, Ashe's mouth fell open.

Moving slowly through the crowd, from opposite directions, Willow and Talon Clay merged in the midst of the onlookers. They exchanged bemused glances and peered about for Ashe. Then Willow noticed Tanya and her own blood began to beat faster as she watched her sister perform.

"She's like a Mexican gypsy, a real hot-blooded one," Talon Clay said to himself. Not even Willow heard him, for like the others she was too wrapped up in the *gringa* who danced like a sensuous dream.

Despite his seething anger, Ashe felt the heat travel his thighs and settle in his loin area. She is like a feline in heat, he thought, and all the prowling tomcats are serenading her. Just look at them, following her every sinuous movement, licking it all up . . . and she is leading them on.

Ellita Tomás watched the red-haired woman dance, knowing she herself had never been so good; the *gringa* caught on fast. But Ellita's mind was on other matters. An old lover had come to the fandango, a jealous lover who meant to do her harm. Rafael . . . He wanted her back. Her full-lipped mouth was a tempting bud of crimson, but her eyes were frightened. Almanzo thought she was a virgin. Santa María, he would kill her!

Ellita Tomás, had known Almanzo for many years, but she had been surprised to learn that he wanted her for his wife. He frightened her half to death . . . how would she ever? . . . She looked over to where he stood, shrugging his wide shoulders indifferently in response to a question, obviously about the fiery-haired one who danced, that a squint-eyed vaquero had asked. Ellita thought if it were not for Almanzo's flat-brimmed Spanish hat held in place by a thin strap, she could very well have mistaken him for an Indian. She knew he was Kiowa, his many times great grandmother having been an Oglala Sioux, and this made her fear him even more. He was Nightwalker—a savage.

Tanya, now dancing a Texas waltz with Guy Rankin, could not drag her eyes off the bride-to-be for long. Something was amiss, and she felt that it had something to do with her. But how could that be? She hardly knew the woman, so how could they have something in common? She watched the cool, deliberate groom bend to say something in Ellita's ear, saw her nod vigorously, at which Almanzo at once strode from her side.

Still a little breathless from the wilder dance, Tanya felt the ardent gazes of many men flit over her, and she knew she was beautiful and desirable. Even Rankin had complimented her profusely. Indeed, he did so again before he went off to join his wife Rosa at the table where their closest kin were sitting down to eat.

Having found a small, flowered alcove where she could sit down and rest, Tanya looked up at the chunk of yellow moon above. It bathed the open courtyard and the low, tile roof that was supported by rough-hewn posts. She had seen the loosely clustered adobe buildings on the way in, but the rambling house, with dark green ivy clinging to its thick adobe walls, was the sight that had captured her attention. Yet, she would never trade Sundance for Rancho de Rosa. That home would always have a special place in her heart.

"Hiding?"

Tanya jumped as Willow came into view. "Yes . . . of course." She fanned herself with a huge palmetto leaf that had been left on the latticed bench.

A giggle surfaced as Willow said, "I'd hide if I were you. I saw Ashe a while ago, and well"—she cleared her throat—"he didn't look none too happy. Lord, I'd hate to be in your place tonight. You'd just better find yourself a nice big hole in the ground to crawl into!"

The redhead only laughed, loving the idea that Ashe was jealous. Maybe that would make him set an early date for their wedding—in two weeks perhaps. Of course, she would have to plan what to wear . . . among other things.

Rubbing his bristled chin, Carl Tucker stood in the shadows, malicious thoughts running through his head, his colorless eyes shining. He was glad Ma had stayed home with Hester. The dull-witted twit had come down with some kind of fever. It was better this way; he could think more clearly, and by God, their devious scheme was yet in the making. Ashe Brandon was ready to kill Tanya Hayes, he had seen it in the Ranger's eyes. No wonder! She'd been dancing like a Mexican *puta*.

Stepping forth like a stealthy cat, Carl Tucker made his way toward the man who intimidated him a bit. Hellfire, he thought, Almanzo Rankin intimidated just about everyone who came his way. All he had to do was give Rafael a little nudge in the right direction, and Garcia could do the dirty work. All Ashe Brandon needed was a little push over the edge . . . he was almost in his cups now. Yellowed teeth showed as Carl Tucker grinned. Tanya Hayes was going to hate Ashe Brandon in the morning. The man looked ready to take her to the *caballeriza* now, to the stable where the hay smelled the sweetest. What do I care if by morning Tanya is not a virgin any longer? Carl thought. At least she will hate Ashe Brandon. It won't matter that she'll be a little used. One night is nothing. Tanya was beautiful; that was all that mattered to Carl Tucker.

"Gracias, amigo," Almanzo said to Garcia, one of the vaqueros who worked for him, a very faithful man, one he could trust not to lie to him. Stepping from the shadows, every formidable movement of his body in tune with his lethal inclination, Almanzo's silver spurs jangled dangerously as he quit the corridor.

Tanya's head came about, and when she noticed Almanzo, her eyes riveted to the purple glow of the great jewel hanging about his neck on a thick golden chain. But it was his face that caused her to gasp, not the jewel itself. Her throat constricted in alarm. He was now a panther about to pounce on its victim. Indeed, those closest to Almanzo gasped audibly as he stepped into the courtyard and moved, quickly as a striking diamondback, to his nervously smiling bride-to-be.

Willow clapped a hand on Tanya's wrist, her breath caught somewhere between her throat and her chest. Almanzo's steel grip caught Ellita around the throat, yet to all watching, he merely appeared to be passionately caressing her. Tanya and Willow, however, were much closer to the couple, and they clearly saw that he was about to strangle the very life from the beautiful Ellita.

Trembling to the very core of her being, Ellita felt Almanzo's lips, deceptively soft, touch her ear. *"Bruja!* Witch! I wanted you! I loved you . . . and your soft body!"

"Almanzo, no!"

Abruptly, she recoiled as his hand shot out to twist her hair, upsetting the glittering mantilla. Then, to degrade her even further, he pressed his palm to her rouged lips and spread the red makeup all around her mouth and onto her chin, giving her the look of a ravished, disheveled, virgin. But Almanzo knew what she was and he told her.

"Puta! Whore! Ellita Tomás that shall forever be your name, for no one will have you now! You have disgraced the name of Rankin. Get off this land and never come back!" He lowered his face as she clutched at his arm in a frantic, last-minute plea. *"If* you do come back, little *puta*, I will give you to the vaqueros to use as the slut you really are!"

"Santa María!" the Spanish guests whispered, and Ellita's parents, who had come from the dining table, hearing the names their intended son-in-law was calling their daughter, crossed themselves and turned dark frowns upon Ellita, angry that she had become soiled before she could land herself a wealthy husband. But this savage . . . Now they were almost grateful to the one who had revealed her shameful sin. They knew its gravity to one of Kiowa blood. The Kiowas punished infidelity by disfigurement or death.

All laughter had died, and the festive scene had become as somber as a graveyard. Already some folk were moving toward the *caballeriza*, the adobe stable, to hitch up their wagons and head for home. However, those who had come from afar, could do nothing but sit down and commiserate with the wretched parents of the bride and of the groom. Indeed, Rosa María Rankin was wailing and sobbing as though there had been a death in the family.

Shocked and stunned, Ellita sat on the ground in the center of the courtyard, her pretty flushed face burning where Almanzo, the man she now would never wed, had struck her, with his lean, cruel hand.

"El salvaje!" she spat out.

With a sudden, inarticulate sob, Ellita fled the circle of firelight, her parents watching her go, Rosa shaking her head. Guy started after her, but his wife pulled him back although she was still shaking her head and sobbing. However, Guy could not sit still; he went to find his adopted son, intending to learn the truth about what had caused him such pain and made him so furious.

A muscle clenched in Ashe's jaw. He had watched the sorry scene unfold, and now he was watching his own bride-to-be with a new light in his eye. From the shadows beneath the adobe-walled corridor he watched her, studied her, wondering if he would be the first to have her. And have her he would . . . soon.

Snorting softly through his nose, a disgusted sound, Ashe saw Tanya rise to follow the thoroughly disgraced young woman. What would she do? he wondered and took another swig of his drink. Would she tell the wretched soul it was all right? "Look at me," she would say, "I've been with others, that does not mean I cannot marry someday." His expression hardened as he wondered just how many men she had lain with. Did she expect him to believe she was pure—after she had danced like *that*? She wanted to become a bride . . . no wonder.

"Not with this man you won't," Ashe said to himself, raking a hand through his already ruffled hair. He didn't care how he looked; no one was paying him any attention anyway. Everyone was too busy mourning . . . and eating . . . and drinking. He snorted through his well-shaped nose. Pigs, that's what some folk were, stuffing themselves when they were surrounded by terrible unhappiness.

Finding a stone bench and sinking down onto it, Ashe stared at the half-finished bottle that appeared from nowhere, weaving before his eyes like a snake. "What the? . . ." He blinked. "Tucker? Carl Tucker?"

"Yep. It's me all right." Carl's grinning face came into view as he hunkered down before Ashe Brandon. "If this ain't been some night, eh?"

"Where's my brother?" Ashe asked. "You know my brother, don't you?"

"'Course I do. Don't you recall he come to live with us when that slut Garnet kicked him from Sundance property?"

"Don't ever mention that name again!" Ashe's hand shot out and encircled Carl's throat, but he eased it away as the younger man nodded vigorously, his face light purple. "What the hell are you bothering me for? You got something to tell me?" Ashe carefully studied the man. "Yeah, you do. . . ."

Carl's tongue came out to lash his lips, wetting them before he spoke. "Tanya Hayes, it's about her. Wait! Don't get your temper up before I get out what I have to tell you." Carl backed away a step, having foreseen that Ashe intended to shake him like a dog does a hare. "You saw how she danced? She—that gal—knows what she's doin' with that body of hers, sure does." Now Carl did feel that his life was being squeezed from him. "Wait. . . . I ain't the one what had her. . . ." He choked and coughed as his neck was released from Ashe's steely hold.

"You'd better tell me what you mean!" Ashe snarled, going for the gun strapped to his thigh.

"I wouldn't be taking that woman to wife, if that's what you been meanin' to do, Ashe Brandon. I ain't alyin'. Here, have a swig of this." Carl waited while Brandon downed two more slugs of the whiskey Carl had taken from the private stock at Rankin's table.

Two minutes later, however, Carl was lying flat on his back, looking up at the tall, wavy form of Ashe Brandon. To Carl's even greater distress, Ashe had planted a booted foot on his belly and was now tipping the whiskey bottle once again. Carl's jaw ached and his head swam from the aching blow he'd received.

"When you gonna let me up?" Carl asked, vowing to get even with Ashe Brandon, and very soon.

"First, you fat bastard, you tell me all you know about Tanya Hayes."

Ashe cracked the bottle on a fat pillar, sending shards of glass flying in every direction. In his hand he held the jagged neck, and he threatened to use it on Carl Tucker if he didn't speak. To give him a taste of what he meant, Ashe pierced Tucker's chin and sliced sideways, sawing back and forth, while blood trickled onto Tucker's throat.

"No wonder the Mexs call you rangers Texas Devils!" Carl rasped, fearing for his very life. "I tell you . . . *Tanya Hayes is a lying slut just like her ma . . . Garnet Haywood!*"

"*What did you say?*"

Angrily, Carl wiped the drying blood from his chin. "Tanya's a slut, just like her mother. That's what I'm sayin'."

As low as a dying breath of wind, Ashe said, "I don't believe you. You're lying." He straightened, tossing the glass aside, aware of the tom-tom beating of his heart. "Where's your proof?" He watched then as Carl Tucker rolled sideways, reached in his dirty vest pocket, and brought out a yellowed sheet of stationery. "Here, this'll convince you."

Stepping toward a nearby lantern, Ashe glanced at the paper. He immediately recognized the neat handwriting of Garnet Haywood. It was a letter to her children, one that had never been received by them, for it was unfinished, the last word trailing into a squiggle.

His eyes gone storm gray, Ashe casually folded the letter. He was stone-cold sober as he looked down pityingly on the shivering form of Carl Tucker and then unceremoniously stuffed the letter into his belt. As he strode into the darkness, he said with deceptive gentleness: "Where's the preacher?"

Chapter 19

Tanya had no remembrance of how or where the wedding had taken place. She just felt numb. She sat the horse in front of Ashe Brandon, his chest pressed into her back, his long thighs intimately flanking her own.

Married. She absorbed this fact slowly, and a chilling aftershock surged through her. Something was wrong—terribly wrong. Ashe Brandon, her husband now, had spoken only two words to her since the hastily held ceremony: "Let's go."

It seemed hours later when they finally turned into Sundance property. The roiling moonlit mists escorted them to the front of the house, swirling silver-blue about her skirts as Ashe handed her down and then, without a word, wheeled his buckskin toward the back of the house.

The very air seemed to pulsate with approaching doom as a vivid flash of lightning made her wince and seek the relative comfort beneath the gallery. Actually it provided shelter, for it was growing darker and the wind, which had begun to pick up, was tearing at her hair and her skirt.

"Why don't you go inside?" the voice came at her from out of the dark, moving toward her until she sensed Ashe's warm, compelling presence.

Tanya shivered, and said, "How can you even see me? I—"

"Go inside," he ordered coldly, giving her arm a little shove.

Surprising her then, Ashe stepped before her and opened the door himself. Instantly he came alert, his muscles tensing as he shoved her behind him and slowly lifted his Walker Colt from its holster. Tanya could feel deadly power emanating from Ashe; like a diamondback preparing to strike, he was now without fear . . . or mercy.

Tanya could hardly breathe. Flattened against the wall, with Ashe splayed protectively against her, she could draw in only tiny gasps of air. Her lungs and chest felt as if they would soon burst through the tension that imprisoned them. She feared for Ashe's life. Was this the reason why he had treated her with such coldness, because he had sensed a prowler inside? No, that couldn't be, for Ashe would not be so foolish as to put her or himself in danger by walking into a trap.

Tanya heard a click. Now she did hold her breath until a shaky voice filled the awesome silence in the house.

"That you, Ashe?"

Tanya breathed out in a relieved whoosh, and she heard Ashe say, "Oh, for Christ's sake! What the hell are you doing here anyway?" He stowed his Colt and reached for a lamp.

With a blunderbuss cradled gently in his arms, Clem came into the circle of yellow light.

"I was standin' guard." He grinned widely. "I mean I was *sittin'* guard. Someone was snoopin' 'round here the other night. I woulda mentioned it to you, but I didn't want to be spoilin' anyone's enjoyment afore the fandango . . . or during."

Ashe's narrowing eyes went over Clem. "How did you get back here before us?" he asked with a ranger's curiosity.

Clem chuckled. "Got a ride back with the Wyatts. I wanted to make sure no thievin' polecat was snoopin' 'round here again. Heh-heh. I really coulda surprised 'im with Sally here."

Ashe frowned as air hissed through his teeth. "You think *I* wasn't surprised, old man?" He nodded at the blunderbuss. "You should be more cautious with old Sally. If you had had her tucked in the shadows instead of out in the open when that flash of lightning showed, maybe I wouldn't have known someone was here. Still"—He clamped a hand about Clem's shoulders, leading him toward the door— "I'm glad you made a mistake tonight. If you hadn't, one of us would be lying on that floor right now— dead." Ashe didn't say which one.

When Clem had gone back to the bunkhouse, Ashe closed the front door with a finality reminiscent of doomsday, and Tanya watched from the middle of the hall as Ashe turned to face her. His eyes, hazel-dark under thick, tawny brows, mesmerized her, and she felt so small, so vulnerable, that she was beginning to regret her hasty marriage. Actually it

249

had been Ashe who was in haste. . . . She wondered now as she had several hours ago, *Why?*

Unable to bear the tension any longer, she broke the silence, saying, "Are you hungry?" Extremely nervous, she dragged her gaze away from the noticeable bulge in his tight-fitting black trousers and peered down at the hands she was clasping together. "Oh, there isn't any food in the house, *is*—"

"I'm not thinking of food." Ashe shifted a bit, very conscious that his body was sentient with growing ardor.

"The West Yagua will be swollen with rain," she said, worried about Willow and Samson returning home.

"They can wade." He shrugged. "Or wait a few days at the Rankins'. Almanzo will escort them home, don't worry."

"Should we go into the parlor?" Tanya's voice was shaky.

"Upstairs." His reply came on the heels of rolling thunder.

"I . . . I don't understand." She looked at him, not seeing Ashe Brandon at all but a frightening stranger.

"Don't you?" He nodded toward the staircase. "It's our wedding night, Mistress Brandon. Now, if you would care to lead the way, I'll be only too glad to follow."

She spread her hands in frantic supplication, giving utterance to her confusion and fear. "Ashe, not like this . . . you are like a stranger to me. Why don't you say something nice, Ashe, like you used to? Why are you so . . . *so cold* ever since we became man

250

and wife?" She shook her head in dejection and uncertainty. "Ashe, why won't you tell me what is bothering you?" She wanted to rush to Ashe and throw her arms about him. He was troubled and angry, and she desperately wanted to make things right between them. "I love you, Ashe." When he stared right through her as if she wasn't even there, she cried, "Ashe, I mean it, *I do love you!*"

His voice dipped low as he ground out, "Did you love me when you danced like a Mexican *puta* for you caballeros? Did you? Did you love me when your eyes raked like hot coals over Almanzo's body? How about your Spanish lover who taught you how to dance like a slut? Did he get close enough to paw you when the others couldn't see? *Did he?*"

Ashe had been backing her up while he gritted out his hateful tirade at her, a dark scowl marring his handsomely rugged face; and now Tanya stumbled against the bottom stair. When she twisted about to brace herself from falling backward, Ashe leaped forward and caught her about the waist. One arm encircling her midsection while she dangled front and back like a broken puppet, he carried her, with no more care than he would a sack of potatoes, up the staircase. Vulnerable as a dejected, lovely kitten, she looked up and her eyes locked with the ones she found unreadable and emotionless.

Her gaze dropped slightly and fastened on the lean brown fingers of the hand that trailed the staircase railing. That same hand had been so gentle once, so caressing, so eager to please her, but now it was taut and inexplicably hard. Ashe's terrible anger was communicated by his other hand, clear through the material at her waist. Despite her distress she attempted to understand his dangerous mood. She could feel his fingers biting into her and making her ribs begin to ache.

"Ashe, please, you're *hurting* me."

As soon as he heard her aching cry, Ashe relaxed his hand a bit, splayed his fingers more securely and more gently at her back. During the lightning flashes, she watched the floor beneath her go by, saw her cascading hair trail along the border of the carpet runner, saw her husband's booted feet proceed down the hall, turn right, stride down another short hall, and then turn to the right again. To her, each step was like a loud heartbeat presaging the advent of her doom. Another ominous flash of lightning struck. They were in the bedroom now, and she twisted around to glance at his body, only to avert her eyes from the shocking evidence of his bold desire. She shivered uncontrollably, fearing that first angry joining would surely tear her asunder. If only she had been wiser and had not flirted so outrageously with the young men. She groaned inwardly. But had she really acted so badly? She hadn't thought so at the time. Ashe was the only person who had criticized her behavior.

Suddenly Tanya felt her body being tossed into the air, and while she was bracing herself for a fall, she looked down to see the bed moving up toward her . . . no, she was moving toward *it*. As soon as her body contacted the gentle surface, she rolled over, scrambled on all fours to the edge of the bed, and tumbled off, only to land hard on her buttocks.

When she looked up, the room was softly illuminated by the sconce Ashe had lighted above the huge mahogany bureau. He was standing beside it, and the look he shot at her was cold and calculating. Holding the stick in his hand, he pursed his crisp lips and blew softly on its red-hot tip. Then he could not help but lift his lips a little at the comical sight she made. She was plopped on the floor like a disheveled child, a small girl with her skirt spread around her, her lips pouting. Tanya made a slight grimace as she tried lifting her backside off the floor, and Ashe's face hardened, became cruel once more. Again, he saw Tanya as the wily vixen who had attracted all those males, saw her lifting her skirt on one side to show a well-turned ankle—just a peek, but enough to set the crowd to cheering eagerly for more. He, himself, had desired her, had wanted her in his arms, but she had seemed to belong to all those leering men, not just to him.

Tanya rolled onto her left hip, and stayed there, her palms resting on the floor as she studied Ashe. There was something different in his face, something frightening.

"Oh," she said numbly, moving again now. "I hurt myself . . . when I fell . . . off the bed."

"Good, he said, picturing Garnet Haywood as he had seen her last, sitting as her daughter, Tanya, was sitting now, on the floor in the dirt where she belonged. "You deserve it for all your deceitfulness and your lies." He turned on his heel, went out the door, and returned several minutes later, a bottle of brandy in his hand. His eyes glinted wickedly as he looked her over while he poured another stiff drink for himself, and he wondered how the hell he had let

253

her charms get to him so.

Tanya had not moved an inch; she sat, frozen. For the moment, sensation and motion had ceased. She stared at the floor, not able to comprehend the cruelty of Ashe's actions or the reason for his extended coldness.

"Get up," he ordered brusquely. "And when you're up, take your clothes off."

Gingerly she rose to her feet, wavering from weakness and the stress she'd been put through in the last eight hours. She glanced at the window. Dawn would soon be breaking . . . but what would the morning bring?

His voice was low and dangerously quiet. "You haven't taken your clothes off yet." She could not bring herself to meet his eyes, and so he went on. "Do you need some help? I'd be only too happy to come to your aid."

"I can do it," she managed to say, her eyes downcast.

Ashe watched as her dress slipped to the floor, then her petticoat. Only her thin chemise—he could tell it had been patched here and there—remained. Her slim-fingered hands were crossed modestly over her auburn patch of womanhood, and her head was turned so that he could gaze at her winsomely lovely profile. The crimson stain on her cheeks clashed with her hair, making it seem overbright.

Watching her stand like a winsome naiad frozen in time, her beauty so pure she seemed unreal, Ashe experienced the strongest surge of passion he had ever felt. "Take the rest of it off," he said, but there was no gentleness in his voice.

Tanya could not bear being so miserably humiliated any longer. The dam that held her temper in check broke, and she whirled to face him squarely, her long hank of hair quivering like red fire over a heaving breast. Her blue eyes blazed with cold fire, and she stamped her foot. "I will not—*not*. Do you hear me, Ashe Brandon!"

Her words ricocheted off him as he turned his back on her and began to strip off his shirt. What she didn't know was that his self-control was gone, and her body would be the prey of his savage lust. Tanya stared at the rippling male muscles on his chest when he turned to face her, cryptically stating, "All in one throw." Then, faintly curious as to how her moist cup would fit him, one hand went to the fly of his breeches.

A timid virgin and a vengeful man in bad temper make the poorest bedfellows for the ritual called consummation. Ashe had meant to have her "All in one throw," and Tanya had been prepared to fight him, but when he came to stand before her, both were struck full force by a mutual hunger.

"Tanya," he murmured, his voice a painful constricted whisper; but when she looked up she met only a sardonic smile. He muttered a curse, and lowered his mouth to hers, moving with exquisite slowness at first. Then his restrained power broke loose. As his mouth grazed hungrily over Tanya's lips, her throat, her breasts, a flooding excitement washed through her.

Her nipple hardened against his circling tongue, and Tanya heard herself saying desperately, "Ashe, please . . . help me lie down. I-I'm so shaky . . . I don't think I can . . ."

Instantly, he scooped her into his arms, hugging her fiercely against his chest while burying his face in her flowing tresses. All barriers had been swept away like chaff before a wind. He lowered his lips to hers and kissed her more urgently than before, opening her mouth with deep tongue thrusts in a miniature act of intercourse. At the edge of the bed he knelt, then pressed her, with tender urgency, into the downy softness of the fresh bedcovers that Tanya had washed and hung out to dry in the sun just two days before.

"Ashe, my sweet darling, Ashe . . . love me, oh love me," she begged, making strange little moaning sounds deep in her throat.

"As God's my witness, Tanya, I love you . . . *mi alma, mi fuego*," he murmured against her gently rounded breast.

"Ashe . . ." she spoke his name slowly, almost letter by letter, her voice husky and breathless as she plied her body against his. "When, darling, when?"

"Now."

Ember-hot, he came against her, then pulled away to poise above her one last time. Tanya let out a low whimper as his full-blooded staff thrust into her, thinking with that sharp, lancing pain she truly became his. Her natural lubricant gradually laved away the burning ache, and in its wake, exquisite pleasure waves began to course through her.

Ashe knew a moment of guilt and remorse for having believed Tanya was not an untouched maid, and as for the other matter having to do with her mother, he wasn't so sure anymore. For the moment, he could think of nothing but Tanya's silken body writhing and bucking ecstatically beneath his.

"Ashe . . . oh . . . wonderful," Tanya panted, as she was swept into a pleasurable spiral.

The heat of fiery passion burned in Ashe, its flames roaring toward sensual heights. All his thrusts were upward now; he was striving to bring Tanya to intense spasms of delight. Curling over her, Ashe sank his lips into hers, plunging his tongue in and out of her mouth in rhythm with his thrusts. A sharp exclamation escaped Tanya's lips and she was soon gasping for breath.

"Ashe!"

He thrust and wrest, their bodies surging, time after time searing her to him with his heat until the ever-tightening knot in Tanya finally let go as he drove deeper than before, his big body stiffening with the intensity of his release. Tanya experienced wave after wave, spurt after spurt, of piercing, throbbing, mindless ecstasy that soon reached its pinnacle.

Then they lay side by side, Ashe tracing the curves of Tanya's body, his long finely muscled legs entwined with hers. Finally, afraid though she was of what she might find there, Tanya forced herself to look into his eyes, and, in loving splendor, they gazed at each other.

Unexpectedly, Ashe rose to his elbows. Tanya did not know the terrible thoughts running through his blond head as he looked down at her. He was seeing Garnet, the slut who had seduced his father, driven his mother to her grave, and then tried to seduce him too. She had not succeeded with him, but Talon Clay had not been so lucky. His heart must still bear the

257

scars of what she'd done to him when Talon was a mere lad, still wet behind the ears. Then, when the ugliness of what he had done had struck Talon hardest, Garnet had pushed him from the nest. *The bitch!*

Apprehensive again, Tanya stared up at Ashe when he turned his head to look at her, to *glare* at her. She beseeched him sadly, saying, "Ashe, what's wrong? Why are you doing this to me again? Ashe, where are you going?"

Snatching up his discarded clothes and boots, Ashe quit the room, never looking back at her, never realizing she sat in the midst of the bed, hot tears of pain and misery coursing down her cheeks.

Realizing that Ashe had left the one candle aglow, Tanya silently thanked him for that one small kindness. She couldn't stand to be alone in the huge room, not on her wedding night, so she sank slowly back into the mattress, staring with tear-bright eyes at the tiny flame struggling for life. Then she smiled, despite the lament of her young bride's heart. What had she done to make her husband hate her so?

Chapter 20

Sleep came hard that night, and Tanya had just begun to drift off when a sound startled her awake. She soon realized what it was. Rain had begun to fall about the house.

The storm had ceased several hours before, but now rain methodically pattered down again, this time without the fury of the surly rainstorm that had pummeled against the tall French windows while her husband had made beautiful love to her. She would have smiled at the memory if she weren't so sad.

In the gloom of predawn light, Tanya rose from the mussed bed, feeling the chilly air nip her naked flesh. She dressed hurriedly to keep the blood flowing warmly throughout her body. Though she longed for a warm bath, she realized she would not be getting one; her husband would be in no mood to help her fetch water. Indeed, he might not even be at the house. She would have no way of knowing that until she went downstairs. At any rate, she would not be served croissants and fragrant tea in bed like the newly wedded wives in New Orleans. Hester had been more than eager to mention that custom.

Tanya kept her eyes averted from the stains that were witness to her lost innocence as, with a hand that almost shook, she stripped the bed. She was painfully aware that her duties as mistress of Sundance had just begun. But no, she thought, my wifely duties began last night in my husband's embrace. She wondered how often he would come to her, love her so exquisitely, and then leave her feeling desperately alone. It happened last night. It might happen again. For how long would she be able to stand this kind of treatment?

With her arms full of linens and her heart beating frantically, Tanya tentatively descended the stairs. Her blue eyes wide, she scanned the halls, checking each and every door, poking this way and that, until her cautious steps had led her to the foyer. Shifting her bundle to one side, she walked over to peep into the front room, her eyes going across the green-and-rose carpet, skimming the kneehole writing table, and lighting on the settee. It was mussed—as if someone had slept in it.

"Why so surprised?" The deep voice made her jump and whirl around, but her lips thinned angrily when Ashe laughed at her nervous reaction. "Did you think I would pull up a piece of flooring and sleep on that? Why didn't you put on the fresh dress I left on the chair?" he said, studying the dirty sheets tucked under her arm.

Tanya's chin lifted a little higher. "I suppose you had to sleep somewhere since you found my company so repulsive!"

Ashe's lips curled as he said, "Look at you . . . just like her. So haughty, so deceiving . . . but I'll bet you couldn't wait to have me lay into you." He reached out to pinch her chin, placing a finger on either side. *"Could you?"*

"No, Ashe, you're wrong!" Her words tumbled out. "I mean it was . . . it was . . ."

"It was good, wasn't it?" he said, so low she could barely hear the words.

Even though her chin hurt when she moved, Tanya nodded, saying "Yes" in a whisper, then, "Let me go, Ashe, you're hurting me."

As if he hadn't realized the angry force of his grasp, Ashe lowered his eyes and stared at the fingers that were pinching her face so hard her chin resembled a bright red cherry. "Go upstairs and fetch your dress," he said, without emotion. "I left it on the chair by the fireplace. Then you can go out to the laundry room and take yourself a bath." With his back turned to her, he asked, "You do know where the laundry room is, don't you?"

Tanya wondered if he was baiting her. Why in God's name was he being so cruel?

"Yes, I know where the laundry room is. I happened to have cleaned that room too, in case you don't remember."

Unaware that Tanya was waiting for him to lash out at her again, he ground out, "You would know everything about this house, wouldn't you? You've always wanted Sundance for your own." *Just like your harlot mother.* "Well, you've got it—*and all that goes along with it.*"

With that, Ashe turned swiftly to face her, his eyes going up and down her body, stripping her and making her feel cheap and ugly. In a cruelly mocking fashion, his eyes were telling her that he didn't love her, that he hated her! Yet he was taunting her with the hard, cold fact that he could have her anytime he so desired. She was his for the taking, just like a harlot. The preacher had said the words and they had signed the marriage certificate, now in Ashe's possession; but she was merely his kept woman, nothing more.

"Ashe . . . why are you doing this to me?" She spread her hands, unwittingly letting the soiled sheets fall to the floor. "In God's name, what have I done?"

Mesmerized by the smears of blood on the fallen sheets, Ashe stared at them for a moment, seeing only the evidence of her lost innocence. Then he shot forward, scooped up the linens and deposited them in Tanya's arms. While she watched in a daze, he brushed past her, heading for the hall. She heard him stride to the back door. Then it slammed resoundingly, the sharp noise echoing throughout Sundance's lonely halls.

Silently her heart cried out, "Oh, God . . . Ashe, what have I *done?* . . ."

Disheartened, Tanya did not go to the laundry room to bathe, nor did she go to the water shed. Silently she moped about the house, wandering in and out of the rooms, stepping through the French doors onto the gallery and then going back inside, acquainting herself fully with all the lovely appointments in the house.

She paused in the dining room, and her fingers absently ran over a small hickory table. Then as her feet skirted the blue and mauve Oriental carpet, she thought about the epithet Ashe had hurled at her earlier.

"Look at you . . . just like her. So haughty, so deceiving . . ."

Tanya wondered who it was that Ashe had been describing. Who was this mystery woman?

Seemingly of their own volition, her feet took her into the sitting room, her favorite place to relax. There were troubled clouds in her eyes as she lounged in the green velvet chair, staring unseeingly, her eyes cast down toward the gold carpet with the red rose design.

"I don't understand," she whispered to the quiet room, to the clubfoot chairs that flanked the sofa and loveseat. "Just who is *she?*" Tanya clenched her hands in her lap.

She had been utterly bewildered when she had gone over their heated conversation in the front room. She, too, had been angry, blazingly so, but her fury had changed to perplexity when Ashe had tossed the soiled laundry at her and quit the room.

The slanting pink sunlight flickered hauntingly across the carpet, and Tanya gazed steadily at the winking swath of waning light.

She was a married woman. *Married.* It had been like a dream. . . . No, more like a nightmare. She was a married woman, yes, but a very troubled and unhappy one.

When had the trouble first developed? Ashe had been put out over something at the fandango. The dance she had been tutored in? If he had been so cross after seeing her dance with the handsome Spaniard, then why had he been in such a hurry to wed her?

In the circle of firelight Tanya recalled the ceremony. Ashe had stared unwaveringly at her, and she had been aware of a sinking feeling in the pit of her stomach. His voice had been implacable when he'd asked—no, *ordered*—her to take Ellita's place at the marriage altar. A swift ceremony had followed, with only Rankin and his tearful wife standing by as witnesses. She had been allowed no time to go in search of Willow and Talon.

Had Ashe been comparing her to Ellita, the young Spanish beauty Almanzo had intended to marry before he'd learned she had committed the ultimate indiscretion? No. That could not be. Ashe had taken her to the altar *after* the miserable scene between Ellita and Almanzo.

Then what? *What?* Tanya sat, stroking the knuckle of her thumb and staring at the erratic patterns of the shifting sunlight until she realized the horrible truth.

Ashe had found fault with her lovemaking! That must be it, she couldn't think of anything else. Her heart contracted painfully. A foolish inexperienced virgin . . .

"Tanya."

"What? . . .

Guiltily, Tanya jerked her head to the right. Ashe was standing just inside the room, measuring her from head to foot but making no move to come

264

closer. She wanted to die!

He was saying something to her, but she couldn't make out his words. Her world was spinning madly. She saw him raise his brows in an unspoken question, as if he was waiting for a belated answer.

"I-I'm sorry," she stammered. "I didn't hear you."

"I said your bath is ready if you would like to take it now. I've brought the tub to your room and set it up."

"The water's hot?" Her voice was dull, expressionless.

"What do you think?"

"You did that"—sadly she watched him turn and walk away—"for me?" He couldn't hear her, of course, for he was already halfway down the hall.

She was wrong, she had to be. Submerged in the tub up to her shoulders, Tanya luxuriated in the now-tepid bath water, reliving the night before.

She recalled the sharply noticeable evidence of Ashe's desire when they had stood at the bottom of the stairs. He had not been thinking of food, he had informed her. His hunger had been for her, she knew it now. Yet he had been a frightening stranger. He had been jealous. He had said she'd danced like a Mexican *puta* for the caballeros.

She had stumbled then and he had reached her just in time, had caught her about the waist. He *had* to care for her, otherwise he would have let her fall. Still, she had felt his appalling anger. He had been rough with her, then inexplicably gentle before his face had hardened and become spitefully cruel.

Oh, she just could not understand this man she had married!

How could he have found fault with her love-making? How?

He had ordered her to remove all her clothes and he had watched while she'd bared herself to a man for the first time. She would have thoroughly enjoyed doing so for Ashe Brandon, her first love. Would have . . . but it hadn't turned out that way . . . not at first. No. She had been humiliated, by her own husband.

Envisioning his every detail, she remembered how she had stared at Ashe's nakedness. His form was perfect, godlike. It rippled with male muscle. He had approached her then, and how she had trembled!

The water was cooling considerably but Tanya didn't mind. Her body was heated enough as she remembered Ashe's kisses which had swept away all barriers between them. She had begged him to love her. . . . Now Tanya sat bolt upright in the water.

Ashe had said he loved her! Tanya recalled his ardent words. Then he had become cold and indifferent as he'd been before they'd made love. He had hated her all over again.

Tanya stepped from the cool water, shivering now as she reached for the towel Ashe had thoughtfully laid beside the tub. She stood still then, and as on the night before, tears of pain and misery coursed down her flushed cheeks, falling onto her naked breasts.

Chapter 21

"I know you're married to Ashe Brandon, Sis,
but"—Willow shrugged, shading her lovely eyes
with one sun-browned arm—"how come it seems
you two never get together?" Her eyes searched the
landscape for a flicker of horses' tails or a glimpse of
Talon Clay and Almanzo returning from their
mustang hunt. "Before you and Ashe got hitched up,
you were always holding hands under the table,
walking under the moon, or just staring at each other
for long stretches. What happened? Does marriage
make folks hate each other so they can't stand to even
touch? If it does, Lordy, then I never want to get
married!"

A breeze redolent of pine stirred pollen from the
bluebonnet-carpeted fields, flirting with new leaves
and already opened blossoms, and furling line-hung
wash and calico skirts. Walking among the rows of
vegetables, Tanya paused to tuck a long strand of
hair behind her ear. Always the curious virgin,
Willow closely studied her older sister, intrigued by

267

Tanya's married status.

"We touch," Tanya said defensively, but she thought, Only accidently, brushing in the hall, or passing on the staircase . . . She wished that were not all, and her long lashes swept downward as an erotic flush crept over her, as it had so many times since Ashe had made her his . . . how she wished to be truly his in more than just name.

Tanya had been devastated when Ashe had looked at her coolly and indifferently the day before he had gone back to San Antonio. He had looked right through her, and she'd had to turn away quickly lest he notice how frustrated she really had become. She had almost moaned out her feverish desire, *"Take me, Ashe, oh . . . please take me. . . ."* She had recalled the thrilling feel of his kisses, the tender way he had caressed her before entering, her flesh against his upthrusting manhood . . . but that was all over now. One night, their wedding night . . . and two weeks had already passed since the morning when she should have had croissants and tea in bed!

Tanya choked back bittersweet tears, turning her face aside.

Willow wrinkled her pert nose which was becoming lightly sprinkled with freckles from so many hours in the hot sun. "Yes," she said, unaware she was twisting her innocent barbs deeper into Tanya's sore spots, "but where are the little kisses? Where are the words that tell the whole blasted world you two are in love?" She had watched couples at dances, fandangos, barbecues, and weddings—lovers, obviously very much in love. Their feeling for each other had created a yearning in her own young breast.

Tanya gritted her teeth, not cognizant of Willow's own bitter situation as she snapped, "Willow, I told you—*we touch.*"

"You're lying, Sis." Willow stood finally, holding triumphantly the poor excuse for a carrot she had been struggling to free from the summer-hard earth. She giggled, "My first carrot." Then her small face screwed up. *"This is a carrot?"*

"Willow, *please.* I am in no mood for fun and games." Tanya plunged her watering can into the rainbarrel and then went among the rows, sprinkling only the root vegetables that would not burn beneath the hot sun. Really I should not be watering at this time of day, she told herself, but she had so many other chores that needed attention she would never get to this later in the day. Clem had gone to town, Samson was spending the weekend at the Rankins, and Willow had enough to do just keeping the little house in order.

Cuffing the earth with her bare toes, Willow murmured, "I'm really sorry for what I said. I didn't mean to say that you lied."

"Forget it, Willow, I'm just tired."

Willow took a bite of her carrot, spit out the dirt she had sucked from it, and walked sedately over to the corner of the corral where the chestnut mare was munching grass. She poked her head through the cross fencing, murmuring to the horse. The mare at once began to approach the fence, and then stood parallel to it while Willow stroked her rump. "Isn't she a beauty? Talon bought her downriver just last week," she said, as if Tanya didn't already know. "Her owner beat her; but look, she's almost tame again. Whoops!'' Willow screeched when Sonador whirled and tried to nip her. She stepped back, giggling, and then walked straight to the fence. "She wants the carrot, that's all."

"Be careful, Willow." As Tanya said this, she came to stand on the greensward side of the garden, having heard the pounding of approaching hoofbeats. "More horses," she said to herself, still looking for signs of them. The sound was like gentle thunder. "Many more horses," she said to Willow emphatically.

"It sounds like a storm is coming," Willow said, her eyes searching now. *"Holy Moses."*

Now they became visible. Talon Clay and Almanzo were riding in, fleetly ahoof, herding in twenty or so beauties this time, all wild mustangs. "They really weren't kidding, Tanya." Willow grinned, tossing her long hair over her shoulder. "Talon and Almanzo have really become mustang hunters, just like they said they would. I can already see it, they're going to have to put up a bigger corral."

"Almanzo was hunting horses long before this." Tanya exchanged a knowing look with her sister. "Remember, he's an Indian."

"Nightwalker." Willow's eyes filmed over with dream mist. "He's real, and he's become my friend." Willow giggled then. "But he hasn't gifted me with any ribbons or laces . . . yet. Oh, maybe he's going to give me a horse when he catches the right one. What do you think, Sis?"

"Remember, he was almost married once. He has the look of a man who has known many women and been unsatisfied with them all."

270

No, Willow thought, Almanzo's not like Talon Clay. There couldn't be another woman user like him. Almanzo had wanted a wife, but such cozy thoughts never entered the blond head of Talon Clay, she was sure of it.

"Be careful, Willow," was all Tanya said.

Middle summer had arrived. The day was hot and still, not a leaf stirring. Even among the tall cottonwoods the heat was strong, for the relentless sun was shooting straight down and all breezes had ceased. It was high noon when Almanzo and Talon, caked with trail dust, rode toward the corral. Both men were wearing beaded buckskin shirts open to the waist, and both wore their long hair braided, but surprisingly, Talon Clay's was a foot longer than Almanzo's. Tanya watched them approach, wanting to apply the scissors to their heads and make them look civilized instead of savage, for they were both very handsome young men. Talon's skin had become as bronzed as Almanzo's, and Tanya wondered a little at this, at how the blond one tanned so easily.

Tanya continued to watch, as did Willow, the latter seeming to worship both young mustangers. Talon and Almanzo planned to crossbreed thoroughbreds with mustangs and get a hundred dollars a head from the army for each horse. Professional mustanging was just beginning to become popular, but in this area these were the only men who caught wild horses in considerable numbers, gathering the mustangs in Texas and selling them to the burgeoning market in the south. Tanya only wished Ashe could be here to see what was going on. He might just take up raising horses, and when they had enough of

271

them, they could get an outfit of cow hunters to help them with the first drive. Almanzo intended to capture a thousand mustangs, he had informed her. Already his father had captured more than enough horses, and he now sold them on a regular basis.

Willow and Tanya admired the black horse Almanzo rode. It trotted, proudly, black mane waving and tail arcing high, to within a few paces of the new bunch trapped against the corral. Then he halted and snorted triumphantly through his velvety nostrils. With his powerful neck bowed half circle, his ears pointed dead ahead, Almanzo's black Halcón stood and sized up the mares.

Hey, *amigo*," Almanzo called to Talon, "Perhaps we will not have to buy those mares we were looking at in Lampasas. Halcón seems to know his business here."

Talon Clay leaned over the head of his trusty buckskin and laughed. *"Tachón,"* he said. "Stud."

Talon glanced over at Willow and then brought his attention back to the mustangs, having completely missed the mysterious sparkle in her eyes. She knew what that word *tachón* meant, but Talon and Almanzo were too busy watching the black to notice. Halcón impressed the young mares, obviously, for the whites of their eyes shone with interest as the stallion walked back and forth in a lordly fashion, his eyes seeking the first lucky lady of the brood. Jealously the chestnut mare in the corral scolded the princely black stallion, and Almanzo tossed back his dark head and laughed aloud.

"Ahhh, listen to Sonador. She will not take kindly to this brood of beauties, do you think, *amigo?*

Already she tosses her lovely head." His dark eyes caught and held Tanya's, a faint smile curving his sensuous mouth. "She is very willing to love, but Halcón has his mind on all the other fillies too. He cannot decide which one he wants first. It is true he also likes to roam far from his home. . . ." he let his words dwindle into a deep chuckle, his black eyes sparkling brighter than ever.

A hot flush went from the tips of Tanya's ears down to her neck. Abruptly she reminded herself that Almanzo was a savage, rumored to be just as ruthless with his lovers as he was in his dealings with men and horses. He could be gentle, however, for she had noticed him with the mare, stroking her silky mane and soothing her nervousness at being in a new place with a soft and gentle voice. But what had he been insinuating when he'd looked at her? She began to feel a little uneasy with him about all the time. If only Ashe would come home, then everything would be better . . . wouldn't it? She didn't really think so. For some reason, Ashe had grown to hate her.

Drovers and mustangers were riding in now, quietly surrounding the horses, and Tanya wondered how Talon and Almanzo had gotten so many men to work for them in such a short space of time. Someone had to pay them all. She had counted four so far, and with Talon and Almanzo that made six.

"Oh, Lord. No," Willow gasped. "Look who else has joined them—that lecherous Carl Tucker. Let's go, Tanya, I don't want his eyes stripping every stitch of clothes from my body again. He gives me the creeps."

Talon Clay urged his buckskin over to the women

273

as they headed from the garden, dipping his head beneath a cottonwood branch. "Aren't you ladies goin' to stay for the best part and watch us get those mustangs into the corral?" He reined his horse up, curving the big head and neck of the buckskin away from them while its dangerous hooves pranced.

"What? And watch you stuff those poor beasts into one little corral?" Willow quipped, mockery dripping from her words. "No thank you, Clay Brandon."

"Suit yourself," Talon Clay said. Turning his attention to Tanya, he asked her, "How about you, Lady Red?"

"Don't call me that!" Her head came up with an angry jerk and her cheeks flushed a mottled pink.

"Whooo-eeee." The drovers and mustangers hooted and hollered as Talon Clay faced her, his red face clashing vividly with his white-blond hair. "We will have to teach you a lesson," Almanzo said, nodding to his companions. "This one does not know how to treat the ladies. He only knows those little ladies of pleasure, those who cannot tell a gentleman from an ill-mannered clod."

Assessingly, Almanzo studied Willow. She seemed to be in complete agreement with him, but he also saw her draw a long, quavering breath.

Tanya shivered as he dismounted with fluid grace and came to stand before her. From beneath the shadow of his flat-brimmed Spanish hat, his blacker-than-night eyes gleamed, boring into her own. Tanya could not read his look, however, and up this close, she noticed something she had not noticed before. He was tall, true, but his leanness was deceptive, for he proved much taller and broader than at first glance. Moving with the supple grace of a hunting cat, he lifted her hand, Tanya's cheeks growing hot as he pressed a warm kiss into her palm and said in a velvety rich, soft voice:

"You may stay and watch, señora, if you wish. If you do not, then I can understand that you have things to do elsewhere. These fleet, hardy, beautiful animals are a sight to behold. Our mounts will mix with them, as they did in a thicket, and then when the whole herd comes together, they will rush on, and we will have them in the corral before the mustangs realize what is going on."

Tanya was mesmerized by the soothingly tender tone of his voice, charmed beyond understanding her own reaction. Yet starved for attention as she was, Tanya lifted her chin and tossed her head, saying, "I do have chores to do elsewhere, but as long as you put it so nicely, I think we will stay and watch. . . ." She didn't quite know how to address him, so she let her words trail into a delightful laugh that babbled like a springtime brook. "You make it sound so interesting," she found herself blurting out, when he slowly released her hand and watched the lily-white member return to her side.

"You are very beautiful." She watched him mouth these words, feeling her cheeks scorch.

Watching him return to mount his black stallion, Tanya realized something that disturbed her very much. Almanzo Rankin wanted her, and he knew— he had read it in her eyes several times—that she was unhappy, wanting love and not being able to receive it from her husband. Tanya at once chided herself for

275

detecting his lust so readily. She had hoped, at first, that he was only admiring her in the way a man admires the wife of a friend—from afar. Actually it was his father, his adoptive father, who was an old friend of Ashe's family. Whether Ashe would consider Almanzo a friend if he could read such thoughts in the Indian's eyes, Tanya didn't know. Ashe seemed to hate her thoroughly, so maybe he would accept, even encourage, Almanzo's admiration and lust.

Aware of Tanya's melancholy expression as she watched the men rush the mustangs into the corral, Almanzo, on the sidelines, felt a pain lance his own heart. He should not feel this way, he told himself, but she was so beautiful and sad that he wished there was something he could do for her. She was good, pure at heart. He knew this. If only he had met her before Ashe Brandon. . . . But that was ridiculous. He could tell this woman's heart had always belonged to the handsome fair-haired ranger, and that would be the way of it forever, until one of them died.

Tanya and Willow watched as Talon Clay and Almanzo joined the others. After only a few minutes, the mustangs were secured in the corral. That done, Talon roped out one of them and brought her right back out and tied a long rawhide strap to the front feet of the horse. After he worked with the blaze-faced one for a while, he turned her out into the corral. If the mare tried to run off once the gate was opened, the rawhide strap threw her. After a few such falls, the horse no longer tried to run.

This went on for several days, and each morning,

Willow and Tanya came out to watch. The same men were always there, and a few had even begun to bunk down with Clem out back. The old man was very excited by all that was going on at Sundance, and he poignantly recalled the days when Pete Brandon had run the ranch. They had had horses then, too, but none as beautiful as the ones the mustangers were bringing home to Sundance.

When a sufficient number of horses had been caught and herd-broke, the mustangers would drive a bunch to San Antonio, where they had found an already burgeoning market. Almanzo had long ago earned himself the reputation of having caught and handled more mustangs than any other man in Texas. Now the drovers and mustangers were beginning to call him Mustang Man, and the Comanches were also giving him a new name, Dark Horse. So, Almanzo was Nightwalker, Mustang Man, and Dark Horse—besides being called some bad words by competitive mustangers. Always he was seen with a white-haired man riding beside him, one who was as bronzed as he was. That man was called White Horse or White Indian, for he had captured the white stallion, the beautiful one, that was sired by a domesticated horse gone wild, a well-bred stallion whose offspring became prize catches. Cloud was such a prize.

The first time Willow had seen Talon Clay riding in on the freshly broke stallion, a long-bladed knife thumping against his buckskin-clad thigh, his chest naked and smooth and bronzed like an Indian's, his thick braid bleached white by the sun, she had fainted dead away.

When she'd awakened, she'd found herself staring into the blazing green eyes of a white-haired Indian. She had been about to swoon again when he'd spoken her name, saying in a deeper, richer tone of voice than she had ever heard him use before, "Willow, sweet Pussywillow, why are you always lying flat on your back with your consciousness knocked clean out of you?" He turned, his handsome, sun-bronzed face bold and keen in the sunlight. Then he shifted, putting his back to the sun.

"Is that you, Talon Clay?" She blinked up at him, seeing the sun's rays sparkle about his blond head in a hot penumbra so glittering that she couldn't see his face and read his eyes as she wanted to. "It don't sound like you . . . don't look like you. . . ."

"It's me, darlin'."

"You're beautiful," she whispered. Then she felt herself being lifted and carried into the house.

"You are the one that is beautiful," he murmured as he kicked the door open. His knee-high moccasins whispering across the carpet, he brought her to the couch in Ashe's cool study at the back of the house.

"What did you say?" she asked him, her head spinning as she chided herself for having forgotten her bonnet on this hot summer's day.

"Nothing. Just rest."

He went away, returned; and she felt a cool cloth covering her forehead. "I was afraid you wouldn't come back." She lay there on the cool couch of Spanish leather, looking up at him, stretched out on her back. When he remained silent, she said, "You look so different, Talon . . . you even sound differ-

278

ent." She tried to reach his taut, bronzed cheek, and he leaned closer, sitting on the edge of the couch. But he soon found this to be a drastic mistake, for now her cool hand touched his cheek. It lay there, gentle as a butterfly's wing, and he found himself at once comparing her with other women. He discovered that in his mind and heart there was no comparison: she was the blazing sun, the others merely candles.

Talon remembered the sweet fire of her kiss, on that day that seemed so long ago. He'd felt as though a blade had been thrust into his heart when he'd been forced to leave her. Now his muscular body quivered with the intensity of the fiercest desire he had ever known, and from the power of an emotion he was afraid to name.

Her heart skipping beats every so often, Willow continued to feast her eyes on Talon, scanning his bare, bronzed chest, taut and hard; his long finely muscled legs encased in buckskin breeches. Finally dragging her gaze back up to his hair, she reached up and fingered the long silken braid slung over his copper-gleaming shoulder. "You look just like an Indian . . . how did your hair grow so long?" Her eyes slid from the braid to meet his, now a smoldering forest green.

Talon's eyes narrowed to slits as he stared thoughtfully at Willow, a very strange expression on his face. The feel of her weakened him, and he didn't like that. He had always been in control where women were concerned, but for a long time now, he had been without a woman. He tried to tell himself that this was the reason for his weakness. But he didn't want another . . . so what was he going to do?

"I took a scalp," Talon said, trying to smile and make light of the seriously dangerous moment they were approaching.

Willow smiled up at him. "It must have been a woman . . . men don't have hair this long and fair. The whisper of the wind is in this hair," she murmured, lifting the braid and bringing it to rest against her softly flushed cheek, close to her ear. "I can hear the wind of your travels, the fleet hoof of your new white horse. You have already gone far and wide with this horse."

"You silly girl," Talon said and brought his face closer to hers. "You're not holding a sea shell, you know." His eyes sliding downward, he watched her hand come to rest over the left side of his chest. "Now you are holding my heart . . . Pussywillow. . . ."

Their lips brushed in the slightest touch of a kiss.

"Oh, God, Willow . . ." Fierce passion swept through him . . . but he was not ready to acknowledge it yet. Maybe he never would be.

Her heart fluttering wildly, Willow said, "Please, Talon, just kiss me once?" Her breath came in quick panting gasps. "Just once . . . and never again?"

"I can't," he groaned, pressing his forehead against hers, his lips hovering close to the tip of her nose. His eyes had been closed, but now they opened. Upon seeing her flawless skin, his eyes dropped to note her long lashes that lay, like silken fibers, against the pearly flesh beneath her eyes. He felt the gentle quivering of her body against his, and he knew that she was crying. Indeed, her tears rolled down her cheeks and into the golden nest of her hair. "Little darlin'," he murmured, shifting his weight so that he lay down full length, her back against his pounding chest, his body cupping hers.

Both weary from many sleepless, frustrated nights, they soon fell sound asleep.

Willow had cried herself to sleep, in the arms of the very one she loved and couldn't have, while Talon had dreamed. . . .

He walked. His feet were bare, his long yellow-white hair braided. The earth surrounding him seemed full of golden halos and streaks of violet blue, and he seemed to be breathing a thick amber haze reminiscent of mist rising from a watery meadow. He could see his breaths clearly as if he were walking in wintry cold, puffs of it sparkling before him like golden motes. Willow stood naked, ankle-deep in a bubbling spring, so wondrously transparent that the golden halos of sun seemed to shine clear through her body like a white opal, catching shimmers and coruscating gleams. Her gilded hair was braided Indian fashion, the glints in it flaming strands of fire cast in bronze. Her opalescent arms stretched above her head, in ecstasy, while glistening crystal drops of water dripped from her fingers. Her body was riper, her curves and face more mature, and the light of the haloed sun touched her pensive, beautiful face as she turned to look at him. Her arms stretched out to greet him, her face an aching testimony of her joy, and she began to run slowly. Then, while the sun grew brighter all around the glade, Willow vanished before her arms could reach him. Talon Clay awoke, bathed in streams of erotic sweat, a younger, more fragile woman curled against his hungering body.

Fireworks exploded in him when he unwittingly touched her flesh as he began to rise, his hard shaft pressing insistently against the front of his breeches. He left then, before he shamed himself, running swiftly to the creek where the water ran deepest. There, he stripped himself and let the cool water lave the fire from his body and soul.

Chapter 22

Evening was stealing in, wrapped in a translucent gray mist. Thin shreds of the stuff lay over the grounds, while some swirled above the galleries of Sundance. A lone woman sat on the porch, and she rose when she sighted a rider coming up the lane. From a distance, Tanya had seen Ashe and the buckskin breaking through the gauzy haze, and her first thrill of elation was swiftly followed by a wave of fear. Tanya's heart beat a rapid tattoo. She stood there, on the porch, waiting to see if he would come to her or head right for the stable without a word to her.

A small wind, sweet with the scent of bluebonnets and hay, rustled the cottonwoods and postoaks, stirring up the shreds of low-lying fog. Memories came flooding back to Tanya: the beauty of their joining, the nightmare after when Ashe left her so coldly, the painful unearthly nights when she had huddled forlorn in her room. She wanted to run to him, but she dared not. She would only make a fool of herself if he cast her aside. Stirring the low-hanging mist, the horse and rider neared. But he was still too far away for Tanya to read his expression, to know if he would be happy to see her . . . or not.

"Finally he comes."

Tanya turned slightly to the right as Almanzo stepped upon the porch to join her. "Yes," she said softly, "finally."

"You have missed him, *señora?*"

"Of course, what kind of question is that?"

"I have just wondered, that is all."

"Almanzo!" Tanya whirled to face the darkly handsome man.

"Yes?"

"You had better leave me now. You see, Ashe is a very . . . jealous man."

"I understand, *señora.*"

About to step from the porch, Almanzo returned to her side, saying, "I am not a fool, *señora.* If your husband sees my haste to leave your side now that he is coming . . . you do understand that this will look suspicious to him?"

"Yes, Almanzo you are right."

She saw the wisdom in his decision. A man like Almanzo would not step down from the porch and rush out to meet another man, a woman perhaps, but never a man. And he couldn't suddenly go back the way he had come. That, too, would look suspicious, as if he had been dallying with her. No, that would not be understood by any husband—especially by Ashe.

It was true; Ashe was suspicious. That had been his nature, ever since he had fallen in love . . . with the wrong woman. He was bone-weary, hungry, and aching all over. He had thought to find his "good" little wife waiting for him in the parlor, seated there with sewing in her lap, or doing whatever else women did in their spare time. He had been down to Corpus Christi, where he'd learned that five squads of rangers were out searching for Indians whose trail had been discovered. He had met up with Lieutenant King and had followed the trail with him going up the divide between the Madio and Arkansas rivers. The rangers had come upon an encampment of Lipans on the east branch of the Madio, within four miles of ranger headquarters. In the skirmish Lieutenant King had been wounded, and two Indians had been killed. Ashe had sustained another bite on the hand, wondering at the time what there was about his flesh that Indians seemed to like. This time he'd had the wound treated immediately, for human bites—or savage's—could cause as much trouble as those of animals. The morning after the encounter they had hit the trail at daybreak, this time under McCulloch, on a trail they followed for twenty-six miles. The chase had begun in earnest, and mules, saddles, blankets, meat, and broken-down horses, marked the path of the red man for sixteen miles. At a chaparral thicket, where the Indians had finally quit their horses and taken to the brush on foot, the chase had ended. Now he had come home to find his sweet bride strolling in the yard with Almanzo Rankin. Would he never be able to trust a woman again? He didn't think so, not after Garnet Haywood Brandon.

Tanya's heart fell as Ashe passed them without a

word, only nodding and tipping his dusty hat as if they were strangers he greeted on the street of a windswept Texas town. As he took his horse out back, Tanya watched him for as long as she could see his ramrod-straight back. She was upset for she had seen his face darken into a scowl before he'd faded from view.

"You and your husband are not getting along, *señora*? Oh, I am sorry. Please forgive my trespass. This is none of my business. But if you wish to talk about it?"

"Would you like to discuss how you came to live with the Rankins instead of the Kiowas?"

"Ah, you are so right, *señora*."

"I have a feeling you have not always lived in Texas, is this so?"

"I have lived in New Orleans, *señora*. I was in prison there, you see."

"P-prison?"

"Do not fret. You see, I only drew my knife for a good reason."

"Only—"

"You see, I used my knife on a man who was trying to rape a girl, of eight or nine perhaps, I cannot be sure. She did not recover her faculties for a whole year, and I remained locked in jail until she could speak."

"She said you were not involved?"

"Yes, if she had not helped me, I might have died in that prison. The conditions were not fit for a dog, and many were already dying from a swamp fever. There was death all around me."

"Very touching," a deep voice drawled, then a

form detached itself from the shadows.

"Ashe!" Tanya snapped, whirling about. "How long have you been standing there . . . spying on us?"

"Long enough, my dear." Ashe came to stand beside his wife, and placing his hand along her cheek, he said, "You look very pale, and I think you are thinner. Are you tired?"

"Of course!" She slapped his hand away. "How very nice of you to notice that, at least. How long have you been standing there spying on us? I asked you."

"And I think I answered you already."

"Ohhh!"

With that, she left the men standing there, slamming the door as she went inside. Leaning forward, Ashe placed a hand against a fat pillar and sighed deeply. He looked toward the sky where an intermittent moon could be seen now and then, facing the heavens as if he sought some help up there. He groaned as if he were hurting; then he whirled, snarling, "What the hell are you? . . ." He looked around but saw no sign of the Indian. He was alone—very much alone.

The master of Sundance had returned. He had not signed up for another six months with the rangers, so it appeared to one and all that he was home to stay— at least until wanderlust got hold of him again.

From the backyard to the boundary line, fences were being repaired, and the Tuckers, noting this, had come over to snoop. At the moment, Hester was seated out on the front lawn, looking like a picture—or one about to be painted. She picked at the folds of her new dress—mama had bought it for her so she might "catch" herself a Brandon man—and batted her lashes. Willow suspected Hester exaggerated their color by some sort of artifice, and she seethed, as she watched Hester's gaze follow Talon wherever he went. If he leaned against a pillar, her eyes were immediately riveted there. If he went to fetch some refreshments, she waited breathlessly until his return. But something was different about Talon Clay. He now wore his jasmine-blond hair in a long shining braid, and went about bronzed and naked to his waist. Hester began to experience a new feeling for Talon Clay—fear. Still, she wondered what it would be like to have him crush her against that smooth, naked chest.

"Like some refreshment?" Willow stood before Hester, a pitcher of lemonade in her hand. "Ooops, I *am* sorry." As she poured she missed Hester's glass completely, spilling a goodly portion over Hester's new violet dress. "Here, let me help. Oh, I *am* sorry again," she said, acting as though she had tripped over Hester's jutting shoe. "Here. We'll get you cleaned up in a jiffy."

"Don't touch me!" Hester shrieked, holding up her arms as if the sky was falling upon her head. "You get away, Willow Hayes, before you completely destroy my new dress! Shoo!"

Her screeching alarmed the new maid. She came careening about the side of the house, shouting, "What's happenin', what's happenin'! I knows jes' what to do, if someone done gone and fainted dead away! Where dey is, where dey is! I'm acomin'." And she smacked right into Talon Clay, who was leaning negligently against a pillar and watching Willow with sleepy green eyes. He caught the maid as she collided with him, holding her at arms' length. "Unhan' me, young man! Where's de patient? I got jes' de thing!"

Talon chuckled and pointed at Hester, mad as a hatter and wet as a hen. Miss Pekoe herself chuckled. "So dat's what all dat dere racket is about. Well, shoot. I'll jes' take myself back inside and get back to my work."

"Yes, you do that, Miss Pekoe."

"How long ya goin' to hold up that there pillar, boy?" Clem asked as he came around the side of the house, chuckling.

Smiling at the old man who was returning to the bunkhouse, Talon left his pillar and went to seat himself beside Ashe. His brother acknowledged his presence with a nod, but his smiling eyes were trained on Willow and her teasing antics. "She's really letting Hester have it this time, ain't she?" Talon said, but not too loudly, for on the other side of Ashe sat Tanya, and beside her was Janice Ranae. The woman and her daughter had not heard that a hasty wedding had taken place, and Talon wondered why Ashe was suddenly determined that no one else would learn of his marriage to Tanya.

"You never did tell me how you got Miss Pekoe," Talon said, still smiling as he watched Willow and Hester.

"It was down in Galveston. She was just coming off a ship there, looked as if she was running from

289

someone. I guessed she was by the looks of her. Then she told me her new master was going to beat her; she had been told he was a mean old man." Ashe chuckled. "It was hard to tell if she had bruises because her skin is so black, but I bought her a nice warm meal. She was ravenous, and she took to my kindness like a flea to a dog's back. She followed me, and don't ask me how I managed to get her home. There were some outlaws on the trail. Don't know if they were any of the Wild Bunch . . . might've been."

Ashe's eyes glittered strangely as he stared at his brother, also looking back in time and seeing before him a frowning, hurt boy, not the young man who was supposed to be a dangerous criminal.

He saw it as if it were yesterday. After Garnet Haywood had done her evil deed, the boy had waited for her at the bottom of the stairs, his slanted somber green eyes adoring her as she'd come down, buttoning her bodice. Ashe had stood there himself, wondering about her. He had known what had taken place upstairs. Garnet had invited him up there a time or two, but he had never obliged her. It was Talon who had worshipped the woman—the sleazy bitch. Talon's jasmine-blond hair had been disheveled, young cheeks flushed. She had ruffled his hair, patted him on the head, and then walked down the hall, asking where she might find her husband. Ashe had wanted very much to strangle her. He felt the urge even now, but she was gone, dead and buried. Good riddance.

Talon began to frown. He wondered what thoughts were making Ashe appear so angry, but his attention was drawn to the girls on the lawn. Willow was still trying to get Hester to go into the house so she could help her clean her dress before it became stained.

Ashe, who had turned to glower at Tanya, noticed how lovely her profile was, and he reluctantly admired the soft, shapely hand she rested on the arm of the wicker rocker. He summoned a memory of her: Tanya, her flaming red hair in braids, skipping across the creek to try to catch up with him. Pain twisted in his heart, and he suddenly realized that he had been halfway in love with her even then. When he looked up again, he found her staring right into his face, her sapphire eyes wide and full of query.

"Ashe? What is it?" She found hostility in his eyes again. Then she found herself being lifted none too gently from the chair. "Ashe, what do you think you are doing? Please, you are twisting my arm."

"You, my dear, are coming inside with me." He pulled her to his side, his breath hot against her cheek, and whispered for her ears only, "It's about time you resume your wifely duties."

"Ashe, I can't believe you're doing this!" she hissed into his ear, an uneasy feeling creeping over her flesh.

"You'd better believe it, because we're going inside—upstairs to be exact."

Her lashes blinking like a swiftly rotating fan, Janice Ranae picked herself up from her seat. "Well, I never! and those two not married!" She searched about for her daughter, yelling, "Hester! Come along now, we're going home. Oh, Lordy! Hester, what in God's name happened to you! You're a mess! Have you gone down to the creek and got yourself all wet by falling in?"

291

"No, Mama. Oh Lord, Mama, just look at what that Willow Hayes done to my pretty dress. It's all ruined." She heard a deep chuckling coming from the porch and looked up to see Talon Clay ducking his blond head. "I heard you, Talon Clay; you were laughing at me." She looked down at the ruined gown, her blond hair swinging forward to reveal the bits of lemon peel still clinging to it. "Let's go, Mama. Oh, just look at my brand-new dress that you bought me so that I could—" A hand suddenly clamped over her mouth to halt the flow of words.

"You hush up now, hear? You want to be giving it away that you're after one of the Brandon boys?" Janice Ranae's lips were almost pressed against her daughter's ears as she added, "We're going to get Saw Grass joined with Sundance. You just leave it all up to Carl. Your brother's got plans. All we have to do is make sure Tanya and Ashe don't get hitched up. Talon Clay neither."

"But, Mama," Hester groaned, "I can't have both of them." She leaned closer to Janice Ranae. "I can't do that, Mama. I ain't no harlot. Besides," she wailed, "who'd ever want me now . . . after Willow shamed me so. Oh, Mama, I'm going to get back at that little twit."

"What's 'twit' mean?"

"I don't know, Mama, I heard it in New Orleans. One of those Creole gentlemen called me that after I crawled out of be—"

"Hush up, I said. You want to go and ruin everything? You got to make the Brandon boys think you're a virgin, 'cause they don't want to marry tainted stuff. Not like that Tanya Hayes."

"But, Mama, I already been with—"

"*Hush*!"

Just then, the drovers came around the side of the house, some chuckling quietly so the Tucker women couldn't hear. Talon watched the wagon bump along the dusty winding road until he could see it no more, only a restless cloud of dust hovering above the road and then dissipating as the last motes drifted off into the air. As he turned Willow lifted a haughty shoulder in his direction, as if she had been waiting to do just that. He watched her make her way back to the little house, watched until she was nothing but a lonely figure silhouetted against the dark green of the wood and then vanished from view.

"Willow . . . Pussywillow," Talon murmured. "How am I ever going to forget you?" Then, finding himself left to his own devices, he rose to go out back where he knew he would find Clem and Almanzo and a few of the drovers and mustangers entertaining themselves with a game of cards. Why not? He had nothing else to do.

The hard slap resounded in the upstairs bedroom, and Tanya stared at the bold imprint her hand had left on Ashe's face. My God, *what have I done*? she asked herself, the color draining from her face as she backed away from him.

"Don't touch me, Ashe. I don't know what your game is, but I'm beginning to think you're a little crazy. You frighten me at times."

"Don't ever slap me again. If you do, woman, you'll find yourself over my knee."

"Ashe, that's ridiculous," Tanya said, vacillating before him. "I've never done anything to deserve such a punishment."

"You haven't? I think you have, but you wouldn't remember all that, would you?" He was finding the idea of taking her over his knee a very pleasant thought. "Besides, you deserve it."

How like her mother she is, he was thinking. First Garnet Haywood showed up, then she seduced Pete Brandon into marrying her, then she seduced his little brother! Sundance—that was all Garnet ever wanted. And she had got what she wanted. But now she was where she belonged—six feet under. God must have wanted her there, he thought, so she couldn't hurt folks any longer. Now here was her daughter, Garnet's *daughter*. He no longer wondered why the red-haired girl who had come to Sundance had seemed familiar. But Willow . . . He could tell that if she dressed up in slippery silks and did her hair like Garnet, no one could tell them apart. Why hadn't he recognized this before Carl Tucker had given him the information? Three women . . . a mother and her two daughters, all birds of a feather, though their colors were slightly different. Now here they were, come to pick up where their mama had left off. How much had Rob Hayes known about their scheming gold-digging plan? About as much as his own father had known about Garnet's devious ways, no doubt. Ever since he'd known Tanya, she'd wanted to take over Sundance. Well, she could have it. He was going to stuff Sundance property down her lovely throat . . . until she gagged on it!

Backing up against the butterfly table, Tanya

reached behind her and folded her fingers about the vase upon it. "Don't come near me, Ashe, or so help me God, I'll use this on you."

"I do believe you would." He snickered then, saying, "Maybe . . ."

She brandished the vase in a more threatening grip and gritted her teeth.

"Just try me. Come one step closer."

His hand reached for his gun, and Tanya said, "You *wouldn't*." But she could tell he was serious, very serious. Just before she closed her eyes, he warned her to stretch her hand higher, away from her face. Then her lashes shuttered, and she screamed, *"Noooo!"*

Only after the smoke had cleared did Tanya dare to open her eyes. Scattered all over the carpet were shards of the milky white glass, mute testimony to the fact that Ashe kept his word. She had heard it said somewhere that rangers didn't hesitate over an unpalatable matter for very long—be it a loose woman, rotgut whiskey, or warring with Mexicans and Indians. They either "had" it, downed it, or shot it. No in-between.

"I don't believe you did that," she said in a shaky voice.

"There's the evidence." He swept an arm out from his body. "Now, come here. You and I have some unfinished business, my dear."

"Don't call me that. Only *gentlemen* say my dear, and you, Ashe Brandon, are a madman!" She whimpered then, as if she had been hurt, and Ashe, seeing an opening, rushed forward. "Don't touch me!" she screamed. "Don't ever touch me again!"

295

Whirling about and clutching her arms as if she were cold, she cried in choking little sobs. "I don't understand you, Ashe. *No!* I said don't touch me!"

"*Lawsy! Lawsy!*" Miss Pekoe hopped about outside the door; then she went to the banister to call for help. "Someone's done gone and got theyselves shot!" She hung her kerchiefed head over the railing. "Or someone done shot someone! *Help me! Help me!* Oh, Lawdy, someone gots to *help!*" She padded over to listen at the door, saying in a soft frightened voice, "*Anyone be alive in deah?*"

Ashe reached out again to touch Tanya's shoulder, but she wrenched herself away, huddling in a cocoon of misery. "Don't come near me, Ashe Brandon. I never want you to touch me again!" Her face twisted around, misery and helplessness written on it. "*I don't understand you, do you hear me?*"

"What's happenin' in there, mastah? You and the mizzus be all right?"

"Yes, Miss Pekoe, everything is fine now." He turned back to his wife. "Tanya, I think we should have a talk sometime . . . I don't know when. . . ." Running his fingers through his hair, he went on. "It has to be sometime soon, though."

She spun about to face him, barely getting out, "*You don't know when* . . . did I hear you right?" Shoving herself away from the table, she went about the room banging drawers, slamming wardrobe doors. "When you *wish* to talk, Ashe Brandon, you can find me in the little house. I am moving back there now—immediately!"

"I can understand that," he said, still trying to clear his mind of the unwanted vision of Garnet

Haywood. Her hateful, but beautiful, image kept floating before him—a wraith in gauzy white dress, white and shining but tattered at the hem—and all the while she was taunting him, laughing in a mocking sort of way, beckoning him to follow wherever her evil, cunning steps might lead. She was a sorceress come back to haunt Sundance. . . . Tanya was answering him.

"I'm glad you can do *that!*"

Stuffing what few possessions she owned into a satchel, Tanya forced it closed, odds and ends of clothing sticking out this way and that. She backed up to the door and reached behind her for the knob. When she spoke her voice was surprisingly controlled. "I'm leaving you, Ashe. Don't ever try to get me back into this house." She looked around once more, on her face loathing and disgust. "I wouldn't live here with a crazy man like you if you . . . were the last person on earth!"

Having said that, she spun about and slammed out the door. "I'm sorry . . . Tanya," he murmured, staring at the door long after she had gone out. Then he leaned back against the bureau and closed his eyes.

Chapter 23

Brown's Mill was settled in 1848 under the auspices of Stephen F. Austin and Nels Peterson. The settlers had traveled down the San Antonio Road in covered wagons until they'd reached the land owned by Mister Peterson; and not long after a village with a large saw mill and a cotton gin flourished there.

Now, on a sparkling summer day Tanya set out at dawn for Brown's Mill, the reliable Dove pulling Clem's wagon along the San Antonio Road. She would be traveling all day since she must return to Sundance before dark, so she told herself she might as well enjoy the trip into town. The money she had in the deep pocket of her frock was the last of her savings, and what she would do after that was depleted she didn't know just yet. Talon had offered them money to "get along," having found out from Samson—the little tattler—that their savings were dwindling, but Willow had puffed up her frail shoulders and said: "No thank you, Talon Clay. We'll just live off the land. We've gotten along so far

299

without you, and we'll keep right on doing so. I'm going to be a schoolteacher, I'll have you know." Talon had laughed at that, but not too hard and long, for she had gone on to say: "It's not funny, you white-faced Indian. Mister—I mean Preacher—Cuthbert is going to start a church and school combined at the old Nicols place. The barn is going to be the school, and he already asked me—well, first he asked Tanya—to help out . . . but she said she couldn't."

"So then he asked little Pussywillow," Talon had chuckled out the words, shaking his blond head, swinging his silken twilled braid to and fro while he hunkered down Indian fashion. Talon had gazed at Willow in what he thought was concealed adoration, but Tanya had not mistaken the look. The sun had been streaming down, its gentle rays making Willow look ethereal.

"That's right! I'm getting better and better at English. Tanya's been helping me. She wants me to become a teacher too, don't you, Tanya?"

Tanya smiled now in remembrance. That had been a month ago, and now, true to her declaration, Willow was teaching children, even some Samson's age, in the renovated barn and Preacher Cuthbert was giving his sermons at the church. They didn't have a name as of yet—just Church and School. Samson went to school there, and on the Sabbath they all attended church. Tanya had yet to see Ashe and the other males at Sundance come to church, but she prayed that would happen, sooner or later.

They had become as strangers, she and Ashe, still she breathlessly waited to catch a glimpse of him. If

300

she happened to, a force flowed between them when their eyes met. This had taken her by surprise the first time, for after a week had passed, she had thought she was finally getting over him. Yet, there had been no discussion of their situation. In fact, they had not shared two words. The free and easy communication they had known before marriage simply didn't exist anymore.

Turning her thoughts from less painful reflections, Tanya smiled, remembering the day when Talon Clay had gifted her and Willow with a dappled roan mustang, all saddle-broke, tame, and ready to go. But not really so tame, she decided. For when she had taken the frisky mare out for a ride just the other day, the horse had acted as if she had had every intention of bucking Tanya off her back. But Tanya had held on, enjoying her new adventure—riding a spirited horse. She had come to love these everyday outings, and to her delight, Teychas was handling like a charm.

But Willow would have nothing to do with Teychas, which meant Friends to the Karankawa, those ferocious Indians who had settled in the vicinity of Matagorda Bay and who were now almost extinct. When she had turned a cold shoulder to Talon Clay, he had persisted, saying, "We are all teychas" and looking expressly in Willow's direction. "Bah!" she had responded, jumping into the Preacher's wagon as he picked her up for school that day.

Fervently Tanya prayed that something would happen soon; either Ashe would go away again, or she herself, she would . . . Oh God, she just didn't know!

The former ranger was in a decidedly good mood as he tied Lágrimas to the hitching post and entered the mercantile. As Ashe moved across the wood floors, seeking the items he needed, Mr. Granger came around the counter to offer his assistance.

"I think I've found everything, Mr. Granger." Ashe readied himself, knowing what was coming next. The storeman never failed to recount the story every time Ashe entered the mercantile.

The man was already laughing, holding onto his fat belly as if he were carrying a huge barrel out front. "Heh-heh-heh, did I ever tell you what happened when I wanted to join the rangers?"

"I think you might have," Ashe said, humoring the man just the same. "But I'm not sure."

"I was already signed up. Heh-heh. Then I went to meet with Captain John Coffee Hays, and said, 'Ranger Granger reporting, *sir*! Well, old Jack he just looked at me and said, 'You're through!' Shoot, I never even got started, to tell the truth. How about the time. . . ."

Listening to Granger's tall tales, Ashe walked around amid the tables, the racks, and the barrels of foodstuffs. A particular blue shade of calico caught his eye, a brilliant jewel-like color, and he was at once reminded, painfully so, of the woman whose eyes exactly were the same shade of blue. He wondered how she would look clad in a dress made from the material. Beautiful, he thought to himself, simply beautiful. He could already feel a stiffening in his

302

loins. He imagined Tanya walking, coming to him, her heart in her eyes as she begged, *"Please take me back, Ashe. I love you and I want to give you a son. Please, Ashe, I promise to make you forget the past. Hold me, just hold me."*

So engrossed was Ashe in this passionate play of fantasy, that when he heard the bell tinkle it was a moment before he looked about to see who had entered. After one glimpse he turned away, shaken to the core of him. Meanwhile Mr. Granger greeted the new customer, a cheerful smile of adoration on his pasty face. Tanya!

Ashe had the strangest replay of his fantasy, imagining that she would walk up to him and throw herself into his arms, tearfully begging him to carry her back to Sundance on his buckskin charger. He heard her voice, so soft and husky-sweet. His blood began to churn in his veins. This was insanity! Here she was, not twenty feet from him, and he wanted to go to her and crush her in his embrace. Yet at Sundance, where they dwelt so close to each other, he wanted to avoid her at every turn!

"Ah, Ranger Brandon," Mr. Granger said with a belly chuckle, "will that be all?"

As Tanya had been watching where she was stepping when she had first entered the mercantile, then turning to shut the door, she had completely missed the handsome man who had momentarily twisted about to face her. Now she turned, ever so slowly, her face a lovely mask of suspense, of waiting, of wondering. When she saw him look away hastily, then back again after a few moments, she ducked her head coyly, looking down as if examining a bit of

303

calico on the table.

"This is lovely," she said softly. "Such a beautiful shade of blue . . . I wonder . . ." Then she shook her head, as if deciding against the cloth, really not very interested in it though it was a pretty shade and one that would compliment her eyes.

"She's purposely avoiding me," Ashe said under his breath. He pretended to be looking for the right size nails, picking up this can and then that one, although he knew the exact size of the nails he needed for the room he was partitioning off upstairs between the master bedroom and the mistress's suite.

"Oh, *this* is a lovely gun, Mr. Granger."

At the sudden sound of her voice, Ashe's hand jerked and the can of nails he had been holding fell, its contents scattering across the floor. Tanya absently glanced at the nails and then went back to examining the long-barreled shotgun.

"Guns aren't lovely, Mrs. Brandon, they are dangerous," Ashe said, helping Mr. Granger pick up the nails he himself had spilled.

"I know how *dangerous* they are, Mr. Brandon, and I'm looking at a rifle not a gun."

"They're all the same, Mrs."—Mr. Granger's mouth sagged clear to his jowly chin—"Mrs. Brandon!"

"That's right," Ashe drawled. "And give her whatever she wants. Put it on my charge."

"B-But, Mr. Brandon, you don't have a charge here."

Lurching forward to swipe his bagged items off the counter, Ashe ground out, "I do now."

"Thank you, Mr. Brandon, but I'll pay for my

purchases myself, with"—her voice dropped as she turned to see his lean, rugged form just going out the door—"my own money. . . ."

No one noticed the large man who had slipped into the mercantile while the commotion with the nails was in progress. Reaching up to still the bell, he had stealthily made his way, behind the tallest barrels and stacks of goods, to the back of the store. From the shadows, Carl Tucker watched all that went on; then he slipped out the back window, intending to return and have a look at that long-barreled shotgun.

In the deepest part of the woods, Tanya reminded herself to watch out for copperheads as she took her pa's ancient weapon down from Teychas' saddle and looped the horse's reins over a branch. She told herself she would have to rely on the old gun to bring down a rabbit. A big, fat, juicy one would do very nicely for her stew pot, and she had sighted two of them as she'd approached this shady glade.

Choosing a spot in which to await her quarry, Tanya hunkered down beside a patch of sweetly scented violets, resting the gun's bore across her lap. She didn't have long to wait, for soon she heard a rustling in the brush; in fact, it sounded like more than one creature. Twisting about to discover the source, Tanya narrowed her view by squinting reflexively.

Ah, she thought, now something is coming.

Her intense blue eyes leveled then as she firmly put the gun's stock into the hollow of her shoulder, her slim finger already curling about the trigger. She shook her head and a shaft of sunlight found her, turning her hair into a fiery liquid scarlet. A flush appeared on her cheeks. Her muscles tensed. Her breathing all but ceased.

And then, singularly, insanely, an image of Ashe making love to her flashed into her mind right before the shot exploded not more than two hundred yards away.

As Tanya's body gradually responded to the blast, her mind also slowly became aware that the shot had not come from her gun at all, but from another close by. She stiffened in alarm. It had to have come from behind her. Her heart hammered in her chest, and for a dark and terrible interval she believed herself to be someone's target. But who would want to kill her? Surely not . . . no, not him, not Ashe. He could not hate her that much, could he?

As terror released its grim clutch on her, Tanya began to realize that the shot hadn't been meant for her at all. No man was that bad a shot.

"Oh my . . ." Tanya could not even choke out the last word "God" when the figure, dressed all in black, a gunnysack over his head, leaped before her. Unconscious of the man's intent or even of what he was doing, Tanya could only stare up into the beady, evil eyes of the big man. Dry-mouthed, heart thudding insanely, she met a gaze of frenzied hatred. Only when the man had vanished into the woods, did her eyes drift downward, seeing but not wanting to see the long, still-smoking object lying in her lap, somehow familiar but not her own. Her pa's gun was gone.

*　　*　　*

Swearing savagely, Ashe pushed himself back with the heels of his hands until his head was resting against the bole of the tree. His hand felt along the ground until it contacted with his shotgun, and he winced at the pain the movement cost him.

Twisting his head about, Ashe ran his eyes up the bark of the tree until he saw where the shot had made the most damage, ripping away a large slab of brown bark and making a sizeable hole in the now naked wood. He looked at his shoulder. Seeing only a bloody nick, he realized he was fortunate to be alive at this moment. His left shoulder, not far from his heart . . . *Someone really wanted to kill him.*

Hearing a rustle in the woods off to his left, Ashe instantly came alert, rolling up from his back to his feet and hunkering on the balls of his toes, silent as a big cat.

He rose now, noiselessly, making his way in a half-crouching Indian walk, his leg muscles iron-hard, his hunger for retribution became more and more insistent as he stealthily pushed forward. He halted then, straining his eyes across the shady green glade. . . .

At the moment Tanya was still trying to decide what to do with the shotgun on her lap. It just didn't make sense, none of it. A shot was fired, not from her own gun. A man with a gunnysack for a head and maliciously evil eyes appeared, scared the living daylights out of her, and then what did he do? *He put his smoking shotgun in her lap and took her pa's lovely, old gun!*

A feeble ray of sun penetrated the dappled green glade and lay warm and pleasant across her shoulders. Tanya lifted an arm above her head, feeling languid and hot all of a sudden. Then she stood, unaware she was being watched, but very conscious of the strange lethargy stealing over her, seeping into her bones. Clutching the shotgun, she leaned to one side. The man watching her thought she was searching for someone.

"Looking for someone?" a deep voice breathed close to her ear. "Like a body maybe?"

At the same instant she heard the words, she noted a blur of movement as a hard, unrelenting hand clamped over her mouth. Her eyes flew wide. Ashe's face was only inches from hers. His entire face, even his cat-hazel eyes, crinkled into a dangerous smile. "Lady Red," he murmured, his voice the slightest whisper of a foreboding wind.

As if hypnotized, Tanya stared into a countenance that wasn't Ashe's at all, but a lean, dark feral face. Her heart beat so hard she feared it would burst from her breast, and fear tore through her body. It was Ashe—oh yes, she could *feel* that—but she didn't know him anymore.

Her breath came a little easier then, as his hand slid down from her mouth and, capturing her chin, tilted her face up to meet the full force of his hard gaze. Despite his anger and resentment, Ashe was very aware of the thud of his pulse and of the heavy, grinding ache that suddenly poured into his loins. Letting his eyes play lightly over her smoky blue orbs, and then dip to her lips and to the gaping bodice of her dress, he said slowly, "I see you bought the shotgun from Granger's store."

Her frightened clumsy fingers toyed with the shotgun's stock, her mind trying to register those words. Silently she cried out, *My God, he thinks it was I who fired that shot.* Her eyes left his face and took in the bloody tear in his shoulder.

"Ashe . . . I . . . this is not my gun! God, you have to believe me. I would never do that to you." She felt, rather than saw, him unwind her nerveless grip from the shotgun. Frantically her eyes searched his face for a measure of belief and mercy, but there was none. "Ashe, listen, someone, a man with a sack over his head, put this gun in my hands!"

Slowly, methodically, his hands left her to begin unbuttoning his shirt. "Are you wearing a petticoat?" he asked suddenly.

"Yes." Tanya could only stare at the blood dripping from his fingers.

"Take it off." He lifted his head to look at her when she hadn't moved a muscle to do as he asked. "Right now, Tanya."

Leaning against the bole of a huge live oak, Ashe watched, tight-lipped. "You don't mind if I watch?" he asked, having every intention of seeing more of her than her ankles very soon.

The question was drawled nastily, Tanya thought. She decided not to answer, just to do as he requested. When she had the petticoat off, she began to tear it into a long strip, thinking he meant to use it for a bandage.

"No," he said in a coldblooded tone. "Bring it here." When she handed it to him asking if she could help, he again refused her and then tore the hem swiftly, making a neat rip that left most of the petticoat still intact. "Now you can help me. Come closer, you can't do it from there." He slid down and propped himself against the tree, taking the petticoat with him and spreading it on the ground beside his long legs.

Acting as he directed, Tanya laved the wound with water from the small pigskin he had secured to his belt. Being this close to Ashe made her heart pound and she was filled with such sweet longing that her heart ached. "Is that too tight?" she asked, when she was done.

"Come here, Tanya." He reached up to take hold of her shoulders on either side and pull her down close to his face. "I want you," he said angrily, "and I mean to have you."

"No, Ashe, *no*!"

She tried to pull away but he only trapped her wrists in a viselike grip, yanking her against his chest. When she tried to slither off him, one of his hands slipped down to cup her buttock and pull her against his thighs. His voice, husky with desire, rasped in her ear, "Will it be so bad to make love with me?" His fingers went around her slim throat, his thumb pressing the small nub he could crush in an instant if he wanted to.

"Ashe," she gasped when his palm cupped her closer yet, "you don't understand . . . I didn't try to kill you. You must let me explain what the masked man looked like."

His fingers left her lovely throat and dove into the heavy bun at the nape of her neck, at once scattering the pins that secured the loop of hair. Pulling the hank loose, he dragged it over her shoulder to lie against her fast-beating heart. He cupped her breast right through the hair, sliding his fingers sensuously around the underside, his thumb exerting pressure on the hardening crest.

"No!" Tanya cried, jerking her warming body from the relaxed circle of his arms. But his lower positioned hand flexed, clutching a handful of her skirts and halting her escape. "If you do this to me, Ashe Brandon, I swear I *will* kill you!" she hissed through clenched teeth.

Despite his wound, Ashe came up with blinding speed to seize her arm before she could make good her escape, flipping her onto her back so swiftly that Tanya didn't know what was happening to her. Nor did she realize that he had brought her skirts to bunch up around her waist in the same fluid motion. Ashe's face blurred before her eyes as he came close.

"We'll die together, Lady Red. Because I am going to do *this* to you." He pried her long legs apart and cupped her womanhood. "And this . . ."

"You fiend!" Her legs lashed out at him, but he quickly stilled all movement by tossing one of his own over them and bringing his hard loins against her hip. She could feel him plying her delicate tissues, but she could not halt the bittersweet torment because his other hand held her arms high above her head. "Damn you, Ashe . . . you are a devil, just as the Mexicans call you rangers. You think only of yourself . . . think you're lord and master above the entire female . . . sex! *Ohhh, stop that!*" She jerked upward, embarrassed and shocked by what he was doing to her and by what she was feeling.

She blossomed. Despite herself, Tanya pressed upward while he spread her legs wide. When he knew she would no longer struggle, Ashe released his hold on her wrists. Swimmingly Tanya saw Ashe hovering above, his face a contorted wavy mask of passion, his shoulder rolling in a play of muscles as he continued to ply his fingers while cupping her buttocks with his other hand. Left wide open to his heavy stroke, she gasped at the flamelike flash of sensation, the insertion, the withdrawal, over and over until her body was driven to seek satisfaction. Then he left her.

"Ashe!" Tanya burst out, searching frantically for him.

He came back and took her swiftly, placing his strong hands on her slim hips while thrusting deep inside. Her whimpers and cries of ecstasy thrilled Ashe. "Tell me you love me," he said thickly. "Tell me you wanted me . . . as much as I wanted you." Quickening his pace, Ashe continued to thrust deep, swelling and pumping, coming almost all the way out, then plunging again and now carrying her with him when her virginal tightness gripped him.

"Faster Ashe . . . oh *yes!*"

"Say it now, Tanya . . . you love me . . . as I love you!"

Panting breaths and cries of ecstasy quickened in her throat and his, while in one final surge a strange, wild joy accelerated his actions. Responding to his impetus Tanya bucked upward one last time, making his release all the fiercer. Then, as if shot by a catapult, Tanya was shot to an erotic peak where she and Ashe were one.

A long shudder was still shaking Ashe's body when he finally opened his eyes to look down at her and give her a weak, satiated smile. Her chest was rising and falling rapidly, her breathing was loud. Still inside her, he brought her with him, to lay against his side. His tawny eyes coursed over her, coming to rest on a saucily peeping breast, the nipple a swollen blossom of ripe red, her bodice all but torn from her chest.

Ashe hugged his wife close, moving so that he could look at her face and gaze into her eyes. He had poured out his love to her, but she hadn't said a single word about loving him. Yet, absolute fascination shone from her jeweled eyes. He realized he had not tasted her lips fully, and this called for more, he thought, lowering his lips, determined to make her cry out this time that she loved him and never wanted to be separated again.

Then, into his pulsing senses burst the painful reminder that she had tried to kill him. He was about to withdraw when she pulled him back, circling her arms about his neck, offering her lips to him. Slanting a kiss across her moist, heated flesh, Ashe thrust his tongue inside her mouth, silently asking her permission, communicating his request by matching its rhythm with that of his thighs.

"Oh yes, Ashe," Tanya murmured against his mouth, darting her little tongue inside. He groaned, and Tanya could feel him grow inside her, filling her until it almost hurt. And as the flaming sun outside their emerald haven began its descent, sinking, sinking, sinking . . . they began to pleasure each other.

Chapter 24

"*Ashe,*" Tanya whispered softly. Her soft moan of deep contentment echoed in the bedroom as she tried to snuggle closer to the warm, vibrant body next to her. Slowly she opened her eyes, blinking in confusion when the bed was empty. Her eyes mere sated slits of cerulean blue, Tanya realized it was his pillow she had been hugging.

Now, opening her eyes fully to the sun streaming inside and already baking the roof and outside walls of the house, Tanya guiltily bounded from the bed. For one glorious week now she and Ashe slept together, ever since their splendrous afternoon in the woods. They had returned blushingly to the house, at least she had blushed—returned as if it were the most natural thing to do, as if they had not been separated for six agonizing weeks.

Dressing for the day, Tanya told herself, a little disappointedly, that the reason for his previous cruel and indifferent attitude remained a mystery. Often-times she had thought his callousness had to do with jealousy, either directly or indirectly related to the night of the fandango. And there had been the night on the porch with Almanzo, of course, but that, too, had been a purely innocent situation. She wondered now whether Almanzo had meant for it to appear to be a clandestine meeting? Had he also meant for his Spanish friend, the dashing caballero, to teach her the wild, gypsy dance right before Ashe's withering gaze? She thought not, but she couldn't be sure.

Whatever had happened, all that was in the past, and she and Ashe had become lovers. They looked forward to a future with children, to a happy life together. What could be more perfect? she asked herself.

After the noon meal a half-dozen hands were helping Ashe see to the mending of old fences and the making of new ones. The horse population of Sundance had grown considerably, so much in fact that they had made an addition to the stable and had lengthened the corral to five times its original size. When a sufficient number of horses had been caught and herd-broke, the mustangers had driven the bunch to San Antonio, where they'd found a ready market.

As he worked Ashe wondered, How could he have believed his wife wanted to kill him? Whatever else bothered him—her reason for following her mother here, the fact that she never mentioned Garnet

Haywood—he knew she loved him. And now another thing was clear to him: Tanya would have been too young to have understood her mother's motives. He was beginning to think Garnet had left her children when they were very small, and her husband, Rob Hayes, might have come to Sundance looking for her. But he had been too late . . . Garnet had died before Rob could lay eyes on her again. He couldn't be sure, however, for Tanya never spoke of the past. Indeed, she gave him the impression that she might still be hurt by what her mother had done to her and to the rest of her family.

The next questions he pondered were: Who had taken that shot at him and placed the damaging evidence in Tanya's hands? Who wanted to see him and Tanya parted?

Pausing at the end of the section he was working on, Ashe glanced up and saw Almanzo at the far side of the corral. Twenty feet of rope was stretched out between Almanzo's hand and the gray-blue mustang's head. Almanzo stood there with a grin on his dark visage, as he watched the surprised look on the mustang's long face. The mustang had suddenly halted her bucking response to the empty saddle on her back. This was the first time a saddle had been placed on her, and it was no wonder she'd tried to get out from under the thing.

The more Ashe thought about that swirling moon-misted night he'd come home to find Almanzo strolling the porch with his wife, the more annoyed he got—and he'd been pretty mad that night!

He now realized it was futile to think about Garnet

Haywood and how she had insinuated herself into his family. Just the thought of her, even after Tanya and he had reconciled, made him see red.

Ashe stopped his busy hands to watch Almanzo. He had to admit that the Indian knew what he was doing, was, in fact, an expert mustanger. All Indians made good mustangers. As he watched the man, Ashe began to wonder again about the identity of the person who had taken a shot at him.

"Easy now," Almanzo said, walking slowly toward the wild mustang, "and keep your head up, girl."

Blowing her surprise at the man, the horse watched the human approach, her legs spread wide apart and a wild look in her eyes. "He don't know whether to stand his ground and start fightin' or back away," Samson said as he came up beside Ashe to lean against the rail. "*She*," Ashe said with a chuckle and ruffled the lad's red hair, but he kept his eyes trained on Almanzo, a dangerous glitter in them.

"Easy girl," Almanzo spoke slowly, soothingly.

The mustang stood in her tracks, legs wide apart, watching the Indian come on. Almanzo, still murmuring softly, reached out to touch the mustang's head, his hand then moving down to her neck. While Almanzo kept talking to her, Talon Clay moved carefully into view.

There was the squeak of leather as the mustang was led to the other side of the corral, Talon walking in front of the horse. Almanzo rubbed the mustang's ear, and then Talon reached out to do the same. Talon glanced up once to see Willow go and stand beside her brother. "Easy now, I'm going to get up on

318

your back," he said. He spoke just as soothingly as Almanzo had. "Let's see how good you can be, youngster."

Talon reached for the latigo and tightened the cinch. At once a hump appeared in the mustang's back, a hump which made the saddle sit nearly on end. "Let her buck," Almanzo schooled Talon. "You just hang on." The Indian looked over the rails to see Ashe Brandon watching him closely; he wondered what was on the former ranger's mind. A flash of blue came into his side vision, and he watched as Ashe's beautiful wife went to stand beside her husband.

All eyes shifted back to Talon then, although a few of the hands would have rather watched the charming vision. But Carl Tucker, who had just come over from Saw Grass, covertly watched the beautiful redhead. He never seemed to get his fill of leering at her. Ashe, however, hardly gave his neighbor a second look; instead his gaze followed the dark one about as if he were waiting for the Indian to slip up so he could send him packing.

Carl Tucker received frosty looks from the Hayes women. He realized of course that Ashe had taken Tanya to wife the night of the fandango, but he had not told Janice Ranae or Hester yet. Now he thought nastily that he wasn't through with Tanya, even though Ashe had wedded and bedded her. And he would get Ashe. His first plan hadn't worked, but his next one was not going to go awry.

Talon raised his chaps so that the belt would not hinder his leg action; then he pulled the brim of his hat down good and solid. He placed his thumb over the mustang's left eye and pulled the lid down, then he added his weight to that of the saddle, reaching out and blinding the horse again. Willow had been keeping her eyes glued on Talon, but now she noticed that the horse was standing very still, looking like petrified wood.

"Ain't . . . I mean isn't she going to move?" Samson asked the tall owner of Sundance who stood beside him. "She looks all bug-eyed and scared."

"Oh, she's going to move all right," Ashe said with a chuckle, hugging Tanya close to his side. He took a moment to gaze down into her face and notice her happy look. Then he brought his lips close to her ear and breathed huskily, *"I love you."* She mouthed the words in return, and a thrill crept over her as his splayed hand lowered to graze over her hip.

"Ashe," Samson said, tugging on the man's elbow, "watch!"

Instinct directing the mustang to act accordingly because neither human nor leather belonged on her back, she swung her head down, and, with a roaring bellow, her withers went up. Willow, perched lopsided on the rail, slapped a hand over her mouth as the mustang's "hump" caused the saddle to twist like a whirligig. Bunched and braided mustang muscles became one with the human blur that was Talon Clay. The ground shook and the fence shuddered; the man and beast shot into the air, to hang suspended a moment before finally coming down. The two in the corral became all dust and tails and manes and hats and arms. The action was too hard for the human eye to follow.

"Ride 'em Talon!" Samson whooped while the hands placed odds on which one, man or beast, would come out the winner.

The hard-hitting hoofs of the mustang struck the earth again and yet again, each time stirring up dust. Talon felt the mustang's muscles working even through the saddle, when he heard Samson call out, "That horse is a dust devil," the young mustanger knew that was the name for the horse. But for now, the horse became rock hard beneath Talon. The saddle twisted underneath the rocking belly, and he began to wonder if he would stay ahorse.

It was a miracle that Talon was still in the middle of the horse's back when the hard jolts and jumps finally subsided into mere bird hops. The mustang was badly winded, its nostrils flaring wide to pull in the air. When the human ran a hand over her sleek neck, she was wild eyed. But, ears cocked back at Talon, the horse finally stood still and listened to the gentle human voice.

"You done real good, Dust Devil. I would've been mighty disappointed if you'd showed me less spirit, girl." He looked over toward his white horse. The wild one he had captured had put on an even wilder show of spirit than this one. "You are much like Cloud," Talon said. He glanced at Willow who was admiring the little mustang. "And that is why I think we will keep you," he finished.

That night Tanya had the dream again, only this time it was a horrible nightmare. She was running on bare feet, her red braids swinging about her head as she searched this way and that. She carried her baby brother in one arm while pulling her sister along with her other hand. "Mother," she cried, "where are you . . . *Mother!*" Her skirts became muddied and clung wetly to her legs. Oh God, how her legs ached. She couldn't run much farther, the baby was growing heavier by the minute. Odd . . . she seemed to be staying in one place even though her legs ran on and on. "Mother . . . don't leave us! Come back. We need you . . . Mother!"

"Tanya, wake up!"

Having rolled over to try to wake his wife from the nightmare, Ashe saw that she was not coming awake, no matter what he did. He noticed then that she was bent over and was clutching her leg as if it pained her. Taking hold of her long leg, Ashe began to massage it vigorously to release the cramp, while she called for her mother over and over. Hearing the mournful cries, not unlike those of a pitiful little girl, Ashe's heart turned over in his chest and he damned himself for having been so cruel and heartless to this woman. This woman, he thought, smoothing her disheveled hair from her forehead, this woman he loved more than life itself.

"Tanya, love, please wake for me," he murmured against her cheek, holding her close in his embrace though her nightmare went on. "I'm here. I love you, darling. Wake up now."

When Tanya's lashes fluttered open, the first thing she saw was Ashe silhouetted against the soft illumination from the sconce, she twisted in his arms and pressed herself tightly against his wide chest. "Oh, Ashe, the dream was awful this time. I kept running, but couldn't get anywhere, and my leg was hurting terribly."

"I know, darling Lady Red, I know," he said soothingly, just like Talon had talked to the mustang earlier in the day. "You had a cramp, you were holding onto your leg. Is it better now?"

"Yes. Thank you." She was silent for a time, content to be ensconced in the circle of his loving embrace and then she said, "Ashe? What did I say?" She was afraid of his answer, but she had to know.

"Not now." He kissed the top of her head. "Maybe tomorrow." How was he going to talk about the woman he most hated in the world, even though she was dead and buried?

"Ashe, please tell me what I said? I must know or I won't be able to sleep."

"Tanya, this is going to be painful. Are you sure you want to hear about it tonight?" He tipped her chin up so that he could look into her eyes and read her innermost thoughts, as he had been able to do all the past week they had been together. "Sure?" he asked again.

"Was it . . . was it about my mother?" She watched his face grow hard, his eyes flinty. "It was, wasn't it?" She was certain of it. "Ashe, I have the very strangest feeling sometimes . . . that my mother has been in this house. I've even had the feeling at the little house. Has . . . Did you know her? Ashe, why are you suddenly so quiet?"

"Tanya . . ." Ashe moaned, burying his face in her

323

throat and tasting sweet strands of hair on his lips. "Please, don't ask me about her. She, oh God, she's dead and buried, Tanya! Let it lay!"

"Ashe!" Tanya shoved away from him and sat up straight in the huge bed. "You did know her!" Tanya shook her head, looking away from her husband. "Oh God, I just knew it." She twisted about and looked at him hard. "Ashe, she was a bad woman, wasn't she? I mean, in my dreams, she's always with a man, always a different man and"—Tanya choked—momentarily—"she's always running away from us, from Willow, Sammy, and me. Ashe? What did she look like? And how did you know she was my mother? When did you find out?" Her voice dropped as a terrible shock wave rolled over her. "Oh dear God, you just found out she was my mother, didn't you?"

"Yes! For God's sake, that's enough!" He turned on her, and Tanya thought she had never seen him look so savage except for the time she had gone into the room across the hall . . . the room where *she* stayed. "Garnet, that's my mother's name, isn't it? She's the woman you called Jezebel, the woman who stole your father from your mother. Now I know she was bad. Did she look like me, Ashe? Is that why you hated me so? Who in God's name told you she was my mother?"

Ashe wasn't answering Tanya, not because he didn't want to but because all of a sudden he was wondering how Carl Tucker had come to have that letter. How had Carl Tucker gotten a letter not *meant* for him, anyway? It was a letter written for

Garnet's children, one that had never been received by them . . . *and why had that letter never been sent?* Even more strange, why had it never been finished? Had Garnet died from . . . natural causes? At the moment he wasn't sure he had ever heard the cause of Garnet's death.

"Tanya, I'm going out for a while." Ashe bounded from the bed, already jerking on his pants when his feet touched the floor.

"You're *what?*"

"I'm going out . . . to search for some answers." He whirled to face her. Her face was now as white as the sheets. "And perhaps to find a murderer. I have some questions for Carl Tucker."

Dear God, Tanya thought to herself after her husband had gone out, *what have I done?*

The sunlight cascaded into the room, awakening Tanya from a restless slumber. Suddenly she recalled that Ashe had gone out in the wee hours of the morning, meaning to find Carl Tucker and ask him some questions.

Turning over on her side, a pink hue staining her cheeks, Tanya remembered, too, the way Ashe had awakened her from her nightmare, his hands massaging her legs and roaming over her thighs. In the fuzzy light his gaze had been a tender caress, his touch as soft as a lambent summer wind.

"Good morning," the whisper was languorous.

"Ashe!" Tanya sat up. "When did you come in?"

"About an hour ago."

325

Tilting her head and spilling her glistening hair over a provocative shoulder, Tanya murmured, "And you've been sitting there the whole time watching me while I slept?"

"H'm, yes." He smiled.

A tremor went through her as he continued to stare at her with the look of hot desire she had come to know so well. "Did you find anything out?" Her long lashes swept upward and she gave him a flirtatious scan, noting that his white shirt was unbuttoned to reveal the hairs on his chest.

"Keep looking at me like that," he purred deeply, "and I swear I'm going to make love to you in broad daylight."

She giggled. "I'll close the curtains."

"They are already closed, as you can see, ma'am."

Grinning impishly, Tanya propped herself up in bed. "We need heavier drapes if you are planning to make love to me in broad daylight, Mr. Brandon."

Coming lithely to his feet, Ashe began to peel off his shirt. His husky voice a caress, he declared, "I'll make love to you in any light: sunshine or shadow, dusk or dawn."

Tanya's blood began to sing in her veins, and her senses swam dizzily. She realized, blazing light of day or not, that she wanted Ashe badly, so much so, in fact, that she was trembling with desire. Forgotten was the question she had asked and the answer she had not received, as she watched him loosen his thick belt with the holstered six-shooter attached and put it aside. Unhurriedly he peeled off his buff nankeen breeches, his strong arms flexing at the slightest movement of his long, large body.

Her blushing gaze traveled his hard-muscled length, dipping down to linger on the evidence of his desire. Suddenly her embarrassment fled. The bright sunlight was no obstacle.

With a small groan of impatience, Tanya swiftly shed her nightgown and opened her arms to him, crying, "Ashe, make love to me!" And when he at last took her into his arms, she arched her naked body to his, her hands stroking his lean thighs and drawing him closer and closer.

Deliberately prolonging her sweet torment, Ashe rose on an elbow and leaned over her, the palm of his hand slipping over the softness of her stomach to the auburn darkness between her white thighs. He lowered his head to kiss her gently but firmly, his mouth lingering at the corners of her sweet honeyed lips, and then sliding down as he shifted his body to bring his lips to the curve of her breast. Then, hearing her moan, his teeth nibbled at the throbbing auburn tip while his fingers plied her, gently parting the auburn curls and then beginning an erotic rhythm all their own. Unconsciously, Tanya's body began to writhe against the insistent pressure, the slow retreat and thrust driving her into a sensual world of pleasure and awakening her passions.

"Ashe . . . I can't wait . . . any longer."

"Just a little more . . . soon now . . . *something sweet.*"

She came up frantically to meet his hand, feeling the warm smoothness of his touch create an avalanche of pleasure that seemed to begin its grinding ache in her stomach and then to spark embers of lust directly beneath the source of fire, Ashe's hand. Soon she became an inferno of grinding heat, and then, just when she knew she could stand the waiting no longer, Tanya felt Ashe's mouth close over her own and a series of sensual explosions followed so forceful that a low groan rose in her throat.

Bringing Ashe back into focus once again and watching dazedly as those same long fingers curled possessively about her bent knee, Tanya was surprised to find that she wanted Ashe, all of him, knowing that what had just happened to her body was but a tiny taste of what was to come.

Ashe had fought back the grinding demands of his own body. First he had wanted Tanya to experience the sweet volcanic release his hands could give her. Now he whispered, "I love to feel the gardenia-petal softness of your flesh . . . here . . . and here. Ah yes, Tanya, Lady Red, open up for me again." The hair of his chest teased her nipples as he bent to kiss her thoroughly.

Now, as he rose over her, Tanya was damp and properly primed for his big body. He nudged her knees apart, she lifted her hips to receive him, and his probing, hardened length spread her further. At last he slid into her welcoming sheath, his bold lancelike thrust, plunging so deeply that he almost hurt her. His strokes were smooth and sure, meeting their mark and then slipping almost all the way out on the wresting curve to caress the heavy velvet of her inner thighs.

Fevered flesh to fevered flesh, they rocketed and

plunged together, each joining hotter and more replete then the last, Tanya's secret delights widening and stretching to accept every greedily loving inch of him as she answered the bold calling of his thrusts with eager archings of her own hips.

Ashe delighted himself in the moist erotic flavor of Tanya's undulating body, and in her passion. She was like a wildcat, purring one minute and growling savagely the next, digging her sharp claws into his flesh but also touching him tenderly. He made his entries as deep as he could, wanting her to be a captive of his desire, of his heart, and his soul. He witnessed the elegance and beauty of their bodies locked in motion, in loving, and in lust. Her breath came hard against his face, fanning his cheeks and stirring his hair as he dipped his forehead to gaze down the length of their straining bodies, then curled his back and drove into her with all the force and fury of his unleashed love.

They came together, Tanya with a cry of wonder as she flung herself up and clung to him, in ecstasy; Ashe carrying her with him, scooping her against him, as he poured himself out at the mouth of her womb. Tanya quivered, there in the grip of her beloved.

"I love you, I love you," Ashe sighed against her lips.

"And I love you, so very much," she said, caressing his cheek with a slightly trembling hand.

Still joined, Ashe lowered her body and only after he had nuzzled her throat and tenderly kissed her lips, did he withdraw. Hugging her close to his side, with no need for words, Ashe kissed her moist forehead and then they slept entwined.

Ashe hadn't found out anything from Carl Tucker. Janice Ranae had seemed bewildered by some of the questions Ashe had asked her, but she had told him over and over again that her son had taken it upon himself to disappear. He had shown her the letter her son had given him, and just then the rooster had crowed and Janice seemed, suddenly, to awake, as if she had been sleeping the whole time she'd stood at the door conversing with Ashe. Inviting him in, Janice Ranae had sat down after he'd declined a cup of coffee, and with no beating around the bush she'd told him how that letter had come into *her* possession. Now Ashe was relating the story to his wife while they sat on the porch, cooled by the early morning mists that twined about Sundance house.

"Before you and your pa ever came here, long ago, or so it seems long ago," Ashe began, "Garnet was sitting right here with Janice Ranae penning a letter to her husband and children. Do you want to see the letter?" Hesitantly Ashe reached inside his buff vest, waiting to hear her answer before handing it over.

"Yes, Ashe, I'll read it."

With the sun rising ever higher and beginning to burn away the mist, a few tentative rays found the porch and spread a pale swath of yellow across the place where they sat. Ashe allowed his gaze to roam his wife's countenance, appreciating her stunning hair, her gardenia complexion, her sweet coral lips . . . and as he did so his worshipful adoration turned into lust. Just yesterday morning he had loved her, and last night, but this morning she had flatly refused on the grounds that her bruised and tender parts needed to recover . . . at least for one full day.

She looked up then, asking him, "Why are you chuckling? I don't find this very funny. In fact, it is quite quite sad."

"Darling,"—he scooped her chin into the palm of his hand—"I was not laughing at that. I was remembering what you said this morning about your tender parts . . . being bruised. Is there anything I can do to ease your discomfort?"

A gleam of deviltry shone in his beautiful hazel eyes, and then he became very serious. She could tell he had only been trying to lighten the depressing subject of Garnet. Lightly she touched his arm and his eyes immediately dropped to her lily-white hand.

Back up into her eyes he looked, searching for her reaction to the letter. "It is addressed to Rob and my children . . . Tanya first, being the eldest, Willow, and my baby Samson," Ashe began. Then his countenance hardened perceptibly, the sun lines at his narrowed eyes darkening, his lips tautening like a bowstring. "She calls Rob, your father, 'Honey'—"

Tanya picked up the letter. "'Honey, I hope you are taking good care of our children. I might come back to you . . . I say might. I am getting bored with this place, with living here with these folks. I need a change. Maybe we can just pick up where we left off. . . .'" Tanya shook her head, adding, "And then *nothing*. It breaks off right there."

331

Unwaveringly Ashe stared at his wife, saying, "Janice Ranae says that Garnet had been sitting there writing the letter, but she all of a sudden dropped everything she was doing and rushed into the house, gasping for breath. It sounded to her like Garnet was having an attack of some kind. Janice Ranae followed her into the house and found her lying down upstairs. Pete, my father, was out at that time, and so Janice Ranae put a cool cloth on her head and did what she could. She said Garnet begged her not to tell anyone and especially not Pete." Ashe paused here as if it was too painful to go on, but finally he continued. "Garnet said Pete would send for the doctor, twenty miles away, and by the time the doctor arrived, she would be better. Janice Ranae said she pleaded and begged her not to, saying this had happened before and she didn't want to bother him. Well, as it turned out, so Janice Ranae says, Garnet tucked the letter into her skirt pocket so it wouldn't blow away and completely forgot she had it until a year ago."

Tanya shot up out of her chair. "I don't believe it! Something is wrong, Ashe, terribly wrong. I haven't trusted the Tuckers for some time now, but I just could not bring myself to be unneighborly." She whirled to face her husband, blurting out, "Ashe, Carl tried to rape Willow!"

His chair overturned as he rose forcefully, lurching forward to grab Tanya by her shoulders. "Why didn't you tell me before? Damn it, Tanya, that man is crazy and I think"—his eyes glittered with a savage green light—"I think he is our stagecoach murderer."

Releasing her, Ashe spun on his heel and headed

for the door, calling over his shoulder, "Help me get my gear together, Tanya, I'm going after him!"

Tanya released a long-held breath, and muttered, "Carl Tucker. The stagecoach murderer?" Shaking the dust from her feet, she called after her husband, "Ashe, I'm going to see if Willow is all right . . . meet me at the little house!"

Chapter 25

"I said don't touch me like that!"

Willow clutched her skirts and ran for the door to the schoolroom, but Carl Tucker came pounding right after her. As the schoolroom was an old barn, a big old barn, it was a long way from the front of it to where Willow had been working at her makeshift desk. She couldn't veer off to the left, for there were chairs positioned haphazardly in the studying area; and she couldn't go to the right or she would only find herself trapped in a corner by that fiend.

"Leave me alone!" she screamed over her shoulder, not watching where her next running step would fall.

In the instant before she tripped over the chair, Willow's mind retraced the events that had brought her to this horrible moment. As it had been so hot— they were in the depth of summer—the children had been let out early every day. Some were so eager to go to school, even in the summer's heat, that they had bemoaned being released so early and had wanted to stay for a full day.

"It's not even proper for children to attend school in the summer," she had told the preacher, but Cuthbert, seeing that she was concealing her eagerness to be about teaching, said it wouldn't hurt this first year since the children's parents were also eager for them to attend.

At any rate, the children had gone home early while Willow had stayed on to do some copying; she was making extra books for the children who didn't have any. Cuthbert had gotten the thick paper and black ink for Willow, beaming proudly when he'd placed the items into her eager hands.

"Oh, this *is* wonderful," she had cried happily. "Now all the children will have books." She hugged the huge stack of precious paper to her chest, her eyes shining with curious moisture.

Now she lay on the dusty floor upon her stomach, her palms smarting where they had struck the puncheon boards, her misting eyes seeking the outside light beneath the schoolroom's double doors. Hearing a demoniacal chuckle at her back, she risked a glance at her tormentor, her eyes widening as they took in his spread-eagled stance above her, then shifting to the frail rhomboid of light that was her only hope. If only she could reach it before this monster had his way with her . . . She had to think of something—fast.

"I bolted it," Carl Tucker said, punctuating his words with a snorting laugh. "I told that preacher man you was goin' home with me. But we're going to have us some fun first, little gal."

Bolted it? Willow's eyes flew to the door and she

gasped audibly, the huge room magnifying the sound into a small explosion that bounced off the walls until Willow heard her gasp echo and ebb again and again. But it was her great fear that made her hearing abnormal, that and her pulse beating so wildly in her veins.

"You must be *crazy*," she hissed up at him, flipping onto her back and digging her heels into the floor to back away from him.

Like a raging bull, Carl shook his head and growled, "That was the wrong thing for you to say, missy. I ain't crazy, it's the whole damned world what's crazy. Even you, Missy Pussywillow. Yeah, I heard Talon Clay call you that the other day. Too bad he hates you. Sure, I saw him frownin' at your little behind the other day. Thinks you're too skinny for him, that's what. Talon Clay likes women what's got more meat to 'em, not scrawny little chicks like you."

At once Willow picked up on that, speaking calmly so as not to alarm him and lessen her chance of getting away. "Well then, if I'm so scrawny, what do you want with me, Carl Tucker? Shoot, there must be hundreds of more meaty girls just waiting for one look from you." Willow paused, nearly vomiting at the flattering words she'd had to force from her lips. "I'll just bet you could go into town right now, any town, and you'd have girls just dying to have you come acourting."

"I don't want to court no woman, I want to . . ." Alarmingly, Carl leaned down to whisper the most frightening words that little Willow had ever heard a man mutter in all her eighteen years. She trembled at the awful-sounding word, one she had heard Almanzo give utterance only once, when he was tearing angry at a mustang that had stepped on his foot. "That's what I want to do to *you*," he hissed into her ear.

"No, Carl, no!" Willow cried, tears beginning to fill her lovely brown eyes. "I don't know what that word means," she gulped, her voice quavery, "but I know it's got to be mighty bad the way you just said it."

"It's worse than that, I mean it could have been . . . if Talon Clay hadn't got to you first. Now it won't be so bad, little one, because it won't be your first time."

Willow thought for a moment and then her eyes flew wide. "So that's what that word means. That's crude, and Talon Clay never . . . never laid a hand on me. He only kissed me," she lied, for Talon had accomplished a little more than that, albeit at her insistence. Talon Clay would never hurt her, she suddenly realized. He wanted to be friends, and that realization made her decide she had been too nasty tempered when Talon had wanted to give her the blue-gray mare, Dust Devil, as a "friendly" gift. He had said that Tanya had taken so well to Teychas she didn't want to part with her.

"Carl," she said suddenly, "someone is coming!"

When he jerked around toward the door, Willow snatched her chance. With all the strength and vigor her petite body could produce, she sprang from the floor, and sprouting upward and outward like a spindly July wildflower reaching for the summer sun. Realizing that his pretty quarry was escaping,

Carl turned with a roaring growl that sounded like a grizzly's. He pounded after her, laughing like a crazed beast when he saw her running toward the front of the schoolroom where there was no avenue of escape, only a tiny window that wouldn't let a cat through.

Emitting little, high-pitched shrieks of fear that ironically resembled the sounds of small children happily playing games, Willow ranged this way and that, seeking an opening, until she whirled about and saw Carl making a dash right for her. She fought like a tiny wildcat when he got hold of her, kicking, clawing, screeching, scratching, and even spitting in his face. One cruel hand caught her hair, twisting and yanking until her somewhat subdued body was brought up hard against his. As something hard and alien pressed against her stomach, Willow's shrill shrieks began all over again. Talon Clay had been this hard against her, but with Talon she had eagerly welcomed the sweet thrill of his blatant desire for her. Not so with Carl Tucker. She despised this monster with every fiber of her being!

Though she fought for all she was worth, Willow soon began to tire. Finally she pushed futilely against Carl's chest as he all but dragged her over to a shadowy corner of the room. "Why," she gasped, "why are you doing this to me?" She began to weep uncontrollably, sobbing out, "Please . . . please don't hurt me . . . I'm so afraid."

Tossing her into the corner and spreading his legs to prevent any avenue of escape, Carl looked down at the fragile flower he had caught and would soon crush beneath his cruel weight. "I'll tell you why, little one, why I'm going to have you. . . . It's 'cause your uppity sister went and got herself hitched up with a Brandon man—and I hate Brandon men!" He wouldn't tell her that Talon Clay had once been his best friend, and that it was all his own fault that Ashe had married the woman he wanted for himself. Aloud he said, "How was I to know he would want her? Ashe always hated Garnet, and I thought he would hate Tanya even more if he learned who her mother was . . . that harlot what went and taught Talon Clay everything she ever knew about whoring."

Rolling her head against the wall, Willow spoke almost incoherently. "Who . . . who are you talking about . . . what woman?" She felt faint and almost hoped the dark arms of Morpheus would embrace her until the evil deed was done. She would never be the same again . . . Talon Clay . . . the only man she had ever loved . . . the only man she wanted . . . he could not be hers now. . . .

"Wake up, Willow!"

"Ashe, is she all right?" Tanya bent next to her husband as he gently checked to see if it was safe to move Willow. "Oh, I just knew she should not have been here alone after the children left. Where is Pastor Cuthbert anyhow? Doesn't he live right next door in the church?"

"Darling," Ashe said, "I don't know anything about that. But someone was here . . . look at these bruises on her arms. Dear God! she'll be black and blue for weeks to come." Placing Willow across his

340

lap, he smoothed the lacy golden tendrils of hair off her cheeks; then he growled, "I'll find out who manhandled her like this. Tanya, I can't tell if she's been . . . if, you think she's been raped."

"Oh, Ashe," Tanya moaned, "I don't know. . . . There is one way to tell, but that isn't always accurate."

"Blood . . ."

"Yes."

After checking, while Ashe kept his eyes averted, Tanya said, "Nothing, not a drop." Stomping her foot, she hissed, "Oh, where is that preacher? Why isn't he here? He must have seen us coming."

Just then a groan was heard from the doorway, and Pastor Cuthbert staggered in holding his head as if it pained him. Ashe exchanged surprised looks with Tanya, and still holding the unconscious Willow in his arms, he walked over to the dazed man who weaved before the door like a befuddled drunk.

"What happened?" Tanya was the first to ask.

"I don't really know for sure. . . ." Cuthbert began, wiping his slim face with a handkerchief he pulled out of his vest pocket. "One minute I was talking to this pleasant young fellow and the next, when I turned about, I received this lump . . . as if someone . . ." He shook his head, then went on. "Oh surely, surely the young man didn't strike me?" He did not believe that such a nice young man could have done such a thing.

"It appears that he did," Ashe said, as he carried Willow outside into the fresh air. "We'll be needing your wagon, Cuthbert. On the way to Sundance we'll have a talk. Are you up to it?"

341

"Of course! I want to get to the bottom of this just as much as you do, young man!"

That evening, Leon, the new cook Ashe had hired just a week ago, served a delicious roast beef with boiled potatoes and peas, and after the preacher had gone back to his church/home, waiving the temporary use of a bodyguard, Ashe and Tanya sat curled up on the leather loveseat in the sitting room. She loved this room, with its plush red-and-gold carpet, black marble fireplace and emerald-green chair. That chair was the most comfortable in the house, and it was positioned so she could sit and gaze out the tall French doors while enjoying the gentle evening breezes coming through the dark green, louvered shutters.

Willow was still asleep upstairs, having taken only a little broth, and Samson had gone back to the bunkhouse to stay the night with Clem. There were just the two of them in the house.

In her relaxed position in the curve of her husband's arms, Tanya asked, "Do you think it was Carl Tucker? The description Cuthbert gave could fit any of a number of blond-haired young men. What could Carl Tucker possibly have as a motive?"

"You."

Twisting about to look up at him, she smiled slightly and said, "Me? Why me? Carl Tucker never . . . Oh, wait a minute. It is true that he leered at me often . . . and Willow too." She snuggled back into the security his arms afforded and gazed straight ahead to the long sofa across from them. "But Carl

342

went after Willow, not me, Ashe."

"Because he couldn't have you, that's why. You were already taken, and this angered him. I believe Carl Tucker is after something else besides. I'm not sure yet what it is, but I have a powerful feeling, in my gut, that there is much more involved—much more."

"Do you still think he's the stagecoach murderer?"

"Definitely." He took hold of her shoulders and, turning her to face him, carefully said, "Talon Clay was one of them, Tanya, but I don't think he's ever done any killing. Talon's difficulties in life stem from something that happened in his past, a thing that inflamed his anger and made him want to get even with somebody. He's the sort of young man that is not about to let anybody trample on him. As a lad, his most sensitive feelings were hurt and his anger was aroused by someone . . . a woman, let's say. He never forgave her for what she did to him."

"Garnet . . ." Tanya breathed out the name, tears starting to brim over her lids. In a tear-laced voice, she said, "Isn't it odd that Carl Tucker is the one seeking vengeance on . . . I guess you could say Sundance . . . I don't know."

Sundance. It was clear to him all of a sudden, and as Ashe swept Tanya up into his arms, he told himself at first light he would go out and hunt Carl Tucker down.

But now Ashe had other matters on his mind, more pleasant ones.

Caressing her husband's cheek lightly, like the brush of a butterfly's wing, Tanya murmured, "I love you, Ashe."

343

"And I," Ashe growled, nipping the slim column of her throat, "love you, Lady Red."

Upstairs, Willow lay awake, her eyes large wilting pansies. She felt as if her body was one large bruise, yet she wished desperately to go back to the little house. Tanya and Ashe would have none of that, however, and if she did slip out while they were . . . The sounds coming from across the hall were very intimate . . . actually very private, but what could she do, stuff her head into a pillow? If she did slip out, in the morning they would come to the little house and be very disappointed that she had left without consulting with them first.

Willow's cheeks began to burn as the sounds from across the way became louder. A lusty laugh was followed by startled murmurs and hoarse cries of encouragement, then by a series of harsh and gentle endearments. These rolled off their tongues like a foreign language, peaking with the loud cry "*Ashe!*"

Finally, silence . . .

If the circumstances of the day had been different, Willow might have become enthusiastic over what she had just heard, might have been excited over the delights the marriage bed could bring. But such was not the case. Having found Carl Tucker so thoroughly repulsive, she began to wonder if she would ever again feel the sweet, aching desire she had known with Talon.

Just then Talon was lying awake in the bunkhouse, restlessly gazing at the thin sickle moon. He wondered if he would ever get any sleep this night, with Clem snoring up a storm. Shoot! he was going to saw the whole dang bunkhouse down!

Suddenly he was aware of his fast-beating heart, of his thrumming pulses. Willow . . . Why couldn't he forget her . . . Forget that he had ever kissed her and got so tangled up in those velvet brown eyes? She was like a fawn, shy and wild. Where was she now? At the little house? She must be. He had been away all afternoon and hadn't returned until sundown. It would have pleasured his eyes to have seen her before he'd turned in; an important part of the day seemed to be missing if she wasn't in his view at least once . . . in the golden glow of early morning, at high noon, or in the sleepy shade of late afternoon.

Now Talon was struck by a terror worse than that he'd felt when he'd faced twenty Comanches with the Wild Bunch and had been compelled to fight for his life, to kill or be killed. He was in dread of the past catching up with him, of having to leave Sundance now that he'd become somewhat decent. The error of his ways might soon catch up with him. His brother knew he'd been an outlaw; he had seen the awareness in Ashe's eyes long ago. Still, Ashe had not turned him in, and Talon wondered why. Was the old saying true? Was blood thicker than water? Or was there something more to it? He knew that a member of the Wild Bunch had murdered a man on that stage . . . but did Ashe know which man that was?

Life had failed him in his youth. He felt cheated. He had fallen in love with an older woman, and she had cruelly mocked him, even as she justified his manhood at a young tender age. Had he ever driven the shame of being cast aside by her from his mind . . . ever forgotten the pain of being driven out of her life, out of his own family, away from his beloved Sundance?

No. He had revolted and become lawless. His blood had surged like that of a savage's, and he had embraced a world of blood and violence, of fevered lust for money and women, women and yet more women. More often than not, he had bedded three or four women in the same night. He had wandered into a valley of crime, of evil. That other kind of love had not been love at all.

Now here was Willow, and it was too late for them. He couldn't have her, couldn't have the kisses her pale pink lips offered, nor could he run his fingers through her glinting hair. And he could not, surely could not, touch her cameo flesh. The joy he was to taste of must come from memory, the remembered feel of Willow. She would be some happy man's wife someday, sharing all the joys and pains that life had to offer. He would remain alone, tortured, all through the lonely starlit nights. The truth was, he would give his life to spare Willow a moment's pain.

Yet he had been a vicious outlaw, and any day men might come, seeking to throw him behind bars or to kill him—to hang him from a tall tree.

Just then Clem began to talk in his sleep, muttering some words over and over. Talon half-rose onto his elbow, something Clem had said making his mind come alert, making his nerves dance.

". . . Take it out! Can't hide it down in that hole

346

anymore!" Clem smacked his lips. "You'll get caught redhanded, Talon! Don't be a fool, young'un, turn it in . . . they'll get you and be hangin' you from the high neck of a tree. . . ." His words trailed off into a series of snorts and loud sawing snores.

By the time the rose of dawn had bloomed, Talon had the stolen cache in the back of his wagon, and Ashe was seated beside him, mighty proud of what his younger brother was about to do. "This is an act of admission, Talon, and I think you just might be in for a pardon signed by the governor himself." He hid his frown then, from Tanya and Willow. They had come outside, light shawls over their nightgowns, to see the men off. Tanya was smiling her reassurance that all would come out right when they went to Austin. "The only thing that worries me," Ashe went on in a lower tone, "is that stagecoach murder. It's got to hang over someone's head and I just hope it isn't yours!" If only he could catch Carl . . .

Back in the lane that led to the bunkhouses Clem stood, bathed in the early morning rays of pinkish gold, thanking God that his sneaky little scheme had worked—he had never talked in his sleep in his whole life! He knew the noose was tightening around Talon Clay's neck. Committees of vigilantes were being formed to stamp out lawlessness, and horse thieves were being hung at different places along the San Antonio River. This way, at least Talon might be afforded a pardon. Might? What made him go and think that? Of course Talon would be pardoned. *He had to be!*

A strange expression in his eyes and his gaze never

347

leaving the road, Talon asked his brother, "Willow sick or something? She didn't seem to be herself."

Since this wasn't the time to compound Talon's problems, Ashe sat silent for several moments—telling moments to Talon. Ashe, realizing he was hesitating too long, only offered, "I guess she had some trouble at the school yesterday. It will all get straightened out soon. No need to concern yourself."

Talon was not satisfied with that. "What kind of trouble? Something to do with children?" His green eyes shifted back and forth between the road and Ashe's wooden countenance.

"Yeah, something like that." He paused for a moment, then went on in another vein. "Looks like that thunderstorm is going to pass to the south, should be good driving all the way in."

"Should be," Talon muttered, realizing that his brother had expertly evaded the subject of Willow's "trouble" at school yesterday. When he returned to Sundance, however, he was going to get to the bottom of this mystery.

Back at Sundance, Willow was confiding in her sister, and an expression of horrible anxiety crossed Tanya's face at what she had just heard. "Are you sure?" Tanya asked.

"I'm sure, Sis." Willow lowered her head dejectedly. "Carl Tucker done the nasty deed and took my . . . my . . ." She couldn't go on; it was just too much, even to mouth the terrible words.

"But," Tanya began, her voice shaking, "but there was no . . . blood. So how could there? . . ." Recalling what she had once said to Ashe, that there didn't necessarily have to be any blood involved in a loss of innocence, she blanched and stared at her sister as if she were looking at her for the first time in her life. In a trance, she said, *"Oh, dear God . . . help us."*

When Willow was alone that night in the relatively huge bedroom, lying on her back and staring at the ceiling, her blond hair loose and spreading like a golden fan about her, the plan came to her—the very dangerous plan.

Realizing that Carl Tucker might have gone away to lie low until yesterday's incident blew over, that she might become heavy with child, and that Carl might not return at all, she had begun to fret over who would become the child's father. The thought of marrying Carl nauseated her as did the idea of becoming a mother to his child. What was she going to do?

Then the notion had come to her—it was a wild fantasy—to try to make Talon Clay fall in love with her. Hadn't she already tried hundreds of times to do just that? She had told herself over and over she would show Talon . . . she would make him fall in love . . . with her. Already the notion was growing weaker and weaker. There were ways, though, ways she knew of. There were those beautiful dresses she had discovered in the room—*her* room—the hidden room in Ashe's library/study.

Flipping onto her stomach, Willow's fantastic thoughts grew wilder and yet more dangerous. She would *make* Talon marry her, somehow, someway. All of a sudden she felt wicked at just thinking of how she would appear to Talon in those dresses . . . and there was the locket with the pretty gold-haired woman in it. Having seen herself in one of those gowns, her hair done up just like the woman's in the locket, she knew that Talon Clay would take more than one look at her. She had felt absolutely beautiful that day last week when Samson had gone fishing, and she'd been stunned to see how much she resembled the pretty lady in the locket.

What *would* Talon think of her? Maybe he would fall in love with her, madly in love.

Talon had hurt her by shunning her offer of love. He had embarrassed her. He had told Carl Tucker she was a bad woman, that he had had her. No wonder Carl Tucker thought she was so easy!

Even if there was not to be a baby, she was going to make him fall in love with her. Then she would break *his* heart, as he had hers . . . after he was madly in love and begging to hold her, to love her. It would serve him right!

What Willow did not realize at the time was that once she unleashed Talon's already barely restrained passions he would not take no for an answer; and innocent as she was, Willow would not realize until too late the dangerous fire that could quicken in a hot-blooded young man like Talon Clay.

When sleep finally claimed her weary body and mind, Willow dreamed of a young man, his hair a long jasmine braid; his mount a cloud of white; his face, his chest, his legs, all tanned a beautiful shade of bronze. He rode beside a young woman astride a blue-gray mustang, her hair loose and flowing, sun-streaked a snowy blond about her more mature face. Her skin was tanned golden. Her name? . . .

Willow Brandon.

But who was the tall, green-eyed half-breed, his dark brown hair a straight arrow down his back . . . his gaze that never left Talon somewhat sad and poignant? *Who was he?* Willow wondered as she awoke bathed in a chilling sweat.

Chapter 26

Ashe and Talon entered the valley bisected by a sprawling meander of the Colorado River and surrounded by timbered hills and ravines.

Austin was first settled in 1835. Mirabeau Lamar, who became president of the Republic of Texas, stopped in the valley while he was on a hunting trip, and in 1839, it was selected for the capital and named for Stephen F. Austin.

When the Mexicans invaded Texas in 1842, Sam Houston, then president of the republic, moved the capital to Houston. The citizens of Austin, fearing that Houston would become the permanent capital, retrieved the archives from a company of Texas Rangers sent to carry them to Houston. The incident became known as the Archive War. By 1845, the capital was again in Austin.

Talon and Ashe drove past the governor's mansion. The place, set back on green lawns was a splendid example of Southern colonial architecture and it overlooked the capitol. The mansion's eastern façade was decorated with fluted Greek pillars with Ionic caps. These had been shaped from pine logs hauled from nearby Bastrop by slave labor. The capitol, a one-story frame building, had once been protected by an eight-foot stockade, but that had been taken down in 1845.

The word "ranger" first came into use in 1823 when Stephen Austin employed ten men to serve as troubleshooters. Austin had hired the men at his own expense and when the Tonkawas did not give up their thieving way and even made a raid on the Colorado settlements, Austin raised thirty men and went after the Indians. In 1826, Austin held a conference at which it was agreed that a permanent force of twenty to thirty Rangers would be kept in service at all times. These early forces were designated as "mounted volunteers," "spies," "mounted gunmen," and "rangers." It was not until the Mexican War that the existence of a body of men known as the Texas Rangers was recognized. Ashe was proud to have served as one of them. One must be young to serve, so that was all behind him now. He was a married man, very much in love with his young wife.

Before coming to Austin, Ashe and Talon had made a short stop at the Navarro Plantation where Ashe had visited briefly with a man by the name of Jake Reed. His rambling home, built in 1822, was perched on a high bluff on the east side of the Brazos. The house had been fashioned from cottonwood logs, hewn and counterhewn. Somewhat in awe of the place, Talon had admiringly walked about, studying the polished walnut columns that supported the house-length gallery.

Mr. Reed had allowed Talon to roam about the place, pleased that the young man was so taken with Navarro Plantation. Meanwhile, the man had sat visiting with Ashe.

"Lord, I'd like a home like this someday," Talon said to himself as he wandered in and out of the rooms, picturing a dainty woman strolling beside him. She looked so happy. . . . Dreams, nothing but impossible dreams . . .

Each room had a fireplace, mostly fashioned of sandstone taken from the river, and in addition to the main house, there were many separate buildings which included a kitchen, a dairy, a guest house, and off beside a shimmering blue lake, quarters for home slaves and field slaves. There was even a doctor's house on the grounds.

When they continued on to Austin, Ashe filled the interested Talon in on the history of the Navarro Plantation. For the first two years after it had been built, those at the plantation depended on wild game for meat.

"Deer. Turkey—and mustang."

"Mustang!" Talon looked askance to his brother. "Shoot!"

"Yes," Ashe continued, a twinkle in his eye Talon could not see, "often without bread or salt."

"Eating mustang." Talon shook his blond head. "I'll never get so hungry that I'll have to eat a horse!"

"Someday you might have to count on it for your meat." Ashe settled back into his seat, the ribbons held loosely between his slim strong fingers, so like Talon's when they lay side by side that one could not tell his from the other's. There was only one difference; Talon's skin was slightly darker, bronzing more quickly under the hot sun. "Much of the mustang meat is jerked, cut into strips and dried on a scaffold of small poles."

"I've jerked meat before"—Talon laughed—"but never *horse!*" Talon was silent for a moment before asking, "How does Reed send his cotton out?"

"Jake sent his first cotton to Mexico by mule back."

"So, what does he trade it for?"

"Coffee. Tea. And other provisions—besides bags of Mexican dollars."

"Ah."

"Later, though, he shipped his cotton to New Orleans. He's had many visitors to his plantation, including General Sam Houston, who's a friend of the family. Houston's revolutionary army camped on the plantation for two weeks in the spring of '36, also on the Groce plantation."

"Old Jake has a son, doesn't he?"

"How did you know?"

Talon shrugged easily, saying, "I saw a portrait of a younger man. He looks a lot like his father."

"Not really," Ashe said, "but you are right about Walter being the son. He's the younger man in the portrait. He owns the Orleans Plantation, much larger than the Navarro. He had about three hundred slaves at one time."

Talon whistled at that. He was beginning to suspect that Ashe was trying to keep his mind off what waited up ahead in Austin, but Talon was not all that worried. What will be, will be, he thought.

356

"The house is colonial in style," Ashe was saying. "I'll have to show it to you sometime."

"Yeah."

"Why so interested in houses all of a sudden?" Ashe asked his brother as they passed a weather-beaten farm wagon drawn by a horse and a mule.

Talon countered with a question of his own, "Doesn't every man want his own home, his own spread, sooner or later?" He dragged his attention back to the front of the wagon after having looked back over his shoulder to the bearded man half-asleep on the weatherbeaten wagon seat.

"You have a home," Ashe said. "Sundance is yours too, you know."

"Yeah. But I'd like to have my own spread, a smaller Sundance maybe."

"*Le Petit Sundance?*" Looking at his brother sidewise, he saw Talon nod, the green of his eyes matching the rolling hills they were traversing. "There's plenty of room on Sundance property for twenty more spreads. Pick your spot and some day we'll build your *own* house."

"You mean it?"

"Of course. After all, Sundance property is yours too. How many times do I have to say it?"

"I'll think about it, Ashe."

"Good. Now let's find a hotel and then get this vexing matter taken care of. Soon as it's over, the better you'll feel, no matter what the consequences. Then, when you're free, you can start planning *Le Petit Sundance.*"

Talon thought his brother sounded awfully sure of himself. If only he could feel the same way . . .

Part Four

It is the wisdom of crocodiles, that shed tears when they would devour.
—*Francis Bacon*

Chapter 27

Taking a handful of Hester's bodice, Talon shook her, rattling her teeth in her head. "Stupid *puta!*" he snarled into her shocked face, his thick, straight blond hair a loose silken flow in the morning breeze. "Don't ever come here to Sundance again spreading your gossip. They're lies, and I don't want to hear 'em!"

He shoved his angry face close to Hester's until she could only see his stunning green eyes and his slim face with the taut cheekbones.

Mesmerized, Hester could only stare at Talon Clay.

When he shoved her backward suddenly, so hard that she almost fell, Hester glared back at Talon defiantly while clutching the slim railing outside the bunkhouse.

Talon grated his white, even teeth, "Where did you ever hear such a crock of lies?"

Bored already with her silly gossip, Talon pulled his glimmering length of hair over his shoulder and began to braid it, his long fingers as dexterous as any woman's. Meanwhile Hester stared, her mouth agape, at such an uncommon, unmasculine feat.

"All of a sudden you don't remember who told you, is that it?" he drawled, absolute boredom in his deep male voice.

"Ma told me." Hester hugged her shoulders and rocked back and forth as if comforting herself. "She knows everything about everybody. Your pa was a half-breed and his name was Hunter-of-the-Horses. So there!"

"Oh bull!"

"Your pa had Kiowa blood, Ma says. So that makes you a half-breed too."

"Lord!" Talon exclaimed with a jerk of his head.

Her heart hammering away, Hester could only stare at his bare, bronzed chest, but before she could mutter another word, Talon had stepped close to her again, his warm, angry breath fanning her cheeks.

"You and your ma are plain loco, you know that."

"Talon Clay, how can you say that about Ma, when she took you in like you were her own kin?"

"Yeah. And all she ever jabbered about when I lived at Saw Grass was Sundance and what a shame it was that my own folks didn't want me there."

"They *didn't*," she taunted. "At least *she*—" Hester got no further.

Clamping a callous hand over her mouth, Talon snarled softly, "Don't. Don't *ever* say her name around me—ever. Now, you just sashay back home with your pimply-faced drover and tell your ma *she's full of it.*"

Narrowing his eyes and flinging the finished braid back over his shoulder, Talon waited for

362

her reaction.

"Oh!"

But when Hester spun about to do exactly as he said, Talon's hand shot out and grasped her by the wrist.

"Ouch! You let me go, Talon Clay!"

He spun Hester about, meaning to ask her another question. "Whatever is it that you and your . . ." He stared down at Hester as if she had suddenly grown two heads. "Hey, you been calling my ma a whore. Martha never slept with any other man but Pete Brandon, my pa, and she certainly didn't sleep with any half-breed like you been telling me!" He shook her once more for good measure. "So, you just get on home and see that you don't come *whoring* around Sundance again! You do, and I'll round up a passel of guys that'll pump you over real good, hear?"

"*Hear!*" With that, Hester flounced angrily to the waiting wagon and glared at the pimply-faced drover who was staring at her red, pinched face.

Just then Willow appeared in the lane. She saw Hester just leaving, her face hotly flushed as if she had been . . . Oh, she hated to think it. . . . And there was Talon, his chest and his feet bare, still looking lazy-lidded around the eyes.

Nevertheless, Willow was not going to be dissuaded by Hester's presence so she walked right up to Talon and greeted him with a bright good-morning smile. Still, she couldn't help but ask, "You two just get up?" Looking around at the lemony yellow grounds and still smiling, she dared go even further, "What would lovers have to argue about on such a beautiful day?" She heaved a deep, contented sigh.

Talon heard her though he was still watching the Tucker wagon go down the lane and become a mere dust cloud in the distance.

For the second time that morning he was forced to lay hands on a woman. Like an iced-over pond, his eyes shone chillingly as he spun on Willow, his voice scathing. "Don't you ever—" His angry eyes dropped to her shoulder and he frowned.

"Ouch!" Willow had shouted, stepping back. But his grip remained clamped about her bruised shoulder, only loosening a little until she cried, "Talon, let go." She gasped, pain clouding her eyes. "It hurts."

Hands merely hovering at her shoulders now, Talon peered closer at Willow, saying, "Why does that hurt?"

Oh, God. She couldn't tell Talon that Carl Tucker had given her these bruises when he had ravished her in the schoolroom the other day. Nor could she tell him that she could very well be carrying Carl Tucker's seed. She couldn't, for if she did all her ingenious schemes to seduce Talon would go untested. She just had to know how far she could get!

"Let's have a look at that," Talon said, and swift as lightning, he shoved her sleeve upward, whistling and then frowning darkly. His fingers gentled all of a sudden, becoming a soothing touch at the back of her arms. "Tell me who done this to you, Willow. Tell me so I can go after him and kill the bastard!"

Swallowing hard, Willow saw her plans dwindling fast. Think. She had to think of something . . . and fast.

She was still wincing from the unexpected pain,

even though Talon had released her. Giving her long hair a toss, she said breezily, "Oh I got the bruise at school the other day. I was riding one of the kids' half-wild horses, and, well, he threw me." At this last, she shrugged.

Willow had said the magic word—*school*. But Talon still looked at her with suspicion. "So, you fell from a horse, eh? I been riding many wild horses and my bruises never turned out like that one." He frowned. "That looks like a man's—"

Swiftly she cut him off, blurting, "Oh well, this one is not so bad. You should see the—" Willow almost choked on what she'd been about to say. Recovering quickly, she managed, "I fell down more than once!" Now she could not bring herself to meet his accusing eyes.

"You got another bruise? Let's see."

"No!" Willow danced away from him, recalling that his soothing touch, brief though it had been, had caused a raw hunger to flash through her body. "Oh, Talon," she began breathlessly, smiling brightly and charmingly up at him. "I heard you got a pardon. That's *wonderful*. I'm so happy for you." She watched him beam proudly and shuffle his bare feet, the dangerously close moment forgotten. "Say, you wouldn't want to show me that horse again, would you?"

When Talon kept staring at her in his mesmerizing way, she brushed a hand before his eyes, saying, "Wake up, Talon, and let's go take a look at Dust Devil."

Unwaveringly he stared her down, as if trying to come to a decision about something. Then, shaking his head, he walked alongside Willow, his bare feet moving silently through the grass—like an Indian's.

"The mustang moves like lightning," Talon warned Willow as he helped her mount the horse, "so be careful."

"I will." Then she giggled, saying, "*You* be careful. You're barefoot!" Nudging the horse in the side, Willow began to move away from Talon.

He stepped back, admiration in his eyes for the petite blonde astride the blue-gray mustang. Willow gave her long, silky hair a toss, so it could blow free behind her. Seeing this, Talon longed to cup her face and run his fingers through her tresses, touching them lovingly and making the hair tumble about her shoulders and face. He would kiss her, and she would open her arms to him. Then he would nudge her legs apart to receive him. . . . He cursed the quickening in his loins, now when he could do nothing about it. He could not touch Willow. He did not want to soil her with his rottenness.

"She's gentle . . . and handles easy, Talon," Willow called over to him, the birds cavorting above her head against a late-summer sky.

Desperately Talon looked aside. He felt as though his very life was being squeezed from his body sometimes. It hurt terribly to be around her and it hurt to be away from her. This kind of passion, much more complicated than any he'd ever known, Talon was beginning to discover, had its embarrassing moments. He'd been able to control his desire for a woman before, but this was downright inconvenient.

"Look at me, Talon! I adore her and I think she loves me too. Oh, I love riding her!"

"Yeah," Talon said under his breath, "I would love to ride you too." Aloud, he said, "Guess I underfigured you, Pussywillow. You seat a horse pretty good for a woman."

Willow gave her head an impudent toss. "What do you mean—a *woman*? A woman can do anything a man can do—sometimes better!"

Talon threw his hands into the air, shouting agreeably, "You tell 'em, darlin'!" Then he spied the old man just emerging from his bunkhouse, disheveled and scratching his chest with the fingertips of both hands. "Hey Clem! come and have a look at Willow . . . on her new horse." His gaze wandering back to Willow, he said, "Yeah. That's your horse now, little lady. I broke and trained her myself." Catching a bright red-headed streak flash behind him, he reached back to pull the lad beside him tousling Samson's hair. "Sammy, little cork, where've you been?"

Cocking his head to look up at the fair-haired, handsome Talon Clay, Samson said, "How come you're so all-fired cheery today?" Then his face lit up. "Hey, I know why. You got a pardon from some act of retrib . . . reterb—"

"Retribution," Talon offered with a cocksure grin which quickly became a frown when he saw Willow giving him a dubious look.

Then Willow began to laugh so hard that she had to stop the horse and lean forward. "Listen to you two! *Retribution?* You know what that word means? Really, do either of you really know?"

"Oh Lord!" Talon smacked his darkly tanned forehead. "That's something like, uh, revenge. No,

367

Sammy, I didn't get revenge." He looked over at Willow and grinned. "I got . . . pardoned that's all." He chuckled. "*Repentance* is more like it. Actually I was given a second chance and released into my brother's custody."

"Shoot." Sammy exhaled. "It's plain and simple: you turned yourself in and brought the loot back. 'Course your brother being a ranger, a former ranger, and that helped. What about the murderer? Does he go free too?"

Going stock-still, Talon stared straight ahead for several moments before turning to Samson and harshly asking, "How did you know there was a murderer, huh?"

"That's easy. Everyone around these parts knows. They was talking about it at the fandango, at Rankin's. Half Texas knows about it, Talon Clay. Why you looking so grumpy? How did you get away without having the murder pinned on you?"

"Simple, kid. I wasn't the murderer. Ashe told them that."

"Tell me the story," Samson begged, his eyes eager and big.

"Me and a couple of other men held up the stage, and while we were busy getting the loot situated on the horses, a shooting took place back at the stage. I don't know which one of the Wild Bunch did it."

"Wild Bunch! *Wowee!* You was one of them, Talon Clay?"

"Nothing to be proud of, Sammy. Don't you ever go getting the idea that it is. It's"—his eyes strayed over to Willow who was cantering across the greensward—"it's hell to be away from home, to be bad. Especially when you should be knowing there's gold right in your own back yard. Understand, boy?"

"Yeah . . . I guess so." Sammy screwed up his little face, and then he snapped to attention again. "But still! You're a hero."

"No hero, Sammy."

"I mean you're a Texas badman." When Talon grimaced, Sammy bit his lip and said, "Ah, gosh, I meant to say you *was* a badman."

"I'm a reformed bandit."

"Yeah. A bandit."

Samson leaned his elbows on the top rail and hitched his boot on the lower one, aping Talon's actions. Then he gaped downward. "Hey! You're barefoot, Talon Clay. Don't you know you kin step onto one of them there thorny cactuses, or maybe a tarantula?"

Throwing his blond head back, Talon laughed loudly. "I've stepped onto worse than that, Sammy." Turning serious, he stared wistfully, at Willow, his blood nevertheless dancing erotically in his veins. "Damn sight worse than that," he added and stared off into the distance.

Chapter 28

The cornflower blue of Tanya's calico dress flattered the red fire in her hair and the warm golden apricot of her tan as she sat in the wagon beside Ashe. It was a "pretty" day, as Texans say. The sun shone lemon yellow bright. The sky was a heavenly blue.

The wagon rolled along the narrow, bumpy road, flanked by rolling postoak belts and rough-hewed farm fences enclosing fields of straggling corn. To the south, beyond the oak and prairie belt, the horizons broadened into rising plateaus of low, flat, stony-soiled hills and then the enormous seas of grass began. Upon the hills and in numerous valleys grew the forest trees—walnut, hickory, sweetgum, long leaf and short leaf pine. These forest trees offered shade in summer and shelter in winter to both animal and human life.

Farther west and to the north, in the Panhandle, was the buffalo grass. These coarse bunches of grass gave sustenance to the wild herds who thundered across the Plains for untold thousands of years.

Tanya smiled at her husband from beneath her wide-brimmed sunbonnet, saying, "It's a gorgeous afternoon for a picnic. I don't think it could have been more perfect."

Ashe closed his large, sun-browned hand over Tanya's, and said lazily, "That's because you make it perfect, Lady Red. What day could be pretty without you in it?"

Tanya looked down at his hands, hands that knew how to love a woman, how to touch her with thrilling intimacy. Just looking upon them made her feel the pride of possession. This man was hers.

"And all the days that went before?" Tanya inquired, a little jealous at the thought of Ashe alone, without her as his wife.

"They were just days. Busy days."

"H'm. Busy nights too?" Not looking at him, she pressed the long folds of her skirt with a suddenly moist palm.

He nodded beneath his dusty hat brim, his cat-hazel eyes smiling. "You don't want to get into that, do you?" he asked. A shaft of sunlight angled across his chin as he lifted it slightly.

"I suppose it's really none of my business what went before." Idly her eyes studied his long-boned fingers, muscled and firm. How she loved the feel of this man, her husband. Often, at night, she had trembled in anticipation, her blue eyes flaring with desire as he disrobed to display his lean-muscled male beauty. Even now, she checked the impulse to reach over and run her hand up and down his leg . . . later maybe.

"It's better left unsaid," he pointed out. Again the

372

corners of his mouth moved in a little smile. What would be her reaction, he wondered briefly, if he told her about Larrisa, or one of the others? Tragic, he decided.

True, she thought. It is better left unsaid. Still . . . Tanya chewed her lip, wondering how it had been with Ashe and other women. Had they loved him as thoroughly, as faithfully, as she loved him? Did Ashe still think of them now and then?

"They meant nothing, Tanya," he answered her unspoken question. "Nothing."

Yellow sun was pouring down upon the wagon. The muffled clip-clop of the horse's hoofs was a steady, lulling sound. Shadows stretched from the hills. Tanya warmed even further, remembering the night she and Ashe had just spent in lingering love. When she couldn't touch him enough, he had lifted her above him, carefully and inexorably setting her down and fusing her to his man-head in a swift, savage movement. Then she had taken all of him, hot sensuality flowing from her while she rocked above him, delighting in this new sexual joy. Ashe had been her willing captive, she the master of the tempo that set the rhythm of their erotic lovemaking. Afterward she had been so at peace, so replete.

Suddenly those beautiful hazel eyes were devouring her face, and Ashe saying in a lazy tone, "If you don't stop daydreaming about what you're daydreaming about, I'm going to pull this wagon over and have you stripped and stretched on the wagon bed in half a minute."

"I was remembering. Mmmm." Tanya giggled softly, then went on. "Last night . . . and how I'd never seen a man undress so fast."

In a half snarl, Ashe said, "I'd better be the *only* man you've seen undress, wife!"

Tanya set about joking with him, softly mocking as she snipped, "It's better left unsaid."

"Women—married women—don't joke about such things, Tanya."

Tanya lifted her face, setting it at an angle that kept him from seeing her delighted expression. "Neither," she said, "should married men."

"It's different with men."

"Oh?" Her eyes locked on his hat-shadowed profile.

"Tell me, which one of us better suits the role for past experiences, experiences that enable one to teach the other spouse—I'm sorry, *pleasure* the other, and yes, I suppose you have to say teach too." His eyes became darker, his cheeks tauter, as he went on without allowing her a word, "Only whores can be female, Tanya."

"Then . . . I suppose we can call all men *lecherous*."

"I'm not lecherous, love, I've only been experienced by the best . . . a few choice women."

"Whores."

"No. Women who take a bath once in a while and smell pretty . . . clean. Have to look pretty too."

"Whores."

Ashe chuckled, relenting, "If you say so, sweet."

"That's what they are if they are unwed and sleeping around!" Tanya nodded once, vigorously, to emphasize her point.

"Tanya . . . Tanya . . ." Ashe said, clucking his

tongue. "You amaze me."

"Shut up!" she snapped, cuffing him on the shoulder. "Just shut up."

"I'd be only too happy to," Ashe leaned back, whistling a tune, then he quit to ask, "What should we talk about now? H'm?"

"Nothing!" Tanya folded her arms huffily beneath her chest, innocently and unconsciously causing Ashe to lower his eyes to her puffed-up bosom.

He pressed on, "My past? My adventures? My bad—"

"Don't say it, Ashe Brandon." Quickly she added, "You're a rogue."

"What's that, rogue? A horse? Am I a horse, Tanya?"

Tanya's cheeks reddened creating a pink aura about her face beneath the charming sunbonnet.

"That's a mighty beautiful blush, Tanya." Grinning, he shot her a roguish look.

Tanya was experiencing a pleasurable giddiness while Ashe actually flirted with her as he had before they were man and wife.

"What should we talk about now?" she echoed his earlier words as her gaze swept quickly past his hard profile. "I know," she said eagerly, answering her own question. "Tell me about the Indians, Ashe. I've seen so few of them that I feel quite ignorant about them."

"Now, that subject I do know more about than the one of women."

Quickly she plunged in, "Have you killed many?"

"Probably as many as have tried and failed to kill

me. I hardly ever miss, Tanya."

"Haven't you ever liked any of them."

"Not many. Only a few."

"Like Nightwalker?"

"He's not really Nightwalker, you know. His father is, but he's a half-breed, I believe. Dark brown hair. Green eyes." Ashe felt a sudden, unexplicable shiver go through him. "They call him Hunter-of-the-Horses too. Some Indians have more than one name . . . notable Indians."

"Have you ever met this Hunter or Nightwalker?"

"Nope." His voice was very soft.

"But do you like *him*, I mean Almanzo?"

"He's one of the few I told you about. I like him. He grows on a person. I can understand him, you see." Ashe checked the old bitterness before it could surface and destroy the new peace and joy he and Tanya had found together.

"H'm, I know what you mean," she said.

He saw her eyes twinkle mischievously.

"Be careful, Tanya. I'm still a bit touchy on this subject. I'll never forget that Almanzo Rankin has an unusual fondness for you. Somehow you've endeared yourself to the man."

"Yes . . . I have." She wouldn't tell him just how deep that fondness of Almanzo's had run at first. She'd had the strongest feeling, on many an occasion, that Almanzo would have liked nothing better than to spirit her away from Ashe. And she'd almost, had the urge to let him . . . almost.

Switching back to safer ground, Tanya said, "Tell me about the Indians, Ashe."

"The Indians were truly the children of the land.

They had a saying: 'The earth is our mother and the sun our father.'"

"You respect them," Tanya said, "but have no love for them."

"That's about the extent of it."

"How about the different tribes?"

"There're the Eastern tribes, living in permanent villages. They build their wigwams of bark and wood. They make their own pottery, supplement game they kill with squash, corn, and beans."

"The 'Western' Indians?"

"They're nomadic wanderers and they, unlike the Eastern ones who are sedentary, know little or nothing of agriculture. From buffalo hides they make their clothes and their tipis, from bones they make crude tools, from tendons thread, from hoofs glue. Meat serves as their main food."

"It seems to me that the lot of the Plains Indians is harder than that of the timber tribes because the Plains dwellers have to wander about seeking the necessities of life."

"Right. The Plains tribes are constantly shifting about, and they are fierce and ungovernable, always fighting for possession of water and land, for social distinction."

"Something like the whites, huh?"

"True. To the south are the Lipans, an offshoot of the Apaches. They are separated from the main tribe by a Comanche severance. Some say that Night-walker, the father, is truly a Lipan and not half Kiowa."

Deep ruts and sharp, heavy rocks jolted the wagon as Ashe pulled off the main road. "Northward," he

377

went on, "are the Tonkawas, Tawakonis, Wacos, and Witchitas. They're dangerous and troublesome but not very strong. Farther west, ranging from the Plains of southern Texas into Kansas are fierce Comanches of Shoshone stock. West of them, in the foothills of the Rockies and along the Pecos are the main Apache groups. The most troublesome lot so far have proven to be the Comanche and the Apache."

"How about the Tawakoni, the Lipan, and the Waco bands? Are they very dangerous?"

"Among those you forgot to mention the Wichita. They are all troublesome too, but less so. Dangerous, yes."

As Ashe drove along the oak-shadowed path, Tanya didn't ask where he was going to stop for their picnic; she was too interested in their conversation about Indians to give much heed to where they were headed.

"Have you ever heard the story of Sarah Hibbins and the Comanche moon?"

"No. What is the Comanche moon?"

"In the southwestern wilderness, when it was still a part of Mexico, settlements of colonists were smaller than they are now . . . and farther apart." The soft sunlight filtered over the densely wooded trail as Ashe cleared his throat. "There was constant danger of raids by savages looking for horses. Some were looking for scalps." He pressed his hand over Tanya's kneecap when she drew in her breath, as she usually did when someone spoke of the Indians taking scalps. She had heard about the practice often enough, but somehow the thought of blood and hair

378

mingled made her queasy—especially lately when her stomach recoiled easily. "The Indians usually raided when the moon was full. . . ."

"The Comanche moon . . . I see. Well, where does this Sarah Hibbins enter into the picture of the Comanche moon?" Tanya jumped a little when a wild turkey gobbled and scurried into the underbrush between the trees. "Lord!" She placed a hand over her fast-thumping heart.

Ashe chuckled, saying, "Sure you want me to tell the story? It's true, you know. The Texas Rangers involved in it lived to relate the tale. It happened back when Stephen Austin first formed a small group of rangers."

"Just try to get out of the telling now," she said in a mock-gruff voice. "Mr. Brandon, I'll choke it out of your handsome throat if you clam up!"

"Okay. Don't say I didn't warn you. Sarah Creath was a pretty blonde—"

"Creath?" Tanya's brow shot up as she went on, "I thought you said—"

It was his turn to break in on her. "Hibbins. But first, Lady Red, the woman got herself married. More than once too. A farm youth, by the name of John McSherry was Sarah's first husband."

"Oh."

"Texas fever, that's what McSherry had. The colonizers, and Stephen Austin, were offering tracts of land, big tracts, and they were free for the asking. The settlers were coming in in the twenties. There was risk, of course, but wild beasts and redskin raiders didn't seem to keep them away. McSherry was set on making his way to Texas, and Sarah was willing to go with her new husband. They boarded a Mississippi steamer for New Orleans, and from there they took a coastal ship for Texas. It wasn't until '28 that McSherry chose his site on the west side of the Guadalupe and built his cabin out of logs. His nearest neighbors were ten miles up the Guadalupe.'

Ashe began to slow the team. "How does this spot look to you?"

"What? Oh, yes. It's lovely, Ashe. Let's have our picnic here. Promise to tell me the rest of the story while we're eating?"

"Ah . . . better I tell you when we're finished."

Ashe had pulled the team off the trail and drawn them up at the crest of a low, wooded hill. There was a clearing here where they spread the blanket and the repast of cold fried chicken, buttered biscuits, Clem's meat pie, and wildberry tarts. A jug of spring-cooled lemonade to wash down the food completed their picnic spread.

Below the picnickers, the floor of the rising hillside was blanketed with a thick cushion of pine needles and a shallow creek, shimmering intermittently in the sun, wound beneath the redolent green pines. A white-tailed deer leaped the short distance separating the banks and vanished. The wonderfully fresh pine odor enveloped them, mingling with moist earthy smells. All around the sun sparkled. When they had finished eating, Tanya put the scraps and the leftovers into the paper-lined basket, out of the sun.

"We're finished," Tanya announced, flopping over onto her stomach. "Ugh. I ate too much."

Ashe chuckled. "Little Miss Piggy. Not only does she want to fill her belly but her brain at the same time. I've never met a woman—excuse me"—he ran his hand up her skirt and cupped the firm, soft globe of flesh—"a woman who wanted to chatter so much. Lady Red, you've got a nice ass. Did anyone ever tell you?"

Tanya laughed softly. "I hear a warning note in your voice so I'll not be answering *that* question."

Ashe's eyes warmed considerably while they roamed over her curving back, lingering on her soft curves below as he murmured, "God, you've got a sexy behind. If you stay in that position, Lady, you're going to get into trouble."

"Mmmm. Just what kind of trouble?"

"*Mucho* trouble. Want me to show you?"

With a throaty laugh, Tanya said, "I don't think my full stomach could take it."

"Well," he sexily drawled, "flip over then and I'll put something exciting between your legs. We'll go slow."

"Very slow." Tanya rolled onto her back, finding her eyes at once locked with Ashe's.

Her hand reached downward, moving to rest on the front of his straining breeches.

Ashe sucked in his breath as the heat of her touch seared through the thick fabric of his pants. "Ashe," she whispered achingly. "I want you darling."

"And so you'll have me, Lady Red," his voice pulsed in every fiber of her being, "all of me."

As the gnawing ache began in her lower region, she watched Ashe's face soften with the heat of his growing ardor. His eyes ran over her in a slow, thorough perusal that caused her pulses to pound, her senses to reel. Then one hand slid up her leg, and that wild sweet melody began to sing in her. She moaned and arched toward his magical fingers.

Delighting in the silken feel of Tanya's flesh, Ashe lowered his mouth to hers. The kiss was hot, fleshy. He wanted her so much that he'd tasted her that whole day, even this morning after having had her the night before. All she had to do was look at him with her beautiful blue eyes and his body trembled with anticipation. She made his heart pound like a drum. She made his body ache for wanting her.

"I can't get enough of you, Tanya Brandon, not nearly enough. I want to be inside you . . . all the time."

Breathlessly she answered, "You say that now, dearest, but wait, just wait until I'm finished with you. We'll make sure this will hold you"—she laughed sensuously—"for a day or so."

Ashe kissed her again and again, each kiss longer and deeper than the one before. He shivered as Tanya opened his shirt and splayed a tapered hand over his chest, squeezing his pectorals, while her other hand eased the fabric aside now. He found the deep velvet core of her while they continued to kiss, his finger cherishing it, meaning to drive her to mindless ecstasy at the erotic sensations he was creating.

Ashe smiled triumphantly when Tanya's body began to tremble wildly and she threw herself against his manipulating hand. He felt her coming then; her shattering climax opened and closed about his smaller member, and he waited until she ebbed to quiet butterfly pulsations.

"Tanya!" Ashe cried out when he realized she had freed his straining manhood. He groaned, and withdrawing his finger, he turned away. "I have to get . . . get out of these clothes." When he turned back his eyes flared at the sight of Tanya wriggling out of her cornflower blue dress. "Let me," he murmured, helping her with the chemise and the petticoat.

"Free your hair, Lady Red."

Tanya did as he asked. Her trembling fingers loosened the thick braid she had fashioned in a coronet atop her head. When her hair rippled over her shoulders, he pressed her back to the blanket, arranging the tresses about her like a dark red cloud. "Scarlet," he said.

"What?"

"Your hair is scarlet."

"Not *that*—red."

"It's scarlet now," he husked across her cheek, "'cause it's blushing. You blush all over when we make love, Tanya. Even your eyes, like you've had a few strong drinks."

"Oh . . . *Ashe!*"

While they had been discussing the color scarlet, Ashe had slid his hard, manly boldness smoothly into her moist core. She was so ready for him that she hadn't noticed until she felt the thrilling fullness move rhythmically against her. Now he filled her completely, thrusting and grinding her buttocks into the rough blanket beneath her.

Hazily Tanya saw Ashe above her, the lazy sun's nimbus behind his shoulders, his face a shadowed mask, the planes contorted by the unbearable pleasure he was receiving and giving.

Ashe could feel his back tense and flex, its hard muscles quivering beneath Tanya's gripping fingers. Then, with a sidewise bump, Ashe was rolling Tanya off the blanket and into the coarse grass. They tumbled playfully, over and over, all the while thrusting and wrenching erotically, until Tanya came out on top.

"Love me now, Tanya," Ashe ground out softly.

She did just that, wrapping herself around him with the undulating magic of her woman's body. Ashe called out in a deep, hoarse cry as Tanya began to ride him, the silkiest part of her thighs coming to rest on his groin with each relaxing motion.

It was Tanya who whispered words of love above him. It was Tanya whose actions set the pace.

"Tanya. *Tanya!*"

Then they were riding high on the surging, swelling, explosive tide of rapture, losing all touch with reality. They perceived each other only with their senses then.

Finally coming to rest side by side, almost drunk with the aftermath of their boundless pleasures, Ashe pulled her against him. Tanya nuzzled her face into the curve of his neck and smiled a woman's contented smile. Ashe's arms tightened around her waist, and he murmured against her sweat-dotted forehead, "I love you, Lady Red."

"And I love you." She punctuated her words with

soft kisses at the hollow of his throat.

"You know what?" He pressed a knee between her thighs.

"No," she said, her eyes mischievous blue snaps, "What?"

"Something's come up between us again."

"Let me see . . . where was I before I was so thoroughly distracted?"

"You were in the middle of telling me a story." Sighing, Tanya looked from the wagon seat to the rolling hills. Along the quiet road, even the smallest sounds could be heard, and oak and cottonwood leaves whispered along the roadside.

"Ah, yes. Sarah Hibbins and the Comanches."

"Sarah and John McSherry," Tanya put in, smiling straight ahead. "They are now in their new log cabin. Go on."

"I will. But this is not a very happy story."

"Does it end happily?"

"Well . . ."

"I want to know about the Comanches."

Ashe sighed deeply and went on. "John and Sarah were very *happy*."

"That's nice. Go on."

"He—John—cleared patches of land, planting corn and other crops. The baby arrived in '29." If Ashe had felt Tanya stiffen beside him, he pretended not to notice. "The baby was named John, after his father. Sometimes Sarah worried about the Comanches. She had heard grisly tales of Indian

385

attacks. Then, on a pleasant afternoon late in the year, John went out to the spring to bring back a bucket of water to his wife." Ashe turned to Tanya. "Do you know what happened? Can you guess?"

"He was scalped."

"These stories aren't mere idles tales. Do you want me to go on?"

"Ashe." She turned on the wagon seat to face him. "I've told you I want to learn more about the Indians. Now, tell me. I want to determine for myself whether they are the bad creatures everyone seems to think them. I've a strong stomach. Please, I want to know what happened to Sarah."

"How about the baby?" He looked straight ahead again. "Want to know that too?"

"Yes."

"You already know that John McSherry was attacked. Sarah had heard the hellish yells from the cabin and had seen the band of Indians spring from the bushes. Her husband lay lifeless on the grass, his scalp gone."

"How terrible it must have been for her."

"Sarah quickly barred the cabin door and picked up her husband's rifle, meaning to defend herself and the baby."

"Did the Indians get into Sarah's cabin?"

"The Indians soon discovered they could not break in and left. But Sarah, afraid they might be hiding nearby, dared not risk her child's life by going out to the body of her husband. Fortunately for Sarah, that night a man by the name of John McCrabb rode up to the McSherry place. He had no idea there'd been an

Indian raid. He merely hoped to spend the night there. Learning of the tragedy, McCrabb took the young mother and her baby to a neighbors' cabin, and the warm, kind folks did all they could for the shocked woman and her baby. Indeed, Sarah stayed on at the Lockharts until she wed another pioneer settler. John Hibbins was his name."

"Lots of Johns," Tanya remarked, wondering what lay ahead for dear Sarah. Already Tanya felt as if she knew the woman. She felt compassion for her. Ashe was a good storyteller . . . or a great relater of *true* stories. She wondered if all rangers had this ability, since they saw so much in their dangerous work. "Go on, Ashe, I'm eager to hear it to the end."

Dragging his eyes from her attentively curious face, Ashe went on. "Again happiness seemed to be Sarah's lot. She and John were pleased when their new baby arrived. Still, there was always the danger of Indians. As I told you before, there were so many raids that the settlers began to demand better protection. They had some, but it wasn't enough. So, at this time, Stephen Austin formed a small group of rangers. They were landowners, each required to serve for a month . . . or provide a substitute."

"How did it go?" Tanya asked.

"Their efforts were not enough. In 1835, when Texans were preparing to revolt against Mexican tyranny, the colonists made plans to raise a battalion of one hundred and fifty rangers to keep the Indians in check."

"So, where is Sarah now?"

"You sure like Sarah, don't you? Thought you

387

would. She had just left Texas to visit relatives back home in Illinois. With her was her baby and her older child, John. When Sarah returned to Texas, her brother George came along. From New Orleans, Sarah and George went by water to Columbus, Texas, a short distance up the Brazos. It was early February of '36. Her husband met them with an oxcart and they began the tedious ride back to their frontier home. Their route took them to Beason's Crossing on the Colorado River and from there to the Navidad. They followed the Bahia road, making their last camp on Rock Creek, only about fifteen miles from the Hibbin's cabin. Another day's travel would bring them home safely.

"Rock Creek is usually as peaceful as you could want, but not for those folks that day." Ashe cleared his throat. "The quiet was suddenly broken. A band of thirteen savage Comanche braves leaped from the brush to attack the whites. They were caught by surprise. The warriors quickly killed the two men. Then they plundered the wagon. Mrs. Hibbins and her two children were taken captive. She was mounted on a mule and tied there. Seven-year-old John was tied on another. Sarah was almost overcome with grief and fear."

"Oh, poor woman," Tanya said. "Losing two husbands to the Comanches." What about the baby? she wanted to ask but she knew that was coming, sooner or later.

"The Comanches were taking Sarah and the children northward, far from any white settlements."

Did Sarah ever escape? Tanya wondered. Many

captured frontier women had not escaped the Indians. Some had been ransomed, others killed or made slaves. Tanya waited to hear the rest.

"Then," Ashe began slowly, "the fate of her baby was decided. The frightened infant had wailed so much for his mother that one of the irked braves grabbed the baby, bashed its head against a tree and tossed the tiny body aside like so much trash."

"How *awful*. To await the wolves and the buzzards. Poor babe. Poor Sarah." There remained a question in Tanya's voice. . . .

"What happened to Sarah?" Ashe asked her unspoken question. "There is more. After several days on the trail, the Comanches crossed the Colorado River and made camp on Shoal Creek. This was near the site where the capital city of Austin was to rise. A cold norther led them to seek the shelter of a cedar thicket that night. They wrapped themselves in buffalo robes. This time they were not so wise; they didn't bother to tie their prisoners and no guards were put out. Why should they worry? they must have thought. They were far from the settlements now.

"What they didn't count on was that Sarah had not given up hope. It was now or never, she knew, though escape meant that she would have to abandon the only child she had left."

"Oh no." Tanya closed her eyes. Then she lifted her head and brightened. She knew something about Sarah now and this fact made her glad. Only if her child lived . . .

"There might be a chance for her and her child this

389

way. The decision was hard, but Sarah didn't hesitate. The Indians all seemed to be asleep. Sarah took a long look at the boy; she might never see him again. Then she tucked a robe about him and stole away from the Indian camp. She didn't want to leave a trail so she headed for the creek, wading downstream in the cold water. For over two hours she waded on. Rocks, snags, chill—none of these stopped her. Five miles, that is what she thought she had gone. Then she heard young John calling, "Momma! Momma!" She must have frozen dead in her tracks. This creek circled the camp. Her little son had wakened and missed his mother."

Ashe stopped here and Tanya asked, "Does she go back for her boy? Or does she try to go on to find someone who might try to rescue little John?" Her hand was on Ashe's forearm; she didn't know she was squeezing him slightly.

"For now, Sarah closed her ears to her son's cries."

"Oh . . . poor babe."

"She left the creek that circled the camp and headed downstream. Sarah knew there had to be settlements along the Colorado. She walked all night, kept on in the morning. Her dress was in shreds, and her scratches were bleeding, yet she pressed on, driven by a mother's love." Here Ashe looked at Tanya, smiling, thinking of the day when they would have a son, or a daughter; it didn't matter. "Sarah had to find help for her son. All day she pushed on. At times she paused to call out loudly— but briefly. No one answered her call for help.

"By late afternoon, Sarah saw some cows grazing

by the river. She waited to follow the milk cows home, thinking there would be a pioneer house close by. She knew she was right when she heard a rooster crowing, and it was Jacob Harrell's home to which the cows led her. Harrell took her to the cabin of Reuben Hornsby. There, she was given food and clothing. She was only ten miles from the Indian camp, she learned. Only a short while after Sarah arrived at the Hornsby cabin Captain John Tumlinson and his Texas Rangers appeared. Tumlinson was a hardy frontiersman. He had come from North Carolina and had settled at Columbus, farther down the Colorado. When he was chosen to head the first organized company of Texas Rangers, he recruited sixty men. It was the job of the rangers to protect the settlements against Indian raids and to hold the frontier. The regular troops fought the Mexicans.

"The rangers had been planning to camp that night near the Hornsby cabin, but after listening to Sarah's story, they ate a bite and set out. Reuben Hornsby went along as guide. It was dark when they found what appeared to be the Comanches' trail. They didn't want to lose the trail in the darkness, so they camped, waiting for daylight. At dawn, they followed the trail easily enough, and a few hours before noon they caught up with the Comanches. The warriors were about to break camp on Walnut Creek.

"Tumlinson made ready to attack them from two sides. He led one group of men, while Lieutenant Rogers led another. Their guns spitting fire, the rangers rode into the camp, surprising the Indians.

The Comanches fled, grabbing only their weapons and leaving everything else. Noah Smithwick, one of Tumlinson's men, lost control of his frightened horse and was momentarily carried along with the fleeing savages. But Smithwick jumped off his horse and went after a Comanche who had dodged behind a tree and was trying to shoot him. The ranger fired and the Indian fell. Then Smithwick ran on, reloading his gun, but the Indian Smithwick had shot was not yet dead.

"The prone Indian reloaded too, and fired at Tumlinson. He missed the captain but killed his horse. Another ranger, Conrad Rohrer, crept up and snatched the gun from the wounded Comanche. He used it as a club crushing the Comanche's skull. The other Indians escaped through the cedars. Two Rangers had been wounded, but neither seriously."

When Ashe paused, Tanya immediately asked, "Well, what happened to the baby, little John?"

"He was wrapped in a buffalo robe and tied to a mule. The Comanches had been about to take him to their camp. One of the rangers had thought little John was a Comanche, and he had shot at the baby twice." Ashe heard Tanya let out a gasp. "Twice he had missed his target. He had been about to try for a third time when another ranger, one who had recognized the white boy, knocked the muzzle up and destroyed the aim of the foolish ranger."

"Sarah got her baby back," Tanya said, happily clapping her hands together.

"Yes, my inquisitive love . . . end of story."

Tanya had learned one thing: her husband disliked most Indians. She couldn't say the same.

After all, God had put them on this earth and He must have had a purpose.

She had also learned early in the telling that Sarah had not perished. If she had, how could she have related the story Ashe had just told.

If I ever have a baby girl, Tanya decided, she will be named Sarah . . . Sarah Brandon.

Chapter 29

By the time the month of August rolled around and exhibited its sultriest temper, a new and peaceful truce existed between Willow and Talon. Often, in the early morning or late afternoon when relief could be had from the flaming ball of sun, they could be seen riding out together, both fair haired, lithe of graceful limb, and full of the zest that the young and healthy know—full of happiness too.

Tanya and Ashe had become married lovers and friends. They were often seen together in the stables, checking items that needed to be worked on or mended, and noting which ones needed to be replenished. New saddles, Spanish and Western, had been purchased along with bridles and harnesses and just about everything else a thriving horse ranch required. Ashe usually went to San Antonio for these items. Almost anything useful or luxurious could be purchased in San Antonio or Galveston. Items from Europe or the North, usually sent via New Orleans, were available at high prices, and anyone with money could purchase ice, jewelry, finely made gun drugs, clothing, cosmetics, and good liquors. Obv ously, this trade was limited to a small, affluent clas The farmers and ranchers bought salt, powder, an lead, and sometimes a few yard goods on the side

Texas laws against incorporation of banks kep them out of the state, however, so Ashe used th banking services provided by freighting or mercar tile firms, such as McKinney and Williams i Galveston. This business and others like it hel money on deposit and made occasional loans. Whe hard money was essential, the major medium c exchange was old Spanish or Mexican silver pesos c dollars and their fractions. Very little gold or silve U.S. coinage had penetrated Texas, so it wa customary to smash the image of the King of Spai on the older coins with a hammer, or to deface th Mexican eagle. When Willow had seen Talon an Almanzo doing this she had been shocked, but sh had soon learned that such mutilation in no wa damaged bullion value while it did assuage nationa pride.

Sundance's stock of mustangs grew, and som thoroughbreds had been purchased for breedin purposes, from a prominent Louisiana planter b the name of Tyrone Hunter—a man in his "young seventies. Tyrone, having fathered two handsom strapping lads, Brian Hunter, the eldest, and Beau the youngest. Beau had sown his wild oats and wa looking for a bride, a willing bride; for Beau' reputation as a devil-may-care gambler and a ladie man did not endear him to the mamas of "quality daughters.

Ashe had taken a trip to Louisiana expressly for the purpose of purchasing some fine horseflesh, and there, at Cresthaven, he had found just the "black" beauties he had been seeking.

A dainty, silver-haired woman, still gorgeous in her early sixties, Angeline Hunter had received Ashe into their lovely old plantation home that set perched on a bluff overlooking the Mississippi river. Their sons, of course, were running Cresthaven now and they owned some of the finest thoroughbreds in all of Louisiana.

Almanzo and Talon ran Sundance in Ashe's absence. The handsome Almanzo had become a permanent fixture at Sundance and he treated its mistress with all the respect due a true lady. Almanzo and Talon were not at Sundance every day of the week, however, and when they were not out on the range, they occasionally went to a dance with a few of the other men. Sometimes they would go two hundred miles to attend a big dance that might last three days or a weekend. Willow and Tanya had laughed when Talon had said that they had shuffled and double-shuffled, wired, and cut the pigeon's wing, making the splinters fly. When Willow had asked if she could come along next time, Talon had become very quiet, exchanging glances with Almanzo. "Sure," he'd said, "next time."

Horses were not the only stock roaming the fenced meadows of Sundance. Now there were plenty of cows and even a few prize bulls. In addition there were a hundred plump chickens and several noisy cock roosters. Samson had been longing for a pig, a real live pig or a squiggly piglet, but so far no one from Sundance had been able to locate a little porker, at least not the white and "pink" sort Samson had admired over at the Rankins'.

Willow still visited the hidden room, *her* secret room, naturally only when Ashe was not in residence. And she still thought of the room as hers, solely, her one and only secret—except for what she felt for Talon Clay.

Why not? No one had ever cared about it, or even known of its existence. Still, she wondered if she should have told Ashe about it. She guessed she should have.

Well, there were only some old clothes in there—"pretty" clothes that once had belonged to a very beautiful woman. Willow roamed the halls, thinking, the woman must have been beautiful to have worn such appealing colors and to have had such a figure. Most of the frocks and gowns were designed to fit a body with attractive curves.

Willow smiled. She didn't worry much over her lack of bosoms; she had discovered a few plump powder puffs that did the job nicely.

Having seen the blurred portrait of the golden-haired woman in the locket and having studied her face, Willow knew she could make herself look just like that beauty. Willow meant to keep the locket, because she felt somehow . . . close to the woman pictured in it.

Yet, Willow was feeling especially guilty over keeping the "secret room" all to herself one day when the men had gone on a drive to San Antonio.

She and Samson still slept at the "summer house," as Willow called it, and took their breakfast there, but

he remainder of their days were spent at the main
house with their sister. At times, Samson fell asleep
in one of the bunkhouses, usually Clem's and
Talon's, and she just left him there where she knew
he would be safe. There were plenty of men to watch
over the boy and see that no harm came to him.
Besides, Samson enjoyed being one of the "men"
after having lived with his sisters for such a long
time.

An especially gorgeous turquoise gown now
caught Willow's eye. It was stashed at the bottom of
one of the trunks. The color not being one of
Willow's favorites, she thought instantly of how
wonderful it would look on Tanya. It would suit her
blue eyes and fuller figure.

With a grin Willow thought: Tanya will certainly
be needing no powder puffs!

"What a find!" Willow sat on her haunches in the
secret room, poring over all the feminine items:
froufrous, ribbons, laces, and even a stack of ribbon-
bound love letters, letters written in a various
assortment of scrawls that made Willow think not of
women's neat hands but of men's. This woman must
have known many men.

Willow had discovered the secret room purely by
chance one day when she'd been helping Tanya,
when her sister had first come to clean for Ashe
Brandon. While dusting the huge bookshelves in the
library/office, Willow had lifted a peculiar-looking
book from its slot, only to find that the spot where she
was standing was beginning to revolve; then she
found herself inside a very dark, airless room.
Luckily, when she had searched frantically, she had

discovered the butt of a candle and the means to light it right beside her on a small oak table. *Someone* had done the right thing!

Now the library was Ashe's office—the room with a room in it—where he conducted most if not all of his business transactions and met with his employees, the mustangers and drovers. He employed many Indian mustangers, and Almanzo was second boss in charge of them, for it was his proficient knowledge of mustanging that had brought the whole profitable operation into being at Sundance in the first place.

Instant riches had been Ashe's reward for sinking his last dollars into outfitting the first of their mustangs with leathers and feed, and for providing tons of liniment for the bruises and sprains of beast and man. He had also paid and housed and fed fifteen mustangers and many more drovers, and he had purchased the thoroughbreds. In short, he had turned his pockets inside out.

Naturally Willow knew all this and she realized that Ashe had never given Tanya a sparkling dress like the turquoise one. True, he had brought Tanya some lovely frocks from New Orleans, even some very nice clothes for Willow and Samson, but none of those things could be compared to the turquoise gown.

"*I'll* give it to her!" Willow screwed up her little face then, chiding herself. "Silly, all these things in here belong to Tanya anyhow! She's the mistress of Sundance now. What am I doing hogging all these beautiful things for myself when they don't even belong to me in the first place?"

Willow stuck her chin into the palm of her dainty

hand. "I wonder though if I should tell her about this hidden room? It is mine, *especially* mine. *I* found it."

The ribbons and laces she had lied about, and hopefully Tanya had not questioned Almanzo, her friend the Nightwalker. But Tanya wouldn't question the validity of her story. Might she not, however, offhandedly mention the "gifts" Almanzo had given to Willow?

I have really gotten myself into a sticky nest of lies, Willow thought. She sighed.

"Well, I'd just better tell Tanya about this room," Willow mumbled as she began to stuff the fancy clothes back into the trunk, but for two dresses, one for Tanya and one for herself. She chose the amber gown to go with her golden hair and brown eyes. No one would miss it anyway.

As she pressed the disc that would return her to the office, for one terrible moment Willow's heart caught in her throat when she realized what she had done—or hadn't done. She had plumb forgotten to put her ear to the wall and listen for anyone in the office. It had never occurred to her to decide what she would do if someone was out there, especially Ashe. If he were to tarry overlong in the office someday, she would come close to suffocating in the airless storage space. She could just hear herself choking, gasping for her next breath. She knew that would happen because several times she had had to open and reclose the revolving door just to let some fresh air in, even though she had opened all the windows in the office.

Outside the secret room now, Willow, with her precious bundle under one arm, the two gowns draped over the other, stood looking at the magical bookcase, wondering out loud, "Now, why in the world would anyone ever want to go and stick such a room in a house anyway?"

As Willow walked down the hall, she thought excitedly, What if someone had hidden some money in there . . . or somewhere else in the house? Could there be more secret hiding places?

Willow's eyes enlarged to shiny brown saucers, and her lips pursed into a tempting Cupid's bow. If so, it would be an awful lot of money . . . *Brandon money.*

Tanya swirled in front of the tilting dresser mirror, breathlessly perusing the turquoise gown, then, gathering her glossy hair off her shoulders, she swept it atop her head and pinned it there.

"Oh . . ." Willow said softly. "You're beautiful just like . . ." She took hold of her lower lip in her teeth and looked away from the mirror that had Tanya's reflection in it. Then she went to sit on the edge of the bed.

"Like who?" Tanya was still gazing dreamily at her stunningly transformed reflection.

"Ah . . . like a queen or something." Willow had almost said, just like the woman in the locket. But she kept her secret, even though she uncannily resembled the woman's portrait when she put on the amber gown and swept her long golden tresses atop her head.

Willow *had* told Tanya about the secret room . . . but not the locket, not yet.

"Oh pshaw." Even as she said this Tanya trembled

with anticipation, so eager was she to have Ashe see her in the lovely turquoise gown. She wondered if he would be shocked by so much creamy flesh pressed upward above the lacy décolletage of the bodice . . . or by the faint outline of her nipples against the sheer material. In comparison, she had seemed quite dowdy in all her other dresses. The ones Ashe had brought she treasured; but they, too, would pale in comparison to the turquoise gown. It made her think of a blue-green gossamer mist hovering above water.

"I had Miss Pekoe air it and press it," Willow said of the turquoise gown Tanya had tried on and had been reluctant to take off and put away. "But," Willow went on, "it seems as though it's only been worn once or twice. . . ."

"It must have belonged to Martha Brandon," Tanya said ruminatively. That was plausible, though highly unlikely. However, she had never really known Martha Brandon. At any rate, Tanya didn't dwell long on the identity of the former owner of the dress, even though she was thoroughly mystified as to who she was. At the moment, she was too busy making plans for Ashe's homecoming.

Like a pretty bluish-green flower spreading out, Tanya sat beside her sister on the edge of the bed and said chattily, "A celebration is in order—for just you and me—and Ashe. I'll have Miss Pekoe prepare Ashe's favorite meal, and then"—she paused breathlessly—"we'll spring it on him!"

Willow corrected her. "You mean *you* will!"

Tanya laughed. "Coward."

"When it comes to Ashe? Yes!"

Willow was suddenly wishing she could disappear

for two weeks after the telling because she didn't relish the idea of being present when Ashe began his interrogation. How he could interrogate!

Looking up at her sister with beseeching eyes, Willow said, "You tell Ashe that I found the secret room and . . . and you can tell me about it the next day."

"Why, Willow," Tanya said with a shake of her head, "why wouldn't you want to tell Ashe yourself? You discovered the room, not me."

Tanya's eyes narrowed suspiciously as Willow continued to weave her fingers together in her lap. "Willow, ah, tell me something. When *did* you first discover the secret room? Wait." She held up her hand. "Before you answer that, tell me something else. Where did you say you got all those ribbons and laces? Was it really Nightwalker, I mean Almanzo, who gave those things to you right before the fandango? I mean . . . how could he have. Almanzo was planning to get married to . . . Oh, I've forgotten her name."

"Ellita Tomás."

Tanya suddenly realized that she had been unconsciously trying to forget everything that had to do with that day, even though that was the night she had become Ashe's bride. There were some parts of it, naturally, that she could never forget . . . like Ashe's tender loving.

"I . . . I lied, Tanya," Willow blurted out.

"What? Whyever did you do that?"

"Well, I wanted to keep the hidden room a secret, you see. It was my own discovery—something that seemed to belong to me alone. I'd never had anything that was just mine before. We've always had to share everything at the little house."

Embarrassed now, Willow ducked her fair head, wishing she hadn't revealed her true thoughts.

"I see, and I understand," Tanya said. "You had to share everything with Samson, even your bedroom." She smoothed back the blond hair from Willow's sad little face. "You never had anything to yourself—not even time."

"I don't like to always share," Willow confessed. "I want things of my own, Tanya."

Willow thought about the times she had seen Talon and Hester together. She didn't want to share her man either. That was why she knew there could never be a life for her and Talon. She wouldn't want to have another woman take a part of him, and it was wrong as well. She and Talon had smiled and joked together lately; they had even begun to be able to touch without getting frustrated or angry with each other. She wanted to keep it that way. As Talon had said—friends. For now anyway. She didn't know what she was going to do later.

"But you have your own room now." Tanya smiled. "You even have a very nice room here too, anytime you want."

"I know," Willow said, feeling guilty. "You've changed everything for me, Sis. What am I going to do now, though? I've kept the secret room to myself and I'm ashamed. Especially now, now that you tell me there's money hidden in there somewhere." She looked over to the cabinet on a stand, not paying much attention to the antique, but staring at the Oriental scene painted in gold on the lacquer box.

"Tanya, please help me? I've been bad . . . and I don't know how anyone could want to love me!" She hung her head dejectedly and felt tears sting her eyelids. Although they wanted to be freed, she clung tenaciously to the watery pearls.

"Oh, sweetheart." Tanya pulled her younger sister into her arms and hugged her tightly to her bosom. "I love you, no matter what. Don't worry, Willow, your secret is safe with me. Ashe will think"—here she sighed regrettably—"he will be *led* to think that you have only just discovered the room. He'll be so happy to get the money that he won't think of anything else."

Even as she said this and continued to hug Willow, Tanya drew her brow together in a worried frown.

Chapter 30

The next week was a flurry of activity in preparation for Ashe's homecoming. Tanya spent two days diligently making certain that all essentials were in order. Miss Pekoe was busily preparing Ashe's favorite meal: roast beef, tiny Irish potatoes in cream sauce, black-eyed peas, greens and crusty raisin and pecan pie.

For the very first time in her life, Tanya found out what it was like to have a splitting headache. Besides that, she hadn't felt well on several mornings. It must be the excitement, she told herself each time, and let it go at that.

The house was neat and tidy as a pin, its furniture and floors polished to a mirrorlike sheen, its windows thrown open wide to allow the sweet-scented breezes into the rooms. Tanya was so excited she couldn't sit still for one minute; she, too, was ready to greet her husband with open arms. She couldn't wait to tell of the discovery of the secret room where the money was supposed to be hidden.

Of course, Tanya hadn't planned to be wearing the lovely turquoise dress when Ashe returned; she'd planned to put it on later, after Ashe had relaxed a bit and had washed up. As it happened, however, Ashe returned late on the day the drovers had said he would be arriving. The drovers themselves had come on ahead and were already ensconced in the bunkhouses when Ashe, Almanzo, and Talon arrived at Sundance.

The moon seemed very far away and small by the time Ashe left the water shed after washing up. He let himself in the back door. Awash with desire, he was eager to be with his wife once again, to taste her honeyed lips, to feel her arms about his neck, to love her until they were both thoroughly satiated.

Walking along the hall with a towel draped over his glistening naked shoulder, Ashe was about to pass the dining room, thinking his wife awaited him upstairs, when he did a double take. Inclining his head slightly, he noticed that the room was lit by candlelight.

Thinking that Tanya might be waiting for him in the dining room, Ashe felt his body begin to respond, and a passionate fire lit his eyes so eager was he to feast them upon her loveliness. He had gone weeks without her and now craved her. An undeniable, raw hunger coursed through him.

"Tanya?" he called softly into the room, his voice unconsciously sensuous, his nankeen breeches already reaching out to his wife. "What's this?" He spied the covered food laid out on the table, smelled the delicious aromas of his favorite meal, saw a freshly baked pie resting on the sideboard.

A shadowy figure, female, was just rising from a small, cushioned chair in the corner. But this was not Tanya. Then who? . . .

"Mistah Brandon."

Miss Pekoe rubbed her bleary eyes as she came into the frail circle of light cast by the sputtering candles. "That you?" The black woman beamed him a smile, then said, "'Course it is."

"What is all this?" Ashe swept an arm wide when he saw Miss Pekoe's black face shining in the candlelight.

"Oh, Mistah Brandon. The missus done went to bed already. She was waitin' so long for you, but she went to bed 'bout an hour ago." She rubbed her eyes again, saying, "I *think* it was an hour ago anyway." Now she blinked her eyes and stared about the room, adding, "Maybe longer by the looks of dem candles. I tole her I'd be waitin' to see if you be comin' home, 'cause she was so plumb tuckered out from ever'thing."

Fastening his eyes directly on hers, he asked, "What do you mean . . . everything?"

"She wanted this to be a special occasion, Mistuh Brandon." Since Miss Pekoe didn't know exactly what that "special" celebration entailed, she could only relate what she did know of what had been going on in Ashe Brandon's absence. "The missus said it was a 'special' day, that's all."

"Did she say why?" He was more curious now, more than before.

"Nope. She jest been so excited over something, that's all. She gots herself a pretty new dress, and if she didn't look like somepin! Mistah Brandon, she

409

was like a big doll all dressed up. Her and that prett
li'l sister of hers, they been up to something all wee
long."

"Where is Willow now?"

"Oh, she's at the li'l house, I would suppose. Sh
been at the school all day with that preacher man, s
she ain't been around much today." Miss Peko
shook her kerchiefed head and rattled on. "That li'
gal sure be a busy one. Uh-huh! Goin' in and out o
your office all the time."

"My office?"

"Yep. Saw her goin' into that funny li'l room
behind the bookshelves all week long. She sho been a
busy mite, Lawsy." Miss Pekoe watched as Ash
Brandon went stone-cold still. "Mistah Brandon
you know what li'l room I'se talking about, don'
you?"

"I have an idea," Ashe said thoughtfully, "now."

"Oooh, Mistah Brandon!" Miss Pekoe's eyes took
on the look of two plumped-up black raisins. "You
didn't know about the secret room?" She watched
her throat all choked up, as he shook his head very
slowly. "I sho did go and stick my big old foot in i
this time."

Maybe this was about the secret the missus wa
going to reveal, Miss Pekoe thought silently, some
thing to do with that strange old wall that moved
Miss Pekoe would never know what a drastic mistak
she'd made by not informing the mister that thi
could very well be the case, that there was a "secre
room" and there was something very importan
about it. Lawsy, she should have gone on to say a
much, but Ashe Brandon was staring at her as if he

410

were about to throttle her . . . or someone else.

"Go on, Miss Pekoe," Ashe told her, "this is getting mighty interesting."

"I'm sho ashamed for being so nosy, Mistah Brandon, but I was meaning to be dustin' your office when I saw Miss Willow in there before me. She was standin' afore the bookcase and I was just gonna say somepin to let her know I was there, but she jest went *Poof!* and disappeared right inside that old bookcase!"

"Miss Pekoe." Ashe heaved an impatient sigh. "How long has this been going on?"

"Ever since I come here, Mistah Brandon." Miss Pekoe looked as if she was about to burst into tears.

"Does my wife know about this . . . this secret room?"

"Why, I do think so, but I ain't never seen her goin' in there. Li'l Willow give her a pretty blue dress, though, the one the missus was wearin' tonight for your homecoming. She looked mighty pretty all done up. Oh, I even helped her fix her hair real fancy, to go with that dress, Mistah Brandon. I know jest how to do up a lady's hair real fine, yessir!"

"Never mind the dress or her hair, Miss Pekoe. I don't want to hear about either of them—or about her."

As she peered closer at the mister, Miss Pekoe was afraid she didn't like what she was seeing in his cold, brittle eyes. She never had seen him look so steamed up, like he was about to do someone in. She was beginning to wonder about the man she worked for. He was strange at times, like something bad was eating away at him. Why he and the missus had been

411

locked up in their bedroom together when that shot had been fired was still an unsolved mystery to her.

"You ain't angry with the missus, are you?" she asked him, her voice trembling. "You ain't gonna shoot up some more pretty vases or furniture, are you, Mistah Brandon?"

"You can go now, Miss Pekoe."

"Yessuh! But what about all this here food? Should I take it out to the kitchen and see if I can save—"

"I don't give a damn what you do with it, Miss Pekoe. For all I care, you can feed it to the dogs!"

With those harshly cross words resounding in the now-silent room, Ashe strode out the door, leaving Miss Pekoe to gape at his ramrod-straight back. Then, letting her eyes take in the exhausting meal that had taken her all afternoon to prepare, one that would have fed a small army instead of just two people, Miss Pekoe said, as if the mister were still beside her, "But, Mistah Brandon, we ain't got no dogs!"

Seated in his office broodingly nursing a brisk shot of brandy, his long legs stretched out along the top of his massive desk, Ashe leaned back in his black leather chair. His mood was darker than the midnight sky outside.

He was staring across the wood floor at the bookcase. He had discovered not half an hour ago, after some searching and poking about, that it *moved*.

412

How ingenious of his father, Ashe was thinking. No house should be without one.

The secret room ... The only item of interest missing now was the money, his father's legacy to his sons. It could have remained there forever, with no one finding it, which brought him to the question of what his father had been thinking when he'd hidden it there? Why the hide-and-seek games? Was there a reason for such secrecy? Garnet? Could she have been trying to get the money so she could move on to another place, another man? Yes, he thought this was the way it must have been.

His eyes gleamed ominously. But the money wasn't there, of course, and he knew who had gotten to it before him, didn't he?

Who else, but his charmingly deceitful wife ... and his imp of a sister-in-law Willow. Both of them just like their mother, beautiful, charming in an earthy sort of way ... and expert at duplicity!

A very disturbing thought kept reverberating in his brain, and his face hardening to the likeness of leather, Ashe began to ponder the question of how long Tanya had been holding out on him. Probably since she had first "cleaned up" his house, he decided.

No wonder Tanya had been so eager to become his bride. Who could want for more? A pocketful of money, no longer hidden in the secret room, and a cozy house to go along with it—not to mention a husband who had been absent from the place most of the time, and one who would no doubt get himself killed in his dangerous line of business!

413

What an unpleasant surprise it must have been for Tanya to learn that he was no longer going to be a ranger, that he planned to settle down and raise a family, do some ranching and breed horses.

Unwinding his long legs and letting one down to the floor, Ashe smiled nastily to himself while he sipped his brandy. *So*, he thought, she has already gone and bought herself some fancy dresses in my absence, with my money—money we should have shared as man and wife.

Ashe smirked into his near-empty glass. What a lie that was, telling Miss Pekoe that Willow had given her a new dress. Willow could never afford such a luxury, not for herself, not for anyone else. She made very little at schoolteaching.

Just what had Tanya been planning to tell him after going to all the trouble of cleaning the house until it was sparkling and fit for a party? Did she intend to let him know that she and her chiseling little sister had *just* discovered the secret room? Of course. And then she was going to tell him that she had found the money—only he was never going to see the full amount!

Ashe lowered his other leg. Then he drank some more, his glower becoming ever darker. She'd made a sucker out of him. Damn women! Why did all the beautiful women have to be the same?

Pete Brandon's foremost passion in life had been collecting priceless antiques at New Orlean's auctions. From where she sat curled in a deep-cushioned chair, Tanya now looked over at one of them, admiring it as she had when she'd first laid eyes on it, the lacquered Oriental cabinet on a stand.

Tanya had readied herself for bed, removing the turquoise dress reluctantly and draping it carefully over a chair. She had planned to don it swiftly when she heard Ashe's footsteps in the hall, but then she had decided that no one could dress so fast. She had chided her foolishness.

She curled up in the chair, however, just in case Ashe did come home. If he did show up before she climbed into bed, he could wake her and they would go down for a midnight snack . . . after they had spent some time alone together up here. As she let her glance slide over to the bed, Tanya's eyes misted with desire and her heart skipped a beat.

Resting her head against the soft cushion, Tanya went back to studying the Oriental table. Long ago she had decided that the antique must date back to the seventeenth century. Over the ground color of black, a Japanese scene had been painted in gold. The lacquer cabinet was mounted on a stand of distinctly European flavor, and it was fitted with a pair of doors that concealed a multitude of small drawers set within. The drawers, Tanya thought, must have been intended to contain small and precious objects. Tanya owned no small pieces of jewelry—no jewelry at all, for that matter—yet she'd had a glorious time with the cabinet anyhow, gathering all the little, homeless objects from the house and allocating a drawer to this or that.

Suddenly she was reminded that she had better put

away the tiny seed-pearl button that had come loose when she'd removed the turquoise dress earlier that evening. Otherwise, she just might lose it. She left her comfortable chair and went to fetch the button.

Tanya had opened and closed the little drawers so many times that now, when she pulled one out, the little teardrop knob came off and there was no way to open the drawer so she could put the button inside. All the other drawers were full.

"There must be a way to open it." She said aloud. She tried prying it open with her fingernails, but the drawer was just too flush against the sides to budge even a hair. Then, as she was poking about here and there, Tanya discovered the secret compartment.

"What is this?" she asked herself, her wonderment growing. "Another of Pete Brandon's secrets?"

Having a miniature "front door" with its own pilasters and pediment, the small compartment at the center was a perfect hiding place for several priceless necklaces . . . or maybe even . . .

"And what is this?" Tanya asked the cabinet as if it were a human being proffering her the secrets of its heart. "Oh . . ." Her hand came into contact with a very thick wad of paper . . . legal tender—money. Lots of it!

"Brandon's fortune," she said with a breathless catch in her voice.

Just as she was gaping down at the pile of notes in her hands, for the first time in her life aware that a momentary greed had washed over her, Tanya heard footsteps stop right outside her door. Her head jerked up and tiny shock waves danced along her nerves. Oh no, no, *no!*

"*Ashe*," was all Tanya got out when the door swung inward. She looked guilty, consumed with blame, and her face turned a flaming rose color. "I ... I ..."

Like a sharp blade cutting her deep, Ashe's voice sliced into her, "Caught in the act of counting all your money, h'm?"

Chapter 31

"Ashe, it— Oh God it's not what you think . . . *really*!"

"Really," he echoed mockingly, his eyebrows lifted cynically. He gave a low, angry laugh, and asked, "Why didn't you ask me first what I *was* thinking? Maybe I thought that you suddenly found that . . ."

"It's true! I did suddenly find this." Feebly she waved the bank notes before his face. "Just now," she added desperately.

"Of course." He shook his head and glared at her, but his gaze remained fixed on her soft mouth. Just looking at her in her present state of near undress, her robe gaping in a vee down her chest, passionate desire surged through him. Nevertheless he went on, "Do you really expect me to believe that? Give me more credit than that, Tanya. Please. I'm not that stupid."

"That's right," she cheerfully replied, tossing her head, "you were a Texas Ranger and they are supposed to be *the most* intelligent men in *all* of Texas." Making circles in the air, she added, "In the whole South, in fact. *Supposed* to be . . ." She let the words hang.

As if he hadn't heard anything she'd said, Ashe strode over to the chair that had the turquoise dress draped over it. "Tanya," he said, clicking his tongue, "shame on you, couldn't you have hung up your pretty new dress instead of laying it over a chair like a useless rag?"

Tanya stood very still, dismay and uncertainty filling her as she noticed his implacable features. He wouldn't give an inch, would he? He would believe only what he wanted to believe, and until he saw fit to believe otherwise, he would be like a stone god on a pedestal. *Damn* him! she thought frustratedly.

Ashe looked over at her. She still clutched the notes in her outstretched palms. "Why should you care, right?" he went on cruelly. "You'll get plenty more pretty dresses anyway." He shrugged laconically. "What does one measly dress matter when you can buy out the whole damn store with two fingers of what you have there in your hands? Isn't that so?"

An ache began in the region of Tanya's heart, but she was determined to see this out to the end. "I haven't *bought* this dress. I happened to have gotten it from—" She bit off the next words. What was the use? He wasn't listening to her. He was only believing what he wanted to.

Tossing the lovely dress carelessly back on the chair, Ashe walked slowly toward her, each step a threat. Tanya stood her ground, but she was utterly bewildered by his savagely bitter attitude toward her.

She had to force herself to breathe normally as he continued to approach and fastened his eyes directly on hers. All she could think of while staring at his bare chest was how it felt rubbing against her raised nipples. The matt of coarse blond hair invariably spread wildfire in her belly. Although he hadn't touched her, already Tanya's breasts ached and her lips throbbed.

Ashe walked over to her and never once did his smoldering eyes waver from the confounded look on her face. But for a few loose coils at her cheeks, her hair was still swept elegantly atop her beautifully shaped head, in the fashion that the black woman's hands had dexterously created. For just a passing moment it occurred to Ashe that Tanya looked rather regal, like some queen in the springtime of her youth. Her cheeks were aglow, her eyes were bright as precious gems, and her lips were like warmed burgundy wine. He would love to sink his fingers into her flaming red hair, and his lips into . . .

Panther-quick, he grasped her chin and, silken malice flowing from his fingertips, turned her face his way and that. Unthinkingly, he said, "I would rather die than be refused this night with you." Realizing what he had just said, Ashe brought his face close to hers, his nose pressing against hers and his lips merely brushing her mouth. Pushing away from her, he amended his words harshly. "So, I will have to die. . . ." A sharp pain stabbed his chest as he looked down at the money—nothing but paper—clutched in her hands.

"Ashe, please. You don't understand," Tanya said brokenly. She wished he would stop staring at her so hatefully. She wanted him to take her in his arm and make wild, passionate love to her. The long endured pang of suppressed passion was now making itself felt as, standing so near Ashe, an exquisite excitement began to course through her.

In a tight voice, Ashe said, "It seems we thrive on misunderstandings, Tanya."

"I hate that word," she said in a tone that merely simmered while she gesticulated with the piles of notes clenched in her tight fists. "But you're wrong, Ashe. I don't thrive on misunderstandings. *You* do . . . and on displaced trust!"

His face went white and a shuttered look closed over his darkened hazel eyes.

Stepping up to him and thrusting the notes at his chest, she said in a raised voice, "Here! This—this *pile* belongs to you. I don't want to have anything to do with it. It's your money—Brandon money."

Taking the notes, Ashe watched her dully as she headed for the door, then paused. "You don't have to gawk at me like that. I'm not leaving you, Brandon. You're too good a man for that. Besides, I kind of like you when you're sober and when you're much calmer than you are now. I'll . . . I'll just take the room next door, *her* room, and wait until you come to your senses. I know there's a man in you somewhere, Ashe, one that will chase that frightened little boy out of you and drive that cursed ghost from this house!"

Shooting forward and looking right into her face, Ashe said stonily, "Don't ever say those things to me again, hear?" His eyes seemed to explode and emit green smoke.

"Say what things, Ashe? The truth hurts?"

"You're crazy, just like your mother was, you know that?"

Tanya, standing her ground like a spitting tigress before a ferocious lion, glared back at her husband, and trying to sound calm, she said, "You're plagued by the ghost of my mother. That's too bad. Wake up, Ashe, or tomorrow will be too late and you *will* find me gone when the morning sun shines in your face."

"You won't leave Sundance," he returned easily and his lips curled.

"No," she said, "I'll leave *you*."

With that, Tanya went out and Ashe stood there, feeling a helpless rage wash over him as he stared at the closed door; then his eyes dropped to the notes he clutched in his bunched fists. The money . . . suddenly it seemed meaningless to him.

Returning the notes to the concealed drawer Ashe groaned in disgust. "I don't believe this," he said, staring at the hidden compartment. "Sundance should have been named Dark Shadows . . . or something close to that." He cursed the drawer and closed it.

Ashe was almost tempted to burn the house down and start all over again with a brand-new building that had no secrets—and *no* ghosts. Skeletons in the closet . . . how many more were there?

Slumping into the nearest chair, the one that Tanya had vacated not long ago, he found that he could still detect her sweet scent. It reminded him of misty roses. He could almost taste and feel her. . . .

Leaning back and staring at the ceiling, Ashe was painfully reminded of how much he had desired Tanya this night, and on many prior nights too. He

had begun to think of raising a family. He wante
children, sons to carry on his name and keep up th
Sundance property; and he wanted sons with Tany
for no other woman could give them to him.

By God, what foul things had caused him to be s
distrusting of women? If he delved deeply into th
past what would he find? Perhaps Garnet was not th
only woman who had disappointed him. H
mother? . . . Was that why he couldn't trust? He
had no problem with Larrisa, but then he hadn
been in love with Larrisa. She had signified nothir
but a good time.

Love? How passionately attached to Tanya am
really? he asked himself. He had believed himself
be in love with her—so in love that it hurt sometime
And he had wanted their love to be perfect, flawle
that nothing in the world could destroy it. He want
nothing to come between him and the woman h
loved. Not even—now here was the painful que
tion—distrust?

What a fool I am, Ashe thought.

He went back to reflecting on the past and on h
mother, Martha. How well had he really known he
She had seemed to be distant, cool, ethereal, remot
Almost like—he hated to think it—almost like a
Indian squaw.

Had Martha really been captured by those Indian
Had they been Comanches, or some other tribe, dow
from the north to hunt, that seized her. And had sl
been mistreated, or was she merely sunburned? H
mind had wanted to believe she'd been mistreate
but when he really thought about it, her bruis
hadn't appeared until she'd been home for two

424

three days. Did he really know the answers to any of these questions?

And why, Ashe wondered, did he have such a bitter hatred of all Indians? He'd even had a difficult time learning to trust Almanzo, and he didn't fully trust him yet.

Maybe all along he'd been kidding himself and Martha had been no nearer perfection than Garnet had been. Faithfulness, that was what it was all about. Why did it mean so damn much to him?

How the hell was he going to learn to trust Tanya when tonight, for instance, she had been holding the stash, the evidence of her betrayal right in her hands. How was he going to cope with the thought that his wife had been holding out on him?

Then Ashe sought sleep, tossing and turning restlessly, his cheeks and body hotly flushed as he thought of the woman in the other room, the woman who carried his name but not his heart.

In the room across the hall, the bedroom that Ashe hated because it had been Garnet's, Tanya was having similar thoughts, only of a slightly different nature.

In the freshly made bed, Tanya turned yet again in sleeplessness. Her worries, like pesky insects, would not give her one moment's rest but continued to sting and nibble at her brain. Worry, the kind that made the flesh prickle and itch all over, it could drive a person insane.

Insane, that was the key word. Tanya was beginning to suspect that the man she loved and had married was a little crazy. Maybe *quite* insane. He had really frightened her tonight, as he had that other time when he'd pulled out his Colt and shot that vase apart in her hands. He could have blown her hand off . . . if he'd been less accurate in his aim. Now, as she had then, Tanya felt that Ashe would never miss when he fired a gun.

Ashe was a perfect shot—she smiled slightly—and a *very* perfect lover. Though she had no one else to compare to Ashe, Tanya knew that her husband could never be faulted for his lovemaking; in fact, she would wager he was better than most men in that area.

Yet, it bothered her that he didn't believe her when she told him the truth. Where was all the trust that was supposed to go along with marriage? Dear God, had he only married her to get even with a ghost? That was really sick, and that was why he was frightening her lately!

At this point it would be best for her to go away. Maybe she would, if she gathered enough courage to do so. She was truly afraid to stay in this house much longer with a madman—a madman she loved. How strange life is, she thought. There was no telling what he would do next or what he would be accusing her of tomorrow or next week. Maybe a month would pass before he turned crazy again.

She was not a quitter, no, never that, so she desperately tried to pinpoint the source of her problem. Not *her* problem, but Ashe's. Ashe has a serious problem concerning my mother, she told herself. But she had to think of someway to resolve it; she owed herself that much, and Ashe too.

Tanya glimpsed the walls surrounding her moon-it bed as she tucked her chin beneath the sheet. A ;host was nothing . . . but a memory . . . the aura a leceased person might have left behind.

Mama . . . if you are here . . . go away! Ashe is my usband and he belongs to the living . . . to me!

Chapter 32

Sometime in the middle of the night, in the darkest hours, Tanya awoke and reached to the other side of the bed. She could have sworn she was not in bed alone, that Ashe was right here, reaching out to caress her shoulder.

But it was not so. She was alone, very much alone. Only the sounds of nocturnal creatures came to her through the window where the curtains stirred restively. It was going to rain soon. She could smell it, and she could hear a distant low rumble of thunder.

Lying awake, unable to sleep, Tanya's hearing was attuned to the orchestration of the crickets and to the lonesome hooting of a nearby barn owl. She could hear everything, every slow, tiny sound a house made in the night, the creaking of a floorboard as the house shifted. Like a human, Tanya thought, the house moves restively when it should be sound asleep like its inhabitants. What a story a house could tell if it could talk. . . .

Suddenly Tanya came alert and pushed herself slowly to her elbows. There had been a sound, as if someone were pausing outside her door. No. She had *felt* that there was someone outside her door. Her heartbeat picked up and there was a tumultuous throbbing in her chest. *Ashe!"*

She knew it was Ashe. She could *feel* that it was Ashe. He was coming to her.

While he was walking ever so quietly across the room to her bed, Tanya's every nerve and fiber reached out to welcome him into her arms. "I dreamed that you were here with me," she softly said as he came to sit on the edge of her bed.

"And so, Lady Red, I am."

"You smell like brandy."

He bent closer to nuzzle her ear, murmuring, "And you smell like love." Groaning thickly in his throat, he said, "I want you bad."

The moonlight that had sent shafts of silver spilling through the windows was now blotted out as the rains came. Ashe left the bed for a minute, to close the windows. After doing so, he turned, stood for a moment with his silhouette illuminated by the sudden flash of lightning, and then he came to her.

Tanya watched as, beside the bed, Ashe stripped himself of his lawn shirt and cream-colored breeches, only able to see him when the soft lightning illuminated the room. When he joined her in the bed she wound her slim arms about his neck and thrust her hips close to the muscled hardness of his body while he cupped the gentle curve of her buttocks. His lips traveled in feathery kisses across her cheek, then across the bridge of her nose to the other side of her

430

face where he began his descent, to her chin, to the hollow of her throat. There was no need for words. It was better this way, when there were fewer words spoken.

When he took her taut nipple between his teeth, Tanya murmured softly and clutched at strands of his tawny hair. Moistening one nipple he moved on to the next, his lips gently mouthing and rolling the nub between his teeth until that rosy crest also stood hard and erect. Then he shifted, palming her rib cage and then her soft, downy belly, lower and lower, all the while taking delight in her soft moanings and in the hips arching to meet his hand.

His touch was wildly sweet and soon all of Tanya's sensations were blended in a thrilling excitement. Kissing her lips, he rubbed her between her legs, and when his fingers entered and began to move rhythmically, she made the first real audible sound, a tiny gasp which she couldn't hold back. Tanya was on fire now. There was a hollow feeling inside her which needed to be filled, and only Ashe could fill it.

The thunder continued to mutter around them, its loud rumbles vibrating the walls of the house, the windows, and blending with the love sounds that were coming from both their throats. In their sweetly sensuous lust Ashe all but lost his senses. He opened his lips over Tanya's, thrusting in a tiny play of love inside her mouth. Hot and hard, his manhood jutted against the softest part of her thighs demanding entry, and when he couldn't stand to wait any longer, he nudged her thighs apart, satisfied that her most tender parts were moist and properly readied for him. Now he plunged, slowed and halted, listening, delighting in her cry of ecstasy as his own heart leaped to his throat at hearing her receive him so joyously.

Ashe deliberately held back, sinking himself shaft deep and halting all motion. He sought her eyes in the flashes of lightning, seeing her expression wide and questioning. There was something else there too. Was it fear? A bittersweet stinging memory came to him, but he thrust it aside. This was Tanya, his wife, the woman he loved. Then why couldn't he tell her so? Why did the hated memory of that other woman have to come between them again. He shook his head to clear it.

"Ashe?" Tanya questioned breathlessly. "What is it?"

"Nothing, Tanya. Just let me love you."

That unquenchable hunger seized them once again and Ashe lifted himself higher, taking her hips with him as her tightness closed around his shaft; then he plunged over and over. When the slide of their bodies came easier for her and his hugeness stretched her to accommodate him, Tanya met every wonderfully aching thrust, arching her back, softly raking her nails down his back. Almost at the last, Ashe changed position. While she cried out in surprise, fearing that he was leaving her for good, leaving her achingly unsatisfied, Ashe rolled her over and pulled her up against his washboard-hard belly. Then he reentered the throbbing spot he had quit only moments before, lifting her higher, higher than she had ever gone before with him.

No longer did Ashe shock her. Tanya splayed her hands on the bed, her body rocking slightly forward with the slamming force behind her that was driving her to ecstatic heights she'd never before reached. She knew lust then, in its purest form, the wonderful beauty of sexual love between husband and wife, its million-faceted gems shining forth in the darkest, most blissful hours before dawn.

"Tanya!"

She heard his deep cry—the sound of rocks rent asunder—and a groaning husky sound, felt the hot moist thrusting, wrenching, and they mounted the crest together then.

The thunder and lightning, the soft rain, all had ceased. Withdrawing, Ashe rolled to his side pulling Tanya along with him, caressing her in the golden afterglow of their splendid lovemaking. They lay still, listening to the sullen gurgle of the rain being sucked from the eaves by the softest of night winds. The songbird came out, the most mournful of night birds, pealing its plaintive, lonely cry. They held each other for a long time, silently, fanning the glowing embers of ecstasy until nothing remained but the stark white ashes of reality. Tanya slept.

The twilight of dawn played from the windows, purple and forlorn, like dancing gray ghosts in the predawn gloom of the house. Ashe turned at the door before going out, looking back at Tanya. He smiled a little wistfully. Then he went to his room to watch the red sun at its grand and blazing task of rising.

Keeping busy, Tanya discovered, was an absolutely essential remedy for worried reflection and frustration. Ashe was forever going. He was building an outside staircase at the back of the house, in the West Indies' style, and planning a loggia to be added later on.

Now, taking a break from baking pies—pecan pies which she prefered to bake herself—and letting them cool on the windowsill, Tanya walked the gallery, the overhanging roof sheltering her from the late summer sun.

Try as she might, Tanya could not understand what prompted Ashe to remain so cool and remote to her during the day yet to come to her at night as a wonderful, soul-wrenching lover. He didn't seek her out during the day, not for conversation, not for a piece of pie—Miss Pekoe could just as well cut him one—not for anything.

"Tanya?" Willow came from inside the house onto the gallery. She was wearing a lovely rose poplin dress, one she had made, with Tanya's help, from some material that Talon had given her as a gift. There had even been enough left over for Tanya to make a skirt to go with the white blouse Ashe had gotten her from a Spanish woman down in San Antonio.

"What is it?" Tanya studied her sister, noting her crestfallen look.

"I've gotten it."

Tanya's eyebrows lifted. "Gotten *it?*" she said. Then it dawned on her just what Willow meant. "Well, hallelujah! is all I can say to that. But why do you look so unhappy then? You should be glad that monster didn't get you with child." She brushed back the luxurious wave that always drifted over Willow's right eye. "Are you having trouble at school? Ah."

434

Tanya tapped her chin. "Not getting along with Talon Clay? No? That's not it?"

"Well . . . part of it. You see, I wanted to make Talon fall in love with me and marry me."

"Willow, were you thinking about this even though you might have been pregnant?"

"Yes! Why not? I love Talon and he loves me."

"Oh, I see." Tanya sat on a white wicker chair, looking down over the grounds of Sundance from the gallery. "It's wonderful that Talon loves you. You must be very happy."

"Yes." Willow said, her chin sagging. "It's wonderful, but he's never said so."

"Oh. Talon loves you, but he has never . . . told you this?"

"I *know* he loves me. He just doesn't know it yet."

"Willow," Tanya began, a serious note in her voice now. "Sit down here, beside me. I've a story to tell you . . . about Talon and Ashe."

"What is it?"

"I think it's time you knew who Garnet Haywood Brandon was."

"Garnet?" Willow canted her head, causing the golden wave to fall over her eye again and make her look sweetly seductive. She gave her glorious head a shake, and the hair fell back behind her ear. "Did she live here? Is she the lady who owned all those fancy clothes in the secret room?"

"Yes. By the way, Ashe has taken the clothes, all of Garnet's clothes, and burned them."

Her eyes darkening, Willow snapped, "What for? They were so beautiful." She lowered her eyes, not letting her sister see the guilt that was trapped in

435

them. The amber gown was her own, she was neve[r] going to let anyone get that from her! Not the gown, not the little tinted portrait in the locket.

"Ashe didn't like her." Tanya looked away, to th[e] lush green limbs of the cottonwoods and oaks. "Neither did Talon Clay. But that was not always th[e] case."

Curious now, Willow asked out loud, "They like[d] her . . . a long time ago?" She watched her sister no[d] that this was so. "Who was she?"

"She was no relation to the Brandon's. Actually she was Pete Brandon's second wife, though I rathe[r] doubt he ever really loved her. I think he was madl[y] in love with his first wife, Martha. But I have [a] feeling, a very strong feeling, that Martha did no[t] return that love."

"Sure," Willow said. "Otherwise, why would [a] man hide everything? I don't think he truste[d] women." She looked hard at her sister's poignan[t] expression. "You don't think Ashe and Talon trus[t] women either, do you?"

"Ashe can be helped, Willow. But there is no hel[p] for Talon Clay. And that is why I think you'd bette[r] steer clear of him—I mean as far as hoping to hav[e] Talon as a husband someday. He is very bitter, ver[y] hurt, and the hate in him runs deep. You don't kno[w] how deep."

"Tell me, Tanya, tell me what this Garnet did t[o] him. She was bad, wasn't she?"

"Y-Yes. You see, what I believe is . . . Ashe has no[t] been with Garnet, otherwise he would have tol[d] me—at least I think he would have. But you see, h[e] has told me that Talon was with Garnet often. D[o] you understand what I'm saying, Willow?"

Biting the knuckle of her forefinger, Willow answered, "Yes, I understand. She was his stepmother."

"That's right. But"—Tanya tried to go on, but all she could say was—"he was also very much in love with her. She was his *first* love, you see. For Talon Clay, there can never be another. She totally destroyed him for any other woman, but you see, I know there is hope for Ashe. He was never involved with her as Talon was, not as thoroughly, not physically. She ruined that little boy."

Willow stared off into the distance, thinking, He loved her. If he loved her . . . her thoughts trailed inwardly, where they were safe, where she could think them out secretly. *If Talon loved her, and I look so much like Garnet, wouldn't he fall in love with me too?*

"Willow? What are you thinking?"

"Oh . . ." Her eyes darkened to bittersweet brown. "I hate her, Tanya, *hate* her!" Willow rose from the chair, hissing as she clung to the arm of it, "Don't ever tell me about her again. I hate her! *Never!*"

Oh, Lord, what have I done? Tanya watched the rose poplin of Willow's skirts as she whirled and dashed into the house. Dear God, why couldn't I tell her? Why am I such a coward? Now it is too late, she thought. Now it would be impossible to tell Willow who the woman had really been. How could she have known how deeply Willow's love for Talon Clay ran? If she had known, she would never have said what she had this afternoon.

After that day there was a noticeable change in

Willow. She seemed to grow up overnight, and Tanya had a feeling that her sister would no longer say anything silly, would never again "tell" on Samson, and would never chase after Talon Clay again. On the last surmise she was not to know how very mistaken she had been until much later, when it was too late to remedy the damaging situation.

A week passed, and then another. Ashe was hardly ever at Sundance anymore, and when he was, he buried himself amid mountains of work in his office, built this or that to add to the house, or rode out to repair fences with his hands. He had purchased more cattle, and they were growing fat on the lush green grass. The back stairs had been completed, and sometimes at night, when sleep was hard in coming, Tanya would sit on the top stair and watch the stars and moon come out, her senses filled with the night smells, especially the redolent odor of pine which drifted from the northern Piney Woods. Oftentimes, due to her restlessness, she would even be sitting there at dawn, watching the morning star until it could be seen no more.

At night, she often recalled the times when Ashe had come to her at midnight; then thrills of anticipation would run along her spine and her body, as if it had a will of its own, would ready itself to accept her lover. But he never came to her anymore. He seemed to have grown to hate her. She laughed ironically at that. If it wasn't hate on their wedding night, then what could it be called? If it wasn't hate on the night he found her with the Brandon legacy in her hands, what was it?

Sitting out under the moon, Tanya had shaken her

st at the night sky. Garnet Brandon, why don't you
et my husband go? He doesn't love you and he never
eally did. You might have gotten Talon Clay with
he bitter poison of your claws, but you haven't
otten to Ashe. He is *mine* and I shall win!" She had
urned to go back inside, but had lingered on the
pper gallery. "No, Garnet, you're not in Heaven. If
our evil spirit still roams this place, as God is my
itness, I'll banish the terrible hold you have on my
usband's mind and soul!"

Out in the stables, Ashe stroked the mane of the
lky black stallion he had purchased and brought
ack to Sundance from Cresthaven. The strong jut of
she's chin was cast in high relief by the lantern
ght, and his buckskin breeches were stained from
ong hours of toil in the stalls. Talon and Almanzo
ad gone out on the range with the drovers, which
ft only a few hands at Sundance. He didn't mind;
ll he wanted to do was work—work until he was so
eary that he fell exhausted into bed.

But even though he was working himself to a
azzle, there were times when sleep would not come.
: was at these times that he thought of Tanya, of how
uch he wanted her. That was the cold, hard truth.
Ie needed her, wanted desperately to make love to
er. She was driving him crazy and he wanted to take
er immediately, go to her room or wherever she
ight be at these times, throw her down and have his
ay with her.

But he couldn't do it, he wouldn't let himself no
atter how much he wanted to make love to her. He

had caught her red-handed, and she was going to pa
for having deceived him. No man, or woman, wa
going to make an ass out of him by trying to steal hi
legacy, maybe even his home. Wife or no wife sh
could not rest smug and content after the evil dee
was done.

Of course, it was true that the money was in hi
possession now, but that didn't change the fact tha
she had tried to steal it from him, had been holdin
out on him. He had given Talon part of the money
even though his brother had said he didn't need i
because he was making enough on the drives to Sai
Antonio. He had been generous with his wife, too
and had given her everything she needed, and som
things she hadn't asked for, like dresses or new item
for the house. He snorted softly through his nose
spinning the rowels of his silver spurs as he let hi
boot down from the stack of hay on which it had bee
resting.

What did she want from him? Hadn't he given he
enough? Or was she like Garnet, wanting everything
every drop of blood a man had inside of him. H
wondered when she would transform into the imag
of her mother, the tarnished angel, wanting ever
man that came along. It hadn't even mattered t
Garnet that some of her lovers were wet behind th
ears.

Ashe bunched his hands into taut fists. "The bitcl
destroyed my brother, made little Talon Clay,
bitter, jaded lover when he was still in his teens." /
tight sob emerged from his throat, and he groane
out loud, "What kind of woman goes aroun
destroying lives at the drop of a hat? Was she sen

straight from hell to torment the lives of young men and fathers?''

He had been speaking so low that anyone nearby would not have heard the bitterly anguished words he'd been grinding out from between his lips. Besides, his back was turned toward the big doors. Yet someone had just entered, and she had seen him standing there. He spun about brusquely when she spoke.

"Ashe," Tanya said softly to warn him of her presence.

After his eyes indifferently grazed her form, clad only in a rose-colored bathrobe, he turned his face aside, giving her only glimpses of his profile as he went back to forking new hay into a stall.

"You're working awfully late. It's after one . . . Ashe." She bit her tongue, unable to go on and tell him what the doctor she had visited that morning had told her.

"If it's so awfully late, what are you still doing up?" He wouldn't look her way again and be tempted into crushing her in his embrace. He could throw her to the floor, take her here like a crude lover, pressing her soft flesh into the chaff and the biting needles of hay. But it wasn't in him; he didn't relish the thought of punishing her, never physically.

"I . . . I am going to have a baby!" she finally blurted softly.

He made a noise that sounded like a low groan of disappointment; then he snarled softly over his shoulder, "I'll have to tip my hat to you, ma'am. Whose is it?"

Her mouth hung open, and she felt a sudden rush

of tears when he didn't make a move to correct himself, to say he was sorry for being so cruel. But she caught the change in his expression from where she stood, saw his mouth twist in bitter regret . . . and something else.

"It's ours, Ashe," she said brokenly. "How could you say, even think, it was someone else's?" She moved closer to him, reaching out to his shoulder but not touching him. Then her hand fell back to her side and she forced herself to breathe normally. "Well then, it's good-bye, Ashe. I'll be leaving in the morning."

"Try it."

His voice was so low that she leaned her head closer, taking in the masculine scent of him: leather, smoke, horse, and a musky scent that was all his own. "I didn't hear you. . . ."

"I said, Go to bed."

In the morning, her bags packed and ready to go, Tanya made her way to the stable and found Clem there with a few of the mustangers. They had their hands full trying to calm an excited range mare that was terribly frightened of the smell of liniment. One of them was trying to apply the stuff to her sore leg. Without giving the men a second look or taking them from their task, Tanya entered the section where the wagons were kept. Her disappointment was great when she noticed that neither the old wagon nor the new one was there. At the sound of a deep male voice behind her, she started and spun about.

"Looking for something?" Ashe stood there, leaning laconically against the half wall. His eyes

442

raked her from head to foot, taking in the old blue calico, faded and patched; noting her old half-boots. "I noticed your bags by the door. Traveling light, aren't you?"

"Where I'm going, I won't need much." Swiftly she looked aside, away from the sarcastic expression engraved in the deep lines of his handsome face. "Where are the wagons? I need one. Don't look like that. You needn't worry; I'll have it sent back . . . after I get where I'm going."

"And where is that?" Pushing himself away from the wall, Ashe came to stand four feet from her.

"Somewhere where they need a housekeeper. I thought I'd try the preacher first. He might need a housekeeper being as he's—"

"Never mind," Ashe sliced through her words. "I stopped by there a few days ago, checking to see if he'd noticed anyone hanging around since that incident Willow had. He's gotten himself a cleaning lady, a widow, and her two brats. I don't think he's got room for another *housekeeper* underfoot."

"I don't like the way you said housekeeper. What did you think I was going there for, to be the preacher's paid wh-whore?" She finally got the nasty words out, but she paled visibly after she said them.

"Too bad you haven't been to church lately, Tanya, or you'd have noticed her yourself."

"I'm going to church"—she whirled about to make her hasty exit—"as soon as I leave Sundance. It's . . . it's like hell living here!"

He caught her by the arm and spun her around to face him, snarling close to her face, "Garnet and your kind have made it hell, that's why!"

443

Hauling back her free arm, Tanya slapped him hard on the right side of his cheek, leaving a vivid imprint on his freshly shaven face. "I hate you, Ashe Brandon. Don't you look at me like that. I'm leaving here and neither you nor God nor anyone else can stop me!"

"Like I said last night"—he released her arm—"*try it.*" He walked over to the door, leaving her with the parting words, "You won't get very far, *Mrs. Brandon.*"

Chapter 33

For the drovers and the mustangers, life on the range was rugged and often very lonesome, but when work allowed, Talon and Almanzo would ride into town with some of the others. The men visited the barbershop, the saloons, and the gambling halls, but mostly they frequented the dance halls or the bagnios. The only one who had had his fill of the last and who steered clear of any woman resembling or representing such a place, was Talon Clay. And of course, when he went along, Ashe Brandon stayed away from the local bagnios himself.

Dusty, hungry, and filled with insatiable thirsts, the men came riding into Sundance, Talon Clay and Almanzo lagging behind the straggling line of weary horses. Ashe, Clem, and Samson met them out back, lending fresh hands where they were needed. Thrilled to be of service to his "companions," Samson took hold of a few horses and saw to them while the dragging men took themselves back to the bunkhouses, Clem trailing behind and boasting of the enormous kettle of stew he'd cooked up. He'd also made corn bread, honey, and lots of black coffee—Mississippi Mud Clem's coffee was aptly named. The whiskey, he knew, would give out early in the evening.

The topic that arose as Ashe stood around with Talon and Almanzo was cattle. "Some small herds are being trailed to ports on the Gulf Coast," Almanzo was telling his boss, feeling more relaxed in Brandon's presence now that their "differences" had been settled. Actually, no man really made Almanzo feel all that uncomfortable. He respected his boss's intelligence and good head for business matters, but some corner of his brain had been telling him that Brandon thought he had a thing going with his wife. Now he thought he had only been imagining this. Ashe did have problems lately, but it was not for Almanzo to press either Brandon or his wife. Let them work it out themselves, he told himself, even if it broke his heart to see the little lady of Sundance looking so sad at times.

"Yeah," Talon picked up. "Then the cattle's shipped to New Orleans, Havana, or other markets. Some are taken on the hoof into New Orleans or to a few cities up north."

"What about Apache raiders?" Ashe wanted to know, his curiosity piqued. He was already planning new undertakings.

"That is the route to the Pacific Coast," Almanzo informed him. "It is very bad, very dangerous to trail herds that way because of the desert stretches and the savages. Yes, they are Apaches." Almanzo chuckled low then, saying, "We will have to learn some of the

446

técnica from the Mexican vaqueros, *sí?*"

Ashe laughed along with Almanzo, saying, "*Sí!* We will have to do that, my friend. We'll get it down and develop the system of handling cattle, add some new touches to the ancient practices."

"Mustangs and Longhorns—*oooweee!*" Talon hooted as he slapped an arm about Almanzo's shoulders. He was starting to make his way back to the bunkhouses when Samson ran up alongside, his smaller legs trying to keep up with the long galloping strides of his friends. "Hey scruff," Talon reached out to rumple the lad's red hair, "how's it going?"

"I . . . Could I talk to you for a minute, Talon Clay? It's real important."

"Sure, Sambo, what's up?" He continued to walk beside Almanzo, his hands buried knuckle-deep in his tight breeches.

"Ah"—Samson faltered, then went on—"can we talk . . . alone?"

Talon broke his stride, a mock-serious look coming over his deeply bronzed face as he peered down at the waist-high lad. But Almanzo kept on going in long strides, calling over his shoulder, "See you back at the bunkhouse. Later, *amigo.*"

With an easy, carefree manner, Talon led the lad over to a broken-down wagon wheel beneath a wide-spreading branch and then plopped a dusty scarred boot upon the rusted circle. Plucking a leaf, Talon cupped his hands about it and blew into his palms, making an odd screeching sound that never failed to make Samson laugh.

"I still can't do that," Samson said. "It don't

matter." Samson frowned and ducked his head looking embarrassed about something.

"Come on, kid, you can tell me," Talon cajoled tilting Samson's chin upward. "Got a new girl friend you want to talk about? Hey, I know all about girls, you just ask me. I'll tell you what to do, so spill your guts."

"I don't have a girl, Talon. Not yet, anyway. They're too much trouble. At Rankin's fandango I almost threw up when all them little girls giggled in my ear and pawed my arm. Ugh!"

"Ha, kid, you just wait." All of a sudden Talon grew very still and looked off into the distance somewhere.

"Talon?"

"Yeah."

"What's rape mean?"

"Why?" Talon lowered his brow as a grin shaped his full, sensuous lips.

"Well, I just been wantin' to know, that's all."

"You heard the guys bandying the word about?" Talon ran his slim hand up and down the taut leg of his worn breeches.

"No."

"Shoot. What then?" Talon was never impatient with young folk, but now his patience was beginning to thin.

"Well . . . that's what Carl Tucker was going to do to Willow one day not too long ago."

The muscles in Talon's face suddenly became taut and hard. Samson drew in his breath because Talon's expression at once made him think of the implacably fierce desert hawk Almanzo had told him about.

448

"Talon?"

A terrible silence reigned.

"I guess rape is a very bad thing, huh?"

For answer, Talon stared long and mesmerizingly
t the lad before he took slim shoulders in his hands,
et Samson aside, and strode straight to the stables,
rim determination and purposefulness in his every
menacing step. Samson could not see his face now,
ut a cold, deadly purpose was written there.

Inside the house Willow was doing what she loved
est when she came to visit and found her sister busy
t stitching or mending. While Tanya sat with her
vork across her lap, Willow moved about the room
vith an oiled rag rubbing the old furniture until a
iece here or there glowed with a mirrorlike finish.

"Should I take that hearth rug out to beat it?"
Willow asked her sister, wiping her hands on her
pron to remove traces of the lemon oil.

"What?" Tanya laughed. "We ought to hire you
n as Sundance's head housekeeper. No, Willow.
ou needn't do that. Minnie can see to it."

Willow affected small voice. "But Minnie is so
kinny Ah doan know how she can do all dat work.
Iuh!" She put on an imperious pout as Miss Pekoe
ould and pranced about as if she were inspecting
he new black girl that had just arrived at Sundance.
Uh-uh, sho is black and *skineee!*"

Tanya put down her needle and laughed softly,
aying, "Is that what Miss Pekoe said when Minnie
rrived? I wouldn't know, I was in town picking up
ome things with Clem."

"And that isn't all. You should have seen— What' that? Sounds like someone's angry—very angry— slamming the back door like that."

Tanya rose from the settee, placing her sewing down and then straightening. "That someone sounds like the master of Sundance. Here he comes down the hall. Wonder what has happened."

"I *couldn't* guess." Willow stood still and straigh as a statue, just as her sister was doing. They waite for the boom to fall around on their heads.

This was how Ashe found them, in the front room Willow beside the kneehole writing table, Tany. before the settee. The French doors had been left ope to air the room out, for the green and rose carpet ha recently been sprinkled with tobacco to preven moths and crickets from infesting it.

As Ashe opened his mouth to speak, Willow, fo some strange reason, looked over to the French doors Seeing the object of her undying affection racin, down the lane at a killing speed, she drifted over t watch until Talon vanished from sight. For moment she stared at the great cottonwood leave moving gently in the wind; then she turned back t face the couple in the room.

"Where is Talon Clay going?" Willow asked he brother-in-law. "He's going to get killed riding lik the devil himself."

"He *is* the devil himself." Ashe waved an arm i the air in frustrated anger. "He wouldn't even talk t me. He wouldn't even *look* at me. What's gotten int him? I needed him here this afternoon for a job w can't put aside any longer." He stepped closer to hi sister-in-law. "Where was he going, can you tell me

450

He seems aware of every move *you* make, so maybe you can shed some light on his mysterious journey to wherever the hell he's going."

"No . . . I can't." Willow puffed up her dainty shoulders and snapped crisply, "And you don't have to *swear* in the presence of ladies, *Master* Brandon." She let out a "Humph!" and went out the French doors, an arrogant tilt to her little blond head.

A deep chuckle welled up from Ashe's chest. "Damn if she isn't a snippy little sprite." He spoke briskly, then turned back to Tanya, almost having forgotten she was in the room too. "Forgive me, and ask your sister to forgive me too."

Acting very businesslike, he turned to leave the room, but was halted by his wife's equally crisp voice.

"*You* have to do the asking, Brandon. I won't do any of your dirty work for you."

Brushing past him with a swish of her rustling petticoats, Tanya proceeded him into the hall. She headed directly to her room upstairs and did not look back to see him standing at the bottom staring hard after her heels. He swore and reentered the front room, exiting by the French doors.

Three days later the bad news hit Sundance. One of the hands was riding in, hard and fast, barely halting his mount before his feet hit the ground. His horse careened before crashing into the corral fence, reins trailing, front legs dancing away from the wood as it reared up with a frustrated cry. Catching sight of the boss standing near the easternmost section of fence,

his hands cocked on his hips, hat brim set high on hi
frowning forehead, the man cringed when he hear
Ashe's angry voice.

"Roberto," Ashe yelled, "what the hell you tryin
to do, tear down the whole new section in one fe
swoop? Get your ass over here and tell me . . . are w
under attack by Apache or the dreaded Comanches?

Walking over to his boss and dreading what h
must relate to him, Roberto said in a low voice, "It'
Tucker . . . Carl Tucker. He's been killed, murdered
down in San Antonio. Rumor has it Talon Clay di
the job."

Ashe's eyes narrowed to mere greenish-gold slit
"Who said it was Talon Clay?" Even as he asked th
question, Ashe had a sick feeling in his gut.

"Well, nobody really said Talon Clay done i
It . . . it's just rumor."

"Is it *really* Carl Tucker's body that was found
And where did this murder take place?"

"Carl was shot right smack between the eyes, an
then—"

"Then?" Ashe said, urging Roberto to go on.

"And then between the legs. He was shot up re
bad, but they said it was Carl Tucker all right—An
that Talon Clay just rode out."

"Where were you all this time?" Ashe said tersel
his fingers playing with the butt of his Colt.

"I just rode in, after the thing took plac
Everybody was running all over, afraid they w
going to get shot up too. Carl Tucker's face was a re
bloody mess. I almost didn't recognize him myse
where he was laying in the dirt."

"*Did* you recognize him for sure?" His gaze drifte

to the left a little, his wife and her sister coming into focus as they left the back of the house and headed toward them. "Keep it to yourself."

"What?"

"I said," Ashe repeated impatiently, "don't tell anyone else about this. We'll soon know the truth when Talon returns. My brother doesn't lie. And"—he shrugged—"if he did shoot Carl Tucker up; then I'll just have to take him in to jail."

"Your *own brother?*"

"That's right. You heard me."

Ashe joined his wife then, leaving his work for the day. The hands spread out, curious but not questioning Roberto, each going his separate way, to wash up, to rest, or to roll a smoke. That left only one peeping out from behind the barn door. As soon as the others dispersed, Samson looked around, and seeing it was safe to come out from where he'd been hiding and eavesdropping, he made his way to the dining room where he knew Miss Pekoe would have supper waiting on the table for the family.

The meal passed in silence for the most part, with Ashe and Tanya making the usual pleasant conversation. Willow excused herself before desert, graciously putting her chair back into place after she rose from the table. Her only desire was to get away from the constant, inquiring glances Ashe sent her way. She was halfway to the door when Samson's words stopped her dead in her tracks.

"Guess it was my fault Talon Clay went off like that." He hunched his shoulders dejectedly, adding, "But I didn't think he'd ever go and kill Carl Tucker for what I told him."

Tanya's gasp was audible, but Willow just stood trancelike, staring toward the dark windows.

Slowly Ashe laid his fork down beside the half-eaten piece of pie, and his eyes flicking over Willow once, he said, "Do you know what happened at the school?"

"I heard about it." Samson glanced at Tanya, then down again, unable to see Willow with his back turned to her. "He tried to rape her that time too, didn't he?" His round brown eyes leaped to Ashe's inscrutable face.

Ashe leaned back in his chair, saying, "You told Talon about this, and the other time too?" His eyes connected with Tanya's for just an instant before going back to the boy.

"No. I only asked him what rape meant. I wasn't sure."

Staring hard at the boy now, Ashe said, "You wanted to tell Talon about Carl's violation of your sister, didn't you?" It was not really a question.

"Yes." Again Samson hung his head. "I did."

"Why?" Ashe questioned harshly.

"Hopin' Talon would give her some protection in case Carl tried to do it again."

His lips thinning, Ashe lashed out, "Don't you think we all strive to give Willow protection knowing what Carl Tucker tried to do to her?"

With an inarticulate whimper only Tanya could catch, Willow whirled and fled the room. Tanya was assailed by the sudden fierce protectiveness she had always felt for her siblings. She rose from the table, her hands splayed on the cloth below. "Ashe!" she said, regarding him coldly as she leaned forward.

You will stop interrogating my brother. He's only a boy and does not understand what is going on round here. You've already got Willow crying, and ou knew all along she was standing here listening!"

"Willow?" Samson said, his head whirling about n reflex action following his sister's words. "I hought she was gone, Sis, really I did." Tears began o sting his eyes.

"It's all right, Samson. You can be excused."

"Can I . . . take my desert with me?"

She smiled. "Yes. And you can go ask Miss Pekoe or a second piece."

After the boy had left the dining room, Ashe whirled on his wife and, in an implacable tone of oice, said, "If you keep on babying him like that e'll never grow up to become a man. He'll be a sissy, anging onto big sister's skirts. Is that what you vant, Tanya?"

"You were interrogating him as if he were a ommon criminal. Didn't you get enough of that vhile you were a ranger? Or do you miss the field so nuch you wish you were back there instead of with ne?" A quick rush of tears clogged her throat and she urned away, showing him her softening profile.

"Guess I was a little hard on the boy, but"—he ran is hands through his tawny mane of thick straight air—"it's just that I'm worried about Talon Clay. Damn! That brother of mine gets himself into more rouble than a passel of outlaws."

"You still think of him as an outlaw don't you." Tanya did not look at Ashe. "You never can forgive nyone, I'm beginning to think. I would only like to now what crime I've committed, what terrible sin

455

has made you so bitter toward me. If it's because I'r my mother's daughter, then you are wrong in you actions." She was going to add that she was not he mother, she was herself, but she thought better of i He was not looking at her, and she doubted hi thoughts even rested on her. She heaved a deep sigh "How will Talon Clay get out of it this time? Ever lawman and bounty hunter for hundreds of mile around will be after him," she said, but she might a well have been talking to the wall for all the attentio she was getting from her husband.

His thoughts drifted for a time before his attentio returned to the woman beside him. "Did you sa something?" he asked, looking at his reflection in th tall French doors while frowning lightly.

"No," she answered dully. "It was nothing. Goo night, Ashe."

Chapter 34

Carl Tucker rode as if all the demons in hell were nipping at his heels, as no doubt they were. He had just killed two more men, the ones who had seen him gun Butch down in the street a few days before. Butch had asked for it, trying to get him to turn himself in. They had argued, and Butch had been heading down the street to the cantina, and the sheriff.

"I got him though." Carl wiped the chewing tobacco from the corner of his mouth with the back of his hand. "Sure did. And I'm goin' to get anyone else what stands in my way from now on."

When Carl reached a level place outside town below a ridge, he reined up and took shelter behind a scrub oak, staring back in the direction he had come. The past three days were beginning to tell on Carl Tucker. "Damn jaspers," he said of the Mexicans, "why didn't they just mind their own business and leave me to mine. I didn't kill one of their kind." He laughed. "I killed one of *my* kind."

"My luck has been very bad lately." He pulled out

a bottle and tilted it to his lips again, letting the cheap whiskey burn as it went down his throat. He slid along the tree until he was sitting on the earthen floor. "It will get better," he told his horse, waving the bottle and then nipping at it again. "I will see Lady Red again. Soon." As he thought of Tanya, he began to laugh softly.

Willow and Tanya entered Granger's store around eleven o'clock in the morning, meaning to purchase some material for some new petticoats. They much preferred to stitch their own because the flimsier, ready-made garments didn't last the year out, and a bit of embroidered lace or some ribbon made them quite pretty.

"Tanya, have you seen them yet?" Willow asked her sister, unaware that Tanya had looked up several times to try to catch their neighbors' attention. But each time she had, Janice Ranae had looked right past her.

"Just look at her, will you?" Willow said. "Her double chin shows up even more when she's being snooty. How come she's so stuck up, Sis, after you loaned her all that money last week?"

"I don't know, Willow. It's hard to understand women like Janice Ranae. Ignorance, I guess."

"Tanya, she's so extravagant. She spends all kinds of money on Hester, but she has no money left to fix her fences. They're falling down! That's where her money should be going, but it's not. Her cattle are grazing on our side and her drovers don't do a darn thing about it. I wonder if they even get enough to eat.''

"Oh, I'm sure they do." Tanya lightly laughed. "With all those rich gooey desserts she's always baking I don't think any one of them could be on the thin side.''

"I wonder if they ever get any of her desserts. She seems stingy, if you ask me."

Tanya smiled graciously when Janice Ranae continued to look right past her ear; then, when Janice Ranae realized her eye contact was being sought, the older woman directed her gaze elsewhere. Actually Tanya felt rather sorry for Janice Ranae. The woman had lost her husband and had not been able to find herself another. What man would look at her? Her entire body seemed to sag, from her double chin down to her shapeless lower half. She had no derrière whatsoever. Her short blond hair was burned to a crisp from the curling iron and her eyes, once a noticeable blue-green, had lost their luster and color. Janice Ranae was not that old either, but to any beholder, she was a picture of aging lackluster dowdiness.

Tanya could not help but laugh a little when Janice Ranae made a fool of herself in Granger's eyes by continuing to look the other way and snub her. Granger shrugged his shoulders at the lovely sisters, and Tanya turned to Willow, asking, "Do you really know why Janice Ranae's acting so petty and avoiding me?"

"Me?" Willow shrugged. "No. I thought you didn't have any idea either."

"Oh, I do, but that doesn't help me to understand her actions." Tanya sighed before going on. "Janice

459

Ranae is quietly miffing me because I didn't loan her the amount she *really* wanted. She had to buy her little Hester a grand birthday present. I found that out afterward, from one of the drovers."

"What was the amount, Sis?"

"Twice what I did loan her."

Willow almost choked as she whispered, "*Twice.* Dear Lord. You already loaned her—"

"Hush. She's coming this way."

Arms full of packages, lengths of material, jars of hard candy, and many more extravagant items they were hardly able to afford, Janice Ranae and Hester, looking very smug, sashayed toward the door. With a hand plopped over her breast, Willow gaped.

"Look at that, they're walking right out the door without a word to you! I can see Hester snubbing me after I drenched her with lemonade—but not you. Not Janice Ranae snubbing you to the point of—of I don't know what! Sis, do you think you'll ever see your money again?"

"Probably not. They are noted for not paying people back when they borrow. No, I don't mind, Willow, as long as Janice Ranae stays away from our doorstep. She and her offspring have caused enough trouble in our house." She was thinking of the letter Carl had given to her husband, and of the never-ending battle it had begun. At least it seemed that way, as if they could never be truly happy again. Carl had no doubt planned it just that way too. He must have known how much Ashe and Talon had hated her mother.

"What's Ashe going to say when you tell him you loaned all that money to Janice Ranae?"

"I'm not going to tell him—not yet."

"You're too kind to undeserving folks, Sis."

Tanya smiled, a bit painfully, saying, "I only wish someone else thought good of me, Willow."

Willow's bottom lip jutted out in a pink pout, "*Tell Ashe* what you did and how that frizzle-headed witch with the double chin snubbed you. He'll be sure to get you your money back. I know he doesn't like Janice Ranae because just the other day he said she didn't have any class."

"I cannot tell him yet, Willow." Tanya smiled. "Soon though."

They rode in silence for a space then, swaying on the wagon seat as they rolled along the San Antonio Road. On the way to the quiet country town and on the way back, they had spotted many antlerless white-tail deer, some prairie chickens, quail, and wild turkey, and three cock pheasants. If there had been more hunters to take them down, there would have been less to see of the beautiful creatures along the road. But as it was, with families far and few between, wild life was plentiful and roamed free as the wind.

"How did Dan Tucker get himself killed?" Willow, ever curious, wanted to know about Janice Ranae's husband.

Her smiling eyes shaded beneath her sunbonnet, Tanya went on to relate what she had heard. "Clem said Dan Tucker was shot—ambushed so the story goes—because he owed too many folks money. He borrowed all the time, even from his own relatives. Never paid them back either. Dan couldn't stand on his own two feet, he always needed help from someone. He wanted to support his family in a style he couldn't afford, and he was covetous when others made more than him. He could never make enough money, he always had to have more, always had to have some brand new toy. Like you said back in the store, extravagant."

Willow clucked her tongue. "Lord, him and his wife must have been a gruesome pair. No wonder the Tuckers never have friends for very long."

"Willow, folks like that can never be happy. They're always running away from people because they owe everybody money."

"I don't think Talon done away with Carl Tucker, Sis. Even if he was angry with Carl for trying to rape me, Talon would never stoop to murder."

"You're right, Willow. Talon Clay is just not a Tucker, even though he spent most his teen years with them." Her eyes clouded over as she recalled what Ashe had told her about the lad.

"Let's not talk about it anymore, Sis. All right?"

"Sure," Tanya said.

"Will you drop me off at the school?"

Tanya shifted uncomfortably on her seat. "That's where I'm headed." She patted the bundle behind the wagon seat. "I've got some nice things for Preacher Cuthbert, for his new home."

"You're an angel, Tanya."

Willow glanced down at her sister's belly, wondering when the baby was going to show. Tanya caught Willow studying her, and she wrapped an arm about the slim girl, hugging her close to her side.

* * *

Juxtaposed in the midst of a line of postoaks, Carl Tucker stood motionless, staring eastward along San Antonio Road. This was Monday, and Tanya Brandon usually took the wagon into town. She should be coming along any time now.

Carl wasn't exactly sure what he was going to do with Tanya when he ambushed her wagon and pulled it into the woods, but he grinned, knowing what he'd like to do with her. However, he wanted her willing, and for that to happen he first had to woo her, to be nice and gently coax her into doing his bidding.

Tanya and Ashe were not getting along with each other, Carl knew that much. Concealed in the brush and trees near their house, he had been watching them for over a week now. Whenever Tanya came outside for something, Ashe would get busy elsewhere. He wouldn't even look her way. Carl licked his fat lips, hoping that Garnet's letter had done its nasty job.

Carl had long been aware of how deep Ashe's hatred of Garnet Hayes—or Haywood, her phony name—ran and he knew the younger Ashe had almost run the woman off the ranch. He had been a lad himself then, but younger, closer to Talon Clay's age. And then Talon had come to stay with them. His ma had worked Talon hard, but he had developed muscles just like his own. They had been close friends, always hunting together, getting into trouble. He'd never forgotten the time Talon got silly tears in his eyes when Carl tossed Hester's striped kitten into the garbage fire. How that cat had screamed and Talon had looked away when he'd poked his stick in the fire to make sure the fur ball stayed in there until she was roasted alive.

"You'd think sometimes the kid had feelings." Carl said aloud. "But I know he ain't got any and soon's I get what's coming to me, then maybe Talon can have some too. I mean to have me the biggest ranch in all of Texas! Yessir!" he bellowed to the air, making his horse skitter behind him. He reached back to swat the perked ears, growling, "Shut up you skinny nag or I'll roast you too and eat you for dinner!"

Sighting the Brandon wagon just coming over the hill, Tanya's sunbonnet a bright beacon, Carl stepped back a little to drag out his gunnysack and slip it over his head. Eerily his eyes peered from the slits, the lower half of the sack being sucked in and blown out with each deep labored breath he took.

Oh git up, gals, in de mawnin',
Oh git up, gals, in de mawnin',
Oh git up, gals, in de mawnin',

Tanya took a deep breath before singing the rest of Miss Pekoe's favorite song and tossing her head like the black woman:

. . . Jes at the break of day.

Just then a scream ripped from her throat. Teychas

side-stepped, trotted a little, and then reared up in her traces as a masked man came riding down the short hill. Tanya, momentarily aware, thought the man looked like the devil himself, or something just as evil. Then everything became a blur. A gun was pointed at her head as she was urged, in a deep ragged voice, to pull her wagon off the road and up the hill, into the trees.

Doing as she was told, having gotten hold of her worst fears, Tanya sat with the trees surrounding her and her nervous horse. As it was, Teychas did not like pulling a wagon, and she began to struggle in her traces. Her front legs sawing up and down, the mare began to scream in a high-pitched whinny.

"Shut her up!" came the muffled order. The eyes rolled behind the mask, watching her climb down to try to soothe the horse but to no avail. "Keep her still!" The man waved his gun. "Or else I'll shut her up for you!"

Afraid only for her horse, Tanya whirled on the masked man. She gasped as he stepped closer, and she stammered out, "She won't keep still, can't you see that? She's a mustang and hates to be confined this way."

"Then why the hell did you put the ugly beast in here in the first place?"

"Teychas is not ugly! How dare you! She's beautiful!" All the while she was venting her anger, she was stepping closer to Teychas, working at the traces to free her. Backing against her horse as if protecting it, she hissed, "I'll do what I want with her . . . she was a gift. She's mine, not yours!" She had gotten to the other side, the masked man tracking

465

her, only gazing into her eyes, never looking down to see just what it was she did with her hands. "Oh!" She stepped out of harm's way when Teychas broke free, running down the small hill, swift as the wind. "Just look what you've done! Now she's run away."

"She'll head straight for home." A nasty chuckle rose from the hem of the mask. "But you won't be followin'. You're staying right here with me." Quiet for a moment, he then went on, "Think she's goin' to be bringing back help for you, huh, little lady?"

Tanya said nothing.

"Sure hope she does." But Carl would not say what he was thinking next. He was busy making plans for Ashe's inevitable arrival.

Glancing down Tanya noticed that the tip of the man's finger was missing. There was one she knew of . . . Carl Tucker!

Situated on the right side of the wagon, Carl on the other, Tanya covertly slid her eyes to the whipstock. Moving closer to the wagon, she leaned inward, the edge biting into her belly as she swiftly took down the horsewhip. She had never had need of it before . . . but now she would.

She moved quickly, before Carl could react to what she was doing. As he neared her, lifting his rifle in readiness to fire, Tanya slashed viciously at his eyes. He grunted with pain and clutched at his mask, stumbling back. Unemotionally she stared at Carl Tucker, knowing he was in great pain. But her mark had been struck; she had gotten him on one of the openings for his eyes.

As Carl winced and staggered backward clutching his face, he stumbled again, this time over the draw bars. He reeled sideways, the rifle angling upward. Losing his balance, he released the rifle to catch himself, directing every foul word he knew at Tanya's head.

Tanya gasped as the butt of the rifle struck the ground hard, setting of a thundering blast from the muzzle. Confused and upset, Tanya groped backward and fell, her blue eyes staring downward, incredulously, at the bloody gaping hole in the torn flesh.

Back at Sundance, Talon, Ashe, and a few others were busy breaking some new mustangs Almanzo and Talon had brought in. Ashe was about to climb aboard the one with hellfire in his eyes, with a mane like black flame.

Throwing the cloth blinder over the mustang's eyes, Talon grabbed hold of the ears, while Ashe tightened the cinch on the saddle once again and made ready to mount the steed. As he swung up into the saddle and gave the nod to Talon to turn him loose, Talon removed the cloth from the horse's eyes and jumped back, bounding up onto the fence. The hellfire stallion went into the wildest of gyrations leaping into the air on all fours and coming down with bone-crushing thuds.

"Oooo-eee, ride 'em!" Talon shouted, his head coming around as the horse bird-hopped to the other end. He was just about to turn on the fence he had mounted, when he spotted Teychas coming in,

trotting free and riderless, tossing her head proudl
and calling to her familiars.

Leaping from the fence as if in confusion, Talo
divided his glances between Ashe gyrating atop th
mustang and Teychas, Tanya's riderless horse com
ing to a standstill before the rail. Ashe or Tanya, h
tried to quickly decide. Either one of them could b
hurt. Tanya might have been already.

Talon whipped out his arm and grabbed fo
Teychas' halter, pulling the horse from the rail. Nov
he swung back to yell at Ashe, only to see him bein
tossed high into the air and to the left side of th
mustang. Talon watched, as Ashe was buffeted in th
dirt, then landed hard against the fence. Bloo
immediately spilled from a wound on his head
staining his blond hair crimson.

Talon stood frozen, not knowing which way t
turn or what to say. Ashe must have caught sight o
the riderless Teychas.

Some drovers were now over the fence trying t
quiet the still-infuriated mount while others dragge
Ashe Brandon under the fence to safety.

Talon raced to his brother's side, coming down o
one knee. Ashe opened his eyes and looked up a
Talon. Seeing his brother's confusion, he asked
"What's the matter? Haven't . . . you ever seen a ma
get thrown from a horse . . . before?" Before Talo
could say what he was thinking, Ashe tried to stand—
unsuccessfully. His thoughts sped frantically i
every direction, and he reeled back in a haze, grinding
out, "Find her . . . just find my wife. . . ."

*   *   *

468

Carl peered over at Tanya who lay sprawled on the mossy ground, disbelief was written in her clear blue eyes. He whipped the mask from his face, saying, "You already know who I am. I could tell you did . . . right afore the rifle went off." He winced at the pain of the bullet hole in his leg. "Why you lookin' at me like that? Weren't you who caught the triggin' shot!" He cried out as he tried moving.

Tanya now leaped to her feet. She had fallen backward when trying to escape Carl, after she had whipped him in the eye. Then the rifle, on its own, had almost finished off her enemy. Yes, Carl Tucker was without doubt the enemy. He and his family had brought her nothing but pain, trouble, and heartache.

For all his wounds, amazing rage swelled in Carl's one good eye as he stumbled to his feet. Crying out, Tanya began to run, looking over her shoulder, yet slowing to step over a branch in her path or to dodge a big rock or a small tree growing close to the road. Carl pushed on and Tanya kept glancing back, relieved to find that he was not gaining on her. He had stopped to tie his neckerchief about his wounded leg. Then with the rage of a bull seeing red, he charged forward, the makeshift bandage seeming to have given his wounded leg renewed strength.

Tanya's lungs felt as if they were going to burst, but she endeavored to put as much space between them as she could. She had to slow down . . . she felt exhausted, faint. The baby . . . would it be hurt by all this? she wondered anxiously.

"Oh . . . oh God!"

A rider was steadily approaching and Tanya kept

right on crying out her relief to see someone coming
He rode as if pursued by all the demons in hell
racing toward her, ever faster, or so it seemed.

"Talon!" she cried. "Thank God it's you!"

His mount slid to a halt, sending up clouds of dus
with his sharp hooves and almost settling his rear t
the ground. It was Cloud, Talon's magnificen
gallant stallion.

"Talon!" Tanya raced up to grab hold of th
bridle. "It . . . oh God, it's Carl!" She blurted ou
what she could in the few moment's before Talon
raced down the road in hot pursuit of his forme
friend.

Upon reaching the wagon, Talon dismounted
while half-running along the ground beside hi
horse. He looked this way and that but could fin
nothing, only blood staining the ground—Car
Tucker's blood.

Alerted, Talon spun about, but he was too late.

Tanya heard the shot ring out, and at once sh
started back along the path she had recently taken t
escape Carl Tucker. Rounding the bend in the roac
she saw Talon half-crouched and clinging to th
wagon. Fresh blood ran from a wound in hi
shoulder. "Talon . . . no!" She raced toward him
even faster, throwing all caution to the wind.

"Tanya," Talon ground out painfully, "be care
ful . . . get down."

Anger set her lovely face into tight lines, marring
her forehead with a deep frown, as she bent down to
swipe Talon's pistol from his tight-gripping fingers
"Let loose, Talon!" Grimacing, he allowed her to
take his gun. She stood straight as an arrow, pointing

he weapon as she noticed a shadowy figure slink off into the woods. She shot once before Talon yanked her back down beside him.

"What are you trying to do, woman! Get yourself illed?"

"One of these days," she vowed, looking toward he massive oaks hung with moss, the ones Carl had anished into.

"One of these days, yes, I'll get the bastard," Talon aid. "But for now, help me into the wagon before I leed to death."

After she had torn strips from her petticoat to try to top the profuse bleeding, she noticed how pale Talon had become. He looked up at his sister-in-law nd, with a half-smile, said, "Don't worry, Sis, we'll et him later. Help me back to Sundance . . . now." His eyes closed and his head rolled against the vagon.

Ashe had been bandaged. He was standing on the porch, leaning against a tall collonette, his gaze eaching to the stretch of road between the pines and oostoaks. He should see them coming from there . . . f they were coming at all.

As he watched, he began to reflect back to a few lays ago, when he and Tanya had again argued heatedly. It was always the same. He couldn't help it. They both lost. He had walked away and had heard her crying softly later in her room upstairs. He wondered how it was all going to end.

Willow suddenly appeared in the lane, but Ashe hadn't caught sight of her. He had been looking

down at the browning grass and thinking of painfu
memories of himself and of his brother—mostly o
Talon . . . and of the woman who had destroyed him

"They're coming!" Willow shouted, beginning t
run down the lane as she lifted her powder-blu
gingham skirts on either side. Her slim ankle
encased in white stockings, flashed as she ran faste
and faster, lifting her skirts higher, higher. "Talon!
she sobbed. "Tanya! Oh God, oh!" she cried, no
seeing the hands pouring from every quarter to fall i
behind her to meet the wagon. All she could see now
was Talon as the wagon rounded the bend, a strang
horse pulling it, Cloud strung out behind. But it wa
Talon who held her gaze. He was lying down, as if h
had been hurt.

Leaving the road, Tanya guided Carl's horse righ
up onto the lawn, to where Ashe had come to stand
several feet out from the porch. Halting the wago
before him, she tied the ribbons to the whipstock an
climbed down unsteadily. Ashe at once grabbed he
elbow to help her stand erect on the lawn. She swaye
and then fainted dead away in his arms.

"Here, let me." Almanzo rushed forward to tak
Tanya from the man. "I will bring her inside wher
Miss Pekoe can see to her." Seeing that Tanya wa
breathing normally, Almanzo nodded to the back o
the wagon, saying, "Your brother needs you."

For a moment longer, Ashe watched the handsom
Indian carry his wife, gently, his concern obvious i
his bent head, into the house where Miss Pekoe an
the new maid already waited to follow the dark
haired man upstairs into the mistress' bedchambe
Then he limped to the back of the wagon where th

472

men were getting ready to transport Talon Clay to the doctor. First, for the long ride, they had to make Talon as comfortable as possible. The shot had gone clear through, and with Willow's help, Clem had made a fresh bandage. Ashe meant to ride along, in the back of the wagon with Talon Clay.

"I am coming too," Willow said. She had been staring at Talon and he at her. They had hardly looked away from each other while the men buzzed about like concerned females, telling about their own wounds while Clem gently bandaged Talon's shoulder.

"No."

Willow spun about to face her brother-in-law. "Why? Why can't I ride along with him?" She looked into the hard planes of the man's face, hardly recognizing him as the same man, the gentle ranger, who had been concerned enough to lead her back home when he had thought she'd gone astray . . . dressed in manly clothes.

Ignoring her, Ashe grasped Talon's hand in brotherly comradeship. It passed between them, what only brothers know, binding, lasting forever until one of them should die. He stepped back then as two drovers, one with a rifle across his lap, mounted to the wagon seat. Clem climbed in back with his box of bandages and herbs, hastily got from his bunkhouse when he had seen Willow racing down the lane. All of a sudden Samson was there, begging to go along. Willow appeared beside her brother, explaining to him that Ashe didn't want too many to accompany the wounded man.

But Samson turned to face her, his look deter-

mined. "You go, Willow. You go with him." H
smiled, saying low, "You belong with him."

Willow's mouth gaped before snapping shu
Then, impudently, she raced to catch up with th
wagon and hopped aboard, Clem lending her a han
as he glanced back over his shoulder to shrug at th
master of Sundance. Ashe shook his head an
allowed a small smile to play on his lips as he hear
his brother's low chuckle flowing back to him. Ash
turned and entered the house.

After he had seen his wife, asking Miss Pekoe in a
aside if the baby was all right, he went to his office
That night, he climbed the stairs to sleep besid
Tanya, caressing her hair and cheek, but no
intimately touching her. Come morning they wer
strangers once again.

"I'm happy that you are all right," was all he ha
said to her when he'd climbed into bed the nigh
before.

Tanya moped about as usual. Talon returned
alive and well. He and Willow and Almanzo had
been nestled in the hay in the stable loft when Tanya
had come looking for her sister, wondering where sh
had gone off to. In the tall pecan tree outside the high
window the trio had spotted a pair of Barred Owls
The humans, laughing and hugging each other
close, had faked some hooting noises. Since the owls
were talky birds, they hooted back repeatedly, their
sounds like the muffled "woof" of a dog, beginning
with a *w* and not an *h*. They were large, earless owl
with great dark eyes. Talon got right under them
and while he looked at them, they looked at him. The
eye contact was intense. Tanya and Willow laughed

he first a bit wistfully as she longed for Ashe. In the aylight the Barred Owls could be seen to be creamy hite on the head, neck, and underparts, while crisp ark brown marks made up a broken pattern of tripes or bars on the rest of them. They were huge irds, magnificent in flight.

Sounds of gay laughter following her, Tanya eturned to the house, her feet stepping onto the dewy rass freshly scythed that morning. That morning . . . she recalled it as if it happened an hour go. . . .

Having just returned from going over the menus with Cook Leon and Miss Pekoe in the cookhouse, Tanya had slipped in the back way. She was standing t the end of the hall when the door to Ashe's office pened and out stepped Janice Ranae!

The woman spotted her, but as usual, Janice Ranae stuck her stubby nose in the air. Tanya had een surprised, to say the least. What would Janice Ranae want here at Sundance? And coming to see Ashe . . . Aha. Tanya thought she knew; in fact she vas certain of it. She made no move to leave her spot t the end of the hall. She listened.

"Thank you so much, Mister Brandon," Janice Ranae was saying as, down the hall, Tanya grimaced t the sugary words. "Oh," Janice Ranae gushed on, "I mean *Ashe*." Again Tanya made a wry face and clenched her hands into fists at her sides.

Pulling the drawstring on her purse and not giving Tanya a second look, Janice Ranae said, "I'll be forever indebted to you, sir."

Tanya thought to herself, *And so she shall be!*

When Ashe finally had let Janice Ranae out the

door, he'd walked the space that separated him from Tanya. He stood, scowling into her face, noting th chin that did not tremble as it had the day before "How could you?" he bit out at last.

"Let me guess," Tanya threw back at him. "Heste badly needs a brand-new wardrobe. Or maybe it's th sagging fences at Saw Grass, they *always* nee repairing. Yes, that sounds more like it, knowin Janice Ranae. How much did you give her thi time?"

A tawny eyebrow lifted sarcastically as Ash stepped closer to her, taking in the fresh rosewate scent of her clean flesh. He gritted his teeth as h continued. "This time? What do you mean, Tanya?

"Oh, I wonder . . . did you loan her the entire sum she *needed*, or just half of it?"

"Of course the entire sum!"

Before Tanya could brush past him with negligent shrug of her shoulders, Ashe took hold o her wrist. He spun her about to face him, asking he none too gently, "What in hell do you mean, Tanya You didn't answer me!"

"You didn't answer me, Ashe. Why did you sa 'How could you?'" She rubbed the aching spot on her wrist after he'd let her go. She had felt his breath warm on her face for only an instant, it had made her recall warmer reunions. But lately, he had chosen to remain strangers . . . they were always strangers Even when they had made passionate love, they remained strangers.

"The woman asked you to loan her money, right?' he asked harshly. "And you didn't, right?"

476

"Oh God. Is that what she said?" Tanya looked aside and then back at Ashe. "Do you recall, Ashe, that I couldn't account for some of the money you gave me a few weeks ago? You were angry, said I was hoarding it greedily. Remember, Ashe?"

"I . . ." Running his long-boned fingers through his hair, he confessed, "Yes . . . but I don't see—"

"Figure it out, Ashe."

Swishing her skirt aside, Tanya left him standing in the hall, glaring in confused anger as she walked away. When it finally dawned on him, Tanya had paused at the bottom stair and she heard him snarl, "Sick cows hell!" He didn't see her victorious smile as she slowly climbed the stairs to her room.

All week long Ashe did not come near her. At the apex of her thighs she ached for him to fill her, to erase her hunger. Her heart craved him, and her breasts were starved for the sensitive touch of his fingertips. Even her lips longed for his thrilling kisses.

One night they had almost come together as midnight thunder rolled across the rooftop. Passing in the hall, they had come to a standstill for one heartstopping moment. Lightning had carved his face into a silver-blue mask of hollows and planes. Tanya had stared, as the lightning zigzagged from the transom to spark in the hazel depths of Ashe's eyes. He had been about to pull her into his arms, she just knew it. Noticing the slashes that grooved the sides of his mouth, she had thought that he was in pain. Not a word had passed between them. She had returned to her room, but where Ashe had gone was a mystery to her. He was no doubt restless and frustrated just as she was.

Tanya and Ashe, at separate ends of the house, strolled the galleries and the porches, each alone with only memories for company through the long moonlit stretches of night.

Chapter 35

Seated at the antique white dressing table that had belonged to Garnet, her lips reposing in a sensual pout, Tanya studied her reflection. She looked pale and ethereal in the soft glow emitted by the candles, one on either side of the mirror.

Tanya couldn't sleep. She wanted Ashe so much that her body ached terribly. If only he would come to her . . . She would go to him, but she couldn't stand the rejection, he would stare right through her, coldly, as he had all week long. That was what she had thought all the other times . . . but tonight was different.

After a week of sulking about the house, Ashe hovering in the background like some huge, threatening storm cloud, her nerves forever on edge, Tanya finally decided it was time to stop suffering and to stand up and fight.

Tanya had reached the breaking point. She could control her frustration no longer. The situation had to change, otherwise she knew she would go stark raving mad.

Rising from the dressing table and checking herself over one last time, patting her hair to make certain not a strand was out of place, Tanya steeled her shoulders. It was time to face the giant and look him straight in the eye!

The curtains billowed slowly, puffing out like a fat man and then becoming skinny once again; and moonlight streamed in at the open windows.

Ignoring the papers strewn about his huge desk, a cup of cold coffee at his elbow, Ashe stared, not at his mountain of paper work nor his ledgers, but at the tiny hot flame that flickered in the lamp. He stared until his eyelids began to burn, but still he could not pull his eyes away from that tiny sun captured in the glass chimney. The flame that wavered ever so slightly mesmerized him into thinking back over the past week.

He didn't want to think about Tanya. He wanted only to work, to lose himself in it. But he couldn't—*damn!*—he couldn't! Not tonight.

Jerking himself out of his chair he went to pour himself a shot of brandy, downing it in one gulp. The fiery measure didn't even make him blink and it felt good going down—nice and warm, soothing. But nothing in the world, he told himself with a satirical smirk, nothing was as warm and wonderful as making love with Tanya.

A tense muscle jerked in his cheek as he set the empty glass aside and returned to his desk, reluctantly, for he wanted to go upstairs and take Tanya in his arms!

No, he wouldn't do it. Besides, she had ignored him the whole week long. Then again, hadn't he done the same to her? Even though he had steered clear of her, she was there at every corner he rounded: outside as he was passing by the garden; in the stables when she went to visit with her horse, Teychas; in the house, along the hall; in the kitchen, when he went for a snack, there she was chatting with Miss Pekoe. As soon as they caught sight of each other, however, he was the first to turn away . . . or was it he? Neither would give an inch, and he certainly wasn't going to be the first . . .

Why? he asked himself. Why didn't he believe her and why did he blame her? Was he in the wrong? He ran his hands through his already ruffled wheaten hair. Damned if he knew!

He gritted his teeth, thinking she had made an ass out of him. Even the men eyed him strangely lately, peering around him as if they expected to see someone tagging along with him. When they saw that he was very much alone, they exchanged looks and shrugged, then went back to their respective tasks. He'd had to put on a false front all week long, but he had found himself bursting out explosively if a man working beside him made one slip-up. Thoughtlessly, he had turned one man out. But that, he promised himself, was not going to happen again. Never would he allow his personal frustrations to enter into his dealings with his men.

A distant rumble of midnight thunder sounded across the earth and Ashe sat, pulling his thoughts from disturbing mind wanderings to listen as the

481

ominous sound grew ever closer, the curtains beginning to stir more strongly at the windows. Finally he rose from his chair and went to secure them against the rain that would soon begin to fall. Plunging his hands into the pockets of his dark brown breeches, he stood at the window, silent as a shadow, watching the thunderstorm approach. The grounds were illuminated by sudden, intermittent flashes of lightning. The room behind him was dark except for the small, flickering flame from the lamp on his desk. Fascinated by the soft play of lightning in the yard, he didn't hear the door to his office open behind him.

Suddenly unsure of herself, Tanya was about to change her mind and go back upstairs when the still figure at the window caught her attention. Unable to move a muscle, she stared at the tall, dark silhouette framed in the window as the lightning flashed outside in the yard, softly illuminating his stern profile and casting his stronger features in silvered relief.

Just inside the room, Tanya stood uncertainly, in a strange paralysis of fear. With nervous hands she reached back and carefully closed the door behind her shivering form. A short distance separated them but to Tanya it seemed hundreds of miles. In an agony of indecision, she closed her eyes, changing her mind a great number of times.

When he turned about and noticed her standing there, Tanya's heart gave a wild lurch. Tanya was totally unaware of the lovely sight she created. Her hair was swept up elegantly, but a few coiling tendrils hugged her cheeks like live flames of red.

gold fire. And her gown gave her the look of a winsome naiad just rising from a turquoise pool that reflected and shimmered about her curving figure.

All the accumulated thought and painful emotion of the recent days and hours was concentrated in the gaze he fixed on her face. Great gusts swept through his big body as, hazel irises blazing, he studied her, his eyes dropping to the lacy bodice spilling between her gently rounding breasts. He couldn't move, he could only stare. Finally he tore himself from his spellbound trance and went to the corner of his desk, half sitting and half standing, one leg swinging free at his knee.

Midnight thunder sounded again. Tanya's eyes did not waver.

"So," he said, "have you come here to my office to tease and excite me with your lovely body? Or do you have something less exciting to reveal, but just as worthy of consideration?"

Taking a trembling step forward, Tanya halted and stood where she was. "I've come here to tell you who I am," she said, a lump the size of his settee growing in her throat.

Fastening his eyes directly on hers, he said, "You're kidding . . . I don't know who my own wife is?" He gave a harsh, annoyed laugh that was more like a snort. "What's this game you're playing now, Tanya? Have you suddenly run short of funds? Need a new dress already? Isn't the one you have on good enough? Or do you, like that slut Garnet, need a whole wardrobe full of frilly stuff?"

Pain and something else broke across her face as he said, "Take a good look at me, Ashe. *Really* look at me." Moving from the spot she had remained glued to for so long, Tanya walked across the room and stopped before the settee. Once there, she spun about and faced him. "Who am I, Ashe, who am I really?"

Ashe was vibrant with longing. A thousand thoughts raced through his brain and even more emotion coursed through his body. Emotions . . . Memories . . . Desires . . . remembering . . . and then the lightning flashed and reached far into the room charging the atmosphere even more than it was already. In blood, bone, tissue, muscle, heart, and brain, Ashe reached out to Tanya. *Tanya*.

"Are you getting it now, Ashe?"

He shot her a sardonic look, saying flatly, "You . . . are Tanya. My wife. And . . ."

"And?"

He was suddenly lost in his own hell. "You are just like . . . *her*." There, he said it.

"Like who?"

A scowl marred his handsome face as he said in a tight voice, *"Garnet, damn it, Garnet!"*

"No!" Tanya hissed. "Your mind can no more change me than it can change the shape of things to come. Look at me, Ashe. You can't make me out to be someone I am not. I am Tanya, *not* my mother. I am not Garnet." Her breath was beginning to come out in little, heart-wrenching sobs. "Not anything like Garnet at all. Ashe, I am an individual, apart from her. Her child, her daughter, yes. But I am *me*, with my own hopes and dreams and desires. They are mine—no one else's!" She hung her head to stare

484

forlornly at the wood floor, muttering, "You see I'm only a . . . a woman, you know."

Lightning flashed into the room, coloring them silver.

Ashe was spellbound, as much by her words as by Tanya herself. The wonderful fire that had been in her dark blue eyes! The lightning flashed again, stronger than all the other silver streaks that had come before. In the illumination Ashe saw much that had been a mystery to him. His long, loose-limbed body straightened and he strode swiftly across the room to take his wife in his arms.

"Tanya," he murmured against her throat. "What a fool I've been all this time." He tilted her chin, gazing deeply into her eyes, the bitter frustration that had been eating at him now washed away, the hard hatred gone too. A bittersweet memory was fast fleeing from his heart. But he could not tell Tanya, would not hurt her with the hard, cruel fact that the first woman he had ever loved, worshipped, and hated all at the same time had been Garnet Haywood. Just like Talon, he had fallen in love with a tarnished angel . . . and she had been so beautiful, as beautiful as Tanya, her daughter.

Cupping her face with one hand, he kissed and sucked her sweet lips and hugged her to his chest with all the fierce urgency of his unleashed desire. The kiss deepened. His arm about her waist cinched her ever tighter until her round breasts were flattened against him, leaving not a seam separating them.

"Tanya," he breathed at the corner of her heated lips, "Don't ever leave me. Stay with me always, always and forever. Oh Lord," he rasped into her ear,

"I've been such a damn fool. Can you ever forgive me?"

Gently catching handfuls of his thick, tawny hair and leaning back to gaze into his silvered face, she said, "Always I will forgive you, Ashe. Always I will love you. Never could I live without you, darling, you are my very breath . . ."

". . . my very life," he finished for her.

"Ashe, take me now. Make me yours forever. Bind me to you now."

"Yes . . . now."

As he began to work at the tiny pearl buttons at her bodice, Tanya caught his shaking hand and stayed it.

"No, Ashe. Take me now, just the way we are. Darling, I can't wait!"

"Whatever you say, love."

"I have to have you within me. Hurry, Ashe. . . ."

Purposefully, his fingers moved at his breeches' front. In a flash then, his hands were back pulling her savagely against him. His lips still clinging to hers, he backed Tanya to the sofa, pushing up her skirts urgently, pressing her into the cold leather. Bending a knee, he joined with her there, parting her small lips to thrust between them. He entered her and his whole length began to move rhythmically. His tongue was like a hot, red brand inside her mouth while his long, finely muscled legs intertwined with hers. Tanya panted and cried out her love.

The heat spread like wildfire between them and soon they were consumed. Together Tanya and Ashe soared, becoming one with the white-hot element that flashed and rolled around them. Lightning

thunder, the rush of startling movement, all insepa-
rable. Wonderful was the feel of hot, rippling muscle
and soft depression. Breasting the lofty silver peaks,
they sailed on and up, toward glorious never-before-
reached heights. There, far above any earthly realm,
wide-winged and free in the cloudless atmosphere,
they explored it together, in a state of intensely fierce
suspension, the final compelling shocks reaching
them, exploding, rocketing; then they swooped
down like a falling star onto soft down.

Tanya saw golden gleams and streaks of sunset red.
She felt the glory of his pounding heart, his
throbbing pulse, his manhood and all his senses. An
equally fulfilling joy and peace followed which,
compared with all the other times of loving, was as a
blaze of sun to a candle.

Ashe's voice was low and steeped in deep emotion
as he said, "I was so afraid you had been hurt . . . that
Carl Tucker had—"

"Hush," Tanya whispered, threading her fingers
through his hair.

Hugging Tanya tight against his fiercely beating
heart, Ashe knew that for him and Tanya, Garnet
Haywood Brandon was gone forever. "I love *you*,
Tanya Brandon, my spirit, my flame, and I mean it,
from the bottom of my big, foolish heart." He carried
her upstairs and held her close, for a long long time.
Then, naked and entwined in their bed, they slept.

In the morning, after Ashe had washed up, half-
dressed, he knelt beside the bed as Tanya awakened.
He pulled her up against him and held her close, no
words needed this glorious morning to tell her of his
love.

Tanya smiled against her husband's white lawn
shirt where he could not see her . . . a woman's
smile, ecstatic, her heart and soul resounding with
*Oh yes, Mama. I told you I would win what you
could never have.*

Last night Garnet Haywood Brandon had died.

*With this ring I thee wed, with my body I
thee worship,
and with all my worldly goods I thee endow.*
                    —Book of Common Prayer

Epilogue

A romantic picture was unknowingly portrayed as Tanya and Ashe stood together back of Sundance House beneath the spreading pecan tree. His arm was wrapped protectively about her thickening waist, his chin was resting on her forehead, his breath stirred the wisps of Titian hair coiled at her forehead and along her flushed pink cheeks. His loose-limbed body was pressed against her backside, protectively curved against her like a long spoon. But the front of her gave evidence to the babe growing within her. He caressed her gentle roundness, that evidence of their love beneath her apron; then he looked down to the thing on her finger she was so raptly studying.

"I love it, Ashe." She gazed down at the band of gold that shone dully on her third finger, left hand. "It's beautiful," she murmured. "Just like everything you have"—here she smiled as he continued to caress her belly beneath her apron—"given me."

"For you, my love, my wife," was all he said. Then, as an afterthought, "This is where I belong, darling, here at Sundance with you."

For only a moment Ashe allowed his worries and
his hatred to enter their serene time together. Ca
Tucker. He had tried to kill Ashe twice now and if h
wasn't already dead, he soon would be. Ashe aske
the sheriff and the rangers to go after Tucker, and h
revealed him as the stagecoach murderer. Tucke
would be found, either dead or alive. The ranger
stopped at nothing, he thought with a fleetin
reminiscent smile. If they didn't get Tucker, then h
would or Talon.

It was almost too wonderful to be true, Tanya ha
thought for the two whole glorious weeks Ashe ha
continued to treat her like a bit of porcelain on
queen's table. The pink-and-blue cradle waited i
the new nursery upstairs, the one Ashe had buil
between the two bedrooms, the nursery he ha
already been planning the day she'd accidentally me
Ashe in Granger's store. He had known, even the
she would have his child.

Both Tanya and Ashe looked up now, as did th
others gathered in the yard.

The magnificent horses were coming, their back
undulating like the waves of a wild ocean, dust, lik
sea-foam, roiling at their hooves, their mane
blowing back like black fire.

"Hear that, Tanya? It's thunder. Texas thunder
our future."

"Mmm, yes."

Cloud, Talon's gallant stallion, now bare an
riderless, proudly led the herd of mares across th
greensward into the now gigantic corral. Clem wa
awhooping and hollering, dusting his hat off on hi

492

knee. Samson, smiling from ear to ear, rested one foot on the bottom rail and casually leaned against the wooden fence. Tanya tilted her chin and smiled into her husband's eyes, his fervent gaze holding hers.

Across the way, on the other side of the dusty corral, a sweet, willowy blonde watched for a certain form, half-hidden in billowing dust clouds, but tall, fair, handsome, and graceful as an Indian, herding the horses with the others. He was the young man she loved more than life itself. Ever since she had met him she had been dreaming, longing, planning . . . *their future.*

Dear Readers:

Thank you for all your letters of kind words, encouragement, and comments. I also answer all the questions you send my way and truly enjoy hearing from each and every one of my readers. Write again soon—

Sonya Pelton

Angel Enterprises
13628 Square Lake Trail
Stillwater, MN 55082

YOU CAN NOW
CHOOSE FROM AMONG JANELLE TAYLOR'S
BESTSELLING TITLES!

BRAZEN ECSTASY	(1133, $3.50)
DEFIANT ECSTASY	(0931, $3.50)
FIRST LOVE, WILD LOVE	(1431, $3.75)
FORBIDDEN ECSTASY	(1014, $3.50)
GOLDEN TORMENT	(1323, $3.75)
LOVE ME WITH FURY	(1248, $3.75)
SAVAGE CONQUEST	(1533, $3.75)
SAVAGE ECSTASY	(0824, $3.50)
STOLEN ECSTASY	(1621, $3.95)
TENDER ECSTASY	(1212, $3.75)

Available wherever paperbacks are sold, or order direct from the Publisher. Send cover price plus 50¢ per copy for mailing and handling to Zebra Books, Dept. 1714, 475 Park Avenue South, New York, N.Y. 10016. DO NOT SEND CASH.

CONTEMPORARY ROMANCE
FROM ZEBRA

ASK FOR NOTHING MORE   (1643, $3.95)

Mary Conroy lived her life as daughter and wife in the safest way possible—always playing by the rules. But this didn't guard her from cruelty and pain. Mary found a new way of experiencing the world as mistress to a very attractive, but married, man. A world where desires and betrayal were separated only by a plain band of gold.

WINTER JASMINE   (1658, $3.50)

The beautiful Beth wanted Danny and longed to be a part of his exciting life style, but Danny was tired of the fast lane and yearned for stability. Together they shared a searing passion and searched for a world in between.

SOMEBODY PLEASE LOVE ME   (1604, $3.95)

Cat Willingham was every woman's ideal of success. She was smart, wealthy, and strong. But it took Wall Street millionaire Clay Whitfield to bring out the sensuous woman trapped deep inside her, and to teach her the passions that love can bring.

Available wherever paperbacks are sold, or order direct from the Publisher. Send cover price plus 50¢ per copy for mailing and handling to Zebra Books, Dept. 1714, 475 Park Avenue South, New York, N.Y. 10016. DO NOT SEND CASH.